PRAISE FOR

Josie Silver

"A dreamy love story . . . A moving story of grief and finding one's way back."

—*People*

"I read *The Two Lives of Lydia Bird* in a single sitting—crying, laughing, and rooting for the heroine, who reminds us that the people we love, and the people we lose, change us, and that who we are at the beginning of our story is never who we are at the end of it. What a beautiful, emotional gift Josie Silver has given us."

—Jodi Picoult, *New York Times* bestselling author of *Small Great Things* and *A Spark of Light*

"An irresistible love story."

—theSkimm

"In a new twist on the classic love triangle, Silver writes a novel that will make you laugh, cry and think about the precious gift of being in love."

—Today.com

"Bursting with wit and charm . . . heart-wrenching yet hope-filled."

—*Woman's World*

"As much a meditation on healing after loss as it is a gently developed love story . . . with excellent characters who all get a chance to experience growth, Silver's wonderful follow-up to *One Day in December* will be sure to appeal to existing fans and draw in new ones with its humor, heart, and excellent prose."

—*Booklist* (starred review)

"Silver's latest (after *One Day in December*) is a heartbreaking, poignant tale. . . . Through lush prose, expert plotting, and richly imagined characters, Silver offers an achingly real portrait of grief transposed with the character's intoxicating parallel universe. This will stay with readers long after the final page is turned."

—*Publishers Weekly* (starred review)

"At its core, this is a story of love lost and individual growth. But it is also about love found and future happiness. While this is in many ways the complete opposite of Linda Holmes' *Evvie Drake Starts Over*, fans of that book will enjoy it."

—*Kirkus Reviews*

"After her mega-hit *One Day in December*, Silver strikes gold for a second time with this tale of love, loss and addiction. The story of someone losing the love of their life doesn't sound like the most uplifting book, but Silver manages to find a new perspective on grief, and delivers an ending that's as rewarding as it is revelatory."

—Owen Nicholls, Electric Literature

ALSO BY JOSIE SILVER

One Day in December

The Two Lives of Lydia Bird

JOSIE SILVER

BALLANTINE BOOKS
NEW YORK

The Two Lives of Lydia Bird

A NOVEL

The Two Lives of Lydia Bird is a work of fiction.
Names, characters, places, and incidents are the products of
the author's imagination or are used fictitiously.
Any resemblance to actual events, locales, or persons,
living or dead, is entirely coincidental.

2022 Ballantine Books Mass Market Edition

Published in the United States by Ballantine Books,
an imprint of Random House, a division of
Penguin Random House LLC, New York.

BALLANTINE and the HOUSE colophon are registered trademarks of
Penguin Random House LLC.

Originally published in hardcover in the United States
by Ballantine Books, an imprint of Random House, a division of
Penguin Random House LLC, in 2020. The Book Club Guide originally
appeared in the trade paperback edition of *The Two Lives of Lydia Bird* by
Josie Silver, published by Ballantine Books, an imprint of Random
House, a division of Penguin Random House LLC, in 2021.

This work contains an excerpt from the forthcoming book
One Night on the Island by Josie Silver. This excerpt has been set
for this edition only and may not reflect
the final content of the forthcoming edition.

ISBN 978-0-593-49827-9
Ebook ISBN 978-0-593-13524-2

Cover design: Derek Walls
Cover image: © Krisikorn Tanrattanakunl/EyeEm/Getty Images

Printed in the United States of America

randomhousebooks.com

2 4 6 8 9 7 5 3 1

Ballantine Books mass market edition: January 2022

For my sister, forever my best friend.

How lucky we are to have each other. X

PROLOGUE

MOST OF LIFE'S defining moments happen unexpectedly; sometimes they slide past you completely unnoticed until afterward, if at all. The last time your child is small enough to carry on your hip. An eye roll exchanged with a stranger who becomes your life-long best friend. The summer job you apply for on impulse and stay at for the next twenty years. Those kinds of things. So I'm completely unaware that one of my defining moments is passing me by when my mobile rings at 6:47 P.M. on March 14, 2018; instead I curse under my breath because I've got a Velcro roller stuck in my hair and I'm already running late.

"Hello?"

I can't help it; I smile as I tap on speakerphone and Freddie half shouts his greeting over the background road noise.

"I'm here," I say, loudly, bobby pins gripped between my teeth.

"Listen, Lyds, Jonah's got car trouble so I'm going to swing round and pick him up on the way back. It won't make much difference; ten minutes, max."

I'm glad he isn't here to see the look on my face. Was it Princess Diana who famously said that there were three people in her marriage? I get that, because there are three people in mine too. Not that we're married yet; very nearly though. Freddie Hunter and I are engaged, and I'm officially *almost* the happiest girl in the world. I refer you back to my earlier statement to explain why I say "almost" the happiest, because there's me, there's Freddie, and there's Jonah bloody Jones.

I get it. I don't go a day without speaking to my sister, but Elle isn't always here on our sofa drinking our tea and demanding my attention. Not that Freddie's best friend is demanding, exactly; Jonah's so laid back he's almost horizontal most of the time, and it's not as if I don't like him–I'd just like him a whole lot more if I didn't see so much of him, you know? Tonight, for instance. Freddie asked Jonah to the dinner without thinking to check with me first, even though it's my birthday.

I spit the bobby pins out as I give up wrestling with the Velcro and pick the phone up instead, irritated.

"God, Freddie, must you? Alfredo's is booked for eight and you know they won't hold the table if we're late."

I know this from bitter experience: our work Christmas dinner there turned into a disaster when the minibus arrived ten minutes late and we all ended up eating

McDonald's in our Sunday best. Tonight is my birthday dinner, and I'm pretty sure my mum won't be impressed with a Big Mac instead of chicken fettuccine.

"Chill your boots, Cinders; you won't be late for the ball. Promise."

That's Freddie all over. He never takes life seriously, even on the once in a while occasions when, actually, it would be nice if he did. Time is elastic in his world, and he can stretch it to accommodate his needs—or in this case, to accommodate Jonah's.

"Okay," I sigh, resigned. "Just keep your eye on the time, will you?"

"Got it," he says, already turning up the car radio. "Over and out."

Silence fills the bedroom, and I wonder if anyone would notice if I cut off the chunk of hair knotted around the roller currently hanging off the side of my head.

And there it was. My life's defining moment, sliding nonchalantly past me at 6:47 P.M. on March 14, 2018.

2018

AWAKE

Thursday, May 10

FREDDIE HUNTER, OTHERWISE known as the great big love of my life, died fifty-six days ago.

One moment I'm cursing him for running late and ruining my birthday dinner, the next I'm trying to make sense of the two uniformed policewomen in my living room, one of them holding my hand as she speaks. I stare at her wedding ring, and then at my engagement ring.

"Freddie can't be dead," I say. "We're getting married next year."

It's probably a self-preservation thing that I struggle to recall exactly what happened afterward. I remember being rushed to emergency in the police car, and my sister holding me up when my legs buckled at the hospital. I remember turning my back on Jonah Jones when he appeared in the waiting room with barely a scratch on him, just his hand bandaged and a wound dressing over one eye. How is that fair? Two get into the car, only one gets out again. I remember what I was wearing: a new green blouse I'd bought especially for the dinner. I've given it away to a charity shop, I never want it on my body again.

Since that awful day I've racked my brain countless times to try to recall every word of my last conversation with Freddie, and all I can remember is grumbling at him about cutting it close for the restaurant. And then come the other thoughts. Was he rushing to please me? Was the accident my fault? God, I wish I'd told him that I love him. Had I known that it was the last time I'd ever speak to him, I would have; of course I would. Since it happened I've sometimes wished he'd lived just long enough for us to have one more conversation—but then I'm not sure my heart could have withstood it. It's probably for the best if the last time you do something momentous passes you by unheralded: the last time my mother collected me at the school gate, her hand reassuring around my smaller one, the last time my father remembered my birthday. The last time I spoke to Freddie Hunter as he dashed back to see me on my twenty-eighth birthday. Do you know what the last words he said to me were? Over and out. It was a habit, something he'd done for years; silly words that have now become one of the most significant phrases of my life.

I guess it was just so Freddie, though, to go out on a phrase like that. He had this great big lust for life, a lightness of attitude coupled with a killer competitive streak—fun but lethal, if you like. I've never met anyone with such a gift for always knowing what to say. He has, he *had,* a knack of making other people think they'd won when in fact he'd got exactly what he wanted. He is, he *was,* the one who was always going to be someone or do something that would make people remember his name long after he'd gone.

And now he bloody well *has* gone, his car concertinaed against an oak tree, and I feel as if someone has tied a knot in my windpipe. It's as if I can't get quite enough air into my lungs. I'm breathless and perpetually on the edge of panic.

The doctor has finally given me something to help me sleep after my mum yelled at him yesterday in the living room: a month's supply of some new pill that he wasn't at all sure about prescribing because he thinks grief is something I need to "pass through sentiently in order to emerge." I'm not making this shit up; he said those actual words to me a couple of weeks ago, before leaving me empty-handed to go home to his very-much-alive wife and children.

Living around the corner from my mother is a blessing and a curse in varying measures. When she makes her champion chicken stew and brings a pot round for us, still hot off the stove, for instance, or when she's nipped round on her way to work to spray de-icer on my windscreen on a cold November morning—those times our proximity is a blessing. Other times, like when I'm seeing double with a hangover and she appears frowning as if I'm still seventeen, or when I haven't tidied up for a couple of days and she looks down her nose as if I'm one of those extreme hoarders in need of a reality TV intervention—those times our proximity is a curse. Ditto when I'm trying to grieve in private with the living room curtains still closed at three in the afternoon and the same pj's on as when she visited me the day before and the day before that, making me tea I'll forget to drink and sandwiches I'll bury in the back of the fridge when she's upstairs cleaning the bathroom or outside pulling the bins down.

I understand, of course. She's fiercely protective of me, especially at the moment; she had the doctor practically shaking with fear when he wavered over the idea of prescribing sleeping tablets. I'm not all that sure about popping pills either, as it happens, although God knows the idea of oblivion is appealing. I don't know why I'm bringing God into this; Freddie is, *was,* and would have always been a strident atheist, and I'm ambivalent at best, so I don't expect God has had much to do with my being placed on a clinical trial for the recently bereaved. The doctor recommended joining the drug trial, probably because my mother was demanding maximum strength Valium and these new pills are being touted as a milder, more holistic option. To be perfectly honest, I don't really care what they are; I'm officially the world's saddest, most tired guinea pig.

Freddie and I have this fabulous bed, you see. It sounds crazy, but the Savoy Hotel was auctioning off its beds for hardly anything to make way for new ones, and sweet heaven, this bed is a fantasy island of epic proportions. People raised eyebrows at first; you're buying a *secondhand* bed? Why on earth would you do that, my mother said, as aghast as if we were buying a camp bed discarded by the local homeless shelter. Clearly those doubters had never stayed at the Savoy. I hadn't either, in truth, but I'd seen something on TV about their handmade beds and I knew I had to have one. It's the most comfortable bed in a hundred-mile radius, in which Freddie and I have demolished countless Sunday morning breakfasts, laughed and cried and made heart-achingly sweet love.

When my mother told me a few days after the accident that she'd changed the sheets for me, she unintentionally sent me into a sudden, screeching meltdown. I watched myself as if from a distance, clawing at the door of the washing machine, sobbing as the sheets tumbled through the suds, swilling any last lingering traces of Freddie's skin and scent down the drain.

Mum was beside herself, trying to lift me from the floor, calling out for my sister to come and help. We ended up huddled together on the stripped kitchen floorboards, watching the sheets, all of us in tears because it is just so bloody unjust that Freddie isn't here to sleep in them anymore.

I haven't been to bed since Freddie died. In fact, I don't think I've properly been to sleep since. I just nap sometimes: my head on the table beside my uneaten breakfast; on the sofa huddled underneath Freddie's winter coat, as I am now; standing up leaning against the fridge, even.

"Come on, Lyds," my sister says now, shaking my shoulder softly. "I'll come up with you."

I glance at the clock, disorientated because it was broad daylight when I closed my eyes, but now it's shadowy enough for someone, Elle, I presume, to have flicked the lamps on. It's typical of her to be so thoughtful; I've always thought of her as a better version of me.

We're physically similar in height and bone structure, but she's dark to my light; her hair, her eyes. She's kinder than I am too; too kind for her own good a lot of the time. She's been here most of the afternoon and Mum's sister, Auntie June, popped in this morning; I think Mum must have drawn up a rota to make sure I'm never on my own for more than an hour or two. It's probably pinned to the side of her fridge, right next to the shopping list she adds to all week and the food diary she fills in for her slimming class. She likes a list, my mum.

"Up where?" I say, sitting up straighter, clocking the glass of water and bottle of pills in Elle's hand.

"Bed," she says, an edge of steel to her voice.

"I'm fine here," I mutter, even though our sofa isn't actually all that comfortable to sleep on. "It's not even bedtime. We can watch . . ." I bat my hand toward the TV in the corner, trying to remember any of the soaps. I sigh, annoyed that my tired brain can't muster it. "You know, that one with the pub and the bald men and the shouting."

She smiles and rolls her eyes. "You mean *EastEnders.*"

"That's the one," I say, distracted as I scan the room for the remote to turn on the TV.

"It'll have finished by now. Besides, you haven't watched *EastEnders* in at least five years," she says, having none of it.

I screw my face up. "I have. There's . . . there's that woman with the dangly earrings, and . . . and the one played by Barbara Windsor," I say, lifting my chin.

Elle shakes her head. "Both dead," she says.

Poor them, I think, and their poor families.

Elle holds her hand out. "It's time to go to bed, Lydia," she says, gentle and firm, more nurse than sister.

Hot tears prick the backs of my retinas. "I don't think I can."

"You can," she says, resolute, her hand still outstretched. "What else are you going to do? Sleep on the sofa for the rest of your life?"

"Would that be so bad?"

Elle perches next to me and picks up my hand, the pills in her lap. "It would, really, Lyds," she says. "If it was Freddie left here alone rather than you, you'd want him to get some proper sleep, wouldn't you?"

I nod, miserable. Of course I would.

"In fact, you'd haunt him rotten until he did," she says, rubbing her thumb over my knuckles, and I half choke on the permanent ball of tears that's been in my throat since the day Freddie died.

I watch her shake a small neon pink tablet into her palm, my name printed in black capitals on the bottle's label. Lydia Bird, followed by the unpronounceable name of the pills. Is that all it's going to take to put me straight? A few weeks of solid sleep and I'll be shipshape-shiny and good to go again?

Elle holds my gaze, unwavering, and tears slide down my cheeks as I realize how shattered I am; I'm as emotionally and physically low as I can go. Or at least I hope I am, because I don't think I'll survive if there's further to fall than this. Taking the pill with trembling fingers, I put it in my mouth and wash it down. At my bedroom door, I turn to Elle.

"I need to do this on my own," I whisper.

She brushes my lank hair out of my eyes. "You sure?" Her dark eyes study my face. "I can stay with you until you're asleep, if you like?"

I sniff, looking at the floor, crying as usual. "I know you could," I say, catching hold of her hand and holding on tight. "But I think I better . . ." I can't quite find the words I need; I don't know if it's because the tablet is having an effect or simply because there aren't any adequate words.

Elle nods. "I'll be just downstairs if you want me, okay? I'm not going anywhere."

My fingers close around the handle. I've kept the door closed since the day Mum changed the bed linens, not wanting to catch even an accidental glimpse of the pristine bed on my way to the bathroom. I've built it up into this thing in my head, as off-limits as a crime scene crisscrossed with yellow tape.

"It's just a bed," I whisper, pushing the door slowly open. There's no yellow tape blocking my entry, and there are no monsters under the bed. But there's no Freddie Hunter either, and that's every kind of heartbreaking.

"Just a bed," Elle says, her hand soothing on my back. "A place to rest."

But she's lying. We both know it's so much more than that. This room, mine and Freddie's bedroom, was one of the many reasons we bought this house. Airy, bathed in daylight thanks to the low-slung sash windows and honey floorboards, striped by bright slices of moonlight on clear summer nights.

Someone, Elle presumably, has been in already to turn on the lamp on my side of the bed, a pool of mellow light to welcome me, even though the sun hasn't quite set yet. She's turned the bed down too; it's all more hotel than bedroom. The overwhelming scent in here when I close the door is line-fresh bed linen. No traces of my perfume mingled with Freddie's after-shave, no office-crumpled shirts slung carelessly over the armchair or shoes kicked off before they could make it as far as the bottom of the wardrobe. It's neat as a new pin; I feel like a visitor in my own life.

"It's just a bed," I whisper again, sitting on the edge of the mattress. I close my eyes as I lie down, curling onto my side beneath the quilt.

We spent more than we should have on bedding befitting of our Savoy bed; white cotton sheets with a higher thread count than I knew existed. As my body slides against the sheets, I realize they're already warm. Elle's put a hot water bottle in there for me, my lovely sister, taking away the chill of clean sheets. My bed, *our* bed, envelops me like an old friend I feel guilty for neglecting.

I lie on my side of the mattress, my body painful with sorrow, my arms outstretched to find him as always. Then I push the hot water bottle to his side, warming the sheets before I move across and lie there myself, clutching the heat of the bottle to my chest with both arms. I bury my wet face in his pillow and wail like a wounded animal, a noise as alien as it is uncontrollable.

And then, little by little, it subsides. My heart rate begins to steady, and my limbs turn lead-heavy. I'm warm, cocooned, and for the first time in fifty-six days, I'm not lost without Freddie. I'm not lost, because as I slide under the coattails of sleep, I can almost feel the solid weight of him depress the mattress, his body spooned around mine, his breath steady against my neck. Save me from these dark, uncharted waters, Freddie Hunter. I pull him close and breathe him in, as I fall into a deep, peaceful sleep.

ASLEEP

Friday, May 11

YOU KNOW THOSE blissful dawn moments, summer mornings when the sun rises before you do, and you half rouse and then fall back asleep, glad of a few more hours? I turn and find Freddie asleep beside me, and the relief is so profound that it's all I can do to lie perfectly still and try to match my breathing pattern to his. It's not much after four in the morning, too early to get up, so I close my eyes again; I don't think I've ever known such absolute peace and comfort. The bed warmed by our nested bodies, the golden half-light before dawn, the muted music of birdsong. Please don't let me leave this dream.

AWAKE

Friday, May 11

I KNOW BEFORE I open my eyes for a second time that he's gone. The bed is colder, the six A.M. sunlight harsher, the birdsong like nails down a blackboard. Freddie was here, I know he was. I burrow my head into the pillow and screw my eyes tight shut, searching the darkness behind my eyelids for sleep again. If I can only sleep, I might find him.

Panic starts to bubble low in my gut; the harder I try to relax, the more my brain fires up, preparing itself for the day ahead, full of dark thoughts and desperate emotions I don't know what to do with. And then my heart judders, jump leads on a dodgy battery, because I remember; I have sleeping pills now. Pink pills designed to knock me out. I reach for the bottle Elle has placed on my bedside table and clutch it in both hands, relieved, then unscrew the lid and swallow one down.

ASLEEP

Friday, May 11

"MORNING, LYDS." FREDDIE rolls over and kisses my forehead, his arm heavy over my shoulders as our morning alarm informs us it's seven A.M. "Shall we stay in bed? I'll call in for you if you call in for me."

He says something along the same lines most mornings, and for a couple of minutes we always pretend to entertain the idea.

"Will you make us breakfast in bed?" I mumble, sliding my arm around the warmth of his body, burying my face in the soft down of his chest hair. There is a solidity about his body that I love; he's a commanding physical presence with his height and broad shoulders. People at the ad agency where he works sometimes underestimate his business brain because of his stereotypical rugby player build, and he's more than happy to use that to his advantage. He's competitive to the core.

"As long as you want breakfast at midday, yeah." I hear the laugh behind his breastbone as he strokes the back of my head.

"Sounds about right," I say, closing my eyes, breathing him in deep.

We stay like that for a few lazy, exquisite minutes, clasped, half sleeping, knowing we need to get up soon. But we linger, because these are the moments that matter, the ones that make it Freddie and me against the world. These moments are the bedrock our love is built on, an invisible cloak around our shoulders when we are out in the world going about our business. Freddie won't return the interested look from the striking girl on platform 4 waiting for the 7:47, and I never allow Leon, the barista in the café I sometimes buy lunch from, to cross the line from messing around to flirting, even though he's movie-star gorgeous and sometimes writes outrageous things on my coffee cup.

I'm crying. For a few seconds I don't know why, and then I remember, and I suck down great lungsful of air, like someone breaking the surface after falling into deep water.

Freddie startles, jerking up on one elbow to stare at me, concern on his face as he grips my shoulder. "Lyds, what's the matter?" His voice is urgent, ready to help, to soothe whatever pain I'm in.

I can't breathe; my breath burns in my chest.

"You died." I sob out the shocking words, my eyes scanning his beloved face for telltale signs of the accident. There's nothing, no hint of the catastrophic head injury that claimed his life. His eyes are an unusual blue, dark enough to be mistaken for brown unless you're close enough to really look. He sometimes wears a pair of black-framed glasses for important work pitches, clear glass, an illusion of weakness where there isn't any. I stare into those eyes now and run my hand over the harvest-blond stubble on his jawline.

A soft laugh rumbles from him and relief passes through his eyes.

"You daft cow," he says, hugging me in. "You were dreaming, that's all."

Oh, how dearly I wish that were true. I shake my head, so he takes my hand and lays it over his heart.

"I'm fine," he insists. "Feel, my heart's beating and everything."

It is. I press hard enough to feel it jumping beneath my palm, and yet I know that it isn't, really. It can't be. He covers my hand with his own now, not laughing anymore because he can see how distressed I am. He doesn't understand, of course. How could he? He's not real, but wow, this doesn't feel like any other dream I've ever had, either. I'm awake in my sleep. I can feel the heat of his body. I can smell the trace of his aftershave on his skin. I can taste my tears when he leans down and kisses me, tender. I can't stop crying; I try to take shallow breaths as I hold him, as though he's made of smoke and will blow away if I breathe too hard.

"A nightmare, that's all," he whispers, stroking my back, letting me cry it out because there's nothing else he can do.

If only he knew that this is the opposite of a nightmare; nightmares come when you're impatiently waiting for your fiancée to arrive on your birthday, your family already assembled at a table in the restaurant on the high street.

"I miss you. I miss you so very much," I gulp. I can't keep a limb still, and he folds his arms around me, really tight this time, and he's telling me that he loves me, and that he's fine, that we're both fine.

"We're going to be late for work," he says gently after a few minutes.

I lie still, my eyes closed, trying to memorize the feel of his arms around me for when I wake.

"Let's stay here," I whisper. "Let's stay here forever, Freddie."

His hand slides into my hair, and he draws my head back so he can look me in the eyes. "I wish I could," he says, the trace of a smile on his lips. "But you know I can't. I'm chairing that meeting this morning with the PodGods," he says, reminding me of something I know nothing of.

"The PodGods?"

He raises his eyebrows. "The coffee-pod people? Remember, I told you? They all turned up to the pitch wearing Day-Glo-green PodGod T-shirts and baseball caps?"

"How could I forget them," I say, even though I've no clue.

He untangles himself from me, kissing my cheek.

"Stay here this morning," he says, his eyes concerned. "You never take a day off. Do it today, yeah? I'll bring you a cup of tea."

I don't argue with him. I haven't been to work in fifty-six days.

My life has been entwined around Freddie Hunter's

since the first time he kissed me, breathing himself into my DNA one late summertime afternoon. It had been coming between us for a while, building like steam in an engine—his seat always beside mine in the school canteen so he could steal my ice cream, flirty comments batted back and forth across the classroom like tennis balls. He began to walk home the same way as Jonah and me, even though it was out of his way, usually making up some flimsy excuse about collecting something for his mum or visiting his nan. When Jonah came down with chickenpox and had to stay home for a week or two, I didn't stand a chance. I get nostalgic butterflies thinking about it even now; Freddie gave me a yellow plastic flower ring, the kind you get from a vending machine, and then he kissed me sitting on my neighbor's front wall.

"Won't your nan be worried about you?" I asked him, after the five most exciting minutes of my life.

"Hardly. She lives in Bournemouth," he said, and then we both laughed because it was at least a hundred miles away.

And that was that. I was Freddie Hunter's girl, then and always. The next morning, he slid a chocolate bar into my bag along with a note telling me he was walking me home. From someone else it could have come off as possessive; my tender teenage heart saw only thrilling directness.

I watch him move with purpose now, heading into the bathroom to switch the shower on, pulling a clean white shirt off its hanger.

"I don't want to jinx it, but I think this one's in the bag," he's saying, answering a work call briefly, his mobile tucked under his chin as he grabs underwear from the drawer. I watch his everyday moves, my answering smile shaky when he rolls his eyes at me because he wants whoever is on the phone to wind it up.

He disappears into the bathroom, and I sit up and push the quilt back when I hear the water sluicing around his body.

"What's happening to me?" I whisper, lowering my feet to the floor, sitting on the edge of the bed like a hospital patient after open-heart surgery. Because that is what this feels like. As if someone opened my chest and massaged my heart back into working order.

"I don't believe in fairy tales or magic beans," I mutter, biting down on my trembling bottom lip hard enough to taste blood, metallic and harsh.

Freddie emerges from the bathroom on a cloud of steam, shoving his shirt into his trousers as he buttons them.

"I better go," he says, reaching for his phone as he shrugs on his jacket. "If I stick the kettle on, can you make the tea? I'll make the train if I dash."

We chose this house in the town we've always called home for exactly this scenario, mornings when we were running late and Freddie would be grateful to have a train station around the corner. His city center job in Birmingham demands much of his time, so the less added for travel the better.

My own commute to the local community center is shorter; ten minutes and I'm in the car park. I love our listed building, it reminds me of something out of a children's storybook. It's believed to be the oldest structure in town, standing half-timbered and crooked at the end of the high street. Much of the architecture is similar; our little Shropshire town is ancient, fiercely proud of its entry into the Domesday Book. There's much to be said about growing up in such a tight-knit community—many families have been here from generation to generation, cradle to grave. It's easy to dismiss the value of something like that, to feel smothered by the fact that everyone knows everyone else's business, but there's a richness and comfort to it too, especially when someone's in trouble.

It wasn't just location that made us fall for the house though. We viewed it early one spring weekend morning, the sun at just the perfect height to show off the honeyed stone and deep bay window. It's the third house along in a row of eight, and decorating it proved to be a bit of a nightmare because there isn't a straight wall or door in the place. It all adds to the charm, I argued, every time Freddie banged his head on the low exposed kitchen beam. I like to think it has echoes of Kate Winslet's cottage in *The Holiday* inside, all stripped boards and cozy clutter. It's a look I've cultivated carefully at garage sales and flea markets, occasionally reined in by Freddie's preference for more modern things. It's a battle he was always set to lose; my magpie eye loves pretty things and my Pinterest game is strong.

A couple of days ago, after I'd forced myself to get dressed and nip round to the liquor store for wine supplies, I realized that I didn't want to go home. It's the first time I'd felt that way about the house since the morning we collected the keys, and another piece of my heart snapped off at the realization that home wasn't home anymore. I could never have conceived of selling the house, but in that moment, I felt cut adrift and I walked in the other direction, two circuits of the children's play park before I could face going home. And then, curiously, once I was back inside, I didn't want to leave again. I am a mass of contradictions; it's no wonder my family is worried to death about me.

It was *our* house, and now it is mine, though there is little pleasure to be gained from being mortgage-free at twenty-eight when I'm Freddie-free too. At the time, we both thought our financial adviser had stitched us up like a pair of kippers on life insurance; the concept of something happening to either of us before the house was paid for seemed ludicrous. How wonderfully lucky we were to have felt so secure. I pull myself out of my thoughts, realizing I'm close to tears again. Freddie is looking at me questioningly. "Okay now?" he asks, cupping my jaw, rubbing his thumb over my cheekbone.

I nod, turning my face to press my lips into his palm as he kisses the top of my head. "That's my girl," he whispers. "I love you."

As undignified as it would be, I want to cling to him, beg him not to leave me again, but I don't. If this is to be my final memory of us, I want it to seal itself around my heart for all of the best reasons. So I stand up and hold the lapels of his suit jacket and look up into his beautiful, familiar blue eyes.

"You're the love of my life, Freddie Hunter," I say, forcing the words out clear and true.

He lowers his head and kisses me. "I love you more than Keira Knightley." He laughs softly as he plays our game.

"That much, huh?" I say, rounding my eyes because we usually start low and work our way up—to Keira in his case and Ryan Reynolds in mine.

"That much," he says, blowing me a kiss as he backs out of the bedroom.

Panic rises from my gut, hot and bilious, and I curl my toes into the floorboards to stop myself from running after him. I listen to his footfalls on the stairs, the sound of the front door closing, and I run to the bedroom window to watch him half stride, half jog toward the corner. Too late, I open the window, struggling with the old catches, yelling his name, even though I know he won't hear me. Why did I let him leave? What if I never find him again? I clutch the windowsill, my eyes pinned to his back. I almost expect him to fade away, but he doesn't. He just rounds the corner, lost to the world, to some corporate coffee client, to the girl on platform 4, to all the places I cannot be.

AWAKE

Friday, May 11

MY FACE IS wet and my mouth is caked with what tastes like blood when I wake. I grab my phone, and on closer inspection I've bitten the inside of my bottom lip quite badly; I can see the indentations my teeth have left and my lip has swollen. It's not my best look—Freddie would have no doubt found my uncanny resemblance to a puffer fish amusing.

Freddie. I close my eyes, winded by the hyperrealism of my dream, or whatever it was. I can liken it only to when you go into an electrical store and see the latest, flashiest TV, the kind that costs a small fortune. The colors are brighter, the edges sharper, the sounds clearer. It was Technicolor brilliant, like watching a movie at an IMAX theater. No; more like being *in* a movie at an IMAX theater. It was too real to not be. Freddie was alive, and showering, and running late for work, and making Keira Knightley jokes once again.

I rack my brain, trying to dredge up a memory of any mention of a corporate coffee client before he died. I'm sure there wasn't one; it's as if Freddie has been living the last fifty-seven days behind a veil, going about his day-to-day business without a care in the world.

I'm once more overcome with the need to try to fall back asleep, to go back and find him, back to the life where Freddie's heart is still beating, but in that world he's already out slaying his meeting with a flash of his cuff links and a smile. For someone who didn't even want to go to bed last night, I now find myself absolutely unwilling to get up and face the new day. It takes me a good fifteen minutes to convince myself that leaving the bedroom is remotely even a good idea. In the end, I strike a bargain with myself; if I get up and do Friday, if I shower, eat, and maybe leave the house for a while, then I can take another pill. I'll have an early dinner, come back to bed, and then maybe, just maybe, I'll get to spend the evening with my love.

AWAKE

Saturday, May 12

"I'VE BEEN DREAMING about Freddie," I say, wrapping my hands around my coffee mug for comfort rather than warmth. Elle looks at me across the kitchen table, nodding slowly.

"I do that every now and then too," she says, stirring sugar into her drink.

Disappointment twists in my gut. What happened to me felt too intimate to be a run-of-the-mill kind of thing.

"I'd be more surprised if you didn't dream about him, to be honest."

"You would?" I look at her sharply, willing her to look up and pay full attention because this is important. "It's the first time it's happened to me."

Elle glances up at the kitchen clock.

"Ready to go?"

We're going to Mum's for breakfast; it's something

we've started to do most Saturday mornings before I visit Freddie's grave. Mum's way of adding structure to my weekend, I think. Elle doesn't pass comment on my unbrushed hair and yesterday's T-shirt. It's one of Freddie's. My hair was for him too; he loved it long, so I've had barely more than a trim for years now. I mean, I can't sit on it or anything yet, but it's slowly become one of my defining features. Lydia, Freddie's girlfriend, the one with the long blond hair.

Had this been yesterday, I probably would have shrugged on my denim jacket and dragged my hair back into an elastic, tangles and all, and considered myself good to go. But it isn't yesterday. If last night has taught me anything, it's that I am alive, and people who are alive should, at the very least, be clean. Even Freddie, who technically *isn't* alive, took a shower.

"Give me ten?" I shoot Elle the barest of smiles. "I think it's time I put on some makeup." I haven't so much as touched my makeup bag since the funeral.

She looks at me strangely; I can tell that I've surprised her.

"Well, I didn't want to say, but you have been looking a little bit shit lately," she says, making light.

Her joke makes my stomach lurch, because we've always been as close as, I don't know, two close things. Two peas in a pod? I don't think that's quite it, because we aren't very alike to look at. As close as sisters doesn't cut it either, because there are sisters like Julia at work and her elder sister, Marie, who she denies could even be from the same gene pool because she's such a cow, and then there are sisters like Alice and Ellen, twins I went to school with who wore matching clothes and finished each other's sentences, but would throw each other under a bus to get picked to captain the netball team. Elle and me, we're . . . we're Monica and Rachel. We're Carrie and Miranda. We have always been each other's loudest cheerleader and first-choice shoulder to cry on, and it's only now that I catch a glimpse of how much I've withdrawn from her. I know she doesn't for a minute resent it or blame me, but it must have been hard on her; she's lost me as well as Freddie, in a way. I make a mental note that one day, when I'm better, I'll tell her how sometimes, on the dark days, she's been the only light I could see.

"I'll be back in a sec," I say, pushing my chair back, a scrape of wood against wood.

"I'll make myself another drink while I wait," she says.

I leave Elle in the kitchen, comforted by the sound of her running the tap and clattering around in the cupboards. She's always been a frequent and very welcome visitor here. Not near as frequent as Jonah Jones, mind—he spent almost as much time here with Freddie as I did, very often slumped on our sofa watching a movie no one had ever heard of or eating pizza out of boxes because neither of them were exactly Gordon Ramsey in the kitchen. I never said as much to Freddie, but I sometimes felt as if Jonah resented having to share his best friend with me. I guess three is always an odd number.

"NO DAVID TODAY?"

Mum looks past us as she opens the front door. I

sometimes think she's fonder of Elle's husband, David, than she is of Elle or me. She was the same way with Freddie; she enjoys fussing over the men in that way mothers do.

"Just us this morning, sorry," Elle says, not sorry.

Mum sighs theatrically. "You'll just have to do. Although I was going to ask him to change the fuse in the plug on my hairdryer, it's packed up again."

Elle catches my eye behind Mum's back and I know exactly what she's thinking. David is terrible at anything DIY related. It's firmly Elle's department if they have a shelf to go up or a room to be decorated, or indeed a fuse to be changed, but our mother insists on clinging to the outdated notion that David, as the man of the family, will do all the manly things. Mum could change her own fuse perfectly well—she raised us single-handedly, and we didn't die—she knows her earth wire from her live. She seems to think it imbues David with an added sense of self-worth if she looks to him for odd jobs, and he in turn looks to us with panicked, help-me eyes. He can't even climb a stepladder without breaking out in a sweat; I had to keep Mum distracted in the kitchen a few weeks ago while he held the ladder for Elle to clear the guttering outside. It's a game we all play. Freddie was the natural doer of the family, and in his absence, David has been unwillingly promoted to family fixer.

"I'm making cheese and onion omelets," Mum says, as we follow her down the hallway. "Testing out a new pan." She twirls a bright pink frying pan at us. "I've bought Auntie June one too. She never treats herself."

"The shopping channel again?" Elle asks, dropping her bag by the kitchen table.

Mum shrugs. "It just happened to be on. You know I don't usually buy off the telly, but Kathrin Magyar was so impressed by it, and the handle had just fallen off my old frying pan, so it seemed like it was fate."

I bite my swollen lip and Elle looks away; we both know that Mum's kitchen cupboards are stuffed with unnecessary purchases the super-glam TV presenter Kathrin Magyar has convinced her will revolutionize her life.

"Want me to chop the onions?" I say.

Mum shakes her head. "Already done. They're in the mini-chopper."

I nod, noticing it on the kitchen surface. I don't ask if that was from the shopping channel too, because of course it was, along with the motorized cheese grater she's used for the cheddar.

I make coffee instead, thankfully unaided by superfluous gadgetry.

"Did you try the pills?" Mum asks, cracking eggs into a bowl.

I nod, winded by the reminder of Freddie.

She rifles through her jug of kitchen implements until she finds the whisk. "And?"

"And they work," I shrug. "I slept through."

"In bed?"

I sigh, and Elle shoots me a small smile. "Yes, in bed."

Relief smooths the lines from Mum's forehead as she whisks the eggs. "That's good. So no more sleeping on the sofa, okay? It's no good for you."

"No, promise."

Elle lays the table; three place settings. Our family swelled to five, and now it's reduced to four, but in its purest form it has always been three: Mum, Elle, and me. We don't really know our dad. He walked out five days before my first birthday, and Mum has never really forgiven him. Elle was a lively three-year-old; I was a handful, and he decided that life with three females wasn't his gig and moved to Cornwall to take up surfing. He's that kind of man. Every few years he sends news of where he is, and he even turned up on the doorstep unannounced once or twice when we were still at school. He's not a bad person, just a flighty one. It's nice to know he's there, but I've never really needed him in my life.

"I'm thinking of buying a new kitchen table," Mum says as she places our plates down and takes a seat.

Elle and I both stare at her. "You can't," I say.

"No way," Elle says.

Mum raises her eyes to the ceiling. She'd obviously anticipated resistance to the idea. "Girls, this one's on its last legs."

We've sat at this battered, scrubbed wooden table our entire lives, always in the exact same spots. It's seen our school-morning breakfasts, our favorite weekend bacon and beetroot sandwiches, and our family rows. Our mother is by and large a creature of habit; her home hasn't changed much over the years, and Elle and I have come to rely on it staying more or less the same. Come to think of it, you could say the same for Mum; she's had the same ash-blond bob for as long as I can recall. Elle and I inherit our heart-shaped faces from her, and we all share the same deep dimples when we laugh, as if someone screwed their fingers into our cheeks. She is our safety net and this house is our sanctuary.

"We did our homework on this table." Elle lays a protective hand on it.

"Every Christmas dinner I've ever had has been around this table," I say.

"But it's drawn all over," Mum tries.

"Yes," Elle says. "With our names from when I was five years old."

She gouged each of our names deep into the surface with a blue ballpoint not long after she learned her letters. The story goes that she was terribly proud and couldn't wait to show Mum what she'd done. They're still there now, childish capitals beneath our placemats. Barbra, Elle, Lydia, a scrawny little bird after each of them.

"Would you like to take it to your house?" Mum says, looking at Elle, who has a screamingly tidy home where everything matches or complements, and absolutely nothing is battered or gouged.

"It belongs here," Elle says, firm.

Mum looks at me. "Lydia?"

"You know I don't have the room," I say. "But please let it stay. It's part of the family."

She sighs, wavering. I can see she knows it's true; I don't think she really wants to lose it either. "Maybe."

"Omelets are lovely," Elle offers.

A thought occurs to me. "Did Kathrin Magyar sell you a new dining table?"

Mum reaches for her coffee and pats the tabletop like an old friend. "I'll cancel the order."

Kathrin Magyar might be good, but she never stood a chance against the Bird family collective.

I LOOK DOWN at Freddie's grave, at a bunch of cellophane-wrapped roses laid along the base of the headstone, garish beside the bedraggled arrangement of daisies and wild flowers I placed there myself last week. Someone else must have been. A colleague, or perhaps Maggie, Freddie's mum, although she doesn't come that often—she finds it too distressing. He was her beloved only child, so much so that she found it a struggle to include me in her circle of love. She wasn't unkind; it was more that she took underlying pleasure in having Freddie to herself. We've met up a couple of times since Freddie's death, but I'm not sure it does either of us any service. Hers is a different sort of loss, one I can't relate to.

The fact that I don't find it maudlin myself has surprised me. I appreciate having a place to come and talk to him. My eyes flicker back to the roses as I open the fresh flowers I picked out at the florist on the way here. Sweet williams, freesias, and some interesting silvery green foliage. Never anything as obvious as roses. Roses are for Valentine's Day, the romance-by-numbers choice of the unimaginative lover. Throw in a teddy and the job's a good one. Mine and Freddie's love was a world away from card shop clichés and helium hearts. It was big, and real, and now I feel like half a person, as if an artist turned their pencil upside down and erased half of me from the page too.

"Who's been to visit you, Freddie?" I say, settling down on the grass, my bag at my feet. There's something terribly depressing about keeping a bag in the boot of the car with cemetery essentials, isn't there? An empty water bottle I fill up at the tap, scissors to cut the flowers to size, cleaning wipes, those kinds of things.

When I first started to come here, I used to try to prepare in my head what I was going to say. It didn't work. So now I just sit in the silence, close my eyes and imagine that I'm somewhere else entirely. I've conjured all kinds of places for us. I've been at home on the sofa, my feet on Freddie's lap. I've been beside him on a sun lounger in Turkey, an ill-advised package holiday to a god-awful hotel, surviving mainly thanks to endless free shots of raki. And we've been opposite each other in Sheila's small, foggy café around the corner from our house, the one that we used to go to for a hangover-busting full English after a heavy night out, beetroot on mine, specially brought in for my regular order by Sheila. It doesn't take me more than a couple of seconds to decide where we're going today. We're in the safety of our big warm Savoy bed, facing each other on the pillows, the quilt pulled over our shoulders.

"Hey you," I say as my eyes drift closed, a half smile already on my mouth. "It's me again."

Thanks to what happened last night, I don't struggle to bring Freddie's face into focus as I sometimes do. His fingers tangle with mine between our bodies, warm and strong, and in my head he grins and says *"Back already? You're eager."*

I huff gently. "I can't tell you how good it was to see you again," I say, barely more than a whisper. "I've missed you so very much."

He reaches out and strokes the backs of his fingers down my cheek. *"I've missed you too"* he tells me, and we don't say anything at all for a few minutes. I just look at him and he looks at me, in a slow, meditative way we would never have taken the time to do when he was here. *So what's new with you, then?* he says after a while, wrapping a strand of my hair around his finger.

"Not much, really," I say, which isn't an understatement seeing as I rarely leave the house these days. "I've been for breakfast with Mum and Elle this morning. Cheese and onion omelets because Mum wanted to test a new pan she bought off the TV." I pause, then get going again. "Auntie June and Uncle Bob have taken up archery," I say. Freddie always found their ever-changing roster of hobbies amusing. They seem to work their way through the adult-class prospectus, regardless of any innate ability. All in good humor though; they're salt of the earth people, and Auntie June has been a rock for Mum since Freddie died. I suspect she's been the one propping Mum up so she can prop me up. I adore Auntie June; she's uncannily like Mum. They share the same infectious laugh, a sound guaranteed to make everyone around them laugh too.

"Dawn and Julia from work came round a few nights ago, brought a card and some grapes. Grapes! As if I'm ill or something." I hear the scorn in my voice and feel bad for it. "It was kind of them to come though. I'm not the best company at the moment." I pause and then laugh softly. "I don't even like bloody grapes."

I keep my eyes closed as I cast around for more news to share with him. "Elle got herself a new job," I say, remembering my sister's big news. "She's going to be the events manager at that fancy new hotel in town. Lots of free cake, or so she reckons."

What else can I tell him? Very little changes in my day-to-day life. He'd probably appreciate some sports news, football or rugby, but I'm at a loss there.

"The doctor gave me some new pills a couple of days ago," I say, almost sheepish because Freddie had a thing about never taking tablets. "Just something to help me sleep. Mum insisted; you know how she gets." I know that there is no shame in needing some help, but I want him to be proud of how I'm coping. In my head he asks me if the tablets have helped, and I smile, hesitant. "I didn't think they would. I haven't been sleeping in our bed at all, until the other night."

And how was it? he asks.

"I didn't realize you were still here," I breathe out, my heart quickening. "I've been so afraid to go to sleep, not realizing that you were waiting for me." I half laugh, giddy.

"I feel different today, Freddie," I say, quiet, even though there's no one around to hear me. "Every day since the accident has been like I'm moving through a gray fog or something, but today there's a chink of light. It's like, I don't know . . ." I shrug and cast around for a way to explain. "As if you're flashing a torch at me in a complicated sequence from somewhere a long way away, and I'm concentrating really hard to follow the pattern. To find you. What are we doing right now where you are?" I glance at my watch. "Midday on Saturday. No doubt you're going to the football with Jonah."

Wow, I can even be pass-agg to a dead man. It's just that sometimes when I think of Jonah and that fast-fading scar across his eyebrow, I boil with the injustice of it all. Freddie should have just come straight home on my birthday, not detoured to Jonah's. My logical brain kicks in most of the time and tells me that it's hideous to lay even a speck of blame at Jonah's door, but sometimes, late at night, I can't stop the thoughts. I've pretty much avoided him since the funeral; texts have gone unanswered, missed calls not returned.

Don't be so hard on him, Freddie tells me.

I sigh because it's easy for him to say. "I know, I know. It's just . . ." I open the pack of wipes as I pause, because even speaking the words out loud feels too much. "It's just that I sometimes wonder, if you'd only just let him drive himself for once . . ." I huff, wiping the headstone a little too vigorously as I finish the sentence inside my head.

He was my best friend, Freddie reminds me. *And your oldest friend too, remember?*

I push the dead flowers into the rubbish bag, breaking the brittle stems as I shake my head. "Of course I remember," I say. I've known Jonah even longer than I've known Freddie. "But things change. People change."

Jonah doesn't, Freddie says, and I don't tell him he's wrong, even though he is. A light went out in Jonah the day of the accident, one I'm not sure he'll ever find a way to reignite. I sigh and look to the skies, aware that I'm adding to Jonah's burden by distancing myself, and feeling shoddy for it.

"I'll try, okay?" I say. "Next time I see him, I'll make the effort." It's a deal I make with the knowledge that day to day, Jonah isn't someone I run into very often.

"I guess I should get going," I say, gathering my things back into the bag. I subconsciously trace my eyes around the golden letters of Freddie's name. Freddie Hunter. His mum wanted to put Frederick—we came as close to rowing as we ever have about it. I stood my ground. He hated being called Frederick; no way was I having it etched on his gravestone for all eternity.

I linger beside the stone, ready and not ready to go. This is the worst bit about coming here: leaving. I try not to think about it too much, about the reality of what is left of him beneath the ground. There were times in the darkest nights just after his funeral when I seriously contemplated vaulting the cemetery gates and scrabbling in the dirt until my fingers closed around the unassuming black pot that holds my life as well as his inside it. It's a bloody good job we didn't have Freddie buried; I cannot be certain that I'd have been able to stop myself from turning up with a torch and a spade and burying myself beneath the dark earth with him.

I sigh heavily as I push myself up from the ground and peel the damp plastic bag from the bum of my jeans, then kiss my fingertips and lay them silently on his stone. "See you later, I hope," I whisper, crossing my fingers on both hands as I turn away and walk toward the car park.

I stow my bags in the boot and slam the lid, startled by the vibration of my phone in the back pocket of my jeans. Elle's name flashes up when I click the screen.

Meet me at The Prince for an hour? I'm already there; new job jitters! I'm sure you could do with a drink too?

I look at her message curiously, no idea how to respond. I haven't set foot in our local pub since the day of Freddie's funeral. She knows that, of course; I've turned the idea down every time she's suggested it in recent weeks. And it's not just the pub; I've pushed away all suggestions of going anywhere. Then I think back over the course of this morning; Elle's probably taken the fact that I've brushed my hair and put on a little makeup as a sign of my progression from red-hot-poker grief to whatever the next stage is. I don't know the name for it; battleship-gray grief maybe? I know the stages have been given actual names by psychologists, but I think of them in terms of colors. Angry red. Endless black. And now, here, hinterland gray as far as the eye can see. I think about Elle's suggestion. Can I face the pub? I don't have other plans; my Saturday is a blank sheet and I know how nervous she is about her new job. She's given so much of her time to me since the accident, perhaps I can give a little back.

"Okay," I fire off, quickly, before I can let myself say no. "See you in ten."

I FEEL AS if everyone is staring at me as I walk into the pub, like one of those saloon bars in the Wild West where everyone pauses when the doors swing open, and glares at the stranger who's dared to enter their midst. I'm probably over-egging it. In fact I definitely am, given that there's less than twenty people in the place and half of them are pensioners nursing pints of mild and watching the snooker on the tiny TV up in the far corner.

The Prince of Wales is a proper pub, complete with ill-advised green and brown carpet and beer mats from the '70s. Not a flashy menu in sight; Ron behind the bar runs to crusty cheese rolls and pickled onions on match days if we're lucky. But it's our local pub, just round the corner from home with little appeal to the hipster crowd, beloved by the patrons for exactly that reason. I've never once felt nervous coming in here, but I do today. Sickly nervous in fact, and very alone as I scan the room in search of my sister.

I spy her before she sees me. She's standing with David and a few others over by the slot machine, her back angled toward me, wineglass in hand, as she leans in to listen to the guy next to her. I swallow hard as I recognize Freddie's drinking mates: people we went to school with, guys who've been on the fringes of my life forever. David spots me and lifts his hand, nudging Elle to let her know I'm here. She's by my side in a flash, her hand sliding into mine.

"Good girl," she says. It could come over as patronizing from someone else, but not from Elle because I know she gets how difficult this is for me, and I also know how much she misses the things we used to do together. "Let's get you a drink." She squeezes my fingers, a subtle gesture that I appreciate as we make for the bar.

I keep my eyes trained forward, not glancing toward the group by the slot machine, even though I know they must all be looking my way. Truth told, I've avoided going anywhere where people knew Freddie because I haven't been able to face answering questions about how I'm coping, or hearing about their own shock and grief. Is that selfish of me? I just can't summon the emotional wherewithal to be bothered about them.

Ron, the owner, smiles at Elle and reaches for a fresh glass. "Same again?"

His eyes slide to me, and it takes him a few seconds to place me as Freddie's girlfriend. Something akin to panic flashes over his face momentarily before he recovers himself.

Elle nods and turns to me. "Lydia?"

For a moment I feel as if this is the first time I have ever been in a pub, confused and hot under the collar, seventeen again pretending to be old enough to drink. My eyes skate over the bottles too fast and I can feel my heart begin to race.

"Glass of wine?" Ron suggests, already reaching a second glass down from the overhead rack, and it is as much as I can do to nod gratefully. He doesn't ask what I want, just slides a large glass of something chilled and white in front of me, pats my hand briefly, and gives Elle a fierce look when she tries to pay for the drinks.

"On the house," he says, gruff to the point of a growl as he picks up his cloth and polishes the bar, doing his best to act disinterested. I look at Elle and can see that she's a little choked up by the gesture. I'm getting tearful and Ron is in danger of wearing a hole in the bar, so I pick up my glass with a small, appreciative smile and head for a table in the corner. Elle detours briefly to David and the huddle by the slot machine, and I take a gulp of wine and glance across to see who's there. The usual suspects: Deckers and co. sinking a few beers before the football–Freddie's friends of old. Duffy, the tight accountant, is there, his pale blue shirt too formal for a Saturday; and Raj, a guy we went to school with who runs his own building firm these days, I think. There're a couple of others too: Boner–don't ask me why they call him that because I don't even want to know–is hammering the buttons on the slot machine, and there's Stu, I think, who spends most of his life at the gym. I don't make eye contact with any of them, which I'm sure they are entirely grateful for. Death is a surefire way to become a complete social pariah.

"Free drinks," Elle says, sliding onto the stool beside mine at the small, round table. "First time for everything."

She isn't wrong. Everything feels like a first time at the moment. First time I fry bacon without Freddie eating it straight out of the pan before I can get it on the sandwich. First time I sleep in our bed alone. First time I go to the pub as the girlfriend of that poor guy who died. None of the first times I'd envisaged or hoped for at this stage of my life.

"Nice of Ron," I mumble, pulling my already half-empty glass closer to me. I should slow down.

Then the door opens and Jonah Jones walks in, head

to toe in black as usual, his dark hair as unruly as always. I can't help it—it twists me up inside to see him alone, he's like Woody without Buzz. He stops to speak to the guys at the slot machine, his hand on Deckers's shoulder, then heads for the bar. He turns our way, tapping a beer mat against the edge of the bar as Ron pulls him a pint, his smile vague and then sliding right off his face when he finally registers me. Likely he feels a punch in the gut at the empty space beside me too, quickly followed up by unease at the way things are between us now. I last saw him at the funeral, both of us barely holding ourselves together. He looks better today, his fingers instinctively moving to trace the healed wound above his eyebrow as his gaze holds mine. I don't know if I should get up and say hello so I stay nailed to my stool, held there by indecision. I don't think he knows what to do either, which is stupid because we've known each other since we were twelve years old. More than half of our lives, yet we're eyeballing each other across the pub like wary lions unsure if we're part of the same pride anymore.

Jonah picks up the pint Ron places before him and drains almost a third of it, muttering thanks when Ron refills it without comment. I'm relieved when David steps in and unwittingly breaks the moment, joining Jonah at the bar before shepherding him across to join us. He drops down next to his wife as Jonah bends to kiss Elle first and then me, his hand warm on my shoulder as he leans in to my cheek.

"Hey, you," he says, taking the stool on my other side. Jonah had the edge on Freddie heightwise, but he's long and lean rather than rugby broad, a panther to Freddie's lion. "It's been a while."

I could tell him the exact number of days since the funeral, but instead I pick at a loose edge on the laminated table, making it worse. "Yeah."

He knocks back more of his beer and slides it onto the table. "How've you been?"

"I'm okay," I say. Words have deserted me. Jonah is so tied to Freddie in my head, I don't know how to be around him now. David is showing Elle something on his phone, most probably to give Jonah and me a little privacy.

"I tried to call."

I nod, awkward. "I know. I haven't really felt like . . . I haven't been able to . . ."

"It's fine," he says, rushing in. "I get it."

I don't tell him that he can't possibly get it, because I know he's one of the people who misses Freddie most of all. Jonah doesn't have much in the way of family of his own. His mum's most significant relationship has always been with the bottle, and his dad was someone else's husband. No siblings to share the load, no home comforts to look forward to at the end of the school day. I know these snippets secondhand from Freddie rather than Jonah himself—as a child he made vague excuses for his mother's absence at parents' evening, and as an adult he doesn't mention either of his parents at all. I guess Freddie and I were the closest thing he ever knew to real family.

"But you're doing okay?" he asks. Unspoken words sit between us, as his fingers make sure his scar is covered by his slightly-too-long hair.

I shrug. "Okay. Not falling apart at the seams in public anyway, which trust me, is an improvement." I hear the subtle my-grief-is-bigger-than-yours edge to my voice; it isn't fair and I know it. He looks down and rubs his hands along the length of his thighs, restless, and when he lifts his dark, troubled gaze to mine again I get the feeling he's gearing up to say something so I jump in first.

"I'm sorry," I say, fiddling with the stem of my glass. "I seem to have lost the ability to make small talk. Ignore me."

He sighs and shakes his head. "No worries," he says.

Oh, this feels awful, awkward. Jonah taps the edge of a beer mat against the table, a nervous beat. He's musical down to his bones; a self-taught pianist and a dabbler in who knows how many other instruments besides. It was always his thing when we were kids. Freddie wasn't musical at all, except for one brief summer when he decided he was going to be a rock star. It faded as quickly as it began, but every now and then he'd come across his old Fender in the loft and for a few minutes he'd think he was Brian May.

"I'll leave you to it," Jonah says, suddenly decisive, his hand a brief squeeze on my shoulder as he gets to his feet. I almost reach out to stop him because it's on my mind that I should attempt to hold out some kind of olive branch. I told Freddie not an hour ago that I'd try. I open my mouth to say something, anything, and then we all look up distracted as Deckers approaches our table. He was one of the troublesome kids when we were all at school, small and scrappy, probably the bane of the staff room. I haven't really spoken to him very much in recent years, and he's awkward now as he puts a glass down in front of me. I look at him, noticing the twin spots of embarrassed color on his cheeks, at odds with his usual cocksure attitude. Then I look at the drink he's placed down: a spirit of some sort I'd say, vodka or gin. No mixer. I don't know if that's because he feels I need something strong or because he can't imagine why anyone would willingly dilute alcohol.

He doesn't say anything, and for a horrible moment he looks like he might cry.

"Thank you," I all but whisper, and he nods, once and sharp, then saunters back toward the slot machine, rolling his shoulders.

"Another free drink," Elle says, making light. "You can come with us again."

I raise a shaky smile and Jonah takes the opportunity to leave us and head for the bar.

I pick up the tumbler and sniff it. "Vodka, I think."

Deckers looks our way from the safety of the slot machine, so I do the polite thing and throw half of it down my throat. Jesus, it's strong; my eyes are smarting.

Placing the glass down, I look at Elle. "My teeth have gone numb," I say.

She half laughs, half huffs. "Won't do you any harm."

"It's barely midday and I'm drinking neat vodka," I murmur.

At that moment, Boner appears beside our table, lanky and rail thin. A very similar tableau plays out: an unidentified drink for me, a nod of the head.

"Thank you . . . er . . . Boner," I say, sounding like someone's prim aunt.

David picks up his beer and I see him try to hide his smirk in it. Boner breathes a sigh of relief and beats a hasty retreat.

"What's funny?" I mutter.

"It just sounded odd, you calling him Boner."

"What else was I supposed to call him?"

"Pete? It's what most people call him these days."

Shit. "Freddie always called him Boner, I'm sure of it," I say, hot faced.

"It *is* his nickname. It's just . . . I don't know. A lad's thing. He couldn't control himself around girls when he was a kid, always used to get . . ." David breaks off, as if he's trying to decide how to phrase it delicately.

"I get the picture," I butt in, and we both stare down at our drinks. Elle is rummaging in her bag for something to do, and David is far too nice to laugh at my embarrassment.

"I can't drink these," I say, changing the subject, and then I groan under my breath as yet another of Freddie's friends brings me a shot. Duffy, the tight accountant. The fact that he's so tight makes the gesture somehow even more significant.

"I'm sorry for your loss," he says, funeral director formal. It's a phrase I'd happily petition to have struck from the English language, but I know he means well.

"Thank you, that's kind," I say, and he melts away, his duty done.

I get it. They're paying their respects. These were the guys who cheered beside Freddie at the football and who formed an unofficial guard of honor outside the church at his funeral. These drinks are for Freddie Hunter rather than me.

I line the drinks up, wondering in desperation whether it would be a terrible plan to put them all in one glass and down it in one go. When I look up I catch Jonah's eye across the pub and he holds my gaze for a few seconds, whether in amusement or sympathy, I can't tell.

Thankfully, the free drinks parade seems to have ended; the slot machine crew have probably realized that a girl has her limits, or perhaps they're worried I might get overemotional and make a scene.

"Shall I get you a mixer?" Elle pretends solicitousness. "Two liters of Coke should do it."

"You're going to have to drink one for me," I plead quietly.

"You know I can't mix my drinks," she laughs. "It makes me insane."

David nods, backing her up, fear in his gray eyes, forever #TeamElle. I can't rely on him to help me out either; he's strictly a three beers man. I don't think I've ever seen him get stupid-drunk. He isn't dull though; his pithy sense of humor can make me cry laughing and he loves the bones of my sister, which makes him a superstar in my eyes.

I pick up the gin and remind myself that it's famously known as mother's rescue. Or is it mother's ruin? I'm going with rescue, because that's what I need: rescue from my relentless sorrow. My eyes slide to the window, watching a street sweeping machine trundle slowly along the gutters. I wish it could sweep out the dark corners of my mind, the dusty rooms at the back stacked with memories of holidays, lazy mornings in bed, and late nights drinking calvados by the lake in France. Would I really erase Freddie from my memory if I could? God no, of course not. It's just hard to know what to do with all of the stuff in my head now he isn't here. Perhaps in time those memories will be precious, and I'll be able to draw pleasure from taking them out one by one and laying them around me like a carpet. Not yet though.

Wine, vodka, and gin. It's not a great combination in quick succession. "I think I might need a lie down," I say.

"You're hammered, kid. Time to go home, I think," David says, getting to his feet. "We'll walk back with you."

Elle checks no one is looking and then downs the brandy with a shudder.

"Things I do for you," she says under her breath.

I appreciate the gesture, because it would have been rude to leave any of the drinks on the table.

Ron lifts a hand in my direction as we make for the exit, and the boys around the slot machine all fall silent and bow their heads as I pass, as if I'm Queen Victoria, forever in my widow's weeds for Prince Albert.

We blink as we spill out into the weak early-summer sunshine, and David catches my elbow to rein me in when I almost veer off the edge of the pavement.

"Tough gig, that," he says. "You did well, Lyds."

"Thank you," I say, a little overwhelmed and a lot tearful.

Elle and I link arms as we head toward home, swaying in gentle tandem, David a step behind, no doubt to keep a safety eye on us.

"Bloody hard work, grieving," I say.

"Takes it out of you," Elle agrees.

"Will it always, do you think?" I ask her.

She squeezes my arm against her side. "Your life is still your life, Lyds. You're still here, inconveniently breathing, watching the sun go down and the moon come up regardless of whether you think it's got a damn nerve showing its shiny face every day."

She props me up as we walk the last few steps to my pale turquoise front door. We all have different colored woodwork in our row, a pastel paint box chosen to add to the wow factor of the cottages. It was already turquoise when we bought it. One of the super organized people farther down sent a paint chart around and everyone got to choose their shade.

"Need some sleep," I mutter.

David reaches over and takes my keys from my hand, opening the door for me.

"Want us to come in for a while?" Elle says.

I look from one to the other, knowing full well that if I say the word they would. They'd come in, make sure I sleep, make sure I wake up again, make sure I eat, and tempting as it is to let them take care of me, I shake my head. Something shifted inside me when I walked into the pub alone today. Perhaps I was bolstered by my sleep encounter with Freddie, or maybe I discovered a small well of untapped bravery somewhere deep inside, I don't know. What I do know is that the people who love me have been holding on so tight to my hands that

I haven't yet had to walk alone. But sooner or later, I have to. Today, now, is as good a time to start as any.

"You two carry on. I'll call you later," I say, giving them both a quick, on-your-way-now hug. "I need a glass of water and a lie down."

I see Elle open her mouth to argue, but David lays a hand on her arm and speaks instead.

"Okay," he says. "Can I suggest a headache pill too?"

I nod, salute, find a smile from the bottom of my boots. "Good call."

I watch them for a few seconds as they strike out toward home, David's arm around Elle's shoulders. I hold silent the part of me that wants to call out for them to come back, and instead I step inside and close my front door.

ASLEEP

Saturday, May 12

"LYDIA?"

You know that kind of sleep you fall into after a bout of daytime drinking, the sleeping at the bottom of the sea kind? I'm fathoms below when I hear Freddie say my name, and it takes all of my concentration to push myself off the bottom, kicking furiously upward to get to him before he goes away.

"Wow, Lyds, you were dead to the world." Freddie's hand is on my shoulder, shaking me lightly. "Did you and Elle go shopping?"

I scrabble to sit up straight in the corner of the sofa, rubbing the crick in my neck where I'd slumped over. I can't gauge what time it is, if I've been out for five minutes or five hours. My head is pounding; my heart, too, at the sight of Freddie.

"You're looking at me weird."

You would too if you were me, I think but don't say as I clear my throat.

"Would you grab me a glass of water?" I croak.

He frowns and looks at me more closely, then laughs. "Have you two been on the wine already? Jeez, Lyds, that's hard-core even for you."

"Here," he says, coming back through with a couple of pills as well as the water. "Take these."

I accept them one by one, swallowing them down.

"You look like an extra from *Shaun of the Dead*," he smiles, smoothing my hair behind my ear. "You haven't been crying, have you?"

I focus on the clock. It's just after two in the afternoon; I can't have been asleep for long. I backtrack over the time since Elle and David deposited me on the doorstep: the failed attempt to sleep on the sofa, even though my brain ached, the last resort a pretty pink sleeping pill with alcohol still swilling around in my system.

And then this. I'm wide awake in my sleep again, and Freddie is here, taking the piss out of me for drinking too much with Elle. There is very little point in telling him that I was drinking with Jonah Jones too and we couldn't find anything to say to each other, because he won't believe a word, and why would he? I don't actually know what I've been doing here in this world. Maybe I *have* been out for a breezy morning shopping and a couple of lunchtime glasses of wine with Elle.

"Hate to tell you this, Lyds, but you might want to scrape the mascara off your cheeks. Jonah's coming to watch the game with me in about . . ." He breaks off to look at his watch. "Ten minutes ago. Late as usual."

"Do something with me instead?" I say. "Take me somewhere. Anywhere. Just you and me."

"You sound more like Ed Sheeran every day," he says, as he pulls his phone from the back pocket of his jeans, no doubt to text Jonah. But then he shoves it away as we hear the sound of the back door opening.

"Cutting it fine." Freddie grins as Jonah strolls into the living room with a box of Bud under his arm. "Tell me it was for a woman at least."

Jonah glances at me and I'm convinced he's going to say *yes, I was with Lydia.*

"Auditioning for *Night of the Living Dead,* Lyds?"

I stare at him, trying to work out if he's playing a part. If he is, I can't imagine many more cruel things to say. I mean, *come on. Night of the the Living Dead*?

"Knobhead," I mutter, and he does a tiny double take.

"Grumpy," he shoots back, then grins.

"She's just woken up," Freddie says, taking the beer. "She needs five minutes to become her usual sunshine self." He shoots me a wink, laughing as he heads to the kitchen.

Jonah drops down on the other end of my sofa, his arms flung wide across the back. He shouldn't be here; this is *my* dream. I'm pretty sure that means I'm entitled to have Freddie all to myself. I experiment with the idea of being in charge and try to mentally eject Jonah from the living room, half expecting him to spring up and leave backward as if someone pressed rewind on a DVD. He doesn't though. He just lounges in that boneless way he has, perpetually somewhere on a beach with a beer in his hand and his toes in the sand.

"What's new with you then, Lyds?"

Right, so we're doing this. Surely it would be okay for him to break character now Freddie is out of the room?

"You know," I whisper, leaning in, testing him. "In the pub, earlier? Wine, and gin, and vodka, and brandy?"

He stares at me, nonplussed. "This morning? Bloody hell, Lyds, that's going some."

I watch him in speculative silence and realize there isn't a trace of understanding in his clear brown gaze. What's there is puzzlement, and then traces of discomfort as the silence lengthens. Embarrassment, even. I cringe a little and withdraw to my end of the sofa, aware my breath must smell like a pub carpet, and I probably look like someone should stab me through the heart with silver.

"Ignore me," I say, pulling the cushion over my head. "Pretend I'm not here."

The irony isn't lost on me. I cannot possibly be here.

"Shall I stick the kettle on? Coffee might help."

I fight the irrational urge to tell Jonah to piss off for trying to be helpful. Dragging the cushion from my face, I sit up straight and scrub at my cheeks as Freddie comes back in and flops on the chair opposite.

Freddie. I want to climb into his lap. I want to fill my head with the scent of him, for his arms to hold me and his lips to kiss me. I want Jonah Jones to go, even as he accepts the beer Freddie holds out across the coffee table and they fall into easy conversation. I rest against the back of the sofa for a couple of minutes with my eyes closed, feigning disinterest as I watch

Freddie through my lashes. And then my eyes fly wide open as Jonah speaks.

"I'm buying a motorbike."

I'm surprised; dismayed. Freddie was always on about getting a bike, always in a hurry to get farther, faster but Jonah has never struck me as the type. Since Freddie's accident, the idea of anyone willfully putting themselves in any kind of danger on the road fills me with dread. Just getting behind the wheel of the car again was an achievement for me.

"Just fancy a change from the Saab, sometimes," he says, conversationally, man-to-man. Jonah drives an old black Saab convertible, a leather-lined battleship on wheels that he loves for no discernible reason. "It's getting a bit long in the tooth; might shake things up a bit."

"Don't do it," I blurt, too loud, too panicky.

They both look at me, startled by my unexpected outburst.

"Spur of the moment decision. There was a photo pinned to the board in the staff room," he says, looking slowly away from me to Freddie, choosing to let my words go uncommented on. He must think I've lost it. "Off Gripper Grimes, of all people."

Freddie barks with laughter. "You're buying a motorbike off Gripper Grimes?"

Gripper Grimes taught us all maths. He earned his nickname from the way he picked kids up by the scruff of their shirt collar to haul them out of class—Freddie most often of all. It's strange hearing Jonah speak of the teachers who terrorized us as kids as his colleagues now.

"You won't believe this thing when you see it." Jonah's eyes glow. "Classic Norton Manx. He's barely had it out the garage since he bought it new."

From what I recall of Gripper Grimes, he wasn't exactly a wind in his sideburns, open roads kind of man.

"He always drove that knackered old white Volvo," Freddie recalls.

Jonah nods. "Still does, mate."

"No way!"

Jonah nods again. "Serviced twice a year and looked after. Made to last, like his wife, he says."

I'm amazed Gripper is even still alive, let alone making seventies-style jokes about the long-suffering Mrs. Grimes. He must have sailed past retirement age back when he taught us. That he's still teaching, and even more that he's still driving, is a shock.

Freddie flicks the TV over to the pre-match warm up, the pundits on the sidelines in competitively big coats interviewing anyone they can lay their hands on. I'm suddenly hot and feel as if I might be sick; a hangover and talking to your dead fiancé will do that to a girl. Lurching to my feet, I mumble something about the bathroom and make a dash for the stairs.

Ten minutes later I grab the sink and haul myself up off my knees, relieved to have flushed the contents of my stomach down the loo. I rinse my mouth out and stare at my reflection in the mirrored cabinet over the sink. Wow, I look hideous. Fresh tear tracks from throwing up streak through the mascara stains already on my cheeks. And that's when I notice I'm wearing the tiny, enamel bluebird pendant my mum gave me for my eighteenth. I didn't put it on this morning. I couldn't have.

I lost it five years ago.

"BETTER?" FREDDIE SAYS, glancing up at me when I go back downstairs.

I nod and raise a lackluster smile. "Need something to eat, I think."

"Line your stomach," Freddie says, his attention already back on the game.

"Pizza?" Jonah nods toward the box flipped open on the coffee table.

The sight of congealing cheese sets my stomach churning again. "Think I better stick to toast," I say, my fingertips clutched around the bluebird nestled in the space between my collarbones. I'm so glad to see it again. I lost it in a club. I didn't even miss it until the next day. It wasn't especially valuable to anyone but me, but of course no one had handed it in. My brain is trying to piece together what it means that I still have it here.

Sitting at the kitchen table, I lay my head on my folded arms and just listen: to Freddie's animated match commentary and Jonah laughingly telling him to calm down before he has a heart attack, to the clink of beer bottles being opened and slid onto the glass coffee table Freddie loved and I never really liked, to the life I used to take for granted carrying on regardless of the fact that Freddie died fifty-eight days ago.

It's too much for my hungover brain to handle. I don't want toast, or water, or to wake up and find he isn't here, so I just go back through to the living room and sit on the floor beside Freddie's chair, my head against his knee. He absently strokes my hair and makes a joke about me not being able to hold my drink, but he's too engrossed in the game to notice the damp patch on the knee of his jeans from my tears. I hide my face with my hair and close my eyes, too tired to do anything but press myself against his warm solidity. I don't think there can be much time left in the football match. I try to focus on my watch but my eyes are bleary. Go home, Jonah Jones, I think. Go home so I can lay out on the sofa beside Freddie and ask him about his day. I need to listen to the rumble of his chest against my ear as he speaks. He winds my hair around his fingers, and I battle, properly battle, not to fall asleep, but it's no good. My eyelids are lead-lined. I can't seem to lift them, even though I'm desperate to stay awake, because I'm missing him already.

AWAKE

Saturday, May 12

THIS IS HIDEOUS. I've just woken up alone in the living room, water rather than beers on the table, no cold pizza, and no Freddie. *This.* This is why I don't go to sleep. Because waking up and remembering that he's dead all over again is too cruel, too harrowing. The price of dreaming about him is higher than I could ever hope to pay. It's a higher price than *anyone* should *ever* have to pay. For no logical reason, fragments of Tennyson's most famous poem still lodged in my brain from school roll around inside my head as I lie on the sofa trying to summon the will to get up. "'Tis better to have loved and lost than never to have loved at all"—that one, the only one everyone knows. Well, Tennyson, my friend, I bet your wife didn't wrap herself around a tree and leave you on your Billy-no-mates own, did she? Because if she had, you might have thought it more prudent not to love at all. I sigh, feeling uncharitable, because I also recall from my studies that Tennyson wrote the poem whilst grieving for his beloved best friend, so perhaps his heart did go through the wringer somewhat too. I wonder if he cried as much as I have. It's cathartic sometimes, crying, and at other times it's the loneliest thing in the world, knowing no one is coming to give me a consolation hug. I don't fight it when tears run down my face again right now, for poor old Tennyson, and for poor old me.

ASLEEP

Saturday, May 12

"FEELING BETTER NOW?"

I wasn't going to take another pill. I limped through to eight o'clock and then caved in, washing one down as I climbed into bed for an early night.

And now I've woken up on the sofa with my head on Freddie's lap. He's absently smoothing my hair while he watches some police drama on TV, and I've obviously been snoozing off the remains of my headache.

I flip onto my back. "Think so," I say, catching hold of his hand.

"You've missed half of this," he says. "Shall I rewind it?"

I glance at the screen, but I've no clue what show it is so I shake my head.

"You were snoring like a beast, Lyds," he says, laughing under his breath. It's his running joke: he always tells me that I snore loudly and I always deny it. I don't think I snore at all; he just says it to wind me up.

"I bet Keira Knightley snores," I say.

He raises his eyebrows. "Nah. She probably sighs softly, like a . . ."

"Trucker?" I suggest.

"Kitten," he says.

"Kittens don't sigh," I say. "They bite your toes while you sleep."

Freddie considers it for a second. "I quite like the idea of Keira Knightley biting my toes."

"She'd have super sharp teeth," I say. "It'd hurt."

"Hmm," he frowns. "You know I'm not good with pain."

It's true. For a big, competitive man, Freddie is a real wimp when he's hurt.

"Maybe I better stick with you," he says. "Keira sounds too much like hard work."

I lift his hand up and place my own against it, palm to palm, noticing how much bigger his is.

"Even if I snore like a hog?"

He laces his fingers with mine. "Even if you snore like a field full of hogs."

I bring his hand to my face and kiss his fingers. "That's not very romantic, you know," I say.

He pauses the show he's watching and looks down at me, his blue eyes amused.

"How about if I say you're a very pretty hog?"

I twist my mouth, thinking, then shake my head. "Still not romantic."

He nods slowly. "Okay," he says. "Not a hog at all?"

"Bit better," I say, hanging out for more, trying not

to smile as I pull myself up to sit in his lap, my legs stretched out on the sofa.

Freddie holds my chin and looks me deep in the eyes. "If you're a hog, I'm a hog."

I burst out laughing. I've clearly made him watch *The Notebook* too many times for him to bust out that line.

"You have no idea how much I love you, Freddie Hunter," I say, and then I show him how much with my kiss, and I make myself a promise. This place, wherever—whatever—it is, is beautiful, and for however long it lasts, I'm going to make the most of every single moment.

AWAKE

Sunday, May 20

SOMEONE'S RINGING MY DOORBELL. My gaze slides to the clock, irritated at being interrupted doing nothing. Yes, it's turned midday and I'm still in my pj's, but hey, it's Sunday. Plus I *have* actually had a shower. Frankly, I'd like to lay here like a statue until the sofa digests me. That can actually happen; I've seen it on morning TV. The chemicals in your sofa eat you alive if you lie on it for long enough. I indulge in a not wholly unpleasant daydream where the sofa opens up like a big fabric Venus flytrap and swallows me whole, but I don't have the luxury of letting it happen. Elle's peering at me through the bay window and from the way she's rummaging in her bag I can tell she's looking for her keys to let herself in. I didn't actually give my mother or Elle a key to my house. One of them must've appropriated the spare in the raw days following the accident, and evidently they've had copies cut so that any number of people can swan in and interrupt my wallowing whenever they feel the need.

I sit up and try to arrange my face into a less morose expression as Elle deposits her bags in the hall and calls out a hello.

"In here," I say, forcing a brightness I don't feel into my voice.

"Didn't you hear the door?" Elle sticks her head round the doorframe as she takes her boots off. I don't expect people to take their boots off when they come in, for the record. It's just a habit that's been drummed into us both by our mother, ever since she installed a cream carpet in our childhood home. "I knocked twice."

"Dozing," I say, giving myself a little "pull it together" shake as I stand up. "You caught me."

Elle's face falls. "You didn't sleep so well last night?"

"On and off," I say. The truthful answer is barely. I don't want to take the pills to help me sleep at night because visiting my other life when everyone there is sleeping feels like a waste. I did it the other night, and oh my word yes, it was all kinds of lovely to watch Freddie sleep, but on balance I crave his time and his words and his waking love. I've become a nocturnal animal, awake with Freddie when I should be asleep, trying to sleep when I should be awake. I don't explain any of this to Elle though. If I tell her I've found a back door to a universe where Freddie isn't dead she'll think that I've been on the Kool-Aid. Or the vodka. Again.

She follows me through to the kitchen, picking up a canvas shopping bag in the hallway. "Grabbed some bits and bobs you might fancy," she says, laying ready-made pancakes and fresh lemons on the table. Shrove Tuesday was always a big event when we were younger; she's the chef of the family and always made a thing of how good she was at tossing pancakes like a pro. Mine usually ended up on the floor, whereas hers were perfect rounds served up with sugar and lemon.

"Lemons for my gin?"

My lame attempt at a joke doesn't hit the mark; she picks up the little net and places it pointedly on top of the pancakes. It's not as if I'm a huge gin drinker, but she's a worrier so I'm sure she must have awful images in her head of me drinking alone at the kitchen table in the middle of the night. Chicken breasts follow: two in the box. I don't ask her who the other one is supposed to be for. It's not her fault that the world caters to couples and I'm now Lydia-lonesome.

"Cake," she says. "Coffee and walnut, your fave."

It's as if she thinks I'll have forgotten. I look at its fancy wax paper wrapping and nod obligingly. "It is."

She pulls milk and juice from the bag, then bread and eggs and ham.

"You don't need to do this, you know," I say, opening the fridge to stash the things away. The scant contents of my fridge call me out as a liar. Most of the things in there have been bought by someone other than me. Soup in Mum's Tupperware, grapes from my workmates, cheese and yogurt Elle herself put there earlier this week. The only thing I've supplied for myself is the wine and a tub of cream cheese.

"I know I don't, but I like to," she says, handing me the butter. "Coffee?"

I nod, grateful.

"Were we supposed to be doing something today?" I say, catching sight of Elle's haul of bags in the hallway. I hope I haven't made plans with her and then forgotten.

She looks at me oddly for a silent second then shakes her head. "I went into town before coming over here. Didn't think you'd fancy it."

"Next time," I say lightly.

She smiles hesitantly, probably because—last weekend's trip to The Prince aside—that's the first time in weeks I've so much as hinted that I might like to do anything other than ghost around the house like Nicole Kidman in *The Others*.

"Get anything nice?" I ask. "Other than coffee-and-walnut cake?" I pick it up and sniff it to show her how much I appreciate the thought.

"Just some work stuff." She shrugs the question off, even though Mum tells me that she's fizzing with excitement about her new job at the hotel.

"Can I see?"

Honestly, the look she gives me makes me feel as if I am the most shit sister in the world. It's hope coupled with distrust, wary kitten-like, as if I might change my mind and whip the saucer of milk away if she shows too much excitement. Ashamed, I make sounds of approval when she shows me the clothes she's bought, and in truth I do feel a genuine pang of envy over her new shoes—not the shoes themselves, but what they represent. New shoes, new job, new start. I hope she doesn't find a new best friend there too.

"Are you nervous?" I ask, watching her fold the tissue just so over the shoes before she closes the lid. She'd definitely be Monica.

"Massively," she says. "Worried I'll be like the new kid at school that no one likes."

I laugh softly. "I don't think there's a single person who knows you that doesn't like you."

She looks doubtful. "Am I bland?"

"Not bland," I say. "Definitely not bland. Just kind and funny." I screw up my nose. "And a tiny bit bossy sometimes." I hold my thumb and index finger about an inch apart. "This much."

She looks down her nose at me. "Only because you need someone to boss you around sometimes."

"I'm glad it's you."

"It could be worse. It could be Mum," she points out, and we both nod, because we know it's true.

"Will you have to boss people around at work?"

"I'll have about ten staff."

"Ah," I say, sagely. "You won't be the new kid then. You'll be the new teacher. They'll all be trying to impress you, bringing you apples and stuff."

"You reckon? I'll bring them here and make you eat them if they do. You need the vitamins more than I do."

"You're being bossy again."

"Practicing for work."

"You've got it down."

We sit for a second and drink our coffee.

"Cake?" I say.

"I will if you will," she says, a line reminiscent of so many other days of our lives. Sledging down the hill behind the house on winter mornings when we were kids, our backsides on Mum's tea trays: I will if you will. Getting our ears pierced at the dodgy salon in the precinct when we were teenagers: I will if you will. Another drink at last orders, even though we've both had enough: I will if you will. Keep breathing even though you're heartsick: I will if you will.

I reach for the cake and unpick the pretty wrapper. "It's a deal," I say.

CAKE TURNS INTO an impromptu movie fest after Elle flicks on the TV and finds *Dirty Dancing*, and we pass a couple of hours watching an earnest-eyed Patrick Swayze gyrate his snake hips at Baby Houseman. I rack my brain to remember the last time I danced, but I can't. It's as if my life has been split in two: before the accident and after. Sometimes I struggle to bring the details of my old life into sharp relief, and panic tightens my chest at the thought of forgetting us, of forgetting Freddie Hunter. I know I'll always be able to recall the top notes: his face, our first kiss, his proposal—but it's the other things: the late-night scent of his neck, the gritty determination in his eye when he rescued a tiny frog from the main road and pedaled all the way to the local park with it wrapped in his T-shirt, the way he could bend the little finger on his left hand back farther than was normal. It's those memories I'm scared of losing—the incidentals, the events that made us *us*. The last time we danced, for instance. And then it comes back to me, and the knot in my chest slowly unravels. I danced last on New Year's Eve, both in The Prince and along the frost-lit streets on the way home,

Freddie holding me up, even though he was three sheets to the wind himself. I stumbled that same walk last week with Elle making sure I didn't fall in the gutter.

Okay, Sunday afternoon, we're done here. My sister has gone home to her husband, and I have someone else to be with too.

ASLEEP

Monday, May 21

IT TAKES ME a few seconds to recalibrate and realize we're in Sheila's, the tiny backstreet café around the corner from home, and the waitress has just placed two full English breakfasts down on the table, even though it's after twelve. It's our usual order in here. Freddie likes it more than I do and always wolfs half of mine. I'm comforted by the familiarity of sliding back into our old routine.

"Best thing about bank holiday." He forks a sausage from my plate to his. "Extra breakfast."

It's a plastic chairs and chipped Formica kind of café. Milky tea and instant coffee in mismatched mugs. The paint on the sign outside is faded and flaking, but for all its shortcomings, the food is hearty and the welcome warm from Sheila, whose husband hand painted the sign forty years ago. He died a couple of years back, dropped down while flipping bacon in the café kitchen, just as he'd have wanted, by all accounts. It was standing room only in church for his funeral. I remember being squished between Freddie and a neighbor from a few doors down who leaned heavily against me and sobbed that he'd never known anyone more talented with black pudding. I'm genuinely not making this up. I catch Sheila's eye when she appears through the beaded curtain from the kitchen and she throws me a smile. Freddie is treated to a wink, and he sticks his thumb up in reply.

"Better bacon than my mother," he grins, making her preen. "Don't tell her I said so though."

He has a way of doing that, of making people feel like his favorite. I've seen him do it countless times over the years, catch someone momentarily in his spotlight.

"I'm just going to grab the ketchup," I say, compelled to speak to Sheila. I'm on my feet and at the counter in five steps, not long enough to formulate my thoughts into words.

"Everything okay, love?" she asks, glancing around me at my barely touched breakfast. Sheila is a woman who's fiercely proud of her cooking, despite the unpretentious appearance of the café.

I nod, biting my lip.

"More tea?" she guesses, confused.

I shake my head, feeling stupid. "I just wanted some ketchup." I pause and then stumble on. "And to say how sorry I am about Stan."

I've startled her. I see something familiar move through her eyes. I recognize the fleeting rawness, how she takes an extra breath before she speaks, as I often do when someone unexpectedly mentions Freddie's name. She still hasn't said anything so I fill the void.

"It's just . . . I haven't forgotten about him. That's all."

It's my own fears spoken aloud, that the world will forget Freddie Hunter. I won't, of course, but someone else sits at his desk at the office now, and someone else wears his number on the Monday night five-aside football team. It's perfectly right that the world has kept turning, but sometimes I just want people to say they remember, so I say it now to Sheila and then instantly feel as if I've overstepped the mark.

"When you're young you think you've got all the time in the world," she says. "And then suddenly you turn around and you're old and one of you isn't there anymore and you wonder how the years went so fast." She nods toward Freddie and then shrugs. "Make hay while the sun shines. That's all I'm saying."

It's such a pat phrase, and yet it isn't to me anymore because it's a pretty damn accurate way to sum up my waking world: someone turned my sun off. I take the ketchup Sheila holds out to me with a small nod and head back to Freddie.

"Fancy making hay this afternoon?" I say softly, running my hand over his shoulder before I sit down.

"Making hay?" he says, perplexed. "Is that girl code for sex? Because if it is, then yes."

I smile, putting the ketchup I didn't really need in the first place down on the table. Luckily for him, he'll never know what I mean.

"I've got something to tell you," he says. "Promise me you won't go mad."

"I can't promise," I say. "Not until I know what it is."

He butters his toast as he shakes his head. "Uh-uh. Promise first."

That's so Freddie. "Fine," I relent. "I promise not to go mad."

He's instantly wreathed in smiles. "I booked our honeymoon."

My heart lifts with joy and then sinks because it's entirely possible I won't be able to come back here this time next year. All of this could stop tomorrow. I actually feel it tumble, slow-motion somersaulting behind my breastbone.

"You did?"

He looks so pleased with himself. He's bursting out of his skin to tell me. "Do you want it to be a surprise?"

I shake my head, not trusting myself to speak. I hope he takes the sheen of tears in my eyes as joy. "Where are we going?"

He pauses, as if he's seriously considering not telling me, but then he can't keep the words in. "New York!"

Ah, of course we are. I've always wanted to go to New York. I've seen every episode of *Friends,* I want to be bezzies with Carrie Bradshaw, and I long to walk barefoot in Central Park. I don't even chastise him about the cost, because in my head we're already on the ferry to Staten Island. It's ridiculously, perfectly us.

"You couldn't have got it more right," I say, reaching out across the table for his hand. "Don't tell me any more. Let me daydream awhile."

He rubs his thumb over my knuckles. "You're going to love it, Lyds."

I have no doubt whatsoever. I feel like I'm about to cry, so I change the subject.

"So what shall we do this afternoon?"

"You mean it wasn't girl code for sex?" He looks hangdog, and then laughs. "We're going to the movies, remember?" he says, reminding me of a plan I've no knowledge of. "I'm going to snog your face off on the back row."

"Snog?" I laugh. "No one says that anymore."

He reaches across the table and stabs my egg yolk. "I do. Hurry up, film starts at half one."

"Movies it is, then." It's bank holiday Monday, I'm with Freddie, and we're fine. Better than fine; we're how we used to be: him and me against the world. I'm not even furious with him for the egg yolk thing, even though he always does it just to get a rise out of me. We're going to go to the movies and snog like school kids on the back row. We're going to make hay while the sun shines.

AWAKE

Sunday, May 27

I'M SITTING ON the kitchen floor, my sweat-soaked back pressed against the cupboard, the bottle of pills clutched tight in my still shaking hand. I accidentally sent them flying off the countertop a few minutes ago, and then scrambled around on the floor like an addict, grabbing for them before they slipped through the cracks. I got a painful splinter in my index finger for my trouble, but all that mattered in those panicky seconds was ensuring that every last one of the remaining tablets went safely back where they should be.

I've visited Freddie for the last seven days in a row, and I'm utterly exhausted, as if I've been running marathons in my sleep. Holding the small bottle of pills in my shaking hand, I dully acknowledge that this cannot go on. It's not just the physical toll; there is a steep mental price to pay too. My waking hours have become my waiting hours, filled with impatience and anticipation, edged with sickly fear that it may not happen next time, that I might never again experience the rush. It's impossible to explain how it feels to be there. There was a painting in the National Gallery when Elle and I visited a couple of years ago, an Australian landscape by an artist whose name I can't quite bring to mind. It isn't one of the most well-known pieces nor the most spectacular, but there was something about the clarity of color and the intense quality of the light that held my attention more than any other. My sleeping world is there among the brushstrokes and pigments of that painting: alive and bold and spellbinding. Addictive.

I hold my head in my hands, bereft because the incident with the pills just now has forced me to acknowledge the truth that's been lurking just beneath the surface for the last couple of days: I'm putting myself in real danger here.

Every day since Freddie died has been a fresh mountain to climb, and even though I've never been a sporty kind of girl, I've somehow found the strength to put on my walking boots each morning and begin that lonely climb again. For the last few days I haven't bothered to lace up my boots, because it hasn't seemed to matter so much if I cut my feet to ribbons. I haven't watched my step or thought beyond the next bend in the track, because all roads lead to the safety of Freddie waiting at the crest for me.

But like all things, there is an inevitable trade-off. A bargain must be struck, and the realization that the price might be my sanity is seeping into my bones like cold bath water.

I'm starting to resent being awake, and to resent everyone in my waking life too. I snapped Mum's head off a couple of days ago on the phone and Elle said I looked like shit when she called around yesterday morning. I bailed on going to breakfast at mum's with her; I was borderline rude because all I could think about was the pink pill waiting for me on the kitchen worktop. She left after a few awkward minutes, her shoulders slumped and deflated, and I watched her go, feeling like a cow but unwilling to call her back because the siren call of the pill was too loud, too persuasive to ignore. And that's the real problem: I see the road ahead and it's littered with their trampled feelings as I turn more and more away from them in favor of the other place, in favor of Freddie.

I set the bottle of pills down on the kitchen floor beside me, and after staring at it for a few jagged, indecisive seconds I stretch out and move it beyond an arm's length away.

Can I bear to take one every other day? Every three days, maybe? Once a week? I frown, remembering that I took two on Saturday, bingeing on Freddie like a greedy child. And that's what worries me most: that I won't have the strength to resist falling so deeply into my other life that I become more there than here, too immersed to make my way safely home again.

AWAKE

Tuesday, May 29

"I'M THINKING OF going back to work soon."

My mother tries unsuccessfully to mask her surprise. We're in her small and immaculate lounge, barefoot as always in deference to the cream carpet. It's not just in the hall; she loves a bargain, and had it laid throughout the ground floor. Considering this is the lounge, there are quite stringent rules around the kind of lounging that is permitted. Red wine is a complete no-no, as is any kind of nonwhite food. So white wine is allowed, and mash or rice pudding. I'm not even kidding. Elle and I put away tins of the stuff throughout our teenage years, and despite the fact that the carpet is at least fifteen years old, it looks almost as good as new. The sofa covers the only stain that will never come out: a teenage Elle came home off her face on gin and black currant one Christmas morning after visiting her then boyfriend down the road for less than an hour.

Impressive really, until she threw up on Mum's carpet then passed out cold in her Christmas dinner.

"Really?" Mum says. I can see that she's trying to choose what to say next. I imagine her bypassing *about bloody time,* and pausing to consider *thank goodness for that,* before finally settling on what actually comes out of her mouth. "Are you sure you're ready, love?"

I shrug and half shake my head, even though I'm trying to nod. "I can't stay at home on my own for much longer without going round the bend, Mum. And I'm sleeping better now with the tablets."

What I don't say is that I need to give myself something to do, something tangible to focus on in the real world. My job as events manager at the community center isn't rocket science; it's mainly desk-based, but I work with a good bunch of people and the pay is decent. They've been kind and allowed me the time off so far as paid sick leave but it can't go on indefinitely.

Mum comes and perches beside me on the sofa, her hand on my knee.

"You could always come back and stay here for a while. If it'd help?"

I feel my bottom lip begin to tremble, because we both know she'd hate it but she loves me enough to say it anyway. It's not the first time she's offered; she's said it at least once a week since Freddie died. I'd hate it too. I like to eat stain-inducing curry off a plate balanced on my knees in the living room and to fall to pieces when no one's watching.

"I know," I say, covering her hand with mine and giving it a squeeze. "But it's not the right thing to do, you know that. I have to move sentiently through my grief, and I don't think that means moving back in with my mother."

She snorts a little bit. It's fast becoming a stock piss-take phrase in our family.

"I'll pack your lunch for you, then. Just for the first day or two."

I expect she's still got the clear pink lunch box she used to send me to school with. "Okay," I say, "that'd help, Mum." Though I suspect it'll help her more than me.

She nods fast. "I'll get those mint biscuits you used to like, the ones with shiny green wrappers."

I swallow around the lump in my throat, feeling fifteen again, back to the days when I slept upstairs in a single bed in the room I shared with Elle.

"First Monday in June, then?" she prompts, and I think about it, wondering if I can. We're in the last week of May now; she's only giving me a few days grace to get myself together. I expect she's keen to catch the wave in case the next one pulls me under and I change my mind, and because I can't promise that wouldn't happen, I nod slowly.

"First Monday in June, then."

"Good girl." She pats my knee as she stands up. "I'll just nip in the kitchen and add those biscuits to my shopping list."

I watch her go, wondering if she knows that she's one of the guardians of my sanity. My mum and her lists used to crack Freddie up—he used to add random things to them when she wasn't looking: hose pipes or dollhouses or nasal trimmers. The memory makes me smile and then ache, because I've reluctantly decided to try to ration my visits to once a weekend. It's too much of a good thing, as unsustainable as eating tablespoons of sugar. The problem with addiction is that at some point you have to give up whatever it is that's taken you over, or else give yourself over completely to it. I don't want either of those things to happen. I want both of my lives, and for that to happen I need a secure footing here in the real world. Time to lace up my walking boots.

AWAKE

Saturday, June 2

I GUESS IT should come as no surprise that I find the cemetery a peaceful place to be. I can almost hear Freddie cracking a horribly lame joke about the residents keeping themselves to themselves. I've been sitting here long enough to get a numb bum and as I look at Freddie's headstone I notice a white splatter against the gray granite. The pigeons around here clearly have no respect for the dead. Rummaging in my bag for the wipes, I find them missing and sigh, irritated. I can't leave it like that.

"Back in a sec," I say, picking up the old flowers I've removed and my rubbish to ditch in the basket in the car park. "The wipes must be in the boot."

At the car a couple of minutes later, I find I'm right. Locking up, I amble back slowly in the sunshine, taking the long way round because the cemetery is in full bloom and I could use a few minutes to catch my breath. It's just about the only place I can feel truly still. I value that now more than ever, a chance to step out of my smoke-and-mirrors double existence.

When I draw nearer to Freddie's grave again I realize that someone else is sitting on my recently vacated spot in front of the stone. Jonah Jones, his knees pulled up in front of him as he speaks. As I step closer and try to decide what to say, he clears his throat and coughs as if preparing to give a speech to the English class he teaches at the local secondary school.

"I'll try, but no promises," he says, quiet. I pause, wondering what he's told Freddie he'll try to do, unsure whether to interrupt because his eyes are already closed. Perhaps he's doing that thing I do, imagining they're somewhere else right now. At the pub maybe, or about to watch the game, feet up on the coffee table in our living room.

"Saturday again already," Jonah says. "Stressful week at work. Ofsted are in checking up on us, staff shortages, the usual crap. I had to take a PE lesson last week and we all know how shit I am at sport. You'd have pissed yourself laughing."

Freddie and Jonah were at opposing ends of the sport spectrum: if there was a chance of winning something, Freddie was all over it with his arms outstretched for the trophy. Jonah on the other hand doesn't mind a kick-about, but he doesn't have that competitive fire in his belly. He's content to be an armchair sportsman, finding his passion in music and books. They were unalike in lots of ways. Freddie was a doer, Jonah more of a dreamer, a stargazer. For his fifteenth birthday a group of us camped out in Freddie's back garden to try to catch a glimpse of a passing comet, or perhaps it was an asteroid shower. Either way Freddie snored through the entire thing while Jonah and I sat huddled under blankets with our eyes glued to the heavens in the hope of an astral show.

"Could have used a beer with my old mucker last night," Jonah says. "Nothing drastic, just kids winding me up and classroom politics pissing me off. Not to mention Harold gave me a dressing down for not wearing a tie in assembly yesterday." He laughs, his eyes still closed. "Can you believe it? Ten years since we left that place and old Harold's still on my back." He pauses, as if listening to Freddie's reply. "Oh, and I won at darts on Wednesday. Duffy was bloody furious. Lost his bet. Had to buy a round, and you know how tight he is. Everyone ordered a whiskey chaser just to wind him up."

I can't help but smile a little at this. Listening to Jonah's recollection of antics in The Prince is strange but kind of warming. I know I would have heard these same stories firsthand from Freddie had he been here still.

Jonah falls silent, absently picking at the frayed knee of his faded gray jeans, frowning, searching for more words, I expect. Then he opens his eyes and sighs, leaning forward to lay his hand flat over Freddie's name on the cold granite for a few quiet seconds.

"'Til next week, mate."

It's as close as he can get to laying his hand on Freddie's shoulder. I know, because there have been times when I've wrapped my arms around the damn sharp-edged thing and laid my cheek against the golden etched words. Not too many times though; we're Brits after all. There's a certain cemetery etiquette to be observed and it doesn't include having a full-on breakdown every time you rock up.

Much as Jonah did earlier, I clear my throat. He looks my way and double blinks, surprised. "Lydia," he says, and then he frowns. "How long have you been there?"

I hate the idea of anyone overhearing me talk to Freddie, so I lie. "Just a second or two." I pause. "I can come back in a while, if you need more time?"

He gets to his feet, brushing grass cuttings off his jeans. "No, it's okay. I'm done here."

I haven't seen or spoken to Jonah since that afternoon in the pub a couple of weeks ago, and I know I need to make things right. Jonah was Freddie's right-hand man, but in actual fact, he was my friend before Freddie even shot into my orbit. His quiet sarcasm aligned with mine when we were forced to partner up on a chemistry project at twelve years old–I think the teacher held vain hopes that some of Jonah's logic might rub off on me. It didn't. We quickly gave up any hope of me ever learning the periodic table, but we fell into the habit of spending our lunchtimes together with our backs against the old oak tree trunk to watch the school comings and goings, the flash in the pan romances, the occasional overspill of teen temper among the older kids. Our friendship came at a time when I needed it, when most of the girls in the class had decided I wasn't cool enough to hang out with them. Grateful, Mum would sometimes pack an extra mint biscuit for Jonah. He'd always try to refuse it out of politeness, but I knew he liked them and it was a welcome addition to the curling at the edges cheese spread sandwich his mum sent him with every day. This isn't a cute boy meets girl story though; we struck up a genuine friendship, as in "oh, you're someone like me" rather than "oh, you make my stomach feel like a washing machine." I liked knowing he'd be waiting for me come lunchtime, that I could rely on him to make me laugh even if I'd had a crap morning. And then Freddie joined the school—Jonah's new desk neighbor because their names followed each other on the register—and within a couple of weeks, two became three around the oak tree at lunchtime. Freddie Hunter blew into my life and swept me up in his carnival of color and laughter and noise. And with him my cool rating went up and I no longer needed so many of our lunchtime conversations. Which is a good thing, really, because three is inevitably a funny number, and never more so than when two of the three become romantically involved. Freddie probably felt caught between us sometimes; both of us vying for his attention and resenting the other when we didn't get it. We made it work though, somehow, over the years, because our friendship mattered too much to lose. And now that it's just two of us again, I don't know how we work. I'll always care for Jonah; he's been part of my world for too many years to not be important to me. But the accident sits between us, the elephant always in the room.

"I'll leave you to it, then." He digs his car keys out of his jeans pocket. "See you around."

I watch him silently as he nods at Freddie's headstone and then strides away along the avenue of gravestones. But just as I'm about to sit down, he swings around and comes back.

"There's this thing tomorrow morning at the school," he says. "You could, you know, come, if you like."

I stare at him, perplexed. "Thing?"

He shrugs. "You know, a workshop type of thing."

"You're not selling it very well," I say, half smiling because I don't know what else to do.

"It's a grief workshop, okay?" His words come out in a rush, scorn laden, as if it pisses him off that they're leaving his mouth. "Mindfulness, that sort of stuff."

"A grief workshop?" I say it in the same tone I might use if he'd asked me to bungee jump or skydive. Jonah isn't generally the type to focus on his inner chakras, or whatever they do at mindfulness workshops. I expect this kind of stuff from Elle; it's a surprise from Jonah.

"It's being run in the main hall." He couldn't look more uncomfortable if he tried. "Dee, one of the new supply staff is a trained yoga and mindfulness teacher. She's offered to run a session if there's enough interest."

Dee strolls into my head: shiny haired and bendy with an ever-ready smile that borders on pious. I catch myself being unkind for no reason and wonder if that is who I am now, bitter like over-brewed coffee.

"I'm not sure it's my kind of thing." I soften the rejection with an apologetic smile.

"I'm not sure it's mine either," he says, sliding his sunglasses on. "It was just an idea."

I nod, and he nods, and after an awkward silent moment he turns to walk away again, but then he stops and turns back around a second time.

"The thing is, I think it might help."

"Help with what, exactly?" I ask slowly, even though I think I know what he means. I wish he'd carried on walking rather than coming back a second time, because I can feel this conversation straying toward dangerous ground.

He looks skyward, thinking before he speaks. "This," he says, throwing his arm out toward Freddie's headstone and beyond. "Help with handling all of this."

"I'm handling it my own way, thank you," I say. The last thing I want to do is sit in a room full of strangers and talk about Freddie, especially with Jonah there too.

Jonah nods, swallows. "Told you," he mutters, but he's looking at Freddie's stone rather than at me. "I told you she'd say no."

Oh, hang on just a minute. "You told Freddie I'd say no?"

Pink spots fire up on Jonah's cheekbones. "Was I wrong?" He isn't someone who generally raises his voice; he's the natural mediator in any argument. "I told him I was going because I thought it might be good for me and that I'd ask you to join as well. But I told him you'd say no."

"Well, there you go, then," I throw my hands up in the air. "You've done your duty and now you can leave without feeling guilty." I regret the words as soon as they leave my lips.

"Without feeling guilty," he says. "Thanks for that, Lydia. Thanks a bloody lot."

"What do you expect when you gang up against me with my dead boyfriend?" I say.

"It wasn't ganging up on you," he says, more measured than I feel. "I just thought it'd be helpful maybe, but I get it. You're busy, or not interested, or scared, or whatever."

I snort and shake my head, looking away down the row of gray headstones.

"Scared?" I mutter, and he looks my way and shrugs, unapologetic.

"Tell me I'm wrong?"

I snort again and throw in a huff for good measure. I know he's trying to goad me and I can't stop myself from walking straight into it.

"Scared? You think I'm scared of some poxy school hall workshop? I'll tell you what scared looks like, Jonah Jones. It looks like a police car pulling up outside your living room window, and it looks like having to bury the man you love instead of marrying him. Scared looks like standing in Sainsbury's thinking about swallowing every damn pill on the medicine shelf because you just remembered that stupid argument you had in the next aisle over about *biscuits* of all things, biscuits, and it winds you. Physically winds you, right here." I bang two fingers over my heart hard enough to leave a bruise. "Scared looks like knowing how endlessly long life seems without the person you planned on spending it with, and also knowing how shockingly, unexpectedly short it can be. It's like that trick with the tablecloth and the teacups except we're human fucking beings being broken, not teacups, and . . ." I stop and gulp in air because I've lost my thread about being scared and I'm bloody crying with anger, and because Jonah looks ashen and horrified.

"Lyds . . ." he says, reaching out to put a hand on my shoulder.

I shrug him off. "Don't."

"I'm sorry, okay?"

"No. No, it's not okay. None of this"—I gesticulate sharply around the graveyard—"is ever going to be okay."

"I know. I didn't mean to upset you."

I don't know where this landslide of anger has come from. It's as if Jonah moved a rock and caused an avalanche, and now it's pouring out of me, uncontrollable as lava.

"Oh, sure, you didn't mean to upset me," I spit, horrible even to my own ears. "Digging at me via a dead man. What is it, Jonah? Do you need someone to chaperone you and tell the supply teacher that you like her?" He looks confused, as well he might. "Just write it on the damn whiteboard. Or ask her out. One or the other, either works, but I'm not up for holding your hand. I'm not your replacement wingman. I'm not Freddie."

We stare at each other for a moment, then I turn on my heel and march off, furious.

I can't tell Jonah what's really the matter; that my body is knackered and my head is wrecked with the push me, pull me of living life with and without Freddie. I laid awake last night and tried to think of a rational way to explain to someone else what's been happening, but it's impossible. How can I expect anyone to understand that I sometimes get to be with

Freddie when I sleep? I'm not delusional, and I'm not pretending that Freddie's still alive in my everyday life. But there's this . . . this other place where he and I are still together, and it feels like I'm locked in constant battle against its siren call. What will happen when the pills run out? I push the thought aside. I can't contemplate it.

AWAKE

Sunday, June 3

I DON'T KNOW what I'm doing here. I was never particularly fond of school; this is the first time I've stepped foot in the place since I collected my A-level results. Or actually, I do know what I'm doing here—I'm here because I felt like a bitch for storming off on Jonah yesterday and ended up sending him a sheepish sorry text and that maybe I could use some mindfulness after all. He replied that it was either that or anger management because I was in danger of turning Hulk and bursting out of my jeans, and I replied that I'd better try to make it then, seeing as green clashes with my hair. So here I am, dragging my feet across the concrete drive just as I used to when I was fourteen and hadn't done my homework. I'm late, deliberately so. He said ten until twelve and it's already turned eleven. I'm loosely planning to slide in toward the end and hide at the back, then tell Jonah a small white lie that I was there for almost all of it so we can put the bruise of yesterday behind us. We may not see each other every day anymore but I don't want to feel that we've fallen out. It seems terribly disloyal to Freddie to turn against his best friend.

As I push open the school hall door the nostalgic smell of floor polish and stale air transports me straight back to morning assembly. I can almost feel my knees aching from sitting cross-legged on the floor while the headmistress lectured us about appropriate behavior, Freddie on one side loosening his tie, Jonah on the other fiddling with the buttons on his watch. There aren't nearly enough people in the hall to hide my arrival this morning: twenty or so at most, sitting around tables with tea and cake rather than in rigid lines on the floor. Most of them look up when I come in and I pause, unsure, until Jonah stands up and makes his way across to me.

"Thought you'd decided to give it a miss after all," he whispers. "It's okay if you don't want to stay, I shouldn't have pushed you yesterday."

"It's okay." I look around at the gathering, apprehensive. More women than men, a smattering of people around my age but mostly older. A horrible thought strikes me: what if Auntie June and Uncle Bob are here? They love a workshop. I scout around and breathe out a sigh of relief when they're nowhere in sight. "How's it been so far?"

He nods. "Yeah, it's all right. Nice people. Honestly, Lyds, you don't need to stay. It might not be your bag after all." He cricks his neck, something I haven't seen him do in years. He used to do it when he was anxious;

taking exams in this very hall for example. "In fact, I'll grab my phone and come with you."

I look at him, confused. "You asked me to come here," I say.

Jonah opens his mouth to say something else but a woman approaches us, holding her hand out.

"Hi there," she says. "I'm Dee. You must be Lydia."

Ah. So I wasn't too far off the mark with Dee. She's brunette and a little shorter than me, her ponytail swinging as she shakes my hand. She's not terrifyingly svelte, more yoga curvy; I can see why Jonah might be attracted to her. Her sympathetic brown gaze holds onto mine, and I realize she already knows my sob story. Both of her hands clasp around one of mine, slightly too warm. "Welcome."

"Hello," I say, slightly too cold and stiff upper lip, extricating myself. I don't know what's come over me. I just hate the idea of a complete stranger thinking she knows everything about me.

"You missed the mindfulness session, I'm afraid," she says. "But you're here for the cake, which is always the best bit in my opinion."

I keep my churlish thoughts of how cake wouldn't be much help to me to myself. "Maybe Jonah can fill me in on the mindfulness," I say instead.

"Or I can do a one-on-one session some time if you'd find it helpful?" Dee offers, and although I can see she's just being kind, she nettles me again. Am I silently radiating SOS signals? Here I am feeling like I'm holding it together, and there everyone else is shoveling help onto me until I'm squashed flat. I'm coming to realize that I'm quite a private person; I prefer to hide behind a shiny veneer and then fall apart when no one's looking.

"I'll keep it in mind," I say, noncommittal. "Thanks though."

Dee's eyes connect with Jonah's for a few silent seconds, just long enough to mean "your friend is bloody hard work, isn't she?" Or maybe I'm wrong and she was being far more New Age and philosophical in a "your friend clearly has a way to go on her healing journey" way. Or then again, maybe it was just a straightforward "fancy a drink later?" kind of look and I'm in the way. I wish I hadn't come, but it's too late now because Dee's hand is on my elbow, steering me over to the group Jonah had been sitting with.

They shuffle round to clear a seat for me beside Jonah, all of them trying not to stare but anxious to make me feel welcome. Tea is poured for me by the woman opposite; Camilla, she tells me as she places the cup down. She is thankfully unfussy: a tight smile and a nod of comradeship.

"This is Lydia," Jonah says, looking grim.

They nod.

"I'm Maud," an older woman on Jonah's other side leans forward and half shouts, fiddling with her hearing aid. If I were to guess her age, I'd have said at least ninety. "My husband, Peter, fell off the roof trying to adjust the TV aerial twenty-two years ago."

"Oh," I say, taken aback. "I'm sorry to hear that."

Judging by the braced faces of the others around the table, I'd say this isn't the first time today that they've heard about Peter's misfortune.

"Don't be. I wasn't. He'd been having relations with

the woman who worked in the butchers for a good ten years."

Wow. This isn't what I was expecting at all.

"Cake?"

I turn to the lady on my other side, grateful for the intervention.

"It's apple and date. I made it this morning." She holds the plate out. "I'm Nell."

"Thank you," I say, reaching for a paper plate. I'm not sure if I'm thanking her for the cake or for saving me from the pressure of finding a suitable reply. I'm soothed by her quiet presence. She reminds me a little of my mum both in age and stature, and her wedding ring tells me she's married. Or else, she was.

"Sorry about Maud," she says under her breath as she slides cake onto my plate. "You can imagine how much help she was during the mindfulness session earlier."

She catches my eye and I'm relaxed by her humor.

"There're some books," Camilla says. Her cheeks stain dull red, as if the effort of speaking up costs her. "I found this one especially useful." She touches the cover of one of several grief-related books scattered around the table. "In the early days anyway."

"I haven't found reading easy lately," I say. "I've always loved books, fiction mostly, but my mind just doesn't seem to be able to retain a story anymore." I'm not sure where the urge to share came from, but there you go.

"It'll come back," she says. "For a while this stuff was all I could read, but it gets easier." She runs her fingers over a string of pearls around her neck. "It does."

I reach for the book she recommended, grateful.

"How about you, Jonah?" Nell asks. "Do you read?"

"I do," he says. "I'm an English teacher. It kind of comes with the territory." He swallows. "I'm struggling with music, mostly."

This is news to me. Music is Jonah's thing: playing it, listening to it, writing it.

"I couldn't watch TV after Peter died," Maud shouts. "Silly sod snapped the aerial."

I'm torn between laughing and wanting to throttle her.

"It's understandable," Camilla says, looking at Jonah. "You probably still connect it to the accident."

I can't make the link in my head. I'm not sure how much the others around the table have heard about Freddie from Jonah before I arrived, so I break off a piece of cake and let the conversation wash around me.

"Yeah." Jonah doesn't meet anyone's eye. "I can't listen to the radio anymore."

"Give it time." Nell must have noticed his hands were shaking too because she pushes a slice of cake toward him.

"Why do you connect music to the accident?" I ask, my eyes trained on Jonah.

"His pal was changing the radio station in his car," Maud butts in, too loud. "Not looking where he was going."

This is news to me. I struggle to find words in my throat to ask Jonah if it's true.

"But at the inquest . . ." I trail off, because it dawns on me that there's more going on here than I realize.

An uncomfortable silence falls around the table, and Jonah raises his face to study the peeling paint on the ceiling. "I didn't think you were coming," he says. "You were late. I didn't think you were coming." And then he turns and looks me in the eyes, his voice low and only for me. "He was just messing around trying to find something to sing to, Lyds. You know what he was like."

I frown, even though I know full well what he means. Freddie approached driving in the same way he approached everything else in life: full tilt. His car was a sporty model with a throaty exhaust and he liked his music cranked up loud, singing with more enthusiasm than his voice warranted.

"But at the inquest you said he didn't do anything wrong. I sat there and I heard you say he didn't do anything wrong." I hear my voice ratchet through the scales toward high-pitched.

"I didn't want . . . ," he says, so quiet it's a strain to hear him. "I didn't want them to say he died because of careless driving."

"Not as careless as falling off the roof," Maud sniffs, reaching for her tea.

I shoot her a look, ready to snap, but I don't. She's not the real reason my heart is thumping. Jonah and I stare at each other. I wonder what else he hasn't told me.

"You asked me to come here today," I say, rubbing my hand over my forehead. "You asked me to come here, and then you throw this . . . this bomb in, knowing exactly what it's going to do to me."

He's shaking his head even as I speak. "You didn't come, Lydia. I waited for you and you didn't come, and everyone was talking about the people they'd lost and I don't even know why I started talking too. It felt safe, I guess."

I stare at him, at the words falling from his mouth.

"You didn't mention the radio once at the inquest . . ." I'm shaking my head, because ever since the accident I've taken Jonah's brief account of what happened in that car and tried to piece together Freddie's last moments. It was officially recorded as accidental death, one of those freak moments you just can't predict. There was mention of slippery weather conditions. It had been a particularly cold snap and there could well have been ice. I listened, and in my head allowed it to come down to something as mundane as the weather, and now the scene I've built in my head is fragmenting in front of my eyes.

"You lied," I say. "You lied to a room of people, Jonah." I look at Nell beside me. "He didn't tell them about the radio. He didn't."

"People do strange things for good reasons sometimes," she says. "Maybe if Jonah could tell you a little bit more . . ." She looks apologetically at Jonah, who swallows hard.

"I didn't lie," he says. "I didn't. There could well have been ice on the road and it had definitely been raining." He looks at me. "You know that's true, Lydia."

"But you've never mentioned the radio . . ."

Everyone else at the table is quiet now, even Maud.

Beside me, Nell sighs and covers my hand for a second, squeezing my fingers. I'm not sure if it suggests sympathy or calm down.

Jonah makes a guttural, frustrated sound, and his hand clenches into a tight ball on the table. "Why would I? What difference would it have made? It was just Freddie and me there that night; no one else got hurt. There was no fucking way I was going to let the last thing anyone ever said about him be that he caused it himself, that he was careless for even a fraction of time." He glances around the table at the others and shakes his head. "Sorry," he sighs. "For swearing."

His eyes are overbright when he looks back at me. I can see he's hanging on by a thread. "I didn't want to see it in the paper, for them to print that his death was needless, for people to use his story as a cautionary tale to be more careful."

Something's happening inside me. It's as if my blood is heating up. "But you could have told me," I say, slowly. "You *should* have told me."

"Should I?" he raises his voice a little and Camilla flinches at the sight of his pain. "Why? So you could feel even more anguished than you already do, so you could curse him for being such a prat, so you could replay the image of him going a couple of miles over the speed limit and scrabbling around with the stereo?"

And then I can see it exactly. Freddie's foot on the accelerator, his eyes momentarily off the road.

"Going too fast to get to my birthday dinner, you mean? You didn't mention he was speeding either."

Jonah looks out of the window toward the school gates. So many years the three of us spilled in and out of those gates, carefree and sure that life would last forever. I can almost see us, hear the echo of our footsteps and our laughter.

"None of this really matters," he says. "It doesn't change the fact that he's gone."

"But it does matter," I say, fired up by Jonah's ignorance of my feelings. "It matters to me. You let me think he died because of the weather and somehow that dull, everyday reason made some kind of stupid sense." I cast around, trying to understand and articulate my feelings in real time. "And now you tell me that he'd still be here if he'd just been more careful, and that he was speeding?" I break off, anguished. "Don't you dare tell me it doesn't matter, Jonah Jones. He should have just come straight home. None of this would have happened if he'd just come straight back."

"Don't you think I know that?" he whispers. "Don't you think it's the first thing I think every single bloody day?"

We stare at each other. Jonah bites his lip to stop it shaking.

"I never wanted you to know all of this," he says, gaunt, drawing my eyes to his scar as he scrubs his hand over his forehead. "You were late . . . I didn't think you were coming."

"I wish I hadn't," I say.

"Me too," he says, his hands clasped together in a knot on the table.

A hush falls around the table. I think it's time for me to leave.

"My son died a year ago." Maud stares at the ceiling.

"Hadn't spoken to me for thirty-six years. All over something and nothing."

I don't reply, but her words make it into my head anyway. Thirty-six years. They were both alive, and yet they allowed something trivial to push them far enough apart that they never spoke again.

"That's very sad, Maud." Camilla reaches out and pats Maud's forearm.

Maud sets her lips in a thin line, all out of pithy comebacks. I don't think she came here today to talk about her errant husband at all. I'm not sure if she offered the information about her son to help me, but she has, sort of, because I know that if I get up and walk out of here now I might not see Jonah Jones again for thirty-six years, or forever.

We sit rigid, side by side in the silence.

"I should have told you sooner," he says eventually, his gaze on his feet.

"Yes," I say. "But I get why you didn't."

I meet Camilla's tearful gaze across the table and she nods, quiet support that I appreciate. It takes a great deal for me to lay my hand over his on the table, and it takes a great deal for him to not crumble.

"That cake could do with some butter on," Maud says. "Is there any left?"

Nell pushes the tin across the table. "Take it, it won't get eaten at my house."

I dash my hand over my eyes, brisk, and stand up. "I should get going," I say, looking around the table. "It was nice to meet you all."

Jonah looks up at me. "I'll see you soon?" he says.

"Yes," I say, even though I most probably won't. I

can't say I'm glad I came because it isn't strictly true, but it's been cathartic for both of us to be so painfully honest. I hold it together until I reach my car, and then I fall into the driver's seat with my head in my hands. I probably shouldn't drive, but I want to go home. I want to be with Freddie.

ASLEEP

Sunday, June 3

WE'RE IN THE HOSPITAL car park. Freddie is carrying Elle. She's wearing one shoe, and I have the other in my hand as I walk briskly beside them.

"I think it's broken," Elle says, her face contorting with pain when she tries to move her ankle. She tumbled top to bottom of our stairs half an hour back, scaring the hell out of me and Freddie. It's strange seeing her in this abstract world too. I'd got used to it being just me and Freddie, but it seems like everyone else's lives are ticking along here as well. And in this world, today, Freddie is exactly how I want to remember him. In control and very much alive.

"Probably," he says. "Good job you've got me to carry you around."

"It's a bit like that scene from *An Officer and a Gentleman,*" I say, trying not to laugh.

Freddie looks pleased by the idea. "Except I'm better looking than Richard Gere."

"You'd definitely look good in the uniform," I say.

"They sell them in that kinky shop in town," he says. "I can get one if you like."

"Err, hello?" Elle grumbles. "Woman with broken bones here. Can you save this conversation for later?"

"It might not be broken," I say, trying to think positive.

"Crap, I hope not," she says. "I can't be on crutches at work." Though even on crutches Elle would still be the most efficient woman in the room.

There's something about the sight of someone being carried into the emergency department that makes people part to allow us through, and we're in a cubicle far faster than we otherwise might have been.

"Good job you were at home," I say to Freddie, perching on the edge of the bed. The doctor doesn't think Elle's broken any bones, but she's been wheeled off for an X-ray to double-check. "I don't think we'd have been seen so quickly if she'd hobbled in."

"The Freddie Hunter charm works every time." He grins, and I roll my eyes. "Want me to carry you upstairs later?" he asks.

"Only if you buy that uniform," I say.

He glances at the coat peg on the back of the door. "I could steal a doctor's coat. Will that do?"

I start to laugh under my breath. "You know what? I think it might," I say, just as the doctor wheels Elle back in.

"Nothing broken," he says, breezy. "Badly bruised, best stay off it for a couple of days."

Elle struggles to get to grips with the crutches the nurse finds for her, so Freddie swings her up into his arms again and carries her back through the ER. As the exit doors slide open I start to hum, "Love lifts us up where we belong," and Elle kicks me in the arm with her good foot.

"YOU WERE GREAT with Elle today," I say once we're home again.

"I was, wasn't I?" he says, messing, and then he shakes his head. "She's lucky it was just her ankle. The way she came down those stairs it could have been a lot worse."

I shudder, because he's right. My heart was in my mouth as we ran to see what had happened. I'm all too aware of how quickly a normal day can become a nightmare.

"I've never broken any bones," he says. "Can you believe that?"

Oh my love, I think.

"Me neither," I say. "Oh, hang on, I'm lying. I have—I broke my finger at Elle's birthday party when we were little. Mum invited Nicky from over the road, even though he was a horror, and he slammed my hand in the front door."

Freddie winces. "On purpose?"

I shrug. "Probably." I hold my right hand up and touch my index finger. "Right there."

Freddie comes in close and kisses the spot. "What was his last name? I'll find him and exact a horrible revenge for you."

I go with it. "What will you do?"

"I think it's only fair that it involves his fingers," Freddie says. "Shall I chop them off one by one? Or whack them flat with a hammer, Thor style?"

Freddie's big physical presence is part of his identity. He totally buys into the idea of himself as my protector, whether I need him to be or not. He's pretty old school in that sense. He likes to wield a screwdriver when things break down, and he's territorial over the lawn mower, even though we only have a small back garden. I don't mind really; I know it stems back to losing his dad when he was a child. He had no choice but to step into his father's too-big shoes because his mum was a woman used to being taken care of. Freddie has happily gathered the Bird family under his umbrella of care. I don't think Mum has changed a lightbulb in the last decade.

"You're my superhero," I laugh.

"I think we've already established that today." He flops down in his chair. "Have I done enough to earn myself a coffee?"

"And biscuits," I say.

"And sex?" he says, always a trier.

I look at him. "Only if you stole that doctor's coat."

AWAKE

Monday, June 4

I'M SITTING IN the car park at work, my old bright-pink Perspex lunch box on the passenger seat beside me. It was on my doorstep this morning with a good luck note stuck to the lid. I can just about make out the metallic paper of the mint biscuit Mum probably had to go to three supermarkets to hunt down, and a carton of Ribena pokes out from beneath a foiled mystery sandwich. She hasn't packed my lunch in more than ten years, but she's seamlessly slid straight back into it as if I'm still fourteen years old. It's comforting, I find, as I push the lurid box into the top of my bag and try to screw up the courage to walk through the staff entrance of the community center for the first time in over eighty days. They know I'm coming of course and I'm sure they'll bend over backward to make things as easy as possible for me, but all the same I'm fighting to keep my toast down as I take a here-goes-nothing deep breath and climb out of the car.

"Like a boss," I mutter, lifting my chin and lowering my shoulders until my shoulder blades almost touch. "Like a boss." I'm channeling a kick-ass character off one of the American TV programs I love; someone far more sassy and no-nonsense than I am. Meghan Markle in *Suits,* maybe. Up to now, the relaxed dress code of jeans and T-shirts at work has always been a bonus, but right now I'd quite like to hide behind a power suit, spike heels, and a chignon.

I stare at the security lock on the door, and poke halfheartedly at the silver buttons. It doesn't work of course; the code changes every few weeks, for no real reason other than procedure, because there's very little point to anyone bothering to break in. What would they take? Well-read books from the town's library housed on the ground floor? We're probably one of the last remaining places to still rely on the library cards and stamps system. Delia, our octogenarian librarian, wouldn't cope with anything more up-to-date. Our office upstairs isn't much better equipped when it comes to technology—a couple of old PCs and a photocopier is about as good as it gets. Some might call it charming; others might deem it out of the ark. Both are accurate descriptions. There's a pleasing old-school vibe to working here, but it can frustrate the hell out of me when things don't get replaced until they literally fall apart. This bloody security lock, for instance, with clunky buttons you have to stab at as if you're in a foul temper. I'm not in a foul temper, but I *am* fast getting cold feet and considering bolting back to my car, when an arm lands heavily around my shoulders. I find myself pulled into a sideways hug, pressed against the side of Phil, my boss.

"Lydia, thank God you've come back," he says, squeezing me as he reaches over and attacks the security lock with gusto. "The place has gone to pot without you."

It's exactly what I need to hear. No pomp and ceremony, no carefully worded welcome back interview. Phil is one of those bosses everyone adores, full of bonhomie and charisma, a man who naturally connects with people—so much so that he boomingly offered to be Dawn's birth partner if her husband happened to be working away when it all kicked off. Thankfully, she didn't need to take him up on the offer, but we all had a bit of a laugh at the idea of him scrubbing up and getting in there at the business end. I don't doubt that he genuinely would have too, had the need arisen.

"Look who I found trying to break in the back door," he says as he leads me into the upstairs office.

It's stupid to be nervous, but I am. I've worked here for the last five years; these people know me. I know them. But they knew Freddie too, and they're all looking at me round-eyed and I can tell that right now they're thinking *shit, what the hell do we say to her, will she dissolve into tears if I say his name, will she be offended if I don't, I think I'll just look incredibly busy and smile and see how things go after a cuppa.*

"Cuppa?" Dawn asks on cue, and I nod gratefully, as she makes a bolt for the kitchen.

My desk next to the window looks as if it's become the general dumping ground, piled high with brochures and boxes, and my chair is nowhere to be seen. I'm not sure how to feel—relieved no one has jumped in and bagged my plum spot beside the only window in the room, or miserable because they haven't thought ahead enough to make it welcoming. Ryan, twenty-two and prime fodder for a spot on *Love Island*, with his blue-black hair and sunbed tan, looks up and winks, a phone wedged against his ear. My face must have given me away, because he follows the direction of my gaze and jumps to his feet, hanging up on whoever he was on hold for.

"Lydia," he smiles, all veneers, striding across the small room to pull me into a hug. It's not lost on me that both of my male colleagues seem more emotionally equipped to deal with my arrival than my female counterparts. Dawn disappeared pretty much on sight, and at the back of the room Julia lifted a perfectly manicured hand without rising from her chair. Granted, she seems to be on a conference call, but even so she doesn't exactly exude warmth. That's not really fair. Julia and I have worked together for some years now and she can't help coming off as a cold fish, even though I know for a fact she's butter soft. She'd just rather no one knew, and uses her oh so glamorous braided hair and long blood-red nails to terrify people into thinking she's a tough taskmaster. She's easily the eldest of our cohort, an indeterminate number somewhere between fifty-five and sixty; I suspect she'll remain in that bracket until someone challenges it. Which no one will.

"Sorry about your desk," Ryan says, leading me by the hand toward it. "Let's sort it out."

His idea of sorting it out involves sweeping everything up into his arms and dumping the lot on top of the nearest filing cabinet, but I appreciate the gesture all the same. He casts his eyes around for a chair, and coming up with nothing, he wheels his own across and then performs a tiny bow to indicate I should take his seat.

"Your throne, m'lady."

I don't argue. I can't, because the simple gesture of kindness has caught in my throat. He notices, and to his credit, he doesn't panic. He just pats me on the shoulder, finds me a tissue, and nods sagely.

"I know, Lyds," he says. "I'm devastating. I have this effect on lots of women."

I gulp-laugh, glad of his humor, and catch Dawn's relieved eye as she drifts toward me with the promised cup of tea. She's no doubt pleased that I'm smiling, and actually, so am I. I can feel myself slowly settling, my fingers running over the familiar bumps and dinks in my battered old walnut desk. I have a place to be.

"No sugar, too much milk," Dawn says, as she always does. It's subtle, but I hear it. It's *I remember,* it's *you're among friends here,* it's *we've got you.*

Julia appears too and places a small vase of pink and purple sweet peas on my desk.

"Perfume was getting up my nose," she sniffs, her perfectly made-up eyes assessing me, no doubt taking in the fact I've lost some weight and making a mental note to bring cake tomorrow and lie about buying it from the reduced counter.

I look at them, one face to the next, and swallow hard.

"Thank you," I say. "It's good to be back."

"We weren't sure whether to, you know, to say anything, about . . ." Ryan says, his lovely dark eyes full of consternation. Again, I admire him for being the unelected spokesman for a group of people twice his age, even if he did stumble at the last hurdle.

"Freddie," I say, forcing the word out clear and untearful, saying it so Ryan doesn't have to. "You can say his name, it's okay."

They all nod, hovering, waiting for more.

"I'm grateful for the chair, and the tea, and the flowers," I say. "But more than anything else I'm glad of the company. I couldn't spend any more days on my own at home. I'm boring myself stupid."

"Say if you need anything," Dawn says, too fast, trying to stop her bottom lip from wobbling. She feels for a tissue in the pocket of her oversize cardigan. All her clothes swamp her; she's been on a wedding diet for months and not had the spare money to replace her wardrobe. She's let her robin's-wing brown hair grow too; there's an air of the waif about her today.

Julia shoots her a withering look, sliding her horn-rimmed glasses down her nose, letting them hang on the rose-gold chain around her neck. "I've got a list of things you can make a start on, when you're ready."

Ryan hands Dawn a tissue, and she dabs her eyes as she plucks my lunch box from my bag. "I'll put this in the fridge for you."

"Hideous color," Julia mutters.

"Bagsy the biscuit," Ryan says, squinting through the pink plastic.

They drift away, and I let out a slow hiss of relief,

glad to have jumped the "coming back to work" hurdle. Next up, actual work.

Between the four of us and Phil, we run the local community center. Ryan has the gift of the gab so he's in charge of the local community magazine, which mostly involves selling advertising space and the odd outing to photograph prize-winning marrows or locals with unusual hobbies. It's a hit-or-miss affair; he's never fully recovered from his visit to a life painting class featuring his retired physics teacher as the nude model.

Julia handles the business side of things, managing the finances, strong-arming local businesses into contributing toward the upkeep of our building and the town fund. That leaves Dawn and me under the catch-all umbrella of "events management," which really means we plan everything that happens in our historic community center, from summer fetes to Christmas fairs, concerts, dances, and parties. I've heard Phil refer to us as his community programmers, which I guess is pretty much on the money. We timetable Darby and Joan senior clubs on Monday afternoons and Mother and Toddler groups on Friday mornings, and everything possible that goes on in between. It's one of those jobs you kind of fall into as a stopgap and stay forever, because life slides into the cracks around it, cementing it in place. The people become your friends, the building becomes your second home, your chair molds to the shape of your bum. On paper we're a disparate bunch, yet somehow, together, we're more than the sum total of our parts, and the community center has become the thriving hub of the community—a minor miracle on our shoestring budget. I realize as I make a start on Julia's to-do list that she's been covering some of my role, and that Dawn's been doing five days rather than her usual three, even though Tyler's still in preschool and she struggles for childcare. They've managed somehow and no one has breathed a word to me of being pressured. I understand now why my desk hadn't been prepared for me; there simply wasn't the time. They've been up to their eyeballs just holding my place ready for me to come back to, shoring me up from a distance without me even realizing.

Grief is an odd thing. It's mine, and no one can do it for me, but there's been this whole supporting cast of silent actors around me in the wings. I mentally add my colleagues to the list of people I need to thank properly somewhere down the line. My mum and Elle are in capitals at the top of course, and all of my neighbors who nip in for a cuppa, and now Julia, Dawn, Ryan, and Phil. A casserole from the family three doors down, a "how are you coping, lass?" card from the old man over the road who lost his wife not long after we moved in. Even Jonah dragging me to that damned grief workshop.

"I was serious about that biscuit," Ryan says, handing me my pink plastic box when we all decamp to the canteen for lunch. There are five mismatched chairs around the table, and after we're all seated, Phil raises his mug of tea.

"Good not to have an empty seat anymore," he says, and they all nod and lift their cups. Hot tears prickle my eyes, and to cover I open my lunch box and toss the biscuit to Ryan.

“Don’t tell my mum I gave you that,” I say, sticking the straw in my Ribena. The taste takes me straight back to school, to lunch with Freddie and Jonah, and today I choose to smile rather than let the tears slide down my cheeks. If I’m the lead actor, then the show must go on.

AWAKE

Saturday, June 23

"I'VE BEEN BACK at work for three weeks already," I say, sitting cross-legged on the sun-scorched cemetery grass. It's shaping up to be an unusually reliable summer. There's mutterings of a hosepipe ban if the weather doesn't break soon.

"In some ways it feels as if I've never been away. Ryan's on his third date in as many weeks and Julia's still cracking the whip."

Freddie had a bit of a love-hate relationship with Julia. His loud conviviality irritated the hell out of her, and her ruthless, get-it-done-yesterday streak wound him up—probably because he was actually quite similar. Underneath it all though, lay mutual affection; she mothered him and he charmed her. He always reckoned she was one of those women who liked her man to wear a collar and leash in the bedroom, which I have to admit I can easily imagine.

"Mum's finally stopped making my lunch too," I laugh softly. "Good job. I was getting addicted to Ribena."

I've brought sweet peas from Elle's garden today, pink and purple with a heady scent.

"Phil's asked me to be Ryan's line manager," I say, poking a flower into the vase. "I think he's trying to make me feel indispensable." I'm nervous about it, but I'm still trying to channel Meghan Markle. I might have to invest in a jacket with shoulder pads.

"I had my hair cut last week." I take the band out and shake my head, letting my hair fall heavy around my shoulders. "Just a trim, really. No one's noticed." I didn't expect anyone to; I only had the ends off, same as always. Any more than that and I have an identity crisis.

"I haven't seen anything of Jonah lately," I say, because I feel obliged to update him with news of his best friend. I've had the benefit of a few weeks to turn Jonah's revelations at the grief session over in my mind and look at them from every angle, and I can grudgingly understand why he did what he did. No one else was hurt or otherwise involved; the only thing that stood to be permanently tarnished by the truth was Freddie's memory. Loyal to the end, Jonah didn't want his friend to receive a dishonorable discharge from life.

"I left a voice message for him last week, but he hasn't replied."

I'm not all that surprised to be honest. My message on Jonah's mobile was short to the point of curt; I just couldn't summon the right words to express myself. I think I apologized for not being in touch sooner, and I almost certainly said something ambiguous about understanding what he'd done. It probably sounded pious, as if I thought he needed my absolution or something, which wasn't my intention at all but I didn't have it in me to delete and re-record.

"I'm just so angry at the needlessness, Freddie," I whisper. It's been a huge mental adjustment to come to terms with the idea that Freddie's own carelessness was a contributor to his death. He's still gone however you look at it, but there was something almost comforting about blaming it on the weather.

"I haven't told anyone else," I say. "Not Mum or Elle."

What would be the point? I haven't felt any better for knowing the truth, so why burden them with it too? They'll just worry about me even more, and I hate the idea of them thinking even a millionth of a percent less of Freddie. So I've sealed the news up and tossed it into the oceans in my head, a message in a bottle that will hopefully never wash up on the shore for anyone else to read.

"I should probably go," I say, sprinkling the leftover water in my bottle over the parched earth around Freddie's stone. "I'm going into town with Elle this afternoon."

As I sit in the silence, I wonder what we're doing now in my other life. So much happens there that I'm not privy to; my weekly visits are partly spent trying to subtly catch up on what I've missed. I lay my hand on the granite stone and close my eyes, conjuring up Freddie's face, his scent, his smile. I imagine his arms around me, his kiss warm on the back of my neck.

"See you soon, my love."

IT'S SO HOT in here. In fact, I think we can all just declare that we live in a hot country now. We're basically Spain, except we drink more tea and eat dinner earlier. There will be no more winter coats or perpetual moans about the weather because we live in a world of wall-to-wall sunshine and itsy-bitsy clothes.

"What do you think of this?"

Elle holds up a hot pink tube top. It's scattered with glittery cherries made of red sequins that catch the department store lights.

"Fine," I say. "If you're eighteen and in Ibiza."

"I'm not, and I'm not," she says, sliding it back on the rail. "Do you think I look old?"

"You're thirty-one, Elle, not eighty-one." I shake my head. "Besides, you've got one of those faces that never age."

She looks at herself in a nearby mirror. "You think so? I feel about a hundred when I'm on the early shift at work."

Her new job at the hotel has her keeping odd hours; they've catered back-to-back weddings across the long, hot summer. I haven't seen as much of her in recent weeks; I've missed her letting herself in and filling the fridge with things I'll probably forget to eat. I understand, of course. In the beginning everyone was on Lydia-watch 24-7, but trying to fill the Freddie-size hole in my life inevitably created holes in the fabric of their own. Elle and David haven't been married for very long; I suspect that between visiting me and the demands of her job, David has been lamenting the strain of not seeing enough of his wife. The idea of being a burden weighs heavily on my shoulders.

"You need to buy the tube top." I pull it from the rack.

She looks at me, quizzical. "Why?"

"In fact, I'm going to buy it for you."

"Don't be daft." She laughs.

"I'm not," I press on. "I'm serious, Elle. I'm going to buy it, then tonight you're going to wear it with your skinny jeans and skyscraper heels and make David's eyes fall out of his head."

"I am?" She looks doubtful.

"Yes. Yes, you are."

We join the back of the queue at the till.

"Come out with us tonight," she says, linking her arm through mine.

I swipe my damp fringe out of my eyes and wish the shop had air-con. "Okay," I deadpan. "Let me just go and see if they have another tube top first though. One with three wheels on it."

"Don't ever say that," she frowns, quick to correct me. "You're never a third wheel with us."

She means it, and David has been a part of our family for so long that I know he'd say exactly the same, but there is no escaping the fact that sometimes, two's the magic number. No one knows that better than me.

ASLEEP

Saturday, September 8

"YOU'RE GONNA DRIVE me nuts in that dress tonight."

Freddie slides his hand up my thigh as I park the car in the restaurant car park. It's a place we've been to a few times over the years, a trendy kind of bar/restaurant hybrid, all discreet lighting and slightly uncomfortable chairs.

"Did you buy it for my birthday?" he asks, catching hold of my hand as we head toward the entrance.

It was Freddie's twenty-ninth birthday a couple of days ago. I marked it in my waking life with an after-work visit to his grave; I'm marking it in my sleeping life by taking him to his favorite restaurant and evidently by buying a new blue dress.

"Of course," I say lightly. It takes me a couple of minutes to orientate myself, to read the signs and the scenery of my other life. Freddie's wearing a shirt I bought him on holiday last year and the scent of his aftershave mingles with my perfume as we step inside the restaurant.

"Hunter, table for four," he says, smiling at the girl behind the welcome lectern. She checks her list and nods, her eyes lingering on Freddie for a few seconds longer than strictly necessary. I'm not worried; it happens a lot. I'm accustomed to the "you lucky cow" side-eye. Freddie's words register as we follow her through the busy dining tables. *Table for four,* he'd said. I don't have to wonder for long who else is making up the party. Jonah gets to his feet as we approach the corner table, laughing as he embraces Freddie in a manly, backslapping kind of birthday hug. I'm caught behind them momentarily; it's only when they move apart that I see who the fourth person at the table is: Dee. Yoga teacher Dee.

She catches my eye and smiles, then nips round the guys and tugs me by the hand to sit beside her. She looks different this evening from when I last saw her in my waking life. Her dark hair is loose around her shoulders and her sleeveless black shift makes the best of her toned arms. All that yoga is clearly paying off.

"I know it's Freddie's birthday, but sit next to me? You know how these two get when they're together."

Yes, I think, I do, because unlike you I've known them over half of my life. It's not very kind of me and I hope I don't let my uncharitable thoughts show on my face as I slide into the chair beside hers. I'm on the back foot; I don't know how well we know each other here. Are we friends? I doubt we've been having slumber parties and plaiting each other's hair, but we must be familiar with each other if I've asked her to my fiancé's birthday dinner. Freddie sits to my other side at the compact square table, squeezing my hand as he takes his seat.

"Hey, Dee, how's tricks?" He smiles easily in her direction.

She laughs prettily. "Oh, you know. Lots of that touchy-feely holistic stuff you laugh at me for."

"I wouldn't dare laugh at you," he says, mock innocent.

She rolls her eyes toward me, good-natured. "Tell him, Lydia, yoga can be just as demanding as football and rugby."

Freddie throws his hands out to the sides and grins. "Come on. Half an hour of over sixties stretching doesn't compare with ninety minutes of pure adrenaline on the pitch. Am I right or am I right, Joe?"

Freddie is the only person in the world who calls Jonah Joe.

For his part, Jonah looks between Dee and Freddie, both of them hoping that their connection with him sways him over to their way of thinking.

"I'm too compromised to be an honest judge." He laughs as he drinks from his beer bottle. "Looks like it's down to you, Lyds."

There's something different about Jonah tonight, and it takes me a couple of seconds to place it. It's been so long since I saw his face without the hairline scar above his eyebrow or the smudge of shadows beneath his dark, soulful eyes. He looks more alive, somehow; there's color in his cheeks where I've lately grown accustomed to his gauntness. But it's not just that. He looks . . . I don't know, more relaxed? And then it comes to me: Jonah Jones looks like *himself* again. He's got his laid-back, feet-in-the-sand look back, and it's only now that I see him here that I realize how much I miss him in my waking life. I think all of this as they all stare at me, waiting for my answer. I can barely remember the question.

"What's it to be?" Freddie says, bumping his thumb over my knuckles on the tabletop. "Yoga or football?"

Dee looks at his hand on mine and shakes her head. "You're trying to influence her decision. Cheap move, Freddie Hunter."

"I am not," he blusters, faking offense. "I just can't keep my hands off her."

I decide to relax into the evening and go with it. "Well, firstly I'll defend yoga and say there's definitely more to it than just gentle stretching, but because it's your birthday, I pick football."

"Never in doubt," Jonah says, shaking his head as Dee laughingly punches me on the biceps.

"What happened to girl code?" she says.

"Any other day but his birthday," I smile, reaching for the bottle of wine they've already ordered.

"SO HOW'S THE BIG secret romance thing going?"

Freddie looks at Dee as he finishes off my dessert. I wasn't quite done with it but he's had his way because it's his birthday.

She looks at Jonah, brows raised across the table at him, and I swear he practically blushes.

"I think they've probably sussed us," she says. "It's

pretty difficult to keep anything under the radar for long in a school. It's a hotbed for gossip."

"People love to talk," Jonah shrugs. "I don't see that it matters to anyone else, really."

Dee swirls her wine and looks at him under her lashes. "I do quite like the sneaking around though, Mr. Jones."

"Hello," Freddie lays his spoon down and rubs his hands together, interested. "Have you two been up to no good behind the bike sheds?"

Jonah rolls his eyes and looks like he'd prefer to change the subject. Dee doesn't though.

"No . . ." she looks at me conspiratorially, and then back at Jonah. "Well, not *exactly*."

"Don't tell me," Freddie says, enjoying making Jonah squirm. "In the broom cupboard?"

"Cliché," Dee says, then after a beat, she adds "in the chemistry lab!" Her voice rises up the excitement scale, her tongue loosened by wine.

"Dee," Jonah warns, lighthearted. He looks across the table at me and pulls a bit of a "sorry about this" face. I don't know why; he doesn't need to apologize to me. I understand though. Our dynamic has always been that we band together if Freddie is being a wind-up, which right now he is, unwittingly aided by Dee.

"I mean, we weren't *doing it,* or anything, just messing around," she says. "I mean, I was still wearing my—"

"So you two, how's the wedding planning going?" says Jonah. He gives me a pleading stare, so I do him a favor and pick up the bone he's thrown.

"Yeah, all good," I say, glad to have gleaned a few bits of information from a conversation with Elle and Mum when I last saw them here. "We've provisionally booked the barn and our rings are stashed in Mum's safe."

Don't ask me why she has a safe. It's one of those hidden-in-a-fake-book things—from the shopping channel, of course. The worst of it was that she didn't even own a bookcase, she had to buy one plus a set of encyclopedias just to disguise the safe.

"And your dress?" Dee says, shiny eyed.

I reach for my wineglass, put off. The honest answer is I don't have a clue about my wedding dress. I know I've found the one, and that Mum has insisted on paying for it. It's all ordered and not due into the shop for some months, another thing that happened when I wasn't here. I'd so like to have been; I can imagine Mum in tears and Elle not far behind her. I bet Auntie June came too. My mum and her sister are like an older version of Elle and me. She'd have been sitting alongside Mum passing her tissues from her best handbag.

I nod, smiling softly. "I'm keeping it as a surprise."

"IT'S GOOD TO see Jonah with someone like Dee," Freddie says, unbuttoning his shirt in our bedroom later.

"Mm." I perch on the edge of the bed and carefully take my earrings out.

"What?" He pauses, his fingers on the buttons. "I thought you liked her?"

"I do, I do," I say, a little too loudly to be convincing.

"Doesn't sound like it . . ." he presses. He knows me too well, which is a good and a bad thing depending on the circumstance. "Did she say something to you in the loo? Graphic details about shagging like rabbits in the chemistry lab, maybe? If she did, tell me everything."

"No, of course not," I laugh, glad his guess is wide of the mark. "No, they seem pretty good together."

He chucks his shirt on the chair and pushes me back on the bed, his chest a warm, welcome pressure. "Not as good as us," he says, his lips against my collarbone as his hand rucks up the hem of my dress.

"No one is," I whisper, and he raises his head and kisses my mouth, fierce and tender all in one. It's a combination that gets me every time.

"I love you more than Naomi Campbell," he says, and I start to laugh because she'd eat him for breakfast and then spit him out.

"I think you pick Naomi because she reminds you of Julia," I say.

"Julia's way more terrifying," Freddie says, his fingers on the small shell button at the back of my dress.

"I love you more than Dan Walker," I say, throwing the BBC breakfast presenter into the mix.

"He's a new one," Freddie says, musingly.

"He was on the TV with puppies the other morning," I say, smoothing my hands over his shoulders. "It swung it for me."

"Okay," he says. "I love you more than . . ." He's popped the button and slides my zip down the length of my spine. "Carol, the woman who does the weather."

"You can't choose someone else from breakfast telly; it's copying."

He laughs, shrugs. "It's your fault. I can't think straight. Let's skip straight to Keira and Ryan so you can take this dress off," he says, all thoughts of Dee and Jonah long gone. "I like you in it, but I'd like you a whole lot more out of it."

I help him pull it over my head, relieved when we're naked, when his skin is pressed against mine. Our love is too big to hide in a broom cupboard or behind a bike shed or in a chemistry lab. Call me conventional, but there is nowhere on earth I'd rather be than here in my Savoy bed with Freddie Hunter.

AWAKE

Sunday, September 16

"ARE YOU SURE about this?"

It's not much before nine on Sunday morning and Jonah and I are standing outside the local cat rehoming center waiting for it to open.

"You don't sound as if you think it's a good idea."

Phil and Susan adopted a cat from this very shelter a couple of months ago and Phil is relentless in his photo- and funny-story sharing of their sweet blue-eyed cat, so much so that he's convinced me that my life will be all round better if it includes a feline friend. I've roped Jonah into coming with me to help me choose, mostly just for something I could ask him to do with me. We haven't really spent any time together since the grief session. We've texted each other sporadically; he eventually replied to me just as I was on the edge of being offended, and then he sent me a text a month or so back when he was chaperoning his class at a theme park. He's not a huge roller coaster fan. The image he sent me of himself in the front car was accompanied by a "Freddie would piss himself if he could see me now. The kids made me do it" message. He was right. Freddie was always in the "the bigger the better" camp when it came to roller coasters and he found it hilarious if he could talk Jonah onto one with him. We knocked a few texts back and forth that day, but then nothing again, until I bumped into him on my lunch break yesterday. I kind of blurt-asked him to come with me this morning and he couldn't think of a reason to say no, and now here we are and someone has just opened the door for us.

"Do you know what you're looking for?" he asks me as I fill in an application form.

Phil's cat springs to my mind. "Something pretty?" I say. "One who'll sit on my lap while I watch the TV."

"Boy or girl?"

"Girl, I think," I say. I don't know why really. I just fancy having another female around.

We file into the viewing area behind a green-haired girl who can't be more than eighteen. The first pen has a brawl of black-and-white kittens and their tired-looking mother. I bypass it; I don't have the time or the energy for a kitten. Jonah pauses by it, watching them, laughing as one of them hurls itself at the mesh and nips his finger.

Next along is a pair of adult black cats. There's a note written on a whiteboard on the front of their cage telling potential new owners that these brothers need to stay together. Another no-no, so I move along.

"Not these guys either?" Jonah looks in on them. "Sorry, boys."

"I can't manage two," I say, looking into the next cage along. The notes tell me this is Betty, a two-year-old tortoiseshell.

"Hello, pretty lady," I murmur, curling my fingertips through the mesh. "How're you doing?"

She rubs herself against the mesh, all fur and big green eyes. I'm beguiled, and Jonah is too when he stands beside me.

"Oh, she's good," he says. "She's giving you the hard sell."

"It's working," I say, laughing when she headbutts my hand. Betty is ticking all of my boxes.

"Freddie would never have had a cat," I say. He really wasn't a cat fan at all. He was one of those people who felt it necessary to nail your colors to the mast as either a dog person or a cat person, whereas I'm a more even-handed fan of both. All things being equal I'd probably choose to have a dog too, but right now it feels like way too much responsibility. A cat though . . . their relative independence appeals to me, at the same time as giving me something to look after, another heartbeat in the house. Being back at work is great in terms of keeping busy—my days are full on, but it also highlights how quiet it is when I get home. I'm trying not to rely on Elle too much either. She's putting in extra hours at the hotel and has precious little time with David as it is.

"Betty looks like a winner to me," Jonah says. "Although you might have to fight off the tomcats with a big stick."

"I can do that," I say. I can be Betty's defender.

It's almost a done deal when I glance down into the end pen and come eyeball-to-eyeball with a really ragged old boy flat out on the floor, white with one black eyepatch, which presumably accounts for the name written on his whiteboard: Turpin; approximately twelve years old, unsuitable for rehoming with children or other animals (not even fish), female owner strongly preferred.

I squat down for a better look almost against my will, and the rangy old cat stares me in the eyes; Eeyore downbeat. Nothing to see here, girlfriend, he says. I've seen too much and I've heard too much, he says. Just leave me here to wallow around in my own misery, sister, he says. And then he shoves his face under his paw and dismisses me.

"This one," I say.

Jonah hunkers down next to me. "You think so?"

He's too nice a person to say anything mean, but doubt runs clear through his question. "Twelve," he says, as Turpin pulls his head back up to take a look at Jonah. "That's pretty senior in cat years. The vet bills might be more of an issue."

I appreciate his pragmatic approach, and he probably has a point. Turpin is a bit of an old dude.

"My boss would kill me for saying this," the green-haired girl says, peering behind her to make sure no one is listening. "But Turpin's been here for a year or more now. He's pretty unsociable. Betty's a safer bet."

Jonah looks at me, and then we both look at Turpin, who stares back at us with muddy brown eyes. I screw my nose up, about to let my head rule my heart, and then the old boy lets out this bone shaker of an "I knew it" sigh.

"I can be pretty unsociable these days," I say. "He'd suit me."

Jonah hides his smile behind his hand. He'd do the same thing; he's as softhearted as they come.

Green-haired girl shrugs in a your-loss way and reaches for the latch on Turpin's door.

I guess it was the beat look in his eyes that clinched it. I recognized it. I connected with it. It said my black heart has nothing for you, and I wanted to say sure, I get that, bud, but someone I love told me that the sun is going to keep on inconveniently rising so you and I may as well watch it do its infuriating thing together. And now he's here, staring me down in my living room, and I'm beginning to wonder if I had a moment of madness in not choosing the sweet girl who liked me because Turpin doesn't seem to like me much at all.

"Food?" I say, because I was always well aware that the way to Freddie's heart was invariably through his stomach. The rehoming center furnished me with a small supply of Turpin's usual food to get us started, and only after the papers were signed and he was officially mine did they double down on the fact that he isn't a great mixer with other animals.

"It says in his notes that he once mauled a guinea pig," one said.

"And he had a pretty spectacular go at our boss when he first arrived here," another said. "Although we've since realized he's more of a woman's cat." The look on her face suggests this is code for keep him away from men at all costs, but he seemed quite ambivalent to Jonah. He wasn't too much trouble on the car ride home, just lay in his box on my knees as Jonah tried to take the corners carefully. It was good to spend some time with him—Jonah, I mean—though the deep fractures in our friendship are going to take some healing. I've asked him to come with me to Dawn's wedding in a few weeks. I don't want to let her down but I can't face going alone either, and Jonah at least knows most of my work colleagues because the school uses the community center regularly for events. He's agreed; another plaster over the fracture.

Turpin doesn't follow me into the kitchen when I fill up his bowl, and when I head back to see if a shake of the box will entice him I find he's decamped onto Freddie's chair and turned his face away into the corner. He's effectively giving me his furry backside. It feels like a cat insult.

"You should probably choose a different chair," I say, aware that Freddie would spit his teeth out at the sight of a cat in his favorite spot.

Nothing. No reaction. Just an obstinate bum.

"Turpin." I test out saying his name with quiet authority and he completely ignores me. "Hey there, Turpin," I say, Disney chipper. Still nothing. I lay a hand on his back and he does something: I don't know if it's a purr or a low growl. I want to say the former, but I rather fear the latter. I sigh and try not to feel as if I've made a mistake. It's early days.

ASLEEP

Sunday, September 30

BLOODY HELL, WHAT are we doing at a *gym*? This is one area of our lives where Freddie and I were sharply divided, as in he loved it and I'd rather skewer my own eyeballs than try to stay upright on a running machine. It's just not something we generally did together. He used the gym at work and I used the gym nowhere, and I feel the no joint exercise approach has suited us perfectly well. Who in their right mind does this on a Sunday afternoon?

"Okay?" Freddie asks, his hand firm on the small of my back.

Maybe I can suggest we do something else.

"Umm . . ."

He laughs. "You can't get cold feet now we're here, Lyds, just stick to the running machine as usual if you like. You're getting almost good at it."

A shiver of irritation slides over me at the tone of his

voice, together with the realization that I've been coming here for a while now. Am I here on a wedding fitness kick? Or do I genuinely enjoy the gym in this world? I find that a stretch to believe. I swallow and glance around, trying to find something unthreatening to use that isn't the running machine, but I don't have the confidence to try any of it out. Fine. I'll get on the bloody running machine and make out like I love it. I breathe a sigh of relief when I manage to set it to a sedate jog, my eyes on Freddie's back across the other side of the gym as I find my pace.

"How's it going today, Lydia?"

A guy who can't be over twenty pauses beside me. I'm grateful he's wearing a name tag that singles him out as Martin, fitness instructor.

"Yeah, good," I say. "Just putting in some miles."

What am I saying? Just putting in some miles? I think he stifles a snort as he glances at the metrics on my machine. I'll be here awhile if I want to put in some miles.

"Warming up a bit first," I mutter, hot-cheeked.

"Right," he says. "Always best."

He walks away, and after a few negative thoughts, I find strange solace in the fact that things can be less than perfect here too. My life with Freddie wasn't all halcyon days and honeysuckle around the door, so why should everything here be rose-tinted? One thing's for sure: If this place *was* a figment of my imagination, we wouldn't be spending Sunday afternoon at the bloody gym. I grit my teeth and crank up the speed on the running machine, pounding frustration and confusion out through the soles of my feet until I break into a hitherto unheard of exercise-related sweat.

AN ODD THING happens when we leave the gym. I had the car keys in my pocket, and as I reverse out of the car park Freddie rolls his head against the headrest and looks at me.

"What have I done wrong, Lyds?"

"What do you mean?" I ask.

"You were fine on the way to the gym, and then once we were there you acted as if it was the last place you wanted to be. And now this." He gestures at the steering wheel.

"What?"

He huffs. "You. Making a point of driving home."

I glance across at him in the passenger seat and he looks suddenly all kinds of out of place and confused, and I realize that to him I must have had a bit of a Jekyll and Hyde moment this afternoon. Note to self for future visits here: take a second to read the situation more carefully before jumping in with both feet.

"I'm sorry," I say. "If I was a bit pissy back there, I mean. I didn't mean anything. You know I'm not the biggest gym fan." I wince inwardly in case I am a gym bunny here, but Freddie doesn't react. I'd have been more surprised if he had, to be honest.

"I'm sorry too. You know I'm not the best passenger." He reaches over and flicks my indicator on and I bite back the urge to slap his hand away.

* * *

BACK AT HOME I'm making us a cuppa, and the simple action of reaching for two mugs again instead of one takes my breath. I'm coming to realize that there is a price to pay for these moments; I'll pay for this one the very next time I make a single cup of tea.

"Bath's ready, stroppy," Freddie says, sliding his arms around me from behind.

I lean back against him, smiling. "Tea's ready, control freak."

"I just know what I like." He laughs it off, then nuzzles my neck. "And I like you."

"Lucky me," I say, and I mean it.

"You know it."

He earns himself an elbow in the ribs for that one.

"Call me if you need me to wash your back," he says. "You'll have to shout loud though. I might put the game on."

I turn to face him, going along with it. "You mean rugby's more tempting than me?"

His mouth twists as he thinks about it. "It's Bath, babe."

"Your loss," I say, flicking him with the tea towel.

He catches my hand and reels me in. "You know I'm kidding, right?"

"You better be," I say, and he kisses me, laughing.

I'm laughing too, and then I'm not because our kiss slips from messing around to serious, from tepid to scorching, from I'm sorry to I want you.

"The bath . . ." I murmur, when his fingers reach for the waistband of my jeans.

"You need to take your clothes off anyway," he says,

popping the button. "I ran it hot, you might want to give it a few minutes to cool down."

"Is that right?" I say, bunching his T-shirt in my hand to tug him closer.

He tugs my zipper down and any last thoughts of the bath leave my head.

LATER, WHEN I finally get my bath, I think back over the afternoon Freddie and I have spent together. I'm coming to realize that even in the relatively short time since the accident I've already started to fundamentally change. I've had to lose my blinkers in order to survive, and the girl I am now sees the world, *every* world, in a slightly different way from the girl I used to be. I'm 99 percent familiar in this life–I'm walking in my own footsteps after all–yet somehow it's as if my shoes don't quite fit. It's nothing and everything, a small irritation against my heel, but I recently saw (on daytime TV, of course) a piece about a woman who ignored a blister on her heel and ended up with blood poisoning that very nearly finished her off. It is terribly difficult to spend time here in this life with Freddie while also being aware of my life without him, so I come to a decision: when I am here, I'm consciously not going to think about my other life. I am not going to waste any more precious time arguing with Freddie over things the girl I am here just wouldn't be bothered by.

AWAKE

Saturday, October 20

I'M SITTING AT the kitchen table, coffee beside me. Turpin was here when I came down; he wolfed his food and made a bolt for the door. No one could accuse him of being clingy, but I don't begrudge him. I could have chosen Betty, but Turpin's take it or leave it outlook struck a chord with me.

As is often the case, I feel hungover, an aftereffect of the tablets and time spent with Freddie in the invisible world next door. What am I doing there right now, I wonder? Probably not much different from what I'm doing here, lazing around still in my pj's.

It's amazing, scary even, how quickly my brain has adapted to living between worlds. In the first weeks, it was difficult to keep the two timelines separate, but like most things, practice makes perfect. I've been coming and going now for five months or more and with every passing visit it becomes easier to rationalize and compartmentalize the two.

The other place isn't an exact copy of my life here except with Freddie still in it; it's a different version of my life altogether. But I do know that if he were still with me, he'd be accompanying me tonight to Dawn's wedding instead of Jonah. I've seen him a couple of times since the great cat mission. We've developed a hand-over routine of sorts at Freddie's grave—he goes early on Saturday, I go later, and in the middle we sit for a few minutes and talk about nothing and everything. What we're actually doing is mending our friendship, or trying to anyway, because we are important to each other. We have so many shared memories. So many Freddie memories. We all visited the Bayeux Tapestry as teenagers, a school trip to Normandy that mostly involved long coach journeys, illicit alcohol, and ill-advised teenage choices. Much of the trip has thankfully been exiled to the fog of youth, but my one enduring memory is the visit to the tapestry itself. It seemed unfathomably long to me at the time, countless heroes and villains, bloody conquests and battles lost, rich with kings, queens, knights, and fallen soldiers. The tapestry of my life is starting to feel similarly littered; my mum and Elle the heroes, Freddie the fallen soldier.

"READY?"

The taxi has just deposited us outside the wedding venue and my nerves are jangling louder than the bracelets Elle gave me to go with the green dress I bought when we were shopping in town a few weeks ago.

"Honestly, not really," I say. "But this is Dawn's big day and I promised I'd be here."

Jonah nods, not quite meeting my eye.

"Dress is nice." He sounds awkward, and I feel it. But I know he's trying to boost my confidence, so I try to raise a smile.

"Thanks for making an effort too," I say, acknowledging Jonah's dark shirt and his attempt to tame his hair. He's happiest in battered jeans and T-shirt, so it's a jolt to see him scrubbed up. He nods, then puts his hand on my back and reaches for the door.

"Come on. We can do this."

"YOU LOOK BEAUTIFUL," I say, careful not to leave a lipstick mark on Dawn's cheek as I kiss her.

Her eyes are drawn to Jonah beside me, and then she squeezes my hands in hers. "Thank you for coming. I know it can't be easy."

She means because we both began wedding planning at the same time, excitedly flicking through bride magazines on our lunch breaks. I paint a resolute smile on my face and squeeze her fingers right back.

"I wouldn't have missed it for the world," I say, and I mean it. Dawn hasn't had it easy: her mum died when she was a child and the rest of her family couldn't afford to make the journey up from Plymouth. Her new mother-in-law makes her life difficult too, always on hand with a criticism of Dawn's mothering skills.

"Everyone is over in the far corner," she says, nodding toward the crowd from work. They look different somehow in their wedding best with their partners by their sides. Ryan spots me first and grabs two extra chairs from a nearby table. He really is the kindest of boys; I can't quite class him as a man yet; he still lives with his parents and spends as much time on videogames as he does with the many girls he seems to date.

"Here she is," Phil booms, his red bow tie tight around his neck as he stands and plants a kiss on my cheek. "Jonah," he says, pumping Jonah's hand with great enthusiasm. They've met often at work, and of course they are aware of his connection to Freddie. It's one of the things that comes with living in a sleepy, backwater town: most people here know each other by face, if not by name. Freddie would have preferred to move away to a bright city lights apartment like his more cosmopolitan colleagues live in, but we bought locally because I wanted to stay within a cup of tea's distance of Mum and Elle.

Julia smiles as we join them, regal in black and white; and Bruce, her painfully shy husband, catches my eye and then looks away again quickly.

"Drink?" Jonah murmurs beside me, and I nod, grateful. Typically, he offers to buy a round for everyone at the table, and Ryan jumps up to help him at the bar. Belatedly, he looks back at me and introduces his date.

"Lydia, Olivia." He nods between us and grins. "Olivia, Lydia." I'm not sure, but I think I detected the slightest pause before he said her name, as if he was just double-checking inside his own head that he'd got it right.

I take a seat next to the outrageously pretty Olivia and compliment her on her immaculate and extremely long fingernails, ice blue to match her tiny dress.

"Have you known Ryan long?" I say, making conversation.

"Not really," she says, sucking her cocktail up through a straw. "We met at a foam party."

I don't really know how to respond to that. I've never been to a foam party; I didn't know they even existed outside of the Balearics.

"Fun," I say in the end, and she nods, hoovering around her ice cubes noisily.

"How'd you meet your fella?" she asks, her eyes on Jonah at the bar.

I'm momentarily thrown. "Jonah?"

I'm still trying to decide how to phrase what Jonah is to me when she speaks again.

"Nice ass," she says, then laughs. "Sorry."

I shake my head. "We're not together," I say. "He's just a friend."

Olivia looks at me as if I'm lying. "Yeah, right."

"I'm serious. He has a girlfriend, and I—" I frown, because I really don't want to get into this. Jonah's been casually seeing Dee for a while now, low-key but there.

"Whatever you say."

It's pretty clear she doesn't believe me. I don't insist because it would look worse, and it's not as if I need to justify myself. I'm probably misreading her anyway; my social skills have taken a knock, another casualty of spending too much time alone. I'm saved from having to respond by Phil's wife, Susan, who heard the exchange from her position on the other side of Olivia.

"Doesn't Dawn look a picture," she says, leaning in toward us. I try to telegraph a silent thank-you. Susan appears in the office at least once a week, often bearing things she's baked or bought for Phil to dish out among the staff. We all love her to death; me never more so than right now. The swift conversation change is enough to move things along until Jonah and Ryan return from the bar balancing trays full of glasses. I make a thing of jumping up to let Ryan sit beside Olivia again, not wishing to separate love's young dream. He tries to argue with me, and for a moment our eyes meet and we both realize something: neither of us especially wants to sit next to his date. I think Olivia's days are numbered, and given that she was eyeing up Jonah rather than Ryan at the bar, I don't think either of them will be particularly disappointed. All the same, she's Ryan's date and he can sit next to her.

"Okay?" Jonah says quietly, checking in with me as we take our seats. His arm rests easily along the back of my chair, and I'm grateful for his presence. He's one of those chameleon people who can fit into any crowd, easy company and genuinely interested in what others have to say. It's probably what makes him a good teacher. He actually listens when people speak, without constantly looking for a way to bring the conversation back to himself.

"Think so." I take a sip of cold sauvignon.

"What do you make of Olivia?" he asks.

I look at him curiously. "Why?"

He laughs softly into his beer. "Ryan just told me

that he's tried to end it with her twice this week and she won't have it. He's scared stiff of her."

"Rightly so," I say, looking across at the pair of them. Her fingernails are grazing the back of his neck, slow and territorial.

I find I'm laughing when Ryan catches us looking and mouths "help me" over Olivia's shoulder. Jonah raises his glass and I shrug, helpless. This is a lesson the boy needs to learn for himself.

The band strikes up a rock and roll number, and it's as if someone pressed Bruce's activation button. He goes from quietly nursing his pint to Buddy Holly all in one move, hauling Julia up behind him in a way that brooks no argument. We all watch in surprise as they take to the floor. Bruce is firmly in charge as he slings her between his spread legs with a quicksilver confidence never displayed on any previous occasion. Christmas meals and office get-togethers have come and gone without him saying more than ten words to anyone, which goes a long way toward explaining why we're all slack mouthed as they fly across the floor, outstripping any other pretenders for their rock and roll crown. People actually move to the edges of the floor to give them more space, and as I watch them it strikes me that I've never seen this side of Julia either. She's absolutely loving it. I've sometimes wondered how Julia and Bruce gel as a couple, but watching them now it's clear that there is something special about their bond that we're not usually privy to. She's a different woman with him—or maybe she's herself with her husband in a way she isn't with anyone else.

* * *

I'VE HAD ONE too many drinks. We all have. The measures in this place are huge, and it seems you can take the boy out of the foam party but you can't take the foam party out of the boy—Ryan's had us all sinking Jägerbombs, a first for Julia and Bruce, and I suspect Phil and Susan too. I've never been a great fan and it's not Jonah's bag either, but given the fact that Ryan appeared with a tray of eight shot glasses, and the glint of challenge in Olivia's eye, we all knocked them back in one eye-watering *salut.*

In truth I've enjoyed myself far more than I expected to tonight, so much so that I feel almost guilty about it. God, I've laughed. Jonah has too, both of us euphoric on the alcohol, giddy on the company, carried along by the music. There is a lightness to my mood that I want to cling to like a raft on a dark ocean, a reminder of the carefree and unencumbered girl I was before. Is it horribly disloyal of me to say that I feel as if I've taken the night off from my own life? I don't think it is; in fact, I think it's probably necessary to find a release valve every now and then or risk blowing a gasket.

"Dance with me!" Ryan grabs my hand. The DJ's playing "Come on Eileen," doing all he can to keep the dreaded wedding DJ cliché alive and well. I shake my head, laughing.

"Not a chance," I say, anchoring myself to the chair with both hands. "I might fall over."

Ryan moves on to coercing Susan instead, and Jonah looks at me, smiling.

"You love dancing," he says. "You should dance."

He's right. I do love dancing. I always have. Elle and I both get it from Mum, who's always first on any dance floor. I shrug, noncommittal, as we watch Ryan and Susan messing around with their arms high in the air. We sit alongside each other, facing the dance floor, his arm warm across the back of my chair.

"We look like a TV judging panel," he says.

I consider the crowd on the dance floor. "Who's your winner?"

The DJ turns down the music and calls Dawn and her husband to the floor, slowing the music right down to their wedding song of choice. Like millions of other couples around the world this year, they've chosen Ed Sheeran to welcome them into wedded bliss, and as the opening bars play, the DJ asks everyone to join the happy couple. It's not long until Jonah and I are pretty much the only people still sitting down; even Ryan and Olivia are up there. He's probably going to regret this in the morning, but for now he seems to have decided to throw caution to the wind because she has her tongue far enough down his throat to know whether he's had his tonsils removed.

Phil ruffles my hair as Susan pulls him past us to join the dancers—a simple fatherly gesture that says more than words could. I watch them for a moment, and the affection I hold for them brings a lump to my throat.

Jonah looks at me, and I'm sure he can see the battle going on in my head. I don't know what's worse—the idea of dancing, or being the only people in the room *not* dancing.

"Come on," he says eventually, helping me up.

He holds me lightly, linking his fingers through mine, his other hand on my back.

"It's only dancing," he whispers, the ghost of a smile on his lips. We don't speak as we move slowly among the other dancers. I see Dawn and her proud new husband, oblivious to everyone around them, their sleeping son on his father's hip. I have to look away; it's too hard.

"Hey," Jonah says when I swallow a shudder of tears, his mouth close to my ear when he gathers me against him. "I know, Lyds. I know."

I'm trying not to cry, but I'm not making the best job of it. It's just so bloody unfair.

"Oh, Jonah," I gulp, pressing my face into his shirt. He's so physically different from Freddie: taller, lithe. My head fits easily beneath his chin even in my heels, and the familiar, understated amber-warm spice of his cologne reassures me.

"I miss Freddie, and I miss dancing, and I miss love."

He doesn't answer me, because there aren't really any appropriate words. We barely even pretend to dance anymore. We stand still and hold each other in the moment as everyone moves around us. He shushes me, quiet unintelligible words as he strokes my hair, and I try to offer him similar comfort because I remember how he looks in my other life. Joyful, free of guilt, the bruises beneath his eyes nowhere in evidence. Here in my waking life he's as damp-cheeked and heartsore as I am, as lost and in need of a shoulder. I hold him to me and hope we can help each other find the way home.

ASLEEP

Saturday, November 17

"AND THIS IS the barn," Victoria says, opening a huge pair of wooden doors with a flourish. Victoria is the event planner at the place we've chosen to hold our wedding, a rustic country inn with a converted barn. We're standing on the threshold of that very barn right now. Pale winter sunlight streams in through the high windows, illuminating tiny dust motes in the air. My romantic heart sees glitter.

"It's dressed ready for a wedding tomorrow," Victoria says, referring to the thick red and gold garlands around the faded old rafters. "Winter theme, obviously. Next month it'll be wall-to-wall Christmas weddings, but it's best of all in the summer. We fill it with wildflower arrangements and hundreds of white fairy lights, a real midsummer night's dream."

"I love it," I breathe. I must have been here before in this life. I expect we'll have looked at various venues before deciding on this as the perfect place for our wedding. I silently congratulate myself; I can't imagine anywhere more us. "It honestly couldn't be more perfect."

Freddie squeezes my shoulders. "Is the ceremony itself in here too?"

"Yes and no." Victoria strides off toward a door at the other end of the barn. "Your ceremony itself will take place in here."

The smaller side room is built from pale gray bricks that look as if they were hand-hewn in days before machinery even existed. It's been carefully restored to retain its tumbledown charm; straightaway it reminds me of the chapel where Ross married Emily in *Friends*. Cast-iron candelabras hang from the lintels. They're not lit today, but in my mind's eye I can already see how spectacular it's going to look, how it's going to smell of trailing honeysuckle, how Freddie will wait for me right there at the front.

"Still love it?" Freddie says, squeezing my hand.

So much, I think. I turn to Victoria.

"Would it be okay if we have a couple of minutes on our own?"

She puts her hands out to the sides. She knows perfectly well that I'm smitten. "It's pretty special, isn't it? Take as long as you need. I'll be back in the bar when you're ready."

Freddie and I walk slowly along the aisle as the door clicks behind her.

"Next time you walk down here you'll be wearing your wedding dress," he says.

"And you'll be down there in your suit," I say. "Will you be nervous?"

He starts to laugh. "Err, no! Unless you're getting cold feet and might leave me here on my own?"

"I promise I won't," I say. I mean it more than he could ever know, because I know all too well what it's like to be the one left behind.

"Will you be nervous?" he asks.

I nod. "I'll be nervous about a hundred things. Does my dress look okay? Will Elle try to tell Victoria how to do her job? Has Jonah forgotten the rings?"

We've reached the end of the aisle now, the place where countless other couples have stood and made their forever vows to each other.

"Jonah won't forget the rings. I won't let him," he says. "And Elle will chill if she has a couple of glasses of champagne in the morning. She'll be glad to be off duty."

He's right, of course; they're such minor worries in the grand scheme of things. It's so typical of him to not let all the small stuff worry him. He always insisted he'd take care of the honeymoon, but everything else was going to be my domain right from day one. And I never minded, as such, but it would have been nice for him to have at least faked interest in wedding favors and table decorations. Dawn and I used to send each other links to things we spotted online, wedding readings and the like. There's something about wedding planning that is just so pleasurably consuming—it's joyful and full of hope; a state of delicious limbo. I wish I'd been able to experience it here; there's so much about our upcoming wedding that I've no clue about.

It's strange thinking about Dawn's wedding now, remembering that poignant last dance with Jonah as I stand here like this with Freddie.

He reels me in against him. "You're going to be the most beautiful girl in the world in your wedding dress. But I'd marry you right here, right now in jeans, Lydia Bird. Except I'm not wearing my lucky underwear."

"You're an idiot," I laugh, not least because he doesn't have any lucky underwear.

"*Your* idiot," he says.

"Too right," I say, standing on my tiptoes to kiss him. My nose is cold, but every other piece of me is warm. Freddie's hands slide down my jean-clad backside and he lifts me clean off the floor.

"I think you should kiss me like this on the actual day," he says.

"Be a bit impractical in my dress," I say, locking my legs around his waist. He holds me there and looks me in the eyes, laughing.

"You should be ashamed of yourself, getting me going in a place like this."

I hug him, really, really tight. He hugs me back, and for that one golden minute, I'm 100 percent happy.

AWAKE

Tuesday, December 25

"GIN AND TONIC." Elle hands me a drink. "Heavy on the gin."

She touches the rim of her glass against mine, in solidarity rather than celebration. We all knew that today would be hard. For a couple of days last week I wasn't even planning on coming to Mum's at all today. Freddie and I never had that awkward tussle of alternating whose family we would go to for Christmas day, because his mum has spent the festive season in Spain for at least the last decade. Which made the thought of today even worse. I had a bit of a meltdown, truth be told. Christmas is just so in your face, isn't it? On the radio, in the shops, on everyone's lips. The worst of it is that I love Christmas; I'm a total sucker for the movies, the glitter, the food. I start celebrating in October, planning which movies to watch, writing endlessly changing lists of gifts to buy and meals to attempt.

Perhaps it's because Freddie was such a big kid, he really threw himself into the whole season, whipping everyone else up with him. Jonah texted me a photo this morning, one from their teenage years when Freddie bought them both ridiculous Christmas hats with flashing red bobbles. It's silly and joyful, their fraternal bond brighter even than their hats. They were both only children, but in each other they'd found a brother. I called him quickly. It was good to hear his voice and feel able to tell each other how much we miss Freddie today. I cried my first tears of the day when he said he missed me too. He always used to come over to ours for Christmas morning bacon sandwiches. Jonah's in Wales for Christmas this year; Dee has family there. I expect there's an element of running away too, but I can't blame him. I sent him back a photo of the bike Freddie bought me a couple of Christmases ago, because I'd once told him I always had Elle's hand-me-downs as a kid. He hid it outside in the garden with a huge red bow on it. I felt about eight years old. I looked it too, delightedly trying out my new ride up and down the street along with two other shiny new bike owners, both of them under ten. I'm pretty sure my whoops were the loudest.

There's none of that easy joy today. We're all subdued, brittle, smiling because we need to rather than because we want to. I feel bad that my whole family have had their Christmas overshadowed too. It's as if a huge raven has landed on the roof and folded his wings down over the windows, dulling the lights on the tree and underscoring the day with melancholy. At least it's just us, though. My Auntie June tried her best to get us to go to them for a change, which was lovely of her, but we decided to stay put in the end. Going somewhere else wouldn't have lessened the impact of Freddie's absence, and at least here I can sob into my turkey if I need to. I feel a bit bad for Auntie June though. I know she'd have loved to have us all over, if only to water down the acerbic effects of my cousin Lucy.

"Your mum's in a panic that she's forgotten to put the roast potatoes in," David says, coming through from the kitchen wearing his customary Christmas jumper. He and Freddie used to try to out-jumper each other, every year more garish than the last. David wasn't going to wear one at all today; Elle told me so a week or two ago, sending me instantly online to remedy it. I went for one bearing a huge reindeer in sunglasses with flashing antlers–I think it would have been Freddie's choice had he been here. I gave it to David just now and he made a bad job of hiding his emotions as he slipped it over his head. His serious expression makes a strange contrast with Rudolph's crazy grin. I sigh and smile at the same time at the sight of it now.

It's like a stone has been dropped into the middle of a pond: ripple after ripple, concentric circles, hurt spreading outward. Freddie was the stone. I am the tightest circle around him, then his mum, and Jonah, and then outward to everyone else who loved him: my family and the rest of his, Deckers and co. at the pub, his colleagues and friends. All those ripples, all those people who might think of him today.

Anyway. I try to pull myself up out of my thoughts to concentrate on the task at hand: navigate through

Christmas lunch with my family. Afterward I can go home and spend my real Christmas with Freddie.

"No roast potatoes?" I frown. My mum brags insufferably about her roasties, and to be fair she has good grounds. "That can't be right."

In the kitchen, I find Mum facedown in the freezer with her backside in the air.

"What's this I hear about roast potatoes?"

She straightens and turns to me, her deeley boppers flashing red, and tears coursing down her face.

"Don't even look at me, Lydia. I'm being a stupid old woman who sobs into the frozen peas. It's the bloody menopause; I've got the memory of a goldfish. No, worse, a guppy. I just wanted to make it perfect and I've gone and forgotten the bloody roast potatoes and now it's all ruined," she says. "I thought I might have a bag of those horrible frozen ones hanging around, but I haven't even got any of those sodding rotten things."

I feel a smile start to twitch my lips despite myself. "Shall we call the emergency services?" I say, putting my hands on her shoulders. "Declare a potato-related disaster?"

She sniffs. "Don't joke. It's not funny."

"Okay," I say. "I could put some roast chicken crisps in a bowl and we can have those instead? No one will notice once they've gone soggy with the gravy."

She rolls her eyes and I rip off some kitchen roll and hand it to her.

"It doesn't matter, Mum," I say, not joking anymore. "Honestly, it doesn't."

She looks unconvinced, but nods. "No crisps though," she says. "This isn't a student squat."

"No crisps," I say. "No sprouts either?"

It's a running joke: she always hides sprouts underneath other things on mine and Elle's plates because she knows we hate them.

She laughs, halfhearted. "Help me start putting things out on the table."

I carry the turkey through to the dining room and place it down in pride of place, my eyes scanning Mum's gorgeous festive table. It's always the same: fresh flowers, her best crystal, and a Christmas log ornament Elle and I made together at junior school. It's not very impressive; a chunk of sawn-off branch covered with raggedy clumps of spray-on snow, a threadbare robin clinging to the top of it with spindly, wire feet. Mum's dressed it up with fresh holly and a fat, creamy candle as she always does, a silk purse of a sow's ear. I find it comfortingly nostalgic. So many things in my life have changed, but some things will always stay the same.

HALF AN HOUR later the food is in its place and we're all sitting around the table when we hit our next hurdle: who is going to carve the bird.

My mum picks up the carving knife, uncertainty all over her face. It was always Freddie's job.

"Let me," David says, clearing his throat as he gets to his feet. He looks as nervous as he did before his wedding speech.

We all love David, but he is the least practical man on the planet and famously clumsy. Mum's eyes round slightly, as if she can't quite bring herself to hand over the carving implements in case he slips and someone ends up in the emergency department.

"He's been practicing carving from YouTube videos," Elle says softly.

Mum looks at me, and I nod because there is something so endearing about the idea of David studying how to carve a turkey on YouTube. We all watch as he tries not to make a hash of it, poking an experimental fork in before going for it, his teeth sunk into his bottom lip in concentration. It's not a complete disaster; I'd give him a three for technique and a ten for effort, which more than makes up for the splinters of bone in my dinner.

"Pass the roast potatoes?" Elle gives Mum the amused side-eye. I can see how hard she's trying to keep things jolly.

Mum doesn't miss a beat and holds out the sprouts instead.

Elle puts two fingers in her mouth and mimes gagging as Mum places the bowl down. "They're good for you," Mum says. "You could do with some color in your cheeks. You're looking peaky."

Oddly enough, the comment is enough to add an instant stain of color to Elle's cheeks. I suppose we're all feeling sensitive today.

I pick up the wine bottle and pour for Mum first, and then Elle. It's David who gives the game away.

"Didn't you, erm, decide not to drink today, Elle?" he says, and she shoots him furious daggers in return.

He turns as puce as Mum's red cabbage, making a show of carving more uneven slabs of turkey in a bluster to cover his tracks. "You know, you're on that diet . . ."

I meet Elle's panicky eyes across the table; she's never dieted a day in her entire life, and in that instant I know. Mum realizes too, laying her cutlery down and placing her shaking hand flat over the base of her throat.

"Elle," she breathes. "Does this mean . . . ?" She pauses. "Are you . . . ?"

"I'm sorry," David says, grabbing Elle's hand on the tabletop. "It just came out." He looks wretched.

We all fall momentarily silent, staring at one another. Elle cracks first.

"We weren't going to say anything today," she says. "We only found out ourselves a few days ago."

"Darling," Mum gasps, and for the second time today, she's crying. And then so am I, and so is Elle. We huddle round the table, Elle on my left, Mum on my right, David opposite, and we all grip hard onto one another's hands. We sit for a few minutes, half sobbing and smiling, not wanting to let go.

"I guess I better drink for two, in that case." I laugh a little, filling my own wineglass to the top.

Elle nods, her worried eyes searching my face, trying to discern if I'm faking it. I'm not, and I am.

I'm not, because I'm thrilled from the soles of my shoes to the tips of my silly party hat; she's wanted to be a mother since we were little girls pushing our dolls' prams around the back garden. She was far more maternal than I was even back then, her dolls always pristine with their hair brushed; mine were always missing an arm, and had Biro on their faces. I understand why she wasn't going to say anything today, but I'm glad that I know. I don't want her and David to have to hide such life-changing news for fear of upsetting me.

But I *am* faking too, because it's a shock and so strangely life-affirming–a baby. A brand-new life, a razor sharp reminder that Freddie and I will never know the joy of having a child of our own.

I raise my glass. "To you two," I say, and I dry my tears because this is one of their most precious life moments.

"Three," Mum adds, high-pitched hysterical.

We clink glasses and I give Elle's hand an extra squeeze. It's good news.

ASLEEP

Tuesday, December 25

"YOUR MUM IS officially the queen of Christmas dinner. I don't need to eat again until next year." Freddie groans next to me on the sofa.

"I think we both know you'll be gagging for a turkey sandwich by eight o'clock," I say. I presume like all our other years, we'll have come home armed with enough leftovers to make sandwiches, soup, curries, and turkey burgers until at least the middle of February. I try to put thoughts of the Christmas lunch I forced down firmly out of my mind.

"I can't believe Elle's having a baby," Freddie says.

So it's happening in this world too, then.

"I know," I sigh.

"Which means we're going to have a pregnant bridesmaid." He mimes the shape of a huge baby belly. It's closer to Mr. Greedy than a pregnant woman, but I grin all the same.

"It does." In fact I quite like the idea of Elle being all pregnant and glowy in our wedding photographs. A wedding, and now a baby. It feels as if someone in the ether sounded a whistle: all change, girls, all change. Some things *don't* change, thankfully; at Christmas we will always gather around my mum's table. Next year, we'll all just squeeze up to make room for a high chair at the table too. I do of course realize that he or she probably won't be in a high chair by that stage. I'm thinking fancifully, in the deep and meaningful way a slightly sozzled aunt-to-be is fully entitled to.

"Do you think we'll have babies one day?" I say, champagne-wistful as I put my feet up in Freddie's lap. It's such an unbearably bittersweet thought, really.

He flicks on the TV, clicking through the channels. "*Doctor Who*?"

I don't answer. Is he avoiding my question? I don't think he is; we've talked generally about children lots of times. It's kind of a given that we'll go down that road. Isn't it? Or am I jumping to conclusions? I tell myself I'm being daft. Turkey paranoia setting in.

Oblivious to my disgruntlement, he leans over and grabs the tin of Quality Street from the coffee table.

"I thought you were stuffed?" I say.

"I'm never too stuffed for a toffee penny," he says. It's one of the many millions of reasons we're compatible: he eats the toffees, I eat the soft centers. I don't think I could live with someone who made me fight for the orange creams. I'd spend the yuletide period low-level furious.

I shake my head when he offers the tin to me.

"Go on," he cajoles. "You know you can't say no to a strawberry cream."

"Maybe later," I say, and he shakes the open tin in front of me.

"Hey, Lydia!" he says, in a silly voice. "Down here! Eat me! You know you want to!"

"That's a terrible impression of a strawberry cream," I say, amused despite myself.

"It was orange, and you've hurt its feelings," Freddie says, solemn.

I roll my eyes. "Fine," I say. "Give it here."

He shakes the tin again for me to help myself, and when I look down I finally understand why he's being so pushy.

"Freddie," I sigh, plucking the gift out from among the jewel bright sweets. "What's this?"

He shrugs. "Santa must have left it for you."

We agreed not to spend very much on each other this year; the wedding bills are racking up like mad and then there's the house and the car . . . it all feels a bit never-ending at the moment. Still, I think Freddie loved the cuff links I found for him in the vintage shop on the high street. He likes to be best-dressed man in any meeting. He always says it gives him the edge before anyone even starts talking. He likes to arrive first too—a tip he picked up from a Barack Obama documentary. He makes no secret of the fact that he's ambitious, but unlike many of his colleagues, he isn't ruthless with it, which actually just makes him more of a threat.

The gift is beautifully wrapped in printed paper

with tiny sketches of the Eiffel Tower and tied with navy ribbon.

"Open it, then," he says, watching me, clearly desperate for me to get inside the paper.

"Did you wrap this yourself?"

"Of course," he says, but he's smirking because we both know he charmed someone else into doing it for him. Someone at work, probably, knowing Freddie.

I can't lie, I'm excited. "You shouldn't have," I say, pulling the ribbon open.

"Yes, I should," he says.

"But I haven't got an extra gift for you."

"You can make it up to me in another way," he grins, but I can tell he's impatient for me to see what's inside.

I'm one of those people who likes to open presents slowly, picking off the Sellotape and smoothing out the crinkled edges of the paper, no peeping to see if I can guess what it is. Freddie is the opposite; he has a quick feel, declares it a book or a T-shirt or chocolate, then rips the paper off like a five-year-old. I drive him nuts. I'm driving him nuts right now, but I enjoy this bit too much to rush it.

"Want to guess what it is?" he says, keen to move things on.

The oblong box is slender and shallow, about the size of a big bar of chocolate. "A camera? A dinner service? It better not be a dinner service."

"Try again."

I peel off the tape carefully. "A puppy?"

Easing the pretty paper back, I find a plain gray box and I pause, my fingers extra slow now as I shake the lid loose. I'm teasing him, even though I'm actually desperate to get a look.

"Just open the bloody thing," he half shouts, leaning forward as if he doesn't already know what's in the box.

So I do, and then I look up at him quizzically.

"Freddie," I whisper. He's actually taken my breath away. "We can't afford to go to Paris."

He shrugs. "I sold my guitar."

"You didn't!" The words jump from me. His Fender has been with him even longer than I have.

"When did I last play it?" he says. "It was going to waste in the loft."

"But you loved it," I say, still shocked.

"I love you more."

And there he goes again, shining his spotlight on me. It makes my heart clench to know that he'll never play his Fender again, but it makes my heart swell too, knowing that he'd sell it to surprise me. I must have mentioned Paris a million times, but I never expected this.

I look into his eyes and all I see there is star-bright love.

"You've really surprised me, Freddie."

"Just doing my job." He catches hold of my fingertips and kisses them.

I turn my hand over and hold his jaw. "Your job, huh?"

He kisses my palm. "Making you happy."

"You don't need fancy trips to do that."

"You know me, I'm a fancy kinda guy." He grins,

then looks at me, serious. "I wanted to give you something special, that's all."

"Well, you did," I say. "You always make me feel pretty damn special, Freddie."

"Good." He taps me on the nose. "Can I watch *Doctor Who* now?"

WE WATCH THE DOCTOR and then the movie that follows it, a plate of turkey sandwiches balanced on the sofa between us.

"Did you make these pickled onions?" he asks, almost crying at the cheek-clenching strength of them.

"Yes," I lie. In actual fact Susan made them; Phil brought a box full of jars into work and begged us to take them off his hands.

"With battery acid?"

"So rude," I murmur, trying not to shudder as I bite one. They're really, really sharp.

"Good job I'm not marrying you for your cooking," he says.

"Or my ironing," I say. Very little ironing goes on in our house, and the scant amount that does happen is usually done by Freddie.

"I'm an enlightened man," he says.

"*And* you give great gifts," I say.

"Man, you're lucky," he says, sliding the empty plate onto the table.

I lie back, my head in his lap.

"Yes." I'm smiling as I close my eyes. "Yes, I am."

I'm dozing, in that blissed out state you only reach at the end of special days with special people. Freddie's idly playing with my hair, twisting long strands of it around his fingers like a cat's cradle.

"Just so you know, Lyds, the answer is yes," he whispers. "One day, we will have babies. Lots of them. A whole brood, some of them smart like you, some with my big mouth who we'll be forever defending when they're in trouble at school."

For a few precious seconds I can almost see them, almost hear their footsteps on the stairs. Freddie Hunter, I think, more asleep than awake. My heart beats for you.

AWAKE

Monday, December 31

EVEN ON THE HAPPIEST of years, there is always something terrible about New Year's Eve, isn't there? All of that forced bonhomie, the hugs and the backslapping, followed by the inevitable alcohol-induced tears. I've resisted all attempts to get me out of the house tonight—I am resolute in my decision to do my very best to forget all about the fact that it is New Year's Eve at all. I won't be watching Jools Holland bash out "Auld Lang Syne" on the piano with his celebrity friends, and I won't be listening to Big Ben chime midnight, heralded by fireworks and TV crews, and Freddie won't be the first person I kiss to bring in the brand-new year. My family is very unhappy with my insistence on being alone at midnight, so much so that I've agreed to spend midday with them instead, hence the reason I'm now dragging my feet as I approach my mother's cheerful red front door. I don't want to accept that it's New

Year's at all, because much as this year has been an endurance test, come tomorrow I'll have to say Freddie died *last* year. It distances him from me in a way that is wholly and thoroughly unacceptable and makes me full of rage and tears. Since our Christmas together I've been feeling lower than I have for a while. My waking life just cannot compete.

"Love," my mum says, opening the door before I can raise my hand to knock. "Glad you're here."

There's frost on the pavement outside but it's comfortingly warm when I step inside Mum's hallway.

"Mind the carpet," she says, eyeing my winter boots in a way I know means take them off right now before you set even a toe farther into this house. I quite like that she still feels the need to remind me, even though it's as ingrained in me as the days of the week. It's one of the things I can still rely on. She smiles at my cheery Christmas robin socks as I line my boots up neatly beside hers on the low wooden bench provided for exactly that purpose. I put the socks on this morning especially for her; she puts stock in small things like that, watching me for signs that I'm doing more than just going through the motions. I *am* just going through the motions, of course, but for her sake I try to fake it till I make it. Though what happens if you never make it? Do you just keep faking it forever, until you're a completely fake person?

Elle and David are already sitting at the kitchen table when I go through.

"I made you some hot chocolate," Elle says, nodding toward the tall snowman cup on the table. It's piled high with cream and marshmallows and chocolate shavings, the kind of thing you'd pay through the nose for in a café on the high street.

"Is this what we do now you can't drink?" I try out a joke.

She pulls a face. "Don't remind me. I'd kill the lot of you for a gin and tonic."

"It's cold out," I say, rubbing my hands together. "This is perfect."

"You can put brandy in it if you want," she says, begrudging.

I take a sip. It's sweet and hot, fine as it is. Besides, I know I'll have a couple of glasses of wine before bed tonight. If I start drinking this early I might not stop until next year and end up a tearful, raddled mess, rocking on my bathroom floor.

"Has Mum cooked?" I say, taking advantage of the fact that she hasn't followed me into the kitchen to try to gauge how long this gathering is likely to take. I'm not being a bitch; I just want to be at home on my own today.

Elle shakes her head. "Just sandwiches, I think."

That's something.

"Are you sure you won't come with us tonight?" David says, his hands cupped around his mug. "We've still got a spare ticket, just in case."

"We're not planning on staying too late ourselves," Elle adds. "You could come back and stay over at ours."

They're both looking at me warily, hopeful that I might have a last-minute change of heart and join them at The Prince. We've spent New Year's Eve there for the last few years and it's always the same. Packed to the rafters, everyone too overdressed for a backstreet pub, a haze of familiar faces, and dubious drinks pressed into your hands, an undercurrent of barely contained anticipation sweeping everyone toward midnight on a sea of champagne corks and party poppers. I can't think of anywhere I want to be less tonight.

"I'll give it a miss this year," I say, arranging my face into an apology.

They don't press me. I expect they know I won't change my mind.

We look toward the door at the sound of Mum's footfalls on the stairs, and she appears carrying a blue-and-white striped cardboard box. Elle smiles at her, one of those small collaborative smiles that immediately lets me know that she's had a hand in whatever's in that box.

"What's this?" I say, smiling to mask my unease. "New shoes?"

They flick nervous glances at each other as Mum takes a seat, each clearly willing the other one to speak up.

Mum puts her hand flat on the lid of the box and swallows.

"Because it's New Year's Eve, we wanted you to know that none of us will ever forget Freddie either," she says, and already I can hear tears thickening her voice. "We've picked some of our favorite photographs, and other bits and bobs that remind us of him most, and we've put them all in this box for you to keep."

Oh. I look into the depths of my half-drunk hot chocolate and will myself not to cry.

"You don't have to look now if you don't want to,"

Elle rushes in. "We just couldn't let the day slide by without marking it with you."

When I woke this morning, letting the day slide by unmarked was my only intention. Now I don't quite know how to feel.

"I'd like to see," I say.

Mum nods and lifts the lid. Straightaway I see things I recognize: photographs and familiar holiday mementos that cost hardly anything but have been rendered priceless by absence.

Mum picks out a photograph and lays it flat, her fingers absently smoothing a tiny bent corner.

"I think this is the first photograph I have of the two of you together," she says. "You'd have been about fifteen."

"Fourteen," I say softly. "I was fourteen."

She nods, her eyes on the photo. "I worried he was too much of a lad, at first," she says, laughing a little, shaky. "Too likely to break your heart."

I can't recall the photograph being taken, but I can vividly remember our first long, sun-filled summer together. I lived every day on a delicious knife's edge, drunk on a giddy first-love cocktail. I stare into my own eyes in the photograph when Mum pushes it across the table and I briefly wonder if it would have been better if she'd been right about Freddie, if he'd broken my heart that summer instead of fourteen years later. I don't mean that. I can't imagine how my life might have been without him. Colder, certainly, and duller. Less . . . less everything. Just less.

"Look at Jonah's hair." Elle laughs, and I'm grateful to her for trying to lighten the mood.

"Perms were in fashion back then," David offers the lie in Jonah's defense, running a hand over his own already balding head. I can't really remember David with hair; he's blond anyway so his transition from buzz cut to balding wasn't notably stark.

"That's not a perm," I say, a small laugh making its way out. "It's Jonah's actual hair."

"Shit," David mutters into his mug.

Freddie has his arm slung across my shoulders in the photo and Jonah is there too, looking away, distracted by something off camera.

I gaze at it, warmed by vague school memories. Jonah with his big dark curls, my shock of blond hair, and Freddie grinning at the center, already the charismatic front man even at fifteen.

"Remember when he gave me this?" Mum hands me a fragile fan. It's blood-red, made of intricately carved bone and paper.

"He picked it especially for you," I say, remembering him laughing to himself as he rummaged through the different colored fans on a beachside stall in Crete.

"For your hot flushes," I say, at the same time as Mum says, "For my hot flushes."

She shakes her head and swipes away a rogue tear. "Cheeky so and so."

There's another photo from that same holiday too, Freddie in neon-lime swim shorts and a baseball cap, me with scorched shoulders in a pale blue sundress I still have somewhere in the loft because it reminds me of our first foreign trip together.

Elle drags the blue-and-white box toward her. "This is from me," she says, pulling out a birthday card. I remember it easily—it's her thirtieth birthday card from last February. I spent an age searching for the perfect "sister" card, and opening it now I cringe as I read the rambling message I wrote to her after an evening at the pub. But it isn't my message that makes the card box-worthy; it's Freddie's red felt-tip pen missive.

"HAPPY BIRTHDAY SMELLY ELLIE,
MY FAVORITE MAKESHIFT SISTER!
YOU DON'T LOOK A DAY OVER FORTY!"

"Makeshift sister," she whispers, then sighs, juddery and long. "Sorry."

"Don't be," I say, closing the card again slowly. Elle and I have always been content for it to be just the two of us, but over the years Freddie came pretty close to being her brother, much in the same way David has to me. He reaches for the box now and digs out a photograph of himself with Freddie, both of them sporting truly hideous Christmas jumpers.

"This was the one year I was the indisputable winner," he says, unable to keep the note of pride from his voice. I can't argue; he's dressed in a lurid lemon-and-lime-striped hand-knitted jumper that reaches below his knees and is splattered with rainbow-bright woolen 3D adornments: sleighs, Santas, gift boxes, reindeer. It's 100 percent hideous in both style and scale. David had it especially made, right down to the baubles embroidered with all of our names. That jumper quickly became the stuff of Christmas legend in our family. Then David reaches inside the box again and hands me the knitted Christmas bauble bearing Freddie's name.

"I took it off the jumper this morning." He bites his lip. "Wanted it to be in the box."

I fold my fingers around it and a sob rises sharply up my windpipe, urgent and unwilling to stay down, and I find I can't put a brave face on it.

"Oh, love," Mum says, moving to stand behind me with her arms wrapped around my shoulders. She bends to kiss my cheek. "We didn't mean to upset you."

"I know." The words catch on my gulping breath.

"Did we do the wrong thing?"

"No," I say, because even if they did, it was with the best of intentions. "Yes, maybe. Oh, I don't even know." I cry because I can't not and no one says anything. Elle holds my hand, tears rolling silently down her cheeks too. She's a fixer, so I know it kills her that she can't fix this for me.

David puts the things back in the box and closes the lid.

"Another day, maybe," he says. I nod, but I don't reply because all I can think is that sometimes we don't get that luxury, and I burn with an inner rage that has no way to extinguish itself. It's always with me these days, to a greater or lesser degree. Right now it's consuming me, so I make my excuses as soon as possible and leave.

IT'S ELEVEN IN the evening now and I've drunk the best part of a bottle of wine and watched a so-so movie on TV, and successfully managed to avoid all of the jangly, streamer-ridden NYE live specials. Even Turpin has chosen to spend time with me tonight. Since his arrival here a few months back I could count on the fingers of my hands the number of nights he's spent under my roof. He appears sometimes for food when I get in from work, but by all accounts he's taken a shine to Agnes, my neighbor a few doors down. I know for a fact she feeds him. I saw her buying cat food in the corner shop, and she doesn't have a cat. I've spotted him sleeping on her front windowsill too—on the inside. I'm not offended; he didn't make me any promises at the shelter. In fact, he gave me fair warning. But tonight it's like he knows I need a friend. Even if it is a mangy and mostly disinterested one.

All in all, I'm pretty proud of how I've handled myself today. I woke this morning with a knot of sickly dread in my stomach, but I'm ending the night in a mellow, reflective mood. I'm not taking a pink pill tonight. I've gone back and forth in my head on this endlessly over the last couple of weeks, and much as a big part of me would like to, I just don't think I'm emotionally up for it—it's too big an ask of my fragile heart, and I'm reluctantly aware of the need to take care of my mental health. Besides, NYE is only ever what you make it: the momentous passing from an old year into a new one, or just another day. I wrap my dressing gown tighter around me as I turn out the lamps and head for the stairs. It's just another day.

I'VE ONLY BEEN in bed for ten minutes when someone knocks on my front door. I've not taken a sleeping pill but the wine has relaxed me enough to make me momentarily wonder if I've somehow slipped from world to world anyway. I flick on the lamp and everything is exactly as it was when I closed my eyes. The room has none of Freddie's clutter. It's still this side of midnight and someone is absolutely, definitely banging on my front door. Panic twists through my gut. Elle? Has something happened with the baby? Mum? I'm gasping, running for the door, dreading opening it even as I shout out to whoever's on the other side to hang on, I'm coming. *Please not the baby. Please not my sister.* I barely register that I'm speaking the words out loud. *Please not my mum.* I can't lose anyone else. I throw the bolt with fumbling fingers and fling the door open.

"Jonah?"

Jonah Jones is leaning against the doorframe clutching a half-empty bottle of Jack Daniels—or perhaps it would be more accurate to say that the doorframe is holding him up.

"What is it? Is it Elle?" I garble, staring at him, clutching the lapels of my dressing gown.

Jonah looks confused, almost in pain as he tries to decipher my words. And then he understands and his expression shifts toward self-loathing.

"Shit, Lyds," he says, scrubbing his hands over his face. "No. No, it's nothing like that. Elle and David are fine, everyone's fine. I saw them at the pub just now. Jeez, I'm sorry. What a thoughtless twat banging on your door like that, tonight of all nights."

He cuts a defeated figure on my doorstep, and now my heart rate has steadied again, I'm able to speak without gasping.

"What are you doing here, Jonah?"

He turns his back against the wall and looks at the sky.

"I've got no fucking idea," he says, and a single tear slides down his cheek.

"Come inside," I say, but he shakes his head and stays rooted to the spot.

"Can't," he says, his screwed-up face a study of torment. "There's too much Freddie in there for me tonight. I came here because of him, and now I'm too much of a pissing coward to come inside because he's everywhere in there." He circles the bottle toward the door.

"Jonah, you've been here enough times over the months since the accident." I keep my voice low and steady because I can see how distressed he is. "It's okay. Come in, let me make you some coffee."

"But it's New Year's Eve." One side of his mouth lifts in the saddest of smiles. "You can't drink coffee on New Year's Eve, Lydia, it's against the rules." He's slurring a little, as if he's drunk enough to not be able to keep the words in, but not so drunk as to not know what he's saying. "I can't sit in his house, on his sofa, with his girlfriend. Not tonight. Not me."

I may have opted to see New Year's Eve as just another day, but Jonah clearly hasn't allowed himself that kindness.

He stares at me, and then finally, he says what he's really come here to say.

"I'm . . . I'm so fucking sorry for what I did," he whispers, gaunt. "It should have been me." He covers his face with his spread fingers and slides down the wall until he's on his backside. "I wish it had been me."

I sigh deeply. He's clearly not coming inside the house, so I put the door on the latch and take a seat beside him on the cold step. Across the road, noise spills from a brightly lit house.

"Don't say that." I take one of his icy hands between both of mine. "Don't you ever say that again."

"You think it," he blurts.

I stare at him, stricken. "Jonah, I don't, I honestly don't. There isn't a day goes by when I don't wish Freddie was still here, but I swear to God I've never even once wished it had been you instead."

I'm not lying. I've wished a hundred times that Freddie hadn't detoured to pick Jonah up, but that isn't the same thing.

He drinks from the bottle then traces a shaky finger over the scar above his eyebrow. "Just this. I got this, and his beautiful fucking heart stopped beating."

I take the bottle when he holds it out to me and swallow a good slug, feeling the liquid burn its way down my throat. The heat is welcome; it's frost-cold out here tonight. I don't know what I can say to make Jonah feel any less wretched. Then I know.

"Mum and Elle gave me a memory box today. Things in it that remind them of Freddie."

"Like any of us could forget him." Jonah rests his elbows on his spread knees.

"There was a photograph from school," I say. "You, me, and Freddie. We were fourteen or so. We look like babies."

He looks at the floor and laughs softly. "Fourteen. Shit. I teach kids that age now."

"We all grew up."

"And we're all getting older—except Freddie," Jonah says. "I can't imagine him as an old man."

I shake my head.

"Me neither." I drink a little more Jack Daniels. It's strong stuff. I can feel it mingling with the wine already in my system, loosening my tongue and blurring my cold, brittle edges.

"You still look the same as you used to," I say. "Except you had mad hair."

He looks at me, and I make big-hair gestures around my head with my hands. He huffs under his breath.

"Yeah, well. There was never spare money around to get it cut and man buns hadn't been invented yet."

I was never overly aware of Jonah's lack of funds as a kid; he always hid it from me. But then he hid lots of things well back then. It's only in recent years that I learned from Freddie how far Jonah's childhood was from fairy tale.

"You were his greatest friend." I want to find things to say to make Jonah feel better. "You got him out of a lot of scrapes as a kid."

Jonah rests his head back against the wall. "Man, but he was trouble," he says. "The only fight I ever had at school was his fault."

I'm curious now; I don't remember Jonah ever fighting. "Who did you fight with?"

He pauses, tapping his head lightly against the bricks as he thinks. "Nah, it's gone. Some kid who Freddie should have known better than to mess with anyway."

"He never knew when to stop," I chime in, because that was just his nature.

"Fearless."

"Which isn't always a good thing," I say, tempering Jonah's JD-induced hero worship ever so slightly.

"Better than being a coward," he says, bleak as he stares into the depths of the bottle again.

"How's things with Dee?" I ask, more to change the subject than because I'm interested.

He rolls his head sideways on the wall to look at me. "Up and down."

"Is that a euphemism?" Look at me, cracking a joke, rubbish as it is.

"Very funny," he says, not laughing. "To be honest, I'm not sure it's going anywhere. She's just not that into me."

I take the bottle from him and swill some back. "Somehow I find that hard to believe."

"She doesn't think my head's in the right place."

"What?" I'm instantly angry on his behalf. "You lost your best friend earlier this year. What kind of person can't understand that?"

He falls silent. "It's not just Freddie she worries about," he says eventually. "It's you too."

"Me?" I've barely seen Dee since the event at the school, once or twice in passing with Jonah.

He stares at me, and for a moment I think he wishes he hadn't said anything at all. Then he sighs and shrugs.

"She just doesn't get it," he says, trying to explain. "That you and me were friends first, before you and Fred were even a thing. Platronic friends, I mean."

"Plantonic," I say, and misplaced laughter bubbles up in my throat because I can't say it either. I'm half-furious, half-tickled, and then suddenly fireworks start to explode high in the skies above us.

"Must be midnight," Jonah breathes, getting unsteadily to his feet, pulling me up with him.

We stand there shoulder to shoulder on my front step and watch the night sky burst into life, color, and light, and the poignant strains of "Auld Lang Syne" strike up through the open window of the house party across the street.

Should old acquaintance be forgot. I listen to the familiar words, tears sliding down my cheeks. *And never brought to mind.* Freddie is never far from my mind, I think, feeling myself start to crumble. This is exactly the reason I didn't want to go out tonight. I didn't want to hear this song. I didn't want to feel these feelings. And now I am and it's every bit as wretched as I knew it would be.

Jonah and I lean against each other, tearful, holding our silence until the mournful song ends and Happy New Year cheers ring in 2019.

"I can't say it, Lyds," Jonah says, forlorn. I hear the tremor in his voice and my heart breaks fresh for the first time this year.

I bite my wobbling lip. I can't bring myself to say those hopeful words either.

"I'm going to make coffee," I say. "Come inside?"

"I shouldn't have come." He dashes his hands over his eyes and shakes his head. "It's not helping either of us, Lyds."

It cuts me. Our friendship is a small wooden boat that's been tossed around on towering storm waves since the accident, smashed into time and time again by anger and grief and relentless frustration. Sometimes we've crested the wave, clutching each other's hands for dear life, other times we've been hurled to the depths and wondered if the only way to survive is to throw the other overboard to lighten the load. It feels tonight as if Jonah has finally made his choice. This boat isn't going to make it safely home with both of us aboard.

"Sorry," he says. I guess he knows it was hard to hear.

"You're probably right," I sigh, pulling my dressing gown tight around my cold, cold body. Across the street people spill out of the party onto the pavement, a blur of lights and singing and raucous laughter, and the cat takes his chance to shoot out of the house for his preferred choice a few doors down.

"I need to get out of here," Jonah whispers, hollow-eyed. He looks ill, as if he might throw up. And then he's gone, jogging, and then running, putting as much distance between us and our sorrow as quickly as he can.

I move back into the shadows of the house, into my silent, lonely hallway and sit on the bottom step of the staircase, my head resting against the wall. It's nine months now since Freddie died. In nine months I could have grown a whole new human. I didn't though; I lost my favorite human in the world instead, and now, inevitably, I've gone and lost one of my oldest friends too.

2019

AWAKE

Thursday, January 3

I'VE HOLED MYSELF up at home and lied to my family that I've got a rotten case of sickness and diarrhea to stop them from coming to visit me. It wouldn't usually keep them at bay, but Elle's being careful because of the baby and Mum and Auntie June have gone for their customary kick-off-the-new-year-in-style spa weekend. They tried to cajole me into going, hence the fictitious bug I don't want to pass around like a belated Christmas prezzie.

I've missed Freddie intensely these last few days. The times I get to see him are magical, but I've missed him keenly here in my long waking hours. I look at my watch. I've been up for a couple of hours but it's still only eight-thirty in the morning, barely light. I'm going to force myself into basic self-care in a while: take a shower, heat up some soup, watch the last remnants of holiday TV. I've been wallowing since New Year's, unable or unwilling to scoop myself up. I'm kind enough to myself to acknowledge that perhaps I needed to go low, an inevitable reaction to the high emotion of New Year's, but it can't go on. I have to show up for work, and for life, on Monday, so I need to clean myself up, eat, maybe even put a wash on and drag the hoover around. I tried to call Elle just now, but she didn't answer. Morning sickness has kicked in over the last couple of days, so she's probably sleeping.

I sit in the corner of the sofa and pull my knees into my chest. I daren't call Jonah, not after the way we left things on New Year's Eve. He was right, I know—it doesn't help either of us to be around each other anymore. I honestly don't know if that will ever change, a thought that makes me rest my chin on my knees, weary. There's no getting away from it. I'm deeply lonely. My eyes settle on the pill bottle on the mantelpiece and my resolve to spend the day doing productive things evaporates, because there's a place I can go where I won't feel so alone.

ASLEEP

Thursday, January 3

THIS ISN'T OUR BED. This isn't our bedroom. I lie perfectly still in the shaded gray morning light, my eyes sliding over the ornate plaster roses on the high ceiling above us and the full-length silk curtains drawn across the windows. Freddie is sprawled out on the pillows beside me, one arm flung over his face as it so often is when he sleeps. I take a moment to study him in this half-light: he's fast out, his mouth slightly open, his eyes flickering beneath his eyelids as if he's dreaming.

Where are we? I've never seen this elegant room before. It's far too grand to be the spare room of anyone we know—there's no Ikea furniture in here, for starters. It's a hotel, I'm sure of it.

My toes sink into the carpet as I slide out of bed and cross to the window to peep around the side of the curtains. And then I slide my whole pajama-clad body behind the curtain to get a better look, and gasp softly, overcome. It's snowing out there, fat white wonderland flakes, and it's unmistakably Paris. Of course it is. Wow, it's picture-book beautiful. My breath mists the cold glass as a queue forms outside a small boulangerie down below, and before I can think too much, I move around the room and throw my clothes on to go outside and join the throng. I've clearly come here prepared for a winter break; my winter boots and warm coat are by the door, and I wind Freddie's scarf around my neck before I slip quietly from the room. The scent of him fills my head as I bury my face in the soft wool, and for a second I stand still in the hallway and just breathe him in. His scent has faded from almost everything I have in my waking world but this scarf is fresh with his shower gel and aftershave, as if he's standing right beside me. I'm almost undone; I have to push my feet in the opposite direction because they want to tug me back inside the hotel room, back to him. He'll still be there when I come back, I tell myself. I know how this works by now. I have until I fall asleep again, and if we're in Paris, I'm going to wring pleasure out of every last moment.

The hotel seems to be converted from a couple of tall townhouses to create a small boutique hotel. I follow the winding staircase down through the center of the building and into the quiet reception, returning the smile of the receptionist who clearly recognizes me as a resident. Outside, I stand for a few seconds on the stone steps and just soak it all in. It can't have been snowing for all that long. The covering is only a centimeter or two, but it's enough to dust the scene with magic. We're on a side street, and as I stand there on the steps, a giddy, soaring sense of euphoria comes over me. I'm in Paris in the snow with Freddie Hunter. I'm smiling as I cross the street, snowflakes settling on my face as I join the back of the queue outside the bakery. It smells delicious and decidedly French—a killer combination of fresh croissants and hot coffee that you just can't re-create at home no matter how fancy your coffee machine is. I edge my way inside the tiny shop, enjoying the bustle and noise around me as people order over each other, all of us bundled into winter coats dusted with snow. It's only as I get toward the front that I realize I need to try to ask for what I want in French; I haven't said much more than *oui* or *non* since I sat my French oral exam at school. I didn't do all that well then either. Nerves fidget around in my throat as the woman behind the counter finally glances my way, dark-eyed and expectant.

"Deux cafés et deux croissants, s'il vous plaît," I say—or at least I think I say—in very stilted schoolgirl French. Thank heavens that my cheeks were already snow-cold pink, as I'm sure I'm blushing. Luckily for me she's used to people inelegantly mauling her beautiful language, and she slides a couple of croissants into a pale-blue paper bag without requiring more of my pidgin French. I have a flash of panic when she asks me for money, but I find euro notes when I rummage in my coat pockets. I offer silent thanks to my other self for being more organized than usual, pressing myself against the doorframe to squeeze outside, coffee cups clutched in my hands, past the ever-growing queue. Back on the street, a girl across the street slides on the snow, laughing, and the guy she's with catches hold of

her and swoops her in for a lingering kiss. They don't temper it, and I'm torn between my very British "get a room" inner voice and swooning because it's just so damn French. And then I look up at the hotel window to the room where a man waits for me, someone who's going to sweep me off *my* feet in Paris too, and I'm grinning like a loon, veering around the still clinched couple and dashing back inside the hotel.

"YOU'RE MY FANTASY WOMAN," Freddie says, flinging his phone down on the bedside table as I enter the room. He's still in bed but wide awake and propped up on the pillows.

"Is that because I have coffee?"

He nods. "And croissants. I thought you were kidding last night when you said you were going to do the breakfast run."

Blimey. There I was thinking I'd been swept across the street by impulse, and I'd already made the same plan twelve hours ago. How predictable. It's a bit of a depressing thought. I hand Freddie the paper bag. "Take your pick."

He peers into the bag. "Both of them?"

I shoot him a not-a-chance look as I hand him his coffee. "It's freezing out there. Feel," I say, touching my cold hand against his cheek.

He shudders. "Get back in bed?"

It's tempting. It really is. But . . . Paris.

"I'm dressed now," I say, shrugging out of my damp coat. "Let's get out there and see Paris."

Freddie hands me the paper bag as I perch on the edge of the bed, coffee in hand.

"Are you mad you didn't win the toss?" he asks.

I've no idea what he's talking about, so I pull a piece of croissant out from the bag and chew it slowly.

"I won't hold you to it if you're dead set on seeing the Mona Lisa," he says.

I put my head to one side, trying to look engaged and amused, willing him to explain further. Wow, this croissant is *divine.*

"You know me," he says. "I'm just not a museums kind of guy."

I do know him, and yes, he's not a fan of museums. He's not big into history at all really, and, even though I'd really love to wander hand in hand around the Louvre admiring art with him, I know it wouldn't move his soul in the way it would mine. And that's okay; he's not an ignorant man, just a guy who knows what he likes. I wonder what his choice is, though.

"Coffee's good," I murmur, because it is. Scalding and tobacco bitter.

He nods. "Almost as good as PodGods," he says.

"That's very loyal of you." I laugh.

"Sure you don't mind wandering in the snow?" he asks me. I blink a couple of times, thinking, and then I realize. I know what we're doing. Freddie and I have done this before in London. He likes to throw away the guidebooks and just follow his nose, discover his own version of the capital, or Paris, or wherever. In London we found a hidden garden and lay on our backs in the sunshine, and we ate lunch in a backstreet pub that hadn't changed as much as a wall tile since Victoria was on the throne, and he bought me a silver-and-blue-agate bracelet because it was the exact same shade as my eyes. We found our very own London, and today we're about to find our very own Paris.

"Let me think about that for a second," I say, sliding my coffee cup onto the bedside table, next to his phone. "Do I mind walking around the world's most romantic city in the snow with you?" I lift the covers and slip into his arms as he stretches to rest his coffee down next to mine. "Can you promise me hot chocolate?"

"I'll promise you anything if you take your clothes off," he grins.

I press my face into his chest to stop myself from asking him to promise to stay alive. He kisses the top of my head, and we stay like that for a while, the warmth of him seeping into me.

"I CAN'T FEEL my toes," I say, trying to wriggle them inside my boots.

Freddie and I are sitting on a bench along the banks of the Seine. We've had the most glorious morning following our noses down winding streets and through public gardens, all of it accompanied by steadily falling snow. The Eiffel Tower is a looming shadow shrouded in mist, but even brief glimpses of its iconic outline are enough to make me unreasonably happy. We're in Paris. I came here once before on a whistle-stop school trip for a few days, and my prevailing memories are of being herded around the city, and of a sardine-packed visit to Notre Dame. I certainly never imagined I'd come back and walk the same city in a snowstorm with Freddie Hunter; he wasn't even my boyfriend back then. It's a strange thought; I can barely remember a time in my life when his name and mine weren't inexplicably linked together.

"Hungry?" he asks me, and I laugh because I know he's dying for me to say yes because he has the appetite of a herd of wild horses.

I nod, and he pulls me to my frozen feet. "Can we find somewhere warm?"

He pulls my bobble hat farther down to cover my ears. "Yes." His phone buzzes in his coat pocket, and he ignores it.

"Do you need to get that?" I say, because work has been blowing up his phone on and off for most of the morning.

"Nope," he says. "Whoever it is can piss off. I'm in Paris with my favorite girl."

I smile because it's a lovely thing to say, but I shiver too. It may have been the snowflakes settling on the exposed skin at the back of my neck, or it might have been because the Freddie I knew would never have been able to resist checking it wasn't something urgent. Although things in this life often feel exactly the same, they're very subtly different. It's unsettling.

EVERY STREET WE look down seems to have a breathtaking monument lolling nonchalantly at the end of it, all of them calling us to come closer and comment on their grandness. It's a city built to be admired, never more so than today with the snowstorm bleaching the scene grayscale and dramatic. It's as if we're starring in our own black-and-white movie. Parisians wander past us immersed in each other or with heads down, intent on getting where they need to be; the city belongs to them in the winter, before the hordes of tourists move in as soon as it warms up. Today it's theirs, and miraculously, it's ours too.

"Wow," I say, slowing in front of a colossal building surrounded by soaring stone columns. My city map informs me it's La Madeleine, a church.

"It looks almost Roman, doesn't it?" I lay my hand against one of those monumental columns as I wander up the wide steps, irresistibly drawn inside by the sheer scale and grandeur. Freddie joins me and we walk slowly hand in hand across the marble floor, awestruck by the size and beauty of the place. It steals my breath; decadent chandeliers cast a warm glow over the lavish frescos decorating the domed ceilings, and there is an overwhelming sense of peace and reverence, an oasis in the hustle of the city. We're not religious people, Freddie and I, but still I'm moved by the history and the atmosphere of reflection. We reach a bank of white taper candles lit by visitors in remembrance of lost loved ones, and when I glance at Freddie I find him digging around in his pocket for change. I can't manage any words as he slips coins into the donation box and picks up a couple of candles. He rarely talks about the father he lost as a child. He was too young to have many memories to cherish but still his absence has been keenly felt. It's one of the things that used to bug me the most—that he wouldn't open up to me about it. But then that's just how he was brought up. His mum never speaks about the past either, she's very live for the moment. I sometimes think her behavior comes over as selfish, but it's probably more that she is a product of her own upbringing too. She was a beauty queen in her day, very adored and looked after by her own parents and then by Freddie's dad. And then by Freddie.

I'm not sure why he hands me a candle too; for my grandparents perhaps, or out of politeness. I watch him sigh as he chooses a place for his act of remembrance among the other candles. Some stand tall, others have burned down to almost nothing. And then he turns and lights the wick of my candle, and I'll never forget the look in his eyes—it's as if he knows. He holds my gaze, and for a little while we just stand and stare at each other. This is it. This is all of our tomorrows, every day of our love concentrated into one small light that will burn out too soon. My hand shakes as I try to decide where to place my candle. I don't want to let it go. In the end I stand it beside Freddie's.

"Time to go," he says, his arm around my shoulder. When we reach the doorway, I take one long, last look over my shoulder at the candles. Two tall white cenotaphs. One for a much-missed father, one for his beloved son.

"THIS PLACE?"

We pause outside a tiny corner café, its emerald-and-gold striped awnings bowed heavy with snow. It's busy inside but the outside tables are sheltered from the weather, so I nod and home in on a spot near the glow of a space heater. Freddie orders moules frites, but for me it has to be hot chocolate and a cinnamon pastry. I know, croissants for breakfast and pastries for lunch, but I'm in Paris, after all. For a few minutes we sit and thaw out, watching the city slide by, drinking it all in. The traffic crawls slowly thanks to the inclement weather, and the people who pass us by are hunkered down into their jackets and scarves against the swirling snow.

I look away from the scene to Freddie's appreciative smile as the waiter places his lunch down. His eyes light up at the sight of his food, the rich scent of wine and garlic on the air. How I wish I could preserve us just as we are right now inside a snow globe: two miniature forever lovers having lunch beneath the striped awning of a Parisian café. It's one of those press-pause moments, the kind of unexpected perfect you get only a handful of, and because no one knows to appreciate those moments more than me, I do. I press pause in my head and commit it all to memory, every last detail. The exact pattern of the metal lattice chairs, the particular shade of blue of Freddie's scarf, the tiny ceramic floral motif on the heavy silver cutlery, the bronze sugar crust on my pastry. And then, as if to remind me that there's no such thing as perfect, my mobile rattles on the tabletop and a message flashes in from David.

> Sorry to bother you on holiday, Lydia, but I thought you'd want to know this straightaway. Elle lost the baby. She's okay—well, as well as she can be, she's sleeping now. Call me when you can. X

AWAKE

Thursday, January 3

I JOLT UPRIGHT on the sofa, my heart racing far too fast to be healthy, as out of breath as if I've run to catch the last train. I grab for my mobile and scan it quickly but there are no missed calls or messages. I brave Facebook and see the green online dot next to Elle's name, so I fire off a quick message to check she's okay in as vague a way as possible. She replies almost straightaway; she knows it's early days but do I fancy pushchair shopping next weekend?

The relief. I slump back against the cushions. Up to now the sleeping visits have been my saving grace, my way back, my sanity and my sanctuary. But this . . . Elle. I somehow hadn't imagined that bad stuff, *really* bad stuff, might happen there too.

ASLEEP

Sunday, January 6

"HOW IS SHE?" I ask, making David a coffee because he looks knackered. Elle's in the shower so I take the opportunity to find out how she really is before she tells me that she's fine.

He's sitting at the kitchen table and rubs his fingers over his eyes. "Not too bad, mostly," he says. "She was upset this morning, but she ate some of the soup your mum brought round."

I know I resolved to take the pills less frequently but I couldn't stay away when I know what my sister is going through. I spoke to Mum briefly on the way here, and she's worrying herself sick about them both. Their faces on Christmas day, their joy, and now this. It's so cruel.

"And you?" I say, wrapping my arms around David's shoulders.

"I wanted to call him Jack, after my dad," he says. "If it was a boy."

He leans his head into the crook of my arm, and to my distress, he cries. We stay like that for a couple of minutes, and then he reaches for the tea towel and swipes it over his eyes.

"Sorry," he says. "I didn't expect that to happen."

I squeeze his shoulder. "Don't feel like you always have to be the strong one," I say, because I know he'll have been holding it together for Elle.

We turn at the sound of my sister coming downstairs. She's wearing plain navy cotton pj's, and her wet hair is brushed back from her colorless face. She looks about fourteen years old.

"Hiya," she smiles. "You didn't need to come. I told you not to worry. Mum's been here, and David's mum this morning too."

"I know," I say. I want to hug her or something but she's flitting from job to job, straightening cups, replenishing the kitchen roll holder, emptying the dishwasher. I don't push the issue because I've been where she is—heartbroke brittle, not wanting people to touch me in case I lose it. "I won't stay too long."

"Why don't you two go through and watch a bit of telly?" David says. "I'll bring you a cuppa." He looks to me for backup.

I nod. "Sounds good."

Elle follows me into their living room. She went through a nautical phase when she decorated it: all cream-and-blue washed-out stripes with muted orange accents. She's quite like Mum in her decorating tastes, I'm definitely the loose bohemian cannon. I sit in the corner of the sofa, and for a second she stands on the rug in the middle of the room, one bare foot behind her ankle, unsure what to do. I open my arms, and instantly her face crumples and she curls into me on the sofa, crying her harrowed heart out. Hot tears burn the backs of my eyes as I hold her tight, wishing she felt less fragile as she heaves and shudders because the bottom has fallen out of her world. There isn't a damn thing I can say that will help her right now, so I don't try to find any words. I just clutch my lovely sister to me as she sobs.

AWAKE

Thursday, January 17

"SURELY, NO ONE does speed dating anymore?" I say. It's Tupperware central on the lunch table in front of us; I'm still using my old pink lunch box because I find it comforting, despite the fact that Julia went to the lengths of buying me a new clear one for Christmas so she didn't have to look at this pink one anymore. It's a relief to be back at work, away from the confusion and sadness in my other world. Seeing Elle so broken sits heavy on my heart. I've found myself checking up on her even more here, reassuring myself that she and the baby are fine.

"Yeah, but it's not just any old speed dating." He grins, peeling the lid off his yogurt and licking it.

"Don't tell me," Dawn says. "Naked speed dating?"

We all laugh, and I really hope she's wrong. Ryan rolls his eyes.

"As if," he says. "I can't unveil these guns in public, there'd be a riot." He kisses his biceps and grins, making us groan.

"Come on then," I say. "What's so special about it?"

"It's silent."

Dawn frowns, opening a packet of Oreos. Now that her wedding is behind her she's allowed herself back on the biscuits. "So how do you know if you like them or not?"

"I fell in love with Bruce's voice before his face," Julia says. We don't laugh, because it's Julia, and equally we don't question it, because it's Julia.

"You don't have to, like, touch them instead of speaking, do you?" I ask, worried what he's getting himself into.

"When I was younger, they called that an orgy," Phil says, unwrapping a huge sandwich. He always has the best-looking lunch.

Ryan pulls a face that suggests we're all just so out of touch. "Come on, people. What do you take me for? You just sort of stare at each other for a few minutes and then move on to the next table and look at them instead."

Dawn isn't taken with the idea. "So you can't ask them anything at all?"

"You're allowed to make hand gestures."

"Because *that's* not open to misinterpretation," Julia says, sarcastic.

Phil mimes slugging a pint. "I'd be fine."

"I hope no one does any Elvis-style thrusting." Dawn starts to laugh.

We lapse into sandwich silence for a little while, thinking it over. I'm probably the least enthusiastic about my lunch. In an effort to be economical I've made tuna, and I must have over-mayo'd because it's definitely on the wrong side of soggy.

"Where is this dating thing then?" Phil asks.

We all shoot him a look because we adore Susan.

"Bloody miles away," Ryan said. "And it's my turn to drive, so I can't even have a drink."

"It doesn't sound like a barrel of laughs," I say. "No talking, no drinking . . ."

He groans, and I pat him on his slumped shoulder.

"Sounds like the kind of event we could hold in the hall here," Phil says, and I realize with relief that his interest was professional, not personal. And then I also realize that he's looking at me for my opinion as I'm in charge of our events program. Ideas have been a little thin on the ground lately so I give it genuine thought, and I don't tell him that I'd rather arrange a conference on fungal toenails than spend my days thinking about dating and romance.

"Maybe," I say, noncommittal. "I'll look into it."

"You could come with us if you like, get a better idea of what happens?" Ryan says, grimacing before he even ends the sentence because he realizes that it probably wasn't appropriate to offer to take me to a dating event.

Dawn looks away, Phil looks uncomfortable, and Julia sighs and makes the universal gesture for wanker with her right hand. It's so uncharacteristic and out of place on her that we all laugh.

Ryan slowly slides the BabyBel his mum always

packs in his lunch box at me over the table. It's his favorite thing. I pat his hand and push the cheese back toward him with a small smile. He'll be fine tonight. He's got this nonverbal communication thing down pat.

AWAKE

Wednesday, March 13

IT'S MY BIRTHDAY TOMORROW.

Freddie died one year ago tomorrow.

Over the last few days I've grown progressively more restless; in some ways it's almost no different than usual, because I miss him every day, but I've started obsessively looking at the clock and thinking back over what I might have been doing this time last year or working out how many hours of my old life I had left. My heart aches for the girl I was and what she was about to go through. What I wouldn't give to go back and insist Freddie come straight home rather than detour for Jonah.

Mum and Elle want to take me out to dinner tomorrow, but I really can't do it. I don't want to mark the day in any way, not as my birthday, in any case. I'm dully aware that my birthday will forever be marred, not ever really appropriate for celebration. Freddie would be furious with himself if he knew, he always made a big fuss of it—he even sent my mum a thank-you card on my birthday once for giving birth to me, the silly sod. Mum reminded me of it the other day when we were talking about how to spend the day. I think she was trying to make me feel obliged to get out of the house for Freddie's sake, a spot of well-intended emotional blackmail to stop me from moping around. It's okay, I promised her, I'm not going to mope.

And I mean it. I'm going into work, for the morning at least. I've booked a half day so I can spend some time at the cemetery in the afternoon. I'll go and have a chat with Freddie, and then I'll come home again and have myself an early night. I haven't taken a pink pill since January. I've told myself it's because I'm rationing my supply, but if I'm honest, it's probably more because of Elle losing the baby there. Her pregnancy is a very apparent part of my life here in my waking world; she's still got terrible morning sickness, and tossing name suggestions around has become our main thread of conversation. Elle is already sporting a small but perfectly formed bump to show for it. In a few months there will be a brand-new human here who doesn't exist in my other world; it feels like a ticking clock, or perhaps a time bomb.

AWAKE

Thursday, March 14

IS IT ODD to have a picnic at the cemetery? I guess it kind of is, but it's my birthday and I'll do what I want to. It's not exactly a picnic anyway; just the blanket out of my boot to sit on because the ground's cold, and a flask of coffee. I've got a slice of cake too; everyone gathered round my desk just before I left work and sang to me, a little out of tune as they thrust a helium balloon at me with apologetic, hopeful eyes. They gave me flowers and a bottle of something fizzy too. I appreciate the gesture. The wine is back in the car park, a party on the passenger seat of my car, out of place here among the quiet granite. I've brought the flowers out with me to leave with Freddie; I was going to get some from a local florist, but as these were a gift to me, they're now a gift from me to him. Does it sound strange to say it feels like sharing a tiny piece of my birthday with him? I've learned not to question my own actions and thoughts too deeply though, sometimes you just have to go with whatever gets you through the day.

"Hi, Freddie." I wrap my arms around my pulled-in knees. "Just me again."

I close my eyes and allow enough silence to imagine him settling himself on the blanket beside me. I feel the weight of his arm around my shoulders, and I smile as he buries his face in my neck and wishes me happy birthday. It's a cold, clear afternoon, but I can almost feel the warmth of his body pressing against mine.

"What would we be doing tonight, do you think?" I ask him.

He tells me it's a secret, and slow tears roll down my cheeks because I can hear his quiet laughter in the still air around me.

"God, I miss you." It's such a gaping understatement. "I'm okay most of the time. I'm toughing it out, Freddie, I really am. But today . . ." I stop, lost for big enough words. "It's just so bloody hard, you know?" I cover my face with my hands, and in my head he gathers me in and tells me that he feels the same, that he finds every day hard without me too.

"Hey, you."

I startle at the feel of someone's hand on my shoulder. Someone real. I look up and find Jonah. He hunkers down on his haunches beside me and looks at me with his dark, gentle eyes.

"Feel like some company?"

I haven't seen Jonah since he walked away from me on New Year's Eve. I've started to text him once or twice and deleted my words before I could press send, and he's not someone I run into much in my day-to-day life. Except for here, it seems.

"Okay," I say, wiping my eyes as I move across to make room for him to share my blanket.

He doesn't speak for a while, his eyes fixed on Freddie's gilded name.

"A year," he says, eventually.

"Yes." I swallow. "A whole year without him."

"How've you been?" he asks me. I hear it in his low, unsure tone; he means in the long, cold weeks since New Year.

I nod. "Okay, mostly," I say. "Work's keeping me busy, and Elle's pregnancy is knocking her about so I've been there quite a lot too."

It's not a lie; Elle's had a really rough time. I've been going round to see her after work most days to sit with her until David comes in. I know that wasn't what Jonah was asking really, but the logistics of my life are all I have to offer.

"And you?" I ask him. "How've you been?"

He lifts one shoulder, a halfhearted shrug. "Yeah, you know. School . . . all the usual stuff."

I drink some coffee. "Dee?"

Jonah pulls blades of grass out of the hard ground one by one. I watch the movement: sharp, deliberate little tugs as he considers his answer.

"Sometimes," he says. "We're taking it slow, seeing what happens. I like her laugh."

There is more in the words we don't say than the ones we do. He doesn't want to tell me that things are going well romantically with Dee because he knows I am in such a different place in my life.

Jonah mirrors my position on the blanket, his knees drawn into his chest. He's dressed in black, probably because it's his default setting rather than a consciously somber choice for the day. He's wearing a navy knitted hat too, and he pulls it off now and shoves it into his coat pocket.

"I'm sorry, Lyds," he says, bleak, staring straight ahead. "For New Year's. I didn't know what I was saying. I didn't mean it."

I study his familiar profile. He's winter pale, and although his high cheekbones have always lent him a classic gauntness, he looks even more so today. His hair is as unruly as ever, his lashes a dark sweep on his cheek as he stares at Freddie's stone and sighs hard. I don't think I've ever seen him look so beat.

"I've tried to text you. A couple of times actually, but the words just came out wrong so I deleted them," I say.

"Same." He nods, takes a moment before he elaborates. "I tried, because I truly am sorry. For banging on your door like a thoughtless twat, and for not coming inside when you asked, and for leaving you crying alone on New Year's Eve. There. I'm sorry for all of it, Lyds. For everything."

"Did you really mean that being with me makes things worse?"

He pinches the bridge of his nose. "God, no. Being with you reminds me of him," Jonah looks at Freddie's headstone. "And that's hard sometimes, but it's comforting too, you know? This, us. It's comforting."

I hand him my coffee. He warms his hands before taking a drink, and then laughs, hollow.

"I'll go away next new year, make double sure I don't turn up on your doorstep. Somewhere far flung. Lie on a beach and forget all about the fact it's even New Year's Eve at all."

"Okay," I shoot him a sad smile when he looks at me. "It's a plan." Relief loosens the stiff set of his shoulders. New Year's Eve has weighed heavier on both of us than I realized.

JONAH WALKS WITH me back to the car park, holding my blanket as I unlock the car. His Saab is parked alongside.

"It's your birthday; of course it is," he says, embarrassed as he spots the red foil balloon bobbing around in the car beside the cake and gifts. "I didn't think."

"I'm not in the birthday mood, to be honest," I say, distracted as my coffee flask slides out of my grip when I open my door. I bend to catch it before it rolls under the car, and in the mess of scrabbling around, the helium balloon makes a successful escape bid. We both grab for the metallic string but we don't stand a chance against the elements.

"Shit," I say, annoyed with myself more than anything. It isn't that I wanted the balloon, it's just not right that this should happen here of all places. We stand and silently watch it make its way upward, a bright red splash against gray, and then suddenly, actually, it becomes completely right. I'm *so* not a symbolic balloon release sort of person, but it turns out I *am* an accidental balloon release sort of person. We watch it until it disappears, lost in the low-hanging mist.

We're quiet for a few beats, and when I look back at Jonah his eyes are steady on mine.

"You'll always matter to me, Lydia," he says. "Let's not lose our friendship again. We've lost too much already."

I nod, on the edge of tears again, because this is what should have happened on New Year's Eve. This healing conversation between old friends, not that destructive thing that hurt us both.

"You'll always matter to me too, Jonah Jones," I say, and I stand on tiptoes and press my lips against his cold cheek.

He rests a hand on my door as I climb in. "Happy birthday," he says softly, waiting for me to fasten my seatbelt before he closes the door. "Drive safe."

I nod and raise my hand, checking the skies overhead for any last fleeting glimpse of the balloon as I pull out of the car park. It's nowhere in sight.

I'M HALFWAY HOME when I have to pause for someone to cross at a zebra crossing, and as the woman makes slow progress in front of my bonnet I realize it's Maud from the grief session. Her shoulders are rounded, and she's pulling one of those shopping trolleys on wheels.

I glance down at the chocolate cake on my passenger seat, and I don't know what makes me do it but I roll down my window and call out her name when she reaches the pavement.

"Hey, Maud," I say, loudly, pulling my car over beside her. "Fancy seeing you again."

She peers into the car at me. "Never seen you before in my life," she barks.

"You have," I say. "We met at the grief session, you know, up at the school a while ago?"

She moves her jaw from side to side a few times as she dredges up the memory. "Newfangled nonsense."

"Hmm," I say. "It wasn't my favorite morning either, if I'm honest."

She stares at me, making no attempt at small talk.

"Anyway," I say, feeling a bit ridiculous. "It's my birthday today and I . . ."

"Are you that desperate for friends that you're bothering strangers in the street?" she says. "You picked the wrong one. I hate birthdays."

"Well, that's a shame," I say. "Because I remembered you liked cake, and I wondered if you'd like this one." I nod toward the chocolate cake on the seat beside me.

She looks past me at the cake and curls her lip. "Chocolate isn't my favorite," she sniffs.

"Oh, okay," I say. "No worries."

"I dare say I could manage it," she says, already unbuttoning the flap on her trolley. "If I have something to wash it down."

She eyeballs the bottle of fizz on the seat beside the cake, and I can't help but laugh at her audacity. I hand her both the cake and the wine and wait while she stashes them away.

"I could come and help you eat it?" I offer, trying to be kind in case she's lonely.

"Find your own party," she says, straightening up. "It's double yellow lines here you know. You shouldn't even be parked."

And that's that. She trundles off with her trolley, and she doesn't look my way when I call out a cheery "Bye then, Maud!" as I pull off. I'm sure it wouldn't please her to know that she's brightened my day no end.

ASLEEP

Thursday, March 14

"HAPPY BIRTHDAY, BEAUTIFUL."

We're in Alfredo's. *Of course we are.*

"I know we came here for your birthday last year too, but it's just the two of us tonight," Freddie says. "Unless you wish your mum was here to complain about her chicken being cold again." He starts to laugh. "You know I love her to pieces, but I seriously thought Alfredo was going to drag her out of here by her hair."

So that's what happened on my birthday in this life. We sat around a table in this same restaurant, and the prevailing memory of the day is my mum grumbling about her cold dinner. I swallow hard and try to smile at the story I have no recollection of, angry almost that something so silly is the first thing that springs to mind about the day my life changed forever.

We pause to order; Freddie is predictable in his T-bone choice. I shake things up a bit with the salmon special. I usually order chicken here, but I don't want to risk any more comparisons or similarities to last year.

"How did Elle seem this afternoon?" Freddie asks as he fills my wineglass.

I don't know how Elle is coping, so I go for a vague reply. "Okay, I think," I say. I want to ask more but I can't think how to phrase it without it sounding odd.

"Want to hear some happier news?" he says, and we fall momentarily silent as our food is placed in front of us.

"Please," I say as the waiter moves away, reaching for my wine again, glad there is another place, somewhere where Elle's belly is rounding with her healthy child and her heart is intact.

"Jonah's moving in with Dee," Freddie says. "The lease on his place is up soon so they've decided to give living together a proper go. She has a two-bed on that new development by the park; you know the one?"

Yes, I know the one. We looked at it ourselves when we were house hunting and ruled it out on the fact that Freddie could touch the fence on both sides of the back garden at the same time.

I'm surprised, to say the least. Jonah loves his place. He has a ground floor apartment in a graceful old Edwardian house close to the school. He pays over his budget every month to get a bay window big enough to accommodate his piano.

"Will there be room for his piano?" I ask, and Freddie gives me the strangest look. "Who knows," he says. "I doubt that's top of his priority list."

I need to slow down on the wine, but this really isn't turning out to be the birthday I'd hoped it would be.

I'd be literally anywhere but Alfredo's—it was always more Freddie's favorite than mine anyway, truth told.

"They're throwing a party next weekend to celebrate. We're not busy, are we?"

I shake my head, and make a mental note not to take a sleeping pill next Saturday.

"Any work news?" I ask, reaching for the wine to top up our glasses. I haven't really perfected the art of asking casual questions, but I like to try to find out how he's been in the days since I last came here. If I sound a little stilted, he lets it pass.

"Nothing concrete," he says. "PodGods are muttering about possible expansion into Brazil but it's early days."

"Wow, that would be big news," I say. PodGods monopolize much of Freddie's work time from what I can gather. He's been behind an aggressive advertising campaign to grow their brand around the world. His ambition has always been a double-edged sword. Great for his bosses, but every now and then work takes up so much of his time that his home life is compromised. It's happened once or twice with other accounts. I'm starting to feel a small stab of resentment whenever he mentions PodGods. I listen to Freddie speak as I pick at my dinner, concentrating more on him than on my food. I watch his mouth form the words, the way his shoulders move beneath his shirt as he cuts his steak, the definition of his biceps when he lifts his glass. He's had his hair cropped a little closer than usual; I'm not sure if I like it. Or maybe I just don't like anything about him being different here. I tune back in to his words.

"At least he approved my leave before he had his heart attack. Three whole weeks."

I can only assume he's talking about Vince, his boss. "Is he okay?"

"Will be, as long as he stays off the burgers."

That's something. Vince isn't my favorite person, but I don't want him keeling over.

"Three weeks, huh?"

"I leave work on July twelfth and go back a married man." Freddie raises his glass to me. I smile and touch my glass to his, but my heart is with my sister tonight. My life here is rosy, while hers is falling to pieces. I can't shake the feeling that her happiness is the price I'm paying for mine.

AWAKE

Friday, May 17

"WHAT IF NO one turns up?"

Ryan checks his hair on his phone. "They will. We've sold thirty tickets with a free drink included. They'll come for that if nothing else."

I'm always nervous at events I've organized, but in truth I haven't really had to do all that much this time. The company in charge of the silent dating evenings are coming in to facilitate. I've just had to sell the tickets, organize the bar staff, lay out the room, those kinds of things. I've made sure the tickets sold to an equal number of men and women, but beyond that, I'm not sure what's going to happen this evening.

"Do I look datable?" Ryan asks, hand on his skinny-trousered hip, brooding into the middle distance like a moody *GQ* cover. He's excited about tonight, always looking for the next big love of his life to walk in. I sometimes wonder if I should counsel him not to wear his heart on his sleeve with such reckless abandon, but I think that's a lesson you can only learn by bitter experience.

"They'll all be blowing kisses across the table at you," I say.

"I hope I don't know any of them," he says, panto-aghast. "That'd be awkward, staring at someone I ghosted."

"Ghosted?"

He frowns, searching for the words to explain. "You know, like when you don't have the bottle to tell someone it's over so you just disappear. Don't answer their calls, never get back in touch. You just fade out of their lives."

"Oh," I say. I know he's being lighthearted, but I can't help feeling bad for all of the people out there who have been ghosted by people they love. Freddie didn't ghost me, but I know how it feels when someone fades out of your life without warning. It's a shitty thing to do to someone by choice.

"I've only had to do it once myself," he backtracks, and I realize my thoughts must be showing on my face. "And only because she was a full-on stalker. I slept with the lights on for a month afterward."

"Anyway," I say, brisk. "You'll be good, I'm sure."

Ryan's the only staff member taking part tonight. Everyone else is either married or me.

THE MAIN HALL is set out with lightning efficiency once the dating company rolls in. Fifteen tables for two organized into a circuit that would make Ikea staff weep with envy, fifteen cardinal red tablecloths and fifteen vases of faux peonies arranged, all in the time it takes me to make them a coffee.

"How long have you been doing this?" I ask Kate, the boss, as I hand her one of our "only for clients" cups. Plain and white with a gold rim, unlike the chipped collection of "Best Auntie Ever" and corporate mugs we make do with upstairs.

She rests her bum on the old school-style radiator, flicking her jet-black hair as she does. It's pure Uma Thurman from *Pulp Fiction* and she's winged her black eyeliner to match. It's an arresting look; maybe that's the key to speed dating, making yourself difficult to forget. She's short with soft curves, and she's packed herself into leather trousers that can't have fit the cow any better.

"A year or so," she says. "We used to do normal speed dating events then moved on to this to set us apart from the crowd." She sips her coffee. "People will give anything a go once, won't they?"

I think about that. Will they? I'm not in any hurry to try BASE jumping, or bullfighting, or swimming the English Channel.

"Hot," she says. I don't know if she means the coffee, the radiator, or Ryan as he walks past carrying a pile of extra chairs.

"Do you take part yourself?" I ask.

Kate laughs softly. "Not a chance."

It's not exactly a ringing endorsement. "No?"

"I'm not looking for love," she says. "It's overrated if you ask me."

There speaketh the broken-hearted, I think. "You probably shouldn't tell your clients that," I laugh.

"I don't usually." She pulls a caught-out face. "And to give it its due, there's definitely something about silent dating that really actually works. It's science-based; studies have shown that people genuinely can fall in love if they stare silently into someone's eyes for a few minutes."

"Not just any old stranger, though, surely?" I say, because I can't think of even one person I know who I could fall in love with in two minutes. I'm deeply skeptical. Oh no—have I become a love cynic? The love of my life has left me, and now the belief in love has left me altogether.

"Well, I suppose people have to be vaguely attracted to each other," she says, "and available, obvs, but if they're at a speed dating event, that box is generally ticked already."

"I suppose it is," I say, accepting her empty cup as she slides off the radiator.

"Fingers crossed for a full house."

HALF AN HOUR later the main room is packed and there's an air of jittery anticipation as people mill around, sticking doggedly to their friendship groups, free drinks clutched in slightly sweaty hands. I watch, detached but fascinated. I don't have a role in the proceedings now that things are under way but I've stuck around out of sheer curiosity. I listen to Kate give her well-oiled welcome spiel, a more in-depth version of our earlier chat about the science behind the silent dating concept–minus her personal reticence toward love, of course. She certainly knows how to work a crowd; everyone pays attention and people start to flick quick, furtive glances around the room. I'm impressed; by the time she's finished they're fired up and ready to give things a silent whirl. Everyone has been allocated their starting position, and on Kate's cue they head toward their tables, toward their first two minutes of love-inducing silence. I catch Kate's eye; she's frowning, and when I follow her gaze I see a woman ramming her arms through the sleeves of her coat and making a bolt for the door. I can tell by her body language that she doesn't want to talk to Kate's assistant who waylays her close to the exit; her shoulders are too high, clenched up around her bright red ears.

"Balls," Kate murmurs, coming to stand beside me.

I eye the empty seat, and the guy sitting alone at the table, fidgeting. It's embarrassing enough to be stood up in public, but it's a double slap at an organized dating event you've actually paid to attend.

"Jump in, would you?" she says, matter of fact.

I laugh, and then I realize she means it.

"I . . . I really can't, Kate," I say.

"It'd be a big help," she says. "I can't get things started with an odd number." Her tone is businesslike; she's not asking me to be romantic, just to help keep the event I've booked and she's running on track. I look at the empty chair, feeling a bit desperate. All I have to do is make my way around the room and sit in silence; I guess I can manage that. I spend a fair amount of time alone, so God knows I'm well practiced. Then inspiration strikes; if we pull Ryan out it'll balance up the numbers. I scan the tables and spot him across the room. He's facing toward me but he isn't looking at me–his gaze is already fixed on the girl opposite him. My heart sinks. I can't do it; he's radiating sunshine-hope so bright I can feel the heat of it from here. Kate must sense I'm wavering, because she places a hand low on my back.

"It's just silence," she whispers. "Tune out and think about your inbox."

She doesn't actually push me forward, but her hand on my back is a very definite help-me-out-here nudge all the same. I sigh, and she takes it as reluctant acceptance.

"You're a trooper," she says.

How the bloody hell did this happen, I wonder grouchily, even as my feet carry me across the room. I don't want to do this. I *really* don't want to do this. I can't imagine anything worse than throwing myself into the dating scene this way, silent or not. It's been fifteen months now since the accident, and I haven't so much as thought of another man in that way. I can't.

As I pull the chair out, I don't look guy number one in the eye. Even as I ease my bum onto the chair, I still can't do it. He's paid to look into the shiny eyes of hope and romance, and he's getting two reluctant minutes of cynicism and despair instead. Up at the front of the room Kate tells us our wait is over; the time has arrived to look into the eyes of the potential love of our lives. But I know she's wrong. However long or short my life turns out to be, I'll never love anyone more than I loved Freddie Hunter.

Okay. I can do this. I sit on my trembling hands as I

look up. I digested enough of Kate's spiel to know we're able to do whatever feels right as long as we don't break the silence rule. Hand gestures (not lewd) are permitted, smiling is good; we can even hold hands if the mood takes us. *It won't.* The guy opposite looks at me in a disinterested way that suggests I'm not really his type. That's fine; he wouldn't be mine either. If I had to guess his age I'd go for twenty-one at most; he looks fresh out of Uni and as if he hasn't quite learned the grown-up ropes yet. I'm not offended by his none-too-polite boredom, nor by the way he bites his already chewed-to-the-quick fingernails to pass some time. Okay, I am a little bit offended by that. As the minute stretches into two I throw a tight, apologetic, I-could-be-your-mother smile across the table, and he throws me a shrug back. It's safe to say number one won't be ticking the box to get my details afterward.

Number two is closer to my age, and as soon as I sit down I sense he's competitive. He sits bone still and eyeballs me as if we're in a staring contest; it's more adversary than romantic. He reminds me of someone who might take part in one of those extreme survival shows, in a buzz cut and camo T-shirt. I can't look away. I'm unreasonably irritated by him, and if we were able to speak I'd advise him to lighten up a little if he wants any matches tonight, because he's coming off a little bit Norman Bates. I don't get even the smallest hint of who he is from his hard stare, but then I don't think he has the measure of me either. It's a long two minutes.

Three, four, and five all fall into the same here-for-the-beer category. They're clearly mates; they keep checking out who each other is with and I'm almost sure they're scoring people out of five under the table on their fingers. They're backseat-of-the-bus boys, taking their life cues from reruns of *The Inbetweeners*.

I want to take number six home to my mum so she can feed him up; he looks lonely and in need of a decent meal. I could see his nipples through his too-thin polyester shirt. It's not a great look. Who buys mint-green shirts? And worse, pairs them with a *Back to the Future* novelty tie? This guy. Halfway in he fishes in his pockets and pulls out a packet of kids' sweets, Chewits, I think. I politely decline and watch him make a slow show of unwrapping one, then he chews it just as slowly and stares at me through his gold-rimmed glasses. It's like being in a nature documentary. I can almost hear David Attenborough's hushed voice-over as he explains the bizarre mastication mating call of humans.

This isn't so hard, really. I guess it's because I'm not romantically invested in the evening, but it feels almost farcical as I nod farewell to Chewit-man and take a seat at the next table.

I can tell number seven is tall, even though he's seated, and there is a capable ranginess to his shoulders. He's Viking dirty-blond and his pale gray eyes telegraph gentle amusement, as if he somehow took a wrong turn at the bar and found himself here by mistake. I don't belong here either, I think, sitting up a little straighter when he leans ever so slightly inward. I don't know why number seven feels different than the others. He's less easy to dismiss; there's something in his gaze that resonates with me. He isn't a back-of-the-bus kid, and I doubt he's eaten Chewits for at least a decade. He's a man, no hint of boyishness left. I'd say he's got a few years on me—five or so—and I can't help glancing at his hand to check for a wedding band, or signs of a recently removed one. He catches me looking and shakes his head slightly in answer to my question, then glances at my left hand in return. It's bare. These days I keep Freddie's engagement ring on a chain around my neck, always close even if it's not on my finger. After a couple of seconds holding the Viking's gaze, I wordlessly shake my head to confirm that no, there's no one waiting for me at home. He's perceptive enough to read my complicated expression and he frowns a little, and then he breaks one of Kate's cardinal rules and almost inaudibly asks if I'm okay. His unexpected kindness triggers something in the deepest, darkest recesses of my soul. It feels like the spluttering rumble of a rusty engine being turned over. It takes a few moments for me to recognize it for what it is: sparks. Terrifying, completely unexpected sparks.

"Rule breaker," I whisper, and he laughs, glancing away. It's self-conscious, bashful almost, and awareness thuds into me that he's attractive. I find number seven attractive, and I don't know what the hell that means. He doesn't remind me of Freddie. He doesn't remind me of anyone. If we could chat I'd tell him I'm only here to make up the numbers, that I don't have a sheet to tick, and that I'm not looking for love, silent or otherwise. But I can't, so instead I try to convey it all with my eyes. And then it's over, our two minutes are done. Consternation flashes over his face, and just before I get up he reaches out and covers my fingertips with his.

"I'm Kris," he says, breaking the rules again.

No one notices among the scrape and shuffle of musical chairs, and I swallow hard, and although I don't intend to, I say "Lydia."

He gives my fingers the smallest squeeze as I rise to leave. "It was good to meet you, Lydia," he says.

I'm terrified, grateful it's time to leave the table for number eight. Thank goodness, I think, sitting down in front of a stranger whose tight T-shirt and weight lifter's body thankfully do absolutely nothing for my spluttery, sparky engine. I don't do anything for his either, it would appear, given the way he's throwing blatant meet-me-in-the-bar looks toward the girl who's just vacated his table. She returns his gaze head-on and grins, leaving me feeling sorry for the guy sitting opposite her now. We're halfway through our two minutes and I don't think she's looked his way once yet. I mentally check out, but unlike number eight, I have the good manners to feign interest. We're both relieved when it's over.

I could kiss number nine out of sheer relief, because we're getting closer to the end, and because I don't have to look at number eight looking at someone else anymore, but most of all because it's Ryan. I collapse into the chair at his table, and he does a "what the bloody hell are you doing here" double take then leans in across the table, half laughing and incredulous. I shrug, helpless, my hands upturned. For a second, it's weird, and then he swipes his hand slowly down his face and emerges with a serene expression firmly in place. I settle after a few seconds, ready to play the game, and I open my eyes wide and look straight into his, po-faced. Ryan does the same, but then his expression deepens and I can see that he's thinking about what it must have cost me to do this tonight. His brows lower with consternation; he's hurting for me, sympathetic, and I can't do anything but hold his hands tight on the table and stare at him, suddenly stricken because I'm at a dating night and I actually felt something for someone new. Ryan's mouth tightens, and I can see what's on his mind as if he's written it in the air with a lit sparkler. He's proud of me. He didn't think I had it in me to do something like this. He's looking at me as if I'm a warrior princess, and as our second minute ebbs he squeezes my fingers extra hard to send me on my triumphant way. In that moment, I couldn't love him more if he was my flesh and blood brother. I'm a breath away from tears, and he sees it and mouths "piss off, loser" at me to make me laugh. It does the trick; a residual ebb of my inner warrior princess carries me through the last six tables. They are all equally unmemorable, to me at least. There's only one stranger I'll be able to recollect from tonight. Number seven. Kris. Rule breaker. Viking.

KATE AND HER team have the event packed back into their transit just as quickly as they set it up, and Ryan and I stroll across the tiny car park after we've waved them off and locked up.

"What did you think of it?" he asks, unhooking his sunglasses from the neck of his T-shirt as he pulls his keys and phone from the back pocket of his jeans.

"Yeah," I shrug. "It seemed to go well. The tick sheets looked pretty busy anyway."

Kate and her team have taken the completed sheets away to put matched people in contact with each other. I managed a sneaky peep at some of them as they were gathered up. One was peppered with Day-Glo-green highlighter ticks. What does that pen choice say about the user, I wonder? Outgoing, likes to be noticed? Needy and attention seeking? Couldn't-find-anything-else-at-the-bottom-of-my-bag disorganized?

"They do silent discos too," Ryan says.

"Kate told me," I say.

I open my car door and fling in a folder I've grabbed to catch up on some work at home.

"I'm not so sure about the idea," I say, one arm resting on the open car door. "To me music is all about sharing the buzz, dancing to the same beat." Okay, so that sounds more hippy out loud than it did in my head. "Did you tick anyone?" I ask, moving the conversation on.

Ryan gives me a does-day-follow-night eye roll. "Err, yes. All except number four. She scared me. She took her glasses off to stare at me, reminded me of my mother right before she gives me a bollocking." He pauses. "And I didn't tick your number, of course."

"Of course," I say drily. Not that I wanted him to, it's just that his tone makes me sound untickable.

"I didn't mean . . ." he says, making it worse.

I laugh and let him off the hook. "I know what you meant. I was only there to make up the numbers."

He opens his door too. "Were you?"

"Was I what?"

"Just making up the numbers?" Color flares in his cheeks.

I don't understand why he's asking me. For a horrible second I think he's about to falteringly declare himself in love with me and I panic, even though I know it's ridiculous.

"Only there was a guy in there earlier, and he asked if I'd pass this on to you."

For a moment I feel like a relieved fool, glad I didn't jump in and say anything stupid. And then I think about what he's actually just said and what it actually means, and I go suddenly hot-faced as I look at the folded paper in Ryan's hand. I swipe it from his fingers as if it's on fire and shove it in my bag, more to put an end to the conversation than because I want to know what it says.

"I didn't read it," Ryan says, unconvincing. He can't even look me in the eye.

"And I won't either," I say. "I'm leaving now." And because this exchange can't possibly get more awkward, I get in the car and slam the door.

I rev my engine by mistake, furious with myself. I should have just said no when Kate asked me to step in tonight.

ONCE I'M OUT of sight of work I take a deliberate wrong turn onto a barely finished housing estate and pull up by the side of the road. The uniform red-brick houses are faceless and pristine, yet to be personalized with cute pairs of bay trees by aspirational newlyweds or with net curtains by the resident busybody establishing their lookout post. My eyes settle on the sign informing me I'm on Wisteria Close, and I narrow my eyes at the obvious attempt to add a little gloss to this bleak corner of nowhere. Nonetheless, the show-home sign boasts of just two empty houses left, so hope clearly abounds around here. I catch myself rolling my eyes, full of cynicism in the face of all of this optimism. But I'm procrastinating. I can almost feel a pulse radiating from my bag on the passenger seat, as if the note is holding its breath in anticipation of being flicked open so it can set a chain of events in motion. Even as my fingers reach in and find the edges of it, I consider the option of screwing it up without looking at it. I could open my window and be the first person to ever throw litter in Wisteria Close, except I'm not the kind of person who does that. I get infuriated by those who blithely leave flotsam and jetsam behind: buried cigarettes on the beach or discarded sandwich wrappers in the park. So, telling myself it's because I'm not that person, I pull the note from my bag and smooth it out flat against the steering wheel.

Hey Lydia,

I noticed you didn't have a tick sheet so I'm going to hazard a guess that you hadn't intended to take part tonight. For the record, me neither, really. It's not my usual thing, but that's kind of the point—I'm trying to do stuff out of my ordinary because doing my usual hasn't been working out too well for me lately. Anyway. I wondered if I could buy you a cup of coffee sometime, or tea, or a vegan chai-latte-skinny-dip, if that's your bag. I think I'm ballsing this up and I'm running out of space, so here's my number. I'd really like to see you again.

Kris.

His blue ink handwriting is neither scruffy nor meticulous, and there are no sign-off smileys or kisses to feel afraid of or scorn at. It's brief, but as I read it for a second, slower time and hear the words between the lines, I learn several things about Kris. He's been through a tough time of some kind. I find myself doubting he's been through as tough a time as I have, and then I instantly feel bad for it. I should know better than to make those kinds of assumptions.

So I can assume he's had some sort of hiccup, romantic probably, but going on the fact he turned up alone tonight at a dating event, he's managed to hang on to his sense of self-assurance, or he's brave, or a little of both. I don't add desperate, because actually, none of the people at the event tonight seemed particularly desperate. And last, he doesn't appear to take himself too seriously, if his chai-latte-skinny-dip joke is anything to judge him by. It's all I have to go on, and together with our brief meeting, it's enough to allow him to slide his bum onto a seat in the waiting room of my life.

AWAKE

Friday, June 14

"I'M AS FAT as I am tall," Elle grumbles, flopping on my sofa. "I'll have to stay here until I give birth now. I can't get up."

"You look magnificent," I say. "All Earth Mother." I make mudra signs with my thumbs and index fingers and try to look yogic.

"Magnificently round," she huffs. "Are my feet even still there? I haven't seen them for a month. And it's too bloody hot in here."

I turn away to open a window so she can't see me laughing. Elle isn't a glowy, content pregnant woman. She's a grumpy, demanding one. David confided that he's increasingly terrified of her when I saw him at Mum's last week; he described her as occasionally Jekyll but mostly Hyde. Every centimeter their daughter adds to Elle's waistline reduces her patience threshold accordingly. Mum tried to make David feel better by telling him pregnancy had a similarly temporary psychotic effect on her moods too, but then went on to say how she'd fractured two of my father's fingers when she'd twisted his hand during a contraction. If she could have the day I was born over again, I think the only change she'd effect would be to break three. Or four. Or go the whole hog, twist his arm clean out of its socket and scupper his chances of ever becoming a half-competent surfer. Anyway, the point is that poor David now has to add fear of injury during the birth to his already too-long list of worries about Elle and the baby. He's a planner; he really isn't keen on situations he can't control with numbers and damage limitation lists.

"Tea?" I ask.

Elle scrubs her dark fringe out of her eyes with the flat of her palm. "Because I'm not hot enough already?"

I bust out a line of "don't cha wish your girlfriend was hot like me?" even though I know it's only going to make her scowl even more.

"I'll never look hot again," she moans.

"Get over yourself," I laugh. "Iced water?"

She shrugs, with grudging acceptance. "Even though I'll need a wee straight after and I won't be able to get up off this bloody sofa."

"I'll heave you up," I say, heading for the kitchen. It hasn't escaped my notice that our roles have slowly switched around since Elle became pregnant. Last year she pretty much kept me sane; this year I'm trying to return the kindness. In her early months I kept her supply of ginger biscuits replenished, and lately there are always ice cubes ready in my freezer because she's perma-hot regardless of the weather. I know David appreciates it too; safety in numbers as he muttered to me darkly a couple of weeks ago, plus his job pulls him away from home sometimes for a few days at a time. Selfishly, it fills my hours. I appreciate having someone else to focus on instead of eating relentless dinners for one and what to do at the weekend decisions. I never realized quite how dependent I'd allowed myself to become on Freddie. It's only now I have to make every last exhausting decision on my own that I realize how much easier it is to have someone to share the daily load with, even if it's as simple as what's for dinner. Although in point of fact, that was something I used to decide for us both. But having no one else to ask or cook for has made the decision so much duller that sometimes I just can't be bothered and have toast. Or a glass of wine. I'm working on it.

"What's this?"

I turn at the sound of Elle's voice behind me. I didn't hear her come through from the living room, and I also didn't think to hide the note from Kris that's been behind the cups on my kitchen shelf, unacted upon ever since I met him at the silent dating event. I don't know what to do about him, to be honest. I tried to bin the note and then couldn't bring myself to drop it in among the bottles and empty tins, and because I couldn't figure out why, I shoved it behind things on the shelf and left it up there to its own devices. A bad plan, as it turns out, because it's decided that the thing to do is to slide out from behind the cups and lie faceup on the dresser for all to see. Or more specifically, for Elle to see.

"Who's Kris?"

I stand still and stare at her, the freezer still wide open, blasting me with iced air. It does nothing to soothe the heat from my cheeks.

"He's no one," I say, deciding to say as little as possible.

"Umm, no," she says, her eyes scanning the note again. "He's someone who'd like to buy you a cup of coffee."

I put her glass down on the table and close the freezer, taking my time.

"I haven't done anything wrong," I blurt.

Elle takes a seat and pulls the water across the table toward her. "Sit down a sec, Lyds," she says.

I don't want to sit down, and I don't want to talk about the note, but I do as she's asked because she's got a steely glint in her eye and she's rubbing her bump in a menacing way.

"Tell me all about it," she says, firm.

I squirm, as if I've been held back after class by the teacher to explain a note that had been passed across the desks. I blink, too fast, and then let out a slow, long sigh.

"He was just some guy from a silent dating event."

Surprise widens Elle's eyes. "You went to a dating event? When? Where?"

I roll my eyes, exasperated. "Of course I bloody didn't. It was something I organized at the community center. I was doing my job, Elle, that was all. I didn't intend to take part, but then a woman dropped out at literally the last minute and someone had to stand in.

It was me, me, or me. I didn't have any option, and I certainly didn't have any fun either."

I don't intend to sound sharp, but I do.

"Don't do that," Elle says, her eyes serious.

"Do what? I didn't do anything. I just sat and looked at each of them for a couple of gormless minutes, moved around the room as instructed, and that was that, end of story."

"That's not what I mean, you numptie," she says, and I can see the glitter of unspilled tears when she raises her eyes to the ceiling and shakes her head.

"Don't tell anyone?" I say, feeling ten kinds of disloyal. "Especially not Mum."

Elle sucks her cheeks in, exasperated. "For God's sake, Lydia, I'm not mad at you or judging you, or thinking bad things about you, if that's what you think," she says.

She's hit the nail on the head, of course. Great; I think I'm going to cry.

"You know I wouldn't have said yes to standing in at that event if Freddie was still here, right?"

She reaches out for my hand, tears sliding down her cheeks.

"And you know you don't even need to ask me that," she says. "But the fact is he isn't here, and you're too young to be on your own all of the time. We worry about you."

"I'm not on my own," I gulp. "I've got you and Mum, and there'll be the baby soon. And I'm busy at work with, you know, doing stuff . . ." I trail off because I can hear how woeful it sounds. I've other friends, of course, but Elle has always filled the best friend role too well for me to need anyone else. If I wasn't with her, I was usually with Freddie. My life was full to the brim with my tight circle of people; I never anticipated a time when Freddie would be gone, Elle would be about to start her own family, and I'd be knocking around my empty house having wine for dinner.

"You know what I mean," she says. "I've wanted to bring this up for a while now and not known how to say it. You know how much we all adored Freddie, but no amount of missing him will bring him back."

I nod as I swipe my cheeks dry with my fingertips, wishing I could tell her that actually there is a way to bring him back, how exquisite it is to slide into a different reality. I watch Elle struggle, as if she's sorting around inside her head for the exact right phrase.

"So, me and David, and Mum too, actually, we all think it might be a good idea if you broadened your circle a bit."

She winces after she's finished, a silent baring of her teeth, her shoulders raised, braced for my response.

"Broadened my circle?" I repeat the phrase slowly. And then realization dawns, cold as IV saline sliding into my bloodstream. "Oh, I get it. You all think I'm leaning on you too much."

She looks winded. "What? No, not that at all, Lydia. That isn't what I meant."

I'm not listening properly, because all I can hear is that I'm taking up too much of their lives, that Elle and David want their life back to just the two of them, or the three of them, and that Mum is tired of having to worry about me. They all need their normal back, which translates to I need to find other people to be with and other places to be sometimes. Fine. Just fine. I get up sharply from the table and flick the kettle on, messing with the cups for something to do.

"Tea?"

"I don't want tea, and I don't think you're leaning on us all too much," she says, her voice low and steady. "I would never say that and you know it."

I turn, leaning against the kitchen surface. "It's okay," I say, brittle, not able to let the hurt go. "You're right anyway. You're going to be busy when the baby comes, and Mum has this Stef person now, so . . ." I shrug.

Stefan, or Stef, is someone Mum works with. She's dropped his name into conversation a few times over recent months. Stef said this, Stef did that. And then Stef was in Mum's kitchen eating macaroni and cheese a couple of weeks ago when I called in unannounced after work, sending Mum into a puce-faced panic, as if I'd caught them in bed rather than eating dinner and watching *The Chase*. She followed me to the front door when I made my excuses to leave, muttering they were just friends, he'd popped round to have a look at her laptop as it was on the blink, and she'd made too much dinner so offered him a plate. Least she could do, really, considering he'd saved her a small fortune. I wanted to tell her that she didn't need to explain herself to me, that I was nothing but happy to think she might have found someone. Elle and I spent most of our teens and adult lives trying to encourage her toward romance. But I have to admit that right now the timing feels off. That's selfish of me, isn't it? And truly, I wouldn't want her to pass up on a chance that might not come around again. It's just . . . I feel lonelier than ever.

"So what was he like?" Elle taps the note with one fingernail. "This Kris."

I'm grateful she's decided to ignore my antagonism. "I can't even remember him really," I say, offhand. It's true, and then it isn't. "He seemed nice enough."

She nods, swallowing. "Attractive?"

I scowl. Shrug. Lie. "Just normal."

"So that tells me nothing," she says, sarcastic. "Will you call him?"

I shake my head. "Don't think so."

Thankfully, Elle doesn't press me for further details.

"No one will ever be Freddie, but that doesn't mean you'll never be happy again, sis."

"Yeah," I say. I don't tell her that I'm more scared by the thought that, in time, someone *might* make me happy again. I may not remember the nuances of Kris's face, but I remember the feelings he stirred in me, and that in those moments, I wasn't thinking of Freddie Hunter at all.

"He seemed okay, to be honest. Didn't take himself too seriously."

Hope brightens my sister's eyes but she tries to play it cool. "Definitely nothing serious about a cup of coffee."

"You say that. I could spill it down myself and end up with third-degree burns."

She smiles, grateful for my silly joke.

"Or you could just have a perfectly nice time."

"I'll think about it," I say, unwilling to commit.

"Don't leave it too long," she says. "He sounds nice."

I take the note and fold it in half. "Don't go on about it. And I mean it–for God's sake, don't tell Mum."

"Promise not," she says, then looks at her water glass in disgust. "Bloody ice has melted already."

Ah, there she is again.

MY PHONE FEELS like it's burning my palm. Elle left half an hour ago, and I'm still sitting at the kitchen table with Kris's note in front of me and my phone in my hand, trying to decide if I'm brave enough to send him a message. Or if I want to, even. Am I just doing it to please Elle? Probably not, given that I kept the note. What am I supposed to say, though? I read it over again, feeling hot with nerves. I haven't put his number into my phone, so I can open a message window and tap something in without fearing I might accidentally press send.

~~Hi Kris, it's Lydia, remember from the dating night?~~

I huff as I delete it. How many Lydias is he likely to know? And if he's forgotten me already, then maybe I'd be better not bothering anyway.

~~Hey you~~

No, that's terrible.

~~Hi there,~~

Bloody hell! How hard can this be?

Hi Kris, thought I might take you up on that vegan-chai-latte-skinny-dip sometime, if the offer still stands? Lydia ~~(from the dating thing)~~.

I don't think I can do better than that. It's brief, lighthearted, take it or leave it. I type his number in and press send before I can chicken out. And then I lay my head on the table and groan.

It doesn't take him long to reply, ten minutes at most. I appreciate the speed—it tells me that he's not someone who plays games for the sake of it.

Hey Lydia, glad to hear from you. I work from home so I'm pretty free. Let me know when and where's good. I'll be there. K

ASLEEP

Monday, June 17

"HE'S RUNNING LATE at work," Jonah says, placing a coffee mug down for me on the coffee table.

"Did he just text you?" I say.

He nods. "He said to get started without him."

I roll my eyes, both because Freddie is late and because he's taken the easy route of letting Jonah tell me. It's after eight o'clock in the evening, for God's sake. Get started without me means he's not going to make it. It's infuriating. We've had tonight penciled on the kitchen calendar for weeks now, at Jonah's rather than ours, to organize our wedding music. I'm relieved he hasn't moved in with Dee yet. It was supposed to happen weeks ago, but his landlady pretty much begged him to stay for an extra couple of months, until she can find a new tenant. It's so Jonah to put his plans on hold for someone else; she's an elderly woman who pops up from her basement flat every now and then to listen to him play.

I haven't been here very often, he's always been so at home in our living room.

It's a very Jonah space; uncluttered, one wall lined with books and vinyl records, a piano in the ground floor bay window. It's restful. Or else it would be, if I wasn't pissed off with Freddie for leaving yet another of the wedding details to me.

"How's Dee?" I ask, to change the subject.

"Fine," he says. "Already making plans for your hen night."

"Should I ask?"

He grins and shakes his head. "I'm sworn to secrecy."

I'm not sure what to make of that so I don't press him.

"So nothing religious for the music," I say. "It's a humanist ceremony."

"Okay," Jonah says, browsing the wall of records as he speaks, coffee mug in his hand. He's barefoot and wearing a battered Rolling Stones T-shirt, like a rock star at a retreat. "Traditional, or . . . ?"

I shake my head. "No, more personal. Definitely not 'Here Comes the Bride' or anything like that."

Jonah rests his coffee cup on the low windowsill and takes a seat at the piano to knock out a few perfect bars of the wedding march. I curl my bare feet underneath me on his taupe-and-white striped linen sofa and groan.

"Don't, it makes me nervous."

He laughs and segues faultlessly into "Over the

Rainbow," raising his eyebrows at me in question. I look down into the depths of my coffee mug, caught unaware by emotion because there's something painfully apt about the song. Too apt, so I shake my head.

"The Beach Boys?" he says.

"I don't think I know any," I say. When it comes to music, Jonah should really have been around in the sixties. He loves Elvis and the Stones, but he always comes back to the Beatles.

"You know this one, surely?" he says, playing the opening bars of something I instantly recognize.

"I do know that," I say, reaching for the pad and pen I've got ready to make notes. "I like it. What's it called?"

"'God Only Knows,'" Jonah says.

My shoulders sag. "Nothing God related."

"It isn't, really," Jonah says, but I'm not convinced.

"How about something from the Beatles?" he asks. I don't think an occasion exists where Jonah wouldn't think the Beatles to be the most appropriate choice.

"'Help'?" I smile.

He picks out the melody with one finger, coffee mug still in his other hand. There's no place Jonah looks more at home than at a piano. "Maybe not entirely appropriate," he says. "'All You Need is Love'?" He puts his mug down and plays the intro beautifully, but all I can see is the wedding scene from *Love Actually*.

"I don't want anything that reminds Freddie of Keira Knightley on our wedding day," I laugh.

Jonah grins too, aware of Freddie's crush. "Fair enough," he shrugs.

"What if we don't find anything?" I say, scraping my hair up into a bun on top of my head.

Jonah chews the inside of his lip. "Can I try something?"

I nod, grateful for any suggestions.

He plays a few bars of something then stops, shakes his hands out, and starts again. It's another Beatles track I think, one I kind of know but not very well, so I really pay attention to the lyrics. He sings of bright stars in dark skies and of a love that will never die, and a tear slides down my cheek because it's absolutely perfect.

"I love it," I say, at the end.

He nods. "It's one of my favorites too."

I reach for my notepad and write "And I Love Her" down at the top of the list.

AWAKE

Thursday, June 20

"IT'S NICE TO see you again." Dee stands up and brushes a kiss against my cheek. "Thanks for coming. I wasn't sure if you'd think it was a bit weird."

She smiles, wary, and shoots me a self-conscious look from beneath her lashes. We're in a café not far from my work. I was caught off guard by Dee's email this morning to ask if we could meet for lunch. I've seen her out and about on several occasions with Jonah but we haven't exactly built up a close, meet-for-a-natter sort of friendship yet. Here we are nonetheless. I raise my hand in greeting when I spot her at a table in the corner and order a coffee. She stands and kisses my cheek quickly before I slide into the chair opposite hers.

"How've you been?" I ask.

"Okay." She fiddles with the handle of her cup. "Busy at work."

I smile as the guy from behind the counter places my coffee down, casting around in my head for something to say. I don't find Dee all that easy to chat to without Jonah as a causeway.

"I guess you're wondering why I suggested this?" she says.

I appreciate her directness. "A little bit," I concede, but I can't stop myself from politely adding "although it's nice to catch up, of course." How very British of me; I just about manage to stop myself from remarking on the glorious weather.

Dee's wearing a canary yellow vest top and black leggings, her dark hair scraped severely back into a high ponytail. She has the look of someone perpetually on their way to the gym; she'd definitely be Sporty at a Spice Girls fancy dress bash.

"I need to ask you for some advice. Well, some help really," she falters. "With Jonah."

Fear kicks in. "Is he okay?"

She nods, and then shrugs, anxious. "Yes and no. I'm really worried about him, Lydia. He won't talk to me about the accident. He clams up every time I even mention Freddie's name."

I look at her across the table, at the way she's twisting the plastic hair band around her wrist and biting the corner of her lip. It probably took a fair amount of courage for her to ask me here today.

"I never met Freddie," she says. "I mean, I know they were best friends, obviously, and I know some of what happened, but beyond that I'm in the dark. I haven't even seen a photo of him. Can you believe that?"

It's news to me that Jonah is so closed off about

things with Dee. He's always been a talker, much more so than Freddie ever was, but now I think about it, he and I don't talk much about the accident itself. I don't especially want to go over it again, so I haven't noticed his reticence. I sat through his painful account of events at the inquest and then he didn't mention it again until the unpalatable truth tumbled out of him at the grief session. We talk about Freddie often, but the accident itself? Not so much.

I rummage in my bag for my phone and flick through until I find a photo of Freddie and Jonah together. It doesn't take long; I have loads. Dee studies my phone screen when I hand it to her.

"Wow," she says, after a while. "That isn't how I imagined Freddie at all."

"No?" I'm not sure what she means.

"I expected them to look like brothers, I guess," she says, and then she smiles and hands my phone back.

"He was very handsome," she says. "You must miss him terribly."

What do I say to that? It's been sixteen months since he died and yes, I miss him every day? Or of course, I miss him, but I secretly see him in a parallel universe sometimes which eases the pain considerably? Yes, but I'm trying to get on with my day-to-day life; in fact I have a date planned soon with a guy I met at silent speed dating? All of the above are true, but I don't think Dee really came here to talk about me so I just nod and shoot her a tiny, tight smile.

"They might not look like brothers, but they were as good as," I say. "Jonah spent most of his teenage years in and out of Freddie's house."

I don't add that Jonah's home life was less than ideal; she probably already knows about his past, but if she doesn't, it's not my place to fill her in. Maggie, Freddie's mum, once told me she gave Jonah an old BMX from their shed for his fourteenth birthday; it was his only gift. She only realized he couldn't ride a bike when his foolhardy teenage pride saw him swing his leg over the crossbar and attempt to pedal away. She fished him out of the gutter, bathed his bleeding shoulder, and then spent the next week holding on to the saddle while he got the hang of riding it in the privacy of her back garden. It probably isn't a story Jonah likes to think back on, and I don't expect he'd appreciate me sharing it with Dee.

"I think a change of scene might be what he needs," Dee says. She's chewing her lip again, nervous.

"A holiday?" I suggest. "Well if you're going to surprise him, don't go for somewhere too hot because he's not much of a sun-lounger kind of guy. Italy, maybe? Somewhere historic; he'd like that."

She looks uncomfortable. "I was thinking more long-term," she says. "My mum moved to Wales a few years ago and it's so beautiful where she is, Lydia, really pretty walking country."

"Wales?" I say, alarmed. I'm aware Dee has family there–she and Jonah spent time with them over Christmas–but what does she mean by long-term? Surely, not as in moving there?

Dee wraps her hands around her mug and sighs. "Have you noticed the circles under his eyes? He doesn't sleep very well, he barely touches the piano, he's even tuned the radio to those crappy talk stations to avoid music in the car. I can count on my hands the number of times I've heard him properly laugh, it's as if he catches himself and feels guilty."

I only half hear what she's saying because my brain is struggling to get past the idea of Jonah moving to Wales. This town might not mean much to Dee, but it's Jonah's home. He and Freddie forged their friendship on these streets, in these pubs. The DNA of their teenage years, of all of our lives, is here. I'm big enough and old enough to understand that things can't stay the same forever, but so much has changed already, and the selfish part of me wants what's left to stay the same.

"I don't know, Dee. At least here he's surrounded by familiar places and people. Maybe he needs that right now."

"Or maybe he'd find it easier to move on if he was somewhere else," she counters, and then shrugs. "I don't know, I honestly don't. I just know he's miserable, and doing nothing isn't going to fix him."

I drink a little coffee and mull over what she's said. "You can't fix grief. It takes as long as it takes," I say. "My doctor told me you have to move through it sentiently in order to emerge the other side."

We look at each other. "Well that sounds like bollocks," she says, and we both laugh. It's the first moment of real connection we've shared.

"Will you talk to him?" she asks, finally playing her hand. "About Wales?"

Any trace of humor leaves me. My gut reaction is no, I can't possibly advise Jonah to move hundreds of miles away. I don't see him all that often these days; he's gone from being an almost permanent fixture on my sofa to a once-in-a-blue-moon run-in, but there's a certain security to knowing he's around if I really need him. The possibility he might disappear from my life altogether feels desperate, but what if Dee's right? What if fresh Welsh air would blow those purple bruises away from beneath his eyes? What if the shadows here are just too long for him to ever see any light?

"Let me think about it," I say. It's the best I can offer.

AWAKE

Friday, June 28

ON A REGRET scale of one to ten, I'm hovering between eight and eleven, and my nerves are making it hard to swallow my breakfast. I haven't told anyone about my date with Kris today, and I've lost count of the number of times I've picked my phone up to cancel. I'm trying to coach myself not to see it as a date; it can be anything I want it to be, so I'm framing it as meeting up with a friend for a casual drink after work. Even though Kris isn't a friend as such yet, because I've only met him once for a few intense minutes. We've texted quite often in between then and now; he sent me an aerial photo of the coast from the roof of a building he's designed, I sent him a shot of a dinner I'd burned when he asked if I liked to cook. It's all been very lighthearted and on the surface from both sides, which is the only reason I haven't pressed send on any of the various cancellation messages I've written. Well, not the only reason. I guess I feel that if I can get one date, or one "meeting with a friend for a casual drink," out of the way, then that's another necessary hurdle jumped. Or at least limped over with the skin taken off my shins. I'm trying not to overthink things, but I'm honest enough with myself to know I don't want to spend the rest of my days looking at an empty armchair. I eye it now, the blue chair I barely sat on because it was well and truly Freddie's. I very rarely sit on it now either; not because I'm too morose to; it just feels off, somehow. The cushions fit his bum, probably. Piers Morgan is on the TV unnecessarily lambasting a bunch of vegetarians so I get up for the remote control to turn him off, and as I flick, a tacky advert flashes up for PodGods coffee. I catch my breath, and then shake my head and huff, because it's a sure fact Freddie would have made a much slicker job of it. I click the TV off and stand in the middle of the room, then impulse makes me sit on Freddie's chair to finish my toast. I perch. And I wiggle. I make myself sit there for a minute, two at best, before I get up again and stand in front of the fireplace, disconcerted. I bought a couple of new sofa cushions a few weeks ago on a whim, bright and embroidered, and I grab one now and try it out on Freddie's chair. It works. I know for a fact that Freddie would have hated the cushions, and he certainly wouldn't have accepted one on his chair. Pushing the last of my toast into my mouth, I switch the cushion back and head into the kitchen to make my lunch.

I'm halfway to the bus stop when I realize I've left my mobile on the coffee table. I hesitate, torn because I don't want to be late and I don't know the bus schedule well; I only catch it on the occasional days when I'm likely to go to the pub after work. But then I don't want to be without my phone today either in case I decide to cancel my casual drink with Kris. Or he might cancel, which would frankly be a bit of a relief, and I won't know I'm off the hook because my phone is at home. On balance I decide that the only thing worse than meeting Kris is being stood up by Kris, so I dash back to grab it. In the living room I pocket my phone, and then before I can change my mind, I move the bright new cushion onto Freddie's chair again. My fingers linger on the back of his chair, almost an apology, but I leave it there all the same and make a run for the bus.

YOU KNOW HOW sometimes a day feels like a week? Today wasn't one of those days at work—it felt almost as if I went in and out through a revolving door, and now I'm dragging my Birkenstocks toward the café where I've arranged to meet Kris. I wasn't sure what to wear; jeans felt a bit too I've-not-made-any-effort, so I'm hoping my blue-and-white sundress strikes a casual summer vibe. My hair began the day in a pony, hung loose at lunch, and is now in a messy bun because it's too warm to wear it down. Jeez, casual drinks shouldn't feel this much of a minefield, surely? I'm probably not even remotely ready to date anyone; I'm annoyed with myself for getting into this position in the first place, and I'm delving down into my bag for my phone even as I walk. Is it too late to cancel? I know the answer: yes, it's too late—I was due there five minutes ago. Ah, there it is. I check the screen; no cancellation messages. I can actually see the café up ahead as my thumbs hover ready to start typing, and then I spy Kris heading toward me from the opposite direction. Bugger, I can't cancel now, it'd be rude. And actually . . . seeing him makes me remember what it was about him that appealed to me in the first place. He's dressed in dark jeans and a T-shirt, and as he ducks inside the café he slides his sunglasses off and hooks them on his shirt. I don't know what it is about the casual move that calms me. I think I'd built him up in my head to be this scary stranger and in reality he's a normal guy. I can have a coffee with a normal guy, surely? I slip my phone back inside my bag and push a straggle of hair behind my ear, gearing myself up to go inside. I can do this. It's just a drink after work with a friend.

It's blessedly cool inside the café, and although there are a few people grabbing an after-work drink I easily spy Kris at a table over in the corner. He raises his hand when he spots me, and I recognize the look on his face as relief as I thread my way across the room toward him.

"Hi," I say.

He stands to greet me, reminding me of his height. We have an awkward moment where we don't know whether to hug, and for a horrible second we almost shake hands, and then he laughs and drops a casual kiss on my cheek, his hand warm on my bare shoulder.

"You came," he says, sitting back down. "I ordered straightforward coffee, is that okay? I can get something else if you'd prefer? I think they have a license if you fancy wine?"

He indicates a cafetière on the table and two cups.

"Coffee's good," I say, smiling as he pours for us both. Probably better to give my liver a bit of a reprieve.

"Have you been here before?" he asks.

I nod. "Sometimes after work, on birthdays, leaving do's, you know how it is." It's a nice place, sympathetically modernized from an old grain store, all exposed wood and scrubbed floors. They stay open pretty late and serve unpretentious food, a welcome change from the usual chains. "It gets quite busy in the evenings." Wow, I'm being boring.

"So," he says, putting the coffee pot back down. "Shall we stare at each other in silence for a few minutes again, stick with our tradition?"

"Do you mind if we don't?" I laugh as I reach for my cup, the tension broken. "Man, that was a strange evening, wasn't it?"

He looks amused. "Crazy stuff. I don't know why I did it, to be honest."

"Well I know why I did," I say without thinking. "I work at the community center and had my arm twisted to make up the numbers."

Another person might have been offended, but Kris just laughs. "I guessed as much." He picks his coffee up and touches the rim to mine. "I'm glad you took one for the team."

Creases fan from the corners of his eyes as he smiles, relaxed, and you know what? It's actually okay. I lower my shoulders from the brace position, take a sip, and exhale slowly.

"How's the building coming along?" I ask, unsure if I've phrased it correctly. He's an architect; do they build things?

"Yeah, not bad," he says. "Almost there now. A couple of weeks or so should see it signed off."

"It must be rewarding," I say. "Seeing your designs go from paper to reality."

He gives me a sometimes shrug. "It can be. Or it can be a complete pain in the ass from start to finish, depending on the building, and the client."

"Is it what you always wanted to do?"

"Besides a Ferrari test driver, pretty much," he says.

"I expect competition's fierce for that one," I say.

"Helps if you're Italian," he says.

"Ah. You don't look Italian."

"Too tall?" he says. "Half Swedish, actually. Dad's a Brit, Mum's from Stockholm."

"But you've always lived here?"

He nods. "We spent our summers in Sweden as kids though. My eldest sister lives there now, I go over when I can."

"You have more than one sister?"

He grins. "Three, all older. I'm the only son."

Wow. "At least you didn't have to wear hand-me-down clothes then," I say. I don't think I had anything Elle hadn't gone through first until I was old enough to buy it myself.

"Don't bet on it," Kris laughs. "My mother is fairly progressive."

It creeps in around the edges of my consciousness; I'm enjoying his company. He's quick to smile, and he doesn't seem to have an agenda. We talk about his job and mine, the one-eyed cat he's taken in because it pitched up in his garden and didn't leave, Turpin the deserter cat who has pretty much left me for another woman, about the shaky state of the nation. He refills our cups, and I realize hunger has replaced my nerves when he picks up the menu and suggests food. We pick our way over a charcuterie sharing plate and I find myself asking him what brought him to the silent dating event.

He ordered a beer with dinner, and he stares into it now. "Loneliness, I guess. I was married. My wife and I separated a couple of years ago."

"Oh," I say. "I'm sorry." As soon as it's out of my mouth I hate myself for parroting the same trite apology so many people have said to me.

"Yeah, so was I for a while," he says, rueful. "Very sorry for myself anyway. Not so much for Natalie; she moved to Ireland with her boss, who incidentally drives a Ferrari."

"Crap." I chase an olive round my plate with a cocktail stick. "Bastard."

"Yeah," he laughs a little. "Anyway, I got pretty sick of it being just me and the one-eyed cat and somehow I found myself signing up to stare at complete strangers in the community center."

"Did you tick any other boxes in the end?" I ask. Okay, I know I'm fishing.

"No," he says, his eyes alive with humor. "Did you?"

"I didn't have a sheet, remember?"

"Ah. Just doing your job. I remember now," he says, then adds, quietly, "For the record, you were very good at it."

I feel heat flush up my neck when he doesn't laugh to diminish the value of the compliment.

"Thank you. It scared me, but I'm glad I did it." I pause just as he did a second ago, and then add, "now."

"Because of me, right?" he laughs, holding eye contact.

"Because of the olives," I say, and he lays his hand over his heart as if I've wounded him.

He looks at me over the rim of his glass. "Why did it scare you?"

I knew we were going to have to talk about my life at some point this evening, and I've deliberated over how much of the truth to reveal. Not because I want to lie; I just don't want Kris to look at me any differently to the way he does now. He's the first person in my life to treat me normally since the accident, without sympathy or side-eyes to check I'm okay. It's a relief.

"I haven't dated for a long time."

Kris peels a slice of serrano away with the tips of his fork. "No?"

It's a tell me more kind of no, and I pick over the various phrases in my head to find one that fits.

"I was with someone," I say, and then correct myself. "I was with Freddie. We were together for a long time, and he, umm, he died."

There. I've said it. Kris places his fork down and looks at me, unflinching. Please, I think. Please don't say you're sorry for my loss.

"Shit, Lydia, no wonder you were scared," he says. "You must have been to hell and back."

It's an apt description. Some days I've stood too close to the flames, my face burning, but now I feel as if I'm slowly backing away from the heat.

"Something like that," I say. "You're the first. You know, the first man, since . . ."

He doesn't let me falter for long. "Want to talk about it, or not talk about it?"

"Do you mind if we don't?" I say, grateful for the choice and that he hasn't pushed for details. Sitting here this evening with Kris has felt ever so slightly magical; lighter and brighter than my usual nights. I'm not ready to let go of those feelings yet.

"In that case, would you like an ill-advised cocktail from this lurid list?" He hands me a laminated neon turquoise card from the menu card stand.

And just like that, he steers us away from the past and back to now.

"I CAN'T BELIEVE it's ten o'clock," I say, hooking my jacket over my bag because it's still warm when we step out of the café. "I was only staying for an hour."

"Me too," he says. "I'd got my eldest sister primed to fake an emergency if I texted her a code word."

"You hadn't," I laugh.

"I absolutely had; you might have been a hideous person," he says, falling into step beside me. We're heading toward the taxi rank just along the high street, and the pavements are quieter now. It's one of those endless, balmy English summer evenings, all the more pleasurable because they're never a given. "She was going to mysteriously break her arm if I texted the word purple."

"Purple?" I find it funnier than it is, probably because of the wine in my bloodstream. "As in rain?"

He nods, stepping around me so he's closest to the road. "What can I say? I'm a Prince fan."

"I'm going to think of you in a purple velvet suit from here on in," I say, slowing my step as we approach the taxi rank, a couple of cars idling ready for passengers.

He smiles down at me as we come to a standstill, and he reaches out and smooths his hand lightly over my hair.

"I like that you're going to think of me at all," he says, and his eyes tell me that he doesn't expect anything more than that from me right now.

"Thank you," I say, terrified because I think I do want more. "I had a really good time tonight."

"Thank you for letting me be the first," he says, and I catch hold of his hand in mine.

"I'm glad it was you," I say, breathless, and he reads my cues and lowers his head slowly to mine.

"You're trembling," he says.

"Kiss me," I say, and he does, and I close my eyes and feel a million forgotten things. It's strange and beautiful and sexy and melancholy, his hand against the small of my back, his mouth gentle and almost too brief. Something shifts inside me. It's like unstoppering a new bottle of scent; floral undertones of romance and late-night amber. It's a smell I don't recognize; it's not my own, but I think over time I could come to see it as such. I think I could even grow to like it.

"Good night, Lydia," he whispers.

I'm still holding his hand, and he squeezes it briefly as he opens the door of the cab.

I'm awkward as I try to reverse myself in, and he

laughs. "You might find it easier if you let go of my hand."

I look at our hands and then shake my head, laughing too.

"Good night," I say, looking up at him once I'm inside.

"Can I see you again?" he asks, his hand on top of the open door. He doesn't pretend he isn't bothered about my answer.

"I'd really like that," I say, not pretending either as the cabdriver puts his indicator on to pull out. I lay my head back and close my eyes as we move through the dark streets toward home. I can practically see my mum and Elle standing shoulder to shoulder giving me an excited double thumbs-up, as if I've just made it through the first round of a talent show. I breathe in deeply, trying to catch lingering traces of that intriguing scent.

ASLEEP

Saturday, July 6

"I'M NOT WEARING IT."

Elle is standing in front of me laughing, a sister-of-the-bride sash slung around her body. She's sun-kissed and relaxed in a strapless red jumpsuit and heels, and she seems so much more herself than the last time I saw her. I have a twinge of guilt for not coming back more this last month. She's holding out a veil covered in various silly hen-night accessories. A strip of paracetamol. Gaudy fake wedding rings. A champagne cork. I can't see a condom, but I'm willing to bet there's one there somewhere.

"You have to," she says. "Dee made it, she'll be offended."

"Dee made it?"

Elle fiddles with the hair slide attached to the veil, her blood-red nail polish immaculate. "You should be thanking me. She wanted to order everyone matching T-Shirts with neon pink slogans."

"I still think they were a good idea."

I turn at the sound of Dee's voice as she appears in my kitchen carrying a bottle of champagne. She's glammed up to the max in a thigh length blue sequinned dress, her usual ponytail replaced by bouncy Kate Middleton curls. It's not a look I'd have predicted from her. "Thought we'd have a bit of the good stuff before we go." She jiggles the bottle at me, shiny eyed.

Elle claps her hands, already turning to my glasses cupboard behind her. She sometimes takes the piss out of my minor obsession with glassware; I've got the right glasses for all eventualities, my beloved, eclectic car boot and charity shop collection. Cut-glass highballs, spindly flutes, red wine, white wine, champagne saucers and a really pretty set of colored soda glasses from the sixties. It's my thing. I try not to wince as she lifts the champagne saucers, coupes if you want to be fancy, out from the back. I don't often buy incomplete sets, but these three impossible tall and skinny stemmed rose-pink glasses called out to me for help, dirty and balanced precariously among a pile of saucepans and plates at a car boot one cold Sunday morning. Freddie grumbled about carrying them and the woman selling them grumbled about wrapping them up for me, but I bought them nonetheless and love them dearly. Too dearly for the way Elle's waving them around by their fragile stems.

"Let me," I say, taking the bottle, and taking charge.

"I can't believe you're getting married in two weeks,"

Elle sighs, sentimental. "I wish I could get married again."

I look up from picking the seal off the champagne. "Do you?"

Her jeweled hair slide catches the light as she leans back against the kitchen counter. "It's just so romantic," she says, suddenly wistful. "The dress, the ceremony, the flowers . . ."

I love the fact that despite planning weddings almost every weekend at the hotel, she still feels nostalgia for her own.

"Still to David though, right?" Dee asks, sitting down at the kitchen table. Elle rolls her eyes, good natured.

"Obviously."

They both clap when I pop the cork.

"I don't know if I'll ever get married," Dee says.

Elle looks at me, and then at Dee. "I thought things with you and Jonah were pretty serious?"

"They're getting there," Dee says, accepting the glass I hold toward her. "I'm just not sure he's the marrying type."

"But you are?" I ask.

"Everyone's the marrying type," Elle says, before Dee can answer. "Trust me, I've seen all sorts at the hotel. Honestly, there genuinely isn't a marrying type. It's more a case of the right time, right person, and bingo, you're waltzing up the aisle in a meringue."

Dee huffs softly. "Maybe he's just not a bingo fan then."

I'm conflicted. Here in this life, Dee is obviously part of my circle. Quite a close part, given that this is my hen night and she's here in my kitchen with Elle. She's obviously having more success with Jonah here too, if marriage is on her mind. But then the Jonah she knows here is different, openhearted and quick to laugh; the man he used to be.

"Give him time," I say. "He's always been more of a thinker. It'll happen when he's ready, I'm sure."

She doesn't look convinced. "Maybe."

"Jonah Jones," Elle says his name with relish, and then laughs. "I had a secret crush on him when I was about sixteen."

"You did not!" I laugh, shocked. She's never mentioned anything of the sort before.

Pink spots appear in my sister's cheeks. "I never told you. I was embarrassed!" She drinks half of the contents of her glass and then waves it around. "What can I say? He has that whole brooding thing going on, all hair and cheekbones."

I turn away and reach for the bottle to give myself a moment to process the thought of my sister and Jonah Jones. Nope. Not happening.

"He is handsome, isn't he?" Dee says, for all the world like a moony teenage girl.

Elle nods. "He's grown into his face."

I shoot her a look. "Grown into his face?"

She laughs. "You know what I mean. He has that whole . . ." she points toward her mouth. "Mick Jagger thing going on, doesn't he?"

I can't say I've ever looked at Jonah and thought of Mick Jagger, but I start to laugh because I know what Elle means. His mouth is a fraction too big for his face, and he has a kind of louche charisma that can hold a room. Not in the same way Freddie does; he's energy and heat to Jonah's laid-back cool. Together they're night and day, two sides of the same coin. Maybe that's what's missing from Jonah in my waking world; he's lost his heat source.

"I do love him though," Dee says.

Elle and I take a seat on either side of her. I smooth my hands over the skirt of my black dress. It's summer short, party ready, and inoffensive, yet I don't much like it. It's not something I'd usually choose, and I wonder how I've ended up with slightly cool, more conservative clothing tastes here. I'm usually a jeans and T-shirt kind of girl, boho at best. It occurs to me that I've still got no clue what my wedding dress is like; how strange and bizarre to not know something so wedding-relevant on my hen night. I don't even know where it is. At Mum's, presumably, as I haven't seen it anywhere here.

"Want Lydia to say something to him for you?" Elle offers my service without consultation.

God, I hope she says no.

Dee shakes her shiny curls. "How desperate would that make me sound?"

"Not necessarily, if it's subtle," Elle says. "A little nudge to test the waters wouldn't hurt."

Dee brightens a bit and looks at me. "Do you think so?"

I want to say no, I don't think so, actually Dee. I don't think so at all, because if I push you two together you're highly likely to piss off to Wales in the none too distant future for a hill-walking Welsh life in the Welsh valleys with your Welsh mother. I don't say that though.

I smile, nod a little and refill our glasses instead and we clink them, a silent toast to my tentative agreement to broker Jonah and Dee's engagement. How on earth did that happen?

"I WISH YOU wouldn't order duck, Elle, you know how I feel about it."

Mum turns the offending dish away from her on the lazy Susan and pauses to help herself to a battered prawn. Despite being a committed carnivore for her entire life, she always has a shudder at the idea of people eating ducks.

"Double standards," Elle says, wielding chopsticks like a pro.

We're in the local Chinese restaurant, a place I've been to many times over the years. Mum and Elle are here, of course, and Dee, plus Julia and Dawn from work and Auntie June, my mum's sister. Sitting on her other side is my cousin Lucy, who was in the year between Elle and me at school, when she could be bothered to turn up. I've no real clue why she's here; she's always looked down her slightly-too-long nose at me in a way that suggests she thinks she's a cut above us. She isn't, for the record. So there's eight of us altogether, each wearing a sash that declares our place in the bridal party. Bride! Mother of the Bride! Chief Bridesmaid! I sneak a glance at Auntie June's and find she's a "Hen on a mission!" What on earth does that mean, I wonder? What would a hen on a mission do? Steal eggs? Spy on a rival coop? I have no clue where that ridiculous train of thought is going but start to laugh under my breath regardless, largely thanks to Dee's champagne, followed by the wine now being thrown at me as if I'm going to have my liver removed in the morning and will never be able to touch a drop again. As it happens I'm quite fond of my liver so I'm trying to pace myself, but I'm fighting a rising sauvignon tide and fear I might go under at some point in tonight's proceedings.

"What are you laughing at?" Elle asks, next to me.

"These stupid sashes," I say, plucking at the one I'm begrudgingly wearing. Being marked out as the hen has already earned me wolf whistles from a car full of boy-men and the offer of a snog from the barman in the pub we went to before dinner. It didn't help that there was a red foil condom packet dangling between us on my veil. (Yes, I found the condom. Dee helpfully stapled it so it hangs right between my bloody eyes.)

Elle plucks a sachet from the back of the veil. "Cinnamon?"

Dee reaches across and taps it. "A natural picker-upper, apparently." She pauses for dramatic effect, and then faux whispers, really loudly, "For men." Her accompanying rising hand action leaves us in no doubt as to what she means. "Just in case of wedding night jitters."

"Cinnamon, are you sure?" Auntie June's eyebrows hit her hairline. She's already on an ill-advised third glass of wine and she rarely drinks. She rarely leaves the house without my uncle Bob either—they're usually to be found doing jigsaws in their dining room or learning some new hobby together. Last time I visited I sat on the chair they'd reupholstered, eating cake they'd made at their afternoon baking class at the local secondary school, drinking elderberry wine uncle Bob had brewed in his man-shed. They're people who like to get involved in the community, and always as a pair. Bob and June. June and Bob. Right now Auntie June is making a rare solo appearance and the cinnamon revelations have just turned her face an unbecoming shade of purple. "Well that explains something, at least."

Elle starts to laugh beside me, quicker on the uptake than I am. "Ooh Auntie June, has Uncle Bob been getting a bit cinnamon-frisky?"

My mum shoots her sister a raised-brows look as Lucy tries not to gag on her prawn toast.

"We've been trying to master cinnamon whirls lately, they're Bob's favorite," Auntie June says, twisting the silver St. Christopher necklace she's worn for as long as I can remember.

"Well, you know what they say, June," Dee says, deadpan, as she spoons special fried rice onto her plate. "Cinnamon in the morning makes Bob a sexy boy."

I start to laugh because Dee has never met my cardigan wearing, giant-vegetable-growing uncle Bob. "Dee, literally no one in the world has ever said that."

"I think you'll find June just did," Dawn says from across the table. "I might buy some cinnamon on the weekly shop. My *'Bob,'*" she makes air quotes around the name to infer that she's protecting the innocent, pointlessly in this case because we all know who she's talking about, "and I are trying to get pregnant again, and it's got to the point where he'd do literally anything to avoid doing the deed ever again. He's exhausted."

"Poor Bob." Julia shakes her head, barely eating anything but doing a sterling job on the wine. "Well, I for one don't need the cinnamon aisle." I look away to hide my smile as the memory of Julia and Bruce dancing at Dawn's wedding slides into my head; they're definitely in tune with each other.

"Me neither," Elle rolls her eyes. "My 'Bob' is more than peppy enough, usually at six in the morning when I'm trying to stay asleep for the last half an hour before the alarm."

She shoots a belated look at Mum, as if she'd forgotten she was there. "Sorry, mother."

"Oh Bob," I laugh. "How indiscreet of you to discuss his bedroom habits over pork balls."

Lucy lays her chopsticks down and reaches for her wine. "Please, Uncle Bob's my father, and I'd rather talk about something else entirely, thank you very much."

We all fall about laughing at her clipped delivery, but Lucy isn't even a small bit amused. To spare her niece any further blushes, Mum reaches into her handbag and pulls out a small, gift wrapped package.

"I've been waiting for the right time to give you this," she says, handing it to me.

The laughter simmers down as everyone watches, interested. It feels like a jewelry box of some sort.

"It always bothered me that your father and I didn't give you girls a good example of marriage when you were growing up," Mum says.

Elle and I both jump in at once.

"You were brilliant," I say, at the same time as Elle says, "Mum and dad all in one."

"We didn't miss him," I add, and I mean it.

"Surfing at his age," Auntie June mutters, throwing her palms up in disgust.

"Anyway." Mum pushes on. "Despite my own romantic woes, I hope your grandparents, *my* parents, helped to show you that sometimes marriage can be just right."

Elle and I didn't have any relationship with our paternal grandparents, but Mum's family provided the much-needed backbone of our childhood. Their neat-as-a-new-pin home a few doors down was practically an extension of ours, their dinner table the scene of most of our evening meals. If I try really hard, I can still almost capture the smell of their house, a welcoming mix of furniture polish, roast dinners, and pipe tobacco. Even Lucy looks nostalgic.

"I miss them so much," Elle says, wine-tearful.

I nod. We all miss them, Mum and Auntie June most of all.

"Open it then."

I'm glad of Dee's interruption. We were in danger of descending into maudlin for a moment there.

"Okay," I say, shaky fingered as I pick the silver and white ribbons open.

Inside there's a small, square red velvet box, worn to threadbare on the corners. When I open the lid I find a small, familiar marcasite peacock brooch looking up at me with flinty green eyes. It's of very little financial value but worth a great deal to Mum, and to me too. It was my gran's favorite, worn to every wedding, christening, and funeral. I have a distinct memory of falling asleep on her lap at some family party or other, tracing the raised feathers of the peacock with my fingertip as my eyes closed. When I think about it now I can almost smell her perfume, even though I can't have been more than five at the time.

"It was the first gift your grandad ever gave your gran, she was about sixteen," Mum says.

Elle touches the brooch lightly. "She wore this at my graduation. I can see it now pinned to that purple suit she used to like."

Elle herself wore Gran's watch on her wedding day, another priceless family piece of little financial worth. I sometimes notice her wearing it at family things.

Because I'm too misty eyed to reliably answer, I pass the box to Dee on my other side to have a look at. She does her best, but without the memories of it pinned to our gran's lapel on high days and holidays it probably isn't the most impactful sight.

Dawn takes an obliging glance next and hands it on to Julia, who eyes it briefly.

"Some people won't have anything to do with peacocks inside their house," Julia says, brutally honest as usual, passing it round the table to Lucy. "Believe they're bad luck. I brought a single feather home once and my mother went straight outside and put it in the bin."

"Oh," I say, yanked straight out of my sentimental fug into fear of anything that might bring ill fortune my way. I'm anxious not to do anything in this life that might beckon my other world closer. The gulf between the two places is already getting bigger.

"There'll be nothing left for me by the time I get married," Lucy grumbles. "Not that I wanted *that* anyway," she curls her lip at the brooch, "but that's not the point."

Auntie June usually bites her lip around Lucy; she obviously realized early on that the path of least resistance is the easiest option with her only daughter. Not tonight. "Don't worry darling, you can have her false teeth, she was very fond of those."

In the small silence that follows, we all look at Lucy, too afraid to laugh.

"No she can't," Mum says. "I gave them to the charity shop. They were in her good navy handbag."

I laugh so hard that the strawberry condom bats me in the eye.

IT'S AFTER ELEVEN. I'm a glass or two beyond merry, full of hoisin duck, and it would appear that I'm dancing on a table in The Prince of Wales. I guess it was inevitable that we'd end up here, just as it was equally inevitable that Freddie's stag party would do the same thing. The hen party whittled down to a coop of three after the restaurant; Dawn and Julia shared a taxi home, and a still frosty Lucy was designated driver for Mum and Auntie June, leaving me, Elle, and Dee to wind our way through the doors of The Prince just after half past ten with a Destiny's Child–like confidence. I don't know which of us would be Beyoncé. Not me, for certain. But what we lack in talent we make up for with enthusiasm as we lead the pub in a rousing chorus of "All the Single Ladies." I don't actually know the words beyond the obvious lines, but it doesn't really matter because no one else here does either. Elle is waving her arms over her head, Dee is doing a shoulder shimmy as she stabs at her ring finger, and Freddie is shouting that he's putting a ring on it in exactly two weeks' time. Part of me recoils at being referred to only as "it"; when I say as much, Freddie blames Beyoncé and hauls me down off the table.

"Nice dress," he grins, setting me down.

"You think? Not too grown up?"

"You *are* all grown up now, Lydia Bird." He touches the lace neckline of my dress. "It's different on you, but good different."

Yes, I think, it's different. Jonah appears, switching the empty beer bottle in Freddie's hand for a fresh one as he dips in and swerves the condom to kiss my cheek.

"Great singing up there," he lies.

"Mind the . . ." I say, gesturing vaguely toward the veil and its various appendages.

Jonah shakes his head. "I can't believe you actually wore it."

"You knew?"

He reaches out and taps the condom packet. "Stapled that one there myself at midnight last night."

"From your wallet?" Freddie laughs. "Hang on to it Lyds, it might be worth something at the *Antiques Roadshow.*"

I screw my nose up, not impressed. Obviously, I appreciate the effort Dee has made, ably assisted by Jonah. I'm grateful too that Freddie and co. have ended their evening here tonight rather than in town, a last-minute scale-down because Freddie is needed at work tomorrow to prep for an important new client. It's all very hush-hush, someone they're wooing in the hope of poaching them from under their closest rivals' nose. He lives for that thrill, so much so that he's prepared to curtail his own stag night in order to be the most prepared person in the room come Monday. Another life tip cribbed from Barack Obama, no doubt.

Half an hour later and Jonah is on the piano, Elle is in a distant corner on David's knee, and Dee is leaning against me in that "I don't think I can stand independently" way that suggests she's had enough to drink.

"Don't say anything to him," she says, poking her straw into the bottle she's clutching. I've no idea what it is; it's lurid blue and might not have been her best idea this evening.

"To who?"

She pulls her straw from her drink and taps the dripping end against her ring finger. "To Jonah. Elle's right. He's Mick Jagger, and I'm no Jerry Hall."

I laugh, because it's ridiculous. "He's not Mick Jagger, and Jerry Hall would eat him alive."

Dee shakes her head, unconvinced. "I can't even sing, Lydia. He needs Adele, not me. I'll never be Adele."

"You made a pretty good Beyoncé just now," I point out. "Come on, stop feeling sorry for yourself." I give her shoulders a bolstering squeeze. "You've got great hair."

"No, you've got great hair," she sighs, dramatic. "You've got Jerry Hall hair."

"I wish I'd got her money," I joke to keep things light.

We fall silent and watch Jonah. He's not even looking at the piano keys as he plays it, his hands confident and assured, the crowd with him as they always are in here.

"It's in his DNA, isn't it," Dee says. "Music, I mean."

I nod, and I'm suddenly despairing from my hen-party heels to the tips of my ridiculous veil because she's absolutely right. "In his bones," I say, thinking of how lost Jonah is in my waking life. If music is gone from his life, he's in even more trouble than I thought. Maybe Wales is the best place for him after all.

Dee plonks herself down on the table behind us, and I excuse myself to go to the loo.

Locked in the cubicle, I sit on the lowered lid and pull my phone from my bag, as much from habit as the need to check it. I need a breather.

My screen saver flashes up. Paris in the snow, rather than the stock image I've opted for in my waking life. I lean my head against the cubicle wall and stare at it, vividly remembering my numb hands around a cup of coffee, frozen icicles on café awnings, cold-lipped kisses. It feels strange when I think of it, more like a scene from a movie than my own life.

"Okay in there?"

I jump. I've obviously been hogging the only cubicle for too long.

"One minute," I say, shoving my phone back into my bag and flushing, even though I haven't used the loo. The woman waiting gives me a bit of a curious look when I emerge, and I can see why when I see myself in the mirror—I've become a rocky horror bride. Sighing, I rub cold water underneath my eyes with my fingertips to get rid of the mascara streaks. This isn't how my hen night was supposed to end, crying in the bloody loo.

Outside, I stand in the cool, quarry-tiled corridor, unsure if I want to head back into the noisy bar or just call it a night and go home. The bar door opens, letting through a blast of music and raucous noise and Jonah Jones.

"Are you hiding?" he asks, smiling as the door closes behind him, blocking out the noise.

"No," I say, as he draws level with me. "Yes, a bit."

"You're pretty difficult to miss in that thing." He nods toward my veil as he leans his back against the opposite wall.

I nod and untangle it from my hair, wishing I'd binned it in the toilets.

"It isn't from my wallet," he says. "Just so you know."

It takes me a second or two to realize he's talking about the red foiled condom.

"Dee bought them."

Do I want to imagine Dee buying strawberry condoms? Not really. "Nice of her," I say.

"Yeah," he says.

"I like her a lot," I say, wondering if I should try to shoehorn in the fact that Dee wants to marry him.

"She's easy to like," he says.

"Easy to love?" I say, keeping my tone light.

He makes a sound in his throat, a mix of frustration and exasperation. "I don't think I even know what love is, Lydia," he says. "It's easy for you, you and Fred have been together forever. You've grown up together, you know? You have that shorthand. But what if you don't have that history, if you don't have all of those layers of life together to make up a strong foundation?"

It's a lot more of an answer than I expected from him, so much so that I don't have a ready reply.

"Me and Dee, we don't have any of that," he says. "I didn't hold her hair back the first time she got drunk and threw up, and I didn't carry her stupidly heavy rucksack back from school for her. I didn't push her first car home for her when she beached it in a snow-drift, and I didn't let her copy my chemistry homework every Monday morning before class."

He runs out of steam and I've no clue what to say because he's just listed all of the things that have made up our friendship over the years. He held my hair back in this very pub when we were seventeen years old, and he pushed my car in the snow when I called him in a blind panic.

"You don't need all of those things to love someone, Jonah," I say, in the end, not sure what he means. "What happened yesterday, or last week, or ten years ago . . . those things aren't important. What really matters is now; here, today, tomorrow, next year. Some people fall in love at first sight and stay together forever, other people marry their childhood sweetheart and end up in the divorce courts. You can't predict life, Jonah, you can only try to make the best of whatever it throws at you."

I don't know where all of that came from, and I don't strictly believe my own lecture. In my waking life, precious yesterdays are all I have left of Freddie.

Jonah looks at the floor and then back up at me, his

dark eyes unreadable. "What if someone falls in love with their friend?"

I think of Freddie. "Then they're lucky," I say.

Jonah nods, bleak. "I guess so. As long as their friend loves them back."

I open my mouth to say something, anything, but nothing comes out because I'm suddenly afraid where this conversation is heading, of the charge in the air between us.

"Being Freddie Hunter's wingman has been the story of my life," he says, and something inside me twists because a universe away, he said those exact same words at Freddie's funeral. Back there he said it had been his honor and his privilege; I don't think he's about to say that here.

On cue, Freddie barrels through the door from the pub, all smiles at the sight of us.

"Hey, my two favorite people in one place."

"Hey you," I say, standing on tiptoe to kiss his cheek. I realize I'm shaking.

"Shall we go for curry?" he says, leaning against the wall next to Jonah. I'm reminded of them standing exactly like that at school, backs against the wall waiting for me at the end of the day. "I'm starving."

"You're always starving," Jonah says, shaking himself down, shucking our too-close-to-the-knuckle conversation off his skin. "Your night, your choice, pal."

"Lyds?" Freddie turns to me. "Coming?"

I shake my head. "I don't think it's good form for the bride to come on the stag night. I'll go and find Dee and Elle."

"Last spotted ordering tequila shots," Freddie grins. "It's gonna get messy out there."

He disappears into the gents humming something loosely similar to the song coming from the bar, and Jonah and I look at each other, alone in the corridor again.

"Forget I said anything, I'm talking shite." He swallows hard and rubs his hand over the back of his neck. "Too much beer."

I nod, grateful for the lie.

"I better get back out there," I say.

He nods, forces out a laugh as he pushes himself away from the wall. "Tequila and all that."

A couple of girls I vaguely recognize from our school days push the door open and I take it as my cue to leave. I push my way through the busy pub looking for Elle, still troubled even as I try to shove my encounter with Jonah to the back of my mind. I can't easily spot my sister or Dee, so I give up and sit down on an empty stool, my head against the side of the slot machine. Everything feels a few degrees off tonight; Dee is too frothy, Elle too pissed, Jonah too serious, Freddie too laddish. And then there's me at the center of it all in my Conservative candidate black dress and festooned veil. I close my eyes, tired and ready to call it a night. I don't want tequila, or Dee, or Elle, even. Tonight has felt much like trying to walk a tightrope. In fact, that's a good analogy for how life is for me at the moment—I'm constantly standing on an invisible wire between two worlds and hoping like hell that I don't plummet to my death. For a girl with bad balance, it's hard work.

AWAKE

Sunday, July 7

MY HEAD IS POUNDING, and I didn't even have a drink before I took the pill last night. Can I be hungover across universes? My travels are always wearying but today I feel steamrolled, both physically and mentally.

Three paracetamol and two mugs of coffee do little to raise my energy or my spirits. I try a little soup and toast soldier self-care at lunch, an overthrow from my childhood, but it would seem there's no escaping this wretchedness yet. I feel . . . I don't know, bruised, I guess? Bruised on the inside, as if someone had a kick around in there and used my internal organs for goalposts.

An afternoon on the sofa does little to mend me. I'm bone tired, as if I'm convalescing. The news rolls past on the TV, informing me it's Sunday July 7th. My tired brain can't manage the maths so I count manually on my fingers up to July 20th. Thirteen days. In one week and six days' time, Freddie and I will get married in a place where I've never even seen my own wedding dress. Thinking about the wedding brings me to Jonah, Freddie's best friend and best man. That conversation we had in the pub corridor last night in my sleeping life . . . I've been trying not to think about it until now. After all, it doesn't apply here. Well, not really. Does it? He didn't say anything explicit or cross any boundaries, but he walked pretty damn close to the line; close enough for me to hear his unspoken words. I sigh and close my eyes, leaning my head back against the sofa cushions. Why does everything have to be so bloody complicated? Perhaps I misinterpreted what Jonah said. It's possible. But in my heart no, I'm not wrong. There was tension in the air between us, something in his dark gaze that asked questions I didn't have easy answers to. Here in my waking world he would never have spoken so boldly, and now it's going to make things decidedly awkward in my sleeping life.

Maybe he'll suddenly need to be somewhere else on our big day. After what he said last night it'd be easier if he wasn't there, for me at least. But not for Freddie, who deserves to have his best friend beside him on his wedding day. I can't see any way around it but to try to do as Jonah suggested—forget he said it at all.

I'M MORE ASLEEP than awake when my phone buzzes a little after five. I made it as far as the shower a while ago and now I'm back on the sofa in my pj's, clean at least, pretending to watch some movie so awful I haven't even registered the main character's name. I dig my mobile out from among the cushions under my head, and my screen informs me that I have one new message—it's Kris. We've texted a bit recently, but I haven't seen him since our first date. Even though I've wanted to, it hasn't felt right.

Fancy a coffee? Could really use a friend if you're around. K x

My thumbs move to tell a white lie so as not to offend him.

~~I'm at my mum's, a family party thing, will give you a bell tomor~~

I pause and delete. Kris is the one person who plays no dual role in my complicated double life and he sounds as if he's having a rough day. Surely, I can find it in myself to offer something kinder than a brush off?

Hey you. Everything okay? I'm mega hungover at home. You sound low, call me if you want. L x

He replies straightaway.

Would it be totally weird if I come to see you for an hour? Could really do with getting out of the house.

Oh. I wasn't expecting that. I've already played my hand by saying I'm around to chat, so I hesitate, and before I can compose my thoughts another text pings in.

Sorry. Ignore that. Crapshoot of a day, you know how it goes sometimes.

And because I do know exactly how it goes sometimes, I tell him no, it's not weird, and yes, he can come over. And then I panic like hell and throw some actual daytime clothes on.

WE SIT AT my kitchen table and drink coffee, and he tells me that his wife appeared out of the blue this morning. She let herself in with the key she hadn't bothered returning, stayed just long enough to fill an Ikea blue bag with things she wanted, and as she was leaving she told him she's three months pregnant with twins.

"I don't know what to say," I say, horrified for him. He looks like a kicked dog. "Shall I call her some terrible names?"

"Already did that, right after she left," he says. "Didn't help very much."

"And she took the kettle." He drains his coffee. "Who does that, Lydia? Takes the kettle?"

I shake my head. "Was it a special kettle?"

He shrugs. "It matched the toaster."

"Did she take the toaster as well?"

He nods ruefully. "No tea, no toast."

I hold his gaze, glad to see the beginnings of amusement there.

"You can probably get a new set for twenty quid from the supermarket," I say.

"I don't even like bloody toast," he says. "And I don't drink tea, either."

I try not to laugh, but I can't help it because what a ridiculous thing to do, really, turn up and take the kitchen appliances.

"I've been offered a new job," he says, changing the subject. "Or a partnership, actually."

"That's good," I say. "Isn't it? It sounds good."

He nods, but his face is conflicted. "It's in London."

Ah. "Will you take it do you think?" I say tentatively.

"Probably," he says. "It's with a friend from Uni, he's expanding his practice."

"Right," I say. The news that he's leaving changes the dynamic between us in a great rush; I don't think I'll see him again after today.

"Another coffee?" I put my hand on his shoulder as I get up to make us a refill.

"You're just showing off now because you have a kettle."

"Maybe," I say, but I'm not thinking about coffee or kettles anymore. I'm thinking how easy he is to be around, and how his gray eyes have green flecks in them when you really look, and when he reaches for my hand to pull me into his lap, I let him.

He sighs and wraps his arms around me, his face in my hair, and I'm not sure which of us is giving comfort and which of us is receiving. He hasn't come here to talk about his kettle. He's come here because seeing the woman he loved and lost has knocked him for six; I understand that feeling more than he knows. He's here because I'm blessedly separate from every other part of his life; I get that too. We don't know each other's family or friends—we don't even know each other very well—but right now that's precisely what makes this right. I am to him what he is to me; a blank page. I like him a great deal and at a different stage of our lives it might have become a chapter or even a whole book, but he's leaving for London and my life is just too complicated to accommodate someone new in it. This story has just one page; boy meets girl, they save each other, and then they never see each other again.

"Lydia," he says, his hands bracketing my face, and then he pushes his fingers into my hair and kisses me, in a way that vaporizes every rational thought from my brain. His low mood meets my kicked-around heart and we both lose control.

"I didn't come here for this," he says as I pull his T-shirt over his head, and I believe him.

"I know that," I say, shaking as his fingers find the clip of my bra.

"Shall I stop?" he asks, one hand on my bared breast, the other thumbing away a tear as it rolls down my face.

"No," I whisper, kissing him. "Don't."

I've never imagined having sex with anyone but Freddie. Well, not really; I mean I've entertained Ryan Reynolds thoughts every now and then, but not in a serious way. But Kris is everything I need him to be. And it's okay that I cried because he cried too, his forehead resting against mine, his hand warm behind my neck.

We lie still in the quiet of the evening, catching our breath, until finally he lifts his head and looks down at me, serious eyed.

"Well, that took my mind off the kettle."

I bury my face in his shoulder, laughing.

* * *

I'M BACK AT the kitchen table, alone now, breaking my alcohol-ban with a late-night measure of brandy unearthed from the back of the Christmas cupboard. My grief guidebooks warned me that it's normal to do out of character things like this; there's even a list. I won't be throwing myself out of any airplanes or white-water rafting, though I can't rule out the classic getting all of my hair cut off at some point.

I'm going to try hard to not let myself regret what happened with Kris this evening. It was wonderful and all the more powerful because we knew it for what it was: goodbye. Perhaps I should think of him as my metaphorical parachute jump; I couldn't have asked for a softer place to land. He understood the feeling of profound absence when your love is no longer present in your life, how it can feel as if they've taken too many pieces of you with them for you to function. Not as you were anyway. I've had to examine the pieces of me left behind and build a new version of myself, Lydia 2.0, bolting new bits on over time. I've assimilated a small, life-affirming fragment of Kris tonight and I gave him a sliver of myself in return, a fair exchange I hope.

I finish the brandy, and as I fill the dishwasher with our coffee cups from earlier, I wonder why it is that we fall in love with some people and not others, even when we wish we could. Billions of humans, all of us scurrying around the planet, falling in and out of love with each other for no reason explicable by logic or numbers or common sense. How unaccountably strange we are.

AWAKE

Friday, July 12

JONAH CALLED ME at work earlier and asked if he could come over this evening, said he was at a loose end, all very casual, but I think the wedding is on his mind. He probably wants to check in and make sure I'm not privately falling to pieces as the date approaches.

I panicked for a couple of seconds after I hung up, and then I reminded myself that Jonah Jones here is not the same Jonah as in my sleeping universe. Here he is dependable, kind, and undemanding, and I'm more than 90 percent certain he hasn't secretly loved me for years. He'll come over for an hour, chat about things in that circumspect way of his, and then I'll send him on his way to The Prince to find Deckers and co. Or maybe I'll find a way to talk to him about Wales; I'll see how it goes. I've been putting it off if I'm honest, but I'll try to look past my own needs tonight and think about what's best for him. And then I realize; that's what this is. He's coming to tell me that he's leaving.

"OKAY?" I ASK, hovering on the doorstep.

He shrugs, one shoulder higher than the other. "Not too bad."

"Want to come in?" I say, eventually, even though I know perfectly well that he does.

"Ta," he says, following me in, closing the door behind him. I go for the kettle, he reaches for the cups, and between us we make coffee, the TV in the lounge providing welcome background noise. I've never felt this kind of awkward around him before. I've been mad at him, sure, but never been so nervous that it's rendered me silent.

"Sit down," I say, backing my bum down onto the end of the sofa, cradling the mug between my hands.

He drops into the armchair he always sat on, the one opposite Freddie's.

"Nice cushion." He says it with a slight question mark—he knows as well as I do the significance.

"How's work?" I ask, as if he's a passing acquaintance in the doctor's waiting room.

"Winding down for the summer, thankfully," he says.

"Of course," I say listlessly. "Lucky."

Jonah's lengthy school holidays used to turn Freddie green with envy, even though he knew perfectly well that much of Jonah's time was spent catching up on paperwork and doing lesson prep.

"That's kind of what I want to talk to you about," he says. "I'm going away for a while."

Here we go, I think. He's going to tell me that he and Dee are going to spend the summer in Wales, see if it feels like a place he could put down roots.

"It's okay, I already know," I say. "Dee told me about Wales."

He puts his coffee down on the table and rubs his hands over his face. "I'm not going to Wales."

"You're not?"

He's nodding slowly, looking at a spot on the rug. "It's over, me and Dee," he says. "We called it last night. Or, I did."

"Oh," I sigh, lost for words now because I'm not entirely sure where this is leading.

"But I thought . . ." I trail off.

"She wants to live in Wales," he says. "Closer to her family."

"She said," I say. "I think she was hoping you might go with her."

Jonah screws his nose up. "I don't know what I want, Lyds. I'm restless, but not for Wales. Me and Dee . . . we weren't at that stage, you know? I don't think she thought so either, to be honest, but she's landed a permanent post in a school out there so . . ." He shrugs. "So she's going anyway. I guess she thought if I went too we could try to make a proper go of things."

"I'm sorry . . ." I say, and I mean it. "I thought you two might go the distance."

"Yeah," he says, resigned. "I thought so too for a while. I feel like a twat for letting it go on for so long, she deserved better." He drinks his coffee, pensive, and

I get the sense that there's more to come, that he hasn't come here to tell me it's over with Dee.

"I'm going to LA for the summer."

Whoa, hang on a minute.

"LA?" I hear the incredulous note in my higher than usual voice. Of all the places in the world I can imagine Jonah going for the summer, LA isn't one of them. Peru, maybe. Island hopping off the beaten track around the Greek Islands, sure. But LA? I just can't picture him among the rollerblading, buff bodied, Hollywood glitterati. Yes, I know, that's a horrible sweeping generalization, but this is Jonah Jones.

"I've been writing again," he says. "Since the accident."

Another unexpected revelation. When we were younger, Jonah entertained journalism aspirations, but in the end he decided chasing down deadlines wasn't the life for him. He turned instead to writing other things: songs, music, and he dabbled in novels and scripts too. He's creative by nature, which is probably why he makes such an excellent teacher.

"That's good," I say. I don't know how the threads of this conversation come together to make one thing yet. Is he going on a writing retreat in LA? "What sort of stuff are you writing?"

"That's the thing, Lyds," he says, and then he stops and looks at me, really studies my face. "I've written this script, and I sent it to a few agents, and to be honest, things have moved a lot faster than I could have imagined."

His bitty delivery isn't making a great deal of sense yet. I get the feeling there's still more to his news.

"Wow, Jonah," I laugh, blindsided. "This is exciting stuff."

"It's pretty mad," he laughs too, self-conscious, and in that second, I see that this matters a great deal to him.

"So you're going to LA to . . . ?"

"Three production companies are interested," he says, making a bad job of playing it down. "I'm meeting up with them, hearing what their ideas might be for it, that kind of stuff."

"Three studios want to make your script into a movie? Are they fighting over you?"

I'm imagining a low-calorie, no carbs Hollywood bun fight on the sun-drenched terrace of some achingly cool restaurant.

Jonah laughs again. "No, it's not like that. My agent just thinks it's a good idea to get a feel for them, see what feels right. Who feels right, really."

It's a lot to take in. "So come on then, what's this movie about to get everyone so hot under the collar? Have you written the next *Star Wars*?" I slide my mug onto the table. "Oh my God, you have! You're going to buy a house in the Hollywood Hills and be neighbors with Bruce Willis."

I don't know why I picked Bruce Willis. I could have gone for someone younger. I should have gone for Ryan bloody Reynolds. I'm definitely not firing on all cylinders.

"I think you're getting just a tiny bit carried away there," he says. "A script being optioned is a million miles away from it ever being made. It's a foot in the door." And then he does that face again, the one that suggests he's uncomfortable with what he needs to say next.

"Thing is, Lyds, it's sort of about Freddie," he says, holding my gaze steady with his own, watching me closely for a reaction. "In a very roundabout, generalized kind of way anyway. I mean . . . it's more about friendship, and about losing your best friend."

"You wrote a movie about Freddie?" It's such a strange idea to get my head around, and then a horrible thought strikes me. "Does he die in it?" My voice is pinched, high-pitched.

"It isn't precisely about him," Jonah says. "It's more about teenage boys, and male friendship, and how loss feels."

I'm a monster. I must be, because all I can think is what Jonah's actually done is found a way to articulate his own feelings more freely and accurately than I ever could, and in doing so he's made his loss bigger than mine. Rather than be pleased for him, I can't shake the idea that he's profiteering from this unthinkable thing that happened to us all. That happened to Freddie, and then primarily to me, not to Jonah bloody Jones.

"You never said anything, not even once," I frown. "You never once mentioned that you were writing again."

"I didn't tell anyone," he says. "Not even Dee."

But I'm not Dee, I think, I'm Lydia, your oldest friend, and you were writing about Freddie, so you should have told me.

"I started to write because I needed to get some of the shit out from inside my head, you know?" He's searching my face for reassurance. "It was so heavy in me."

Now that I *can* relate to.

"And then as the pages filled up, I started to enjoy the writing process itself, to remember how it felt to create worlds different to mine, to spend time thinking about a story that isn't my own."

He has no idea how much of a chord his words strike. Except I don't need to write my different world; I live it.

"So what, are you the hero of this story?"

It's a low blow, and I dislike myself for implying Jonah was anything but a hero to Freddie in real life.

Jonah's perched forward on the edge of his seat. "It's not that kind of thing," he says. "Like I said, it's not me and Freddie, not specifically. But he inspired it, so I wanted you to hear about it from me."

"Thanks for that," I say, feeling like a cow.

"Do you mind?" he asks.

"Did you think I would?" I don't meet his question with a question to be confrontational. I'm just trying to work out if my selfish feelings are in any way justified.

"I don't honestly know," he says, and I believe him. "I just didn't want you to think I've found a silver lining in all this, I guess."

"I don't think that," I say, and I sigh, because I've just put my finger on my real feelings for what they are and I'm not proud of myself. "I'm jealous of you, if anything."

He looks at me, incredulous. "Jealous?"

It's my turn to struggle for the right words. "I

just . . . it's heavy in me too, you know? You're going to be somewhere else, meet new people, be somewhere where the memories aren't everywhere you look."

He nods, and his eyes tell me that he knows better than most.

"You'll probably go to LA for the summer and decide you love it so much you'll never come home again."

Jonah comes and sits next to me. "I'll come home again, Lydia. I promise."

"You don't know that. They might make you an offer you can't refuse."

He looks doubtful. "It's early days. I could have just as easily had these meetings from here, Skype or something," he says. "I'm going there as much to get away from here as to go there, if that makes any sense."

"Kind of like running away," I say, dully.

"I don't like to think of myself as someone who runs away," he says. "But, yeah, maybe a bit."

We sit in silence for a minute, and I briefly entertain the idea of doing something similar, of catching a plane to the other side of the world for a while to see if life feels lighter there.

"So what? You're loosely planning to go to LA and hope things go well?"

"It feels like time for a change," he shrugs. "LA is as good a place as any."

Dee was partially right then; Jonah does need to get away, but hopefully not forever.

"Good for you, Jonah," I say softly, because I understand that in a roundabout way he's come here today to ask for my blessing. "I hope it's the start of something good for you."

"That means a lot to me," he says, sincere, grabbing my hand. "*You'll* always mean a lot to me, Lyds. I don't want us to ever lose our friendship."

Distant echoes of the hen night, my two worlds brushing close to each other. Here, thankfully, we are as we've always been. Old friends.

"Me neither," I say, squeezing his fingers.

He glances at the chair where Freddie used to sit, and then around my living room. "This place is starting to feel more like yours these days."

"You think?" I say, surprised by the idea. I haven't changed much; a new cushion here, a lamp there, a bohemian mirror I spotted on the way home from work the other day. I sort of understand what Jonah means though. It's inevitable I suppose, a necessary evolution as the shape of my life changes.

We fall quiet again, and then I tell him something I hadn't planned to.

"I've been seeing someone."

Jonah looks at me as if I've just grown a second head. "Seeing someone?"

"We met up a couple of times."

He shakes his head, as if it's the most outlandish thought. "I never imagined you dating someone else."

His judgment stings. "You're not the only one entitled to a life after him, you know."

He drops his arm over my shoulders and pulls me in against his side. "I didn't mean it that way. It's just . . . you and someone else. It feels weird."

He has no idea. "Imagine how it feels to me."

We sit there in silence for a while, his arm a comfortable weight, our heads tipped back against the sofa.

"Big shot movie man."

He laughs softly when I shoulder bump him. It's a familiarity I've missed more than I realized.

"Shall we get pizza?" he asks.

I look at the coffee table. It's held countless pizzas over the years, Freddie and Jonah's standard football dinner.

I guess it could stand one more.

I STAND ON the step and wave him off as he climbs back into the Saab just after nine. Jonah Jones in LA. Who knew? They'll eat him alive. Or maybe they won't. Perhaps he'll switch pizza for egg white omelets and industrial strength coffee for kale shots. As I close the door, I console myself with two things. One, he didn't declare himself in love with me, and two, at least it's not bloody Wales.

AWAKE

Saturday, July 20

IT'S RAINING. IT'S 6:30 on Saturday morning and rain is beating against my bedroom window, the remnants of a tropical storm rumbling its way across the Atlantic from the Caribbean. I'm in bed and today would have been my wedding day. Today is *still* my wedding day, somewhere in a world beyond my own. Is it raining cats and dogs there too? Are we all huddled in Mum's kitchen in our dressing gowns looking out the window, coffee mugs in our hands, cursing the rain-clouded skies? Or are we eating a celebratory early breakfast around the table together, not giving a hoot about the weather because it's my wedding day, and if needs be I'd marry Freddie Hunter in my jeans in a hailstorm? I hope it's that one.

My family has gone with the don't-mention-it approach in the run-up to today. Elle's at work; this is her final wedding at the hotel before she goes on parental leave. She's eight months pregnant now and trying not to let her bump protrude into the edges of people's wedding photographs, and Stef, who I've still to meet properly, has taken Mum away for the weekend. She made an absolute song and dance about telling Elle and me, suggesting that she was going to the Lakes, and that by some unholy coincidence Stef had booked to go to the same place at the same time, so they're traveling together to save on petrol. Even David, who never comments, had to raise the newspaper to eye level so Mum couldn't see him laughing.

Jonah left for LA a couple of days ago too, so all of the major players in my now nonexistent wedding are busy doing other things. Life's weird like that, isn't it? Today would have been full of wedding-related things for everyone; Mum pinning buttonholes on with her rollers in, Jonah nervously checking the rings were still in his pocket, neighbors nipping out into the street in their slippers to wave us off to church. And because none of those things are now going to happen, today has been filled with different things; work and the Lakes and LA, like a shelf in a shop being restocked for a new season. The only person who hasn't refilled the day with something else is me. I don't need to, because I'm still going to my wedding.

ASLEEP

Saturday, July 20

MY DRESS IS so very, incredibly beautiful. I'm standing in front of my mother's bedroom mirror, ready to go, alone and transfixed by the woman gazing back at me. I don't know what time it is, if I have minutes to spare or I'm running late as usual; either way I need a little more time to gather myself together. Someone has styled my hair over one shoulder, loose waves and twists intricately interwoven with fine plaits. I raise my fingertips to touch the twisted wire circlet of silver stars across my forehead; it looks as if it tumbled from the night skies. My dress isn't white; it's delicate shades of seafoam silk overlaid with net so gauzy I'm almost terrified to move. More tiny stars shimmer on the gown when I turn one way and then the other. Who knows where I found it; it's part mermaid, part moon goddess, ethereal and mesmerizing. I run my fingers over the bodice and find my gran's marcasite peacock pinned at my waist.

"The car's just pulled up, Lydia love."

Mum appears behind me in the doorway trying to fasten one of her favorite pearl earrings. She looks amazing in a Jackie O–style boat-neck dress in a deeper shade of seafoam with navy accessories.

"Carol Middleton's got nothing on you," I say, smiling through a film of tears because I now know how my mum looks on my wedding day.

"And you knock spots off Kate and Meghan." She walks forward and holds my hands; I notice her perfect nude manicure and the familiar liver spots she's tried every cream under the sun to get rid of.

"Ready to go?"

I nod. "Think so."

"Come on then." She gives my hands a final squeeze. "The sooner we get you married, the sooner I can get my hands on a gin and tonic."

IT ISN'T RAINING HERE. The skies are the lavender blue of French shutters when Elle helps me out of the car, her dark hair in a chignon at the nape of her neck, lovely in a strapless Mediterranean-blue dress. Victoria, the wedding organizer, is on hand trying to help too, and for a brief moment I feel as if she and Elle are in a tug-of-war and I'm the rope. Elle's eyes meet mine, and I wink to subtly remind her she's one of the wedding party rather than in charge of proceedings today. I see the reluctance in her eyes as she concedes to Victoria. She can't help herself; she's a born organizer and this has brought out her competitive side.

"Is he here?" I ask.

Victoria laughs. "Of course. Everyone's inside waiting for you."

The barn basks in the honey-gold sunshine, its huge doors fastened back to reveal glimpses of the interior as we head toward it. It looks a million times better than all of those staged wedding spreads in the glossy magazines, rustic and romantic and us, filled with flowers and creamy lit candles in the deep shady window recesses. I can smell honeysuckle and pine needles, and I can hear music I can't quite identify, and my heart is beating out of my chest with longing to see Freddie at the altar.

When we reach the entrance, Mum moves to one side of me, and Elle to the other, and we link hands. I don't think we'd planned on walking down the aisle as a three but I can't stop gripping Elle's hand so that's how we proceed. My mum, me, Elle. It was just the three of us so many years; around the breakfast table before school, Saturday evenings squished on the sofa fighting over the remote, piled into Mum's bed when one of us couldn't sleep. It's absolutely as it should be that we make this walk as a three today.

Music begins to play; there's a pianist, and as soon as he begins to sing a Beatles track I realize it's Jonah. Of course it's Jonah; who else would we ask to sing at our wedding?

People turn to see us, a change in atmosphere from relaxed to breath-held, a rustle of expectant voices, the excitement palpable. I'm bathed in shafts of warm sunlight, and up ahead I can see Freddie's back turned toward me. All around me I spy familiar faces; my work people, Phil and Susan beaming as if I'm their own child, Dawn tearful, Ryan almost on the verge too by the looks of him. Julia RSVP'd as soon as I sent out the invites to let me know she couldn't make it; they're visiting family in Ghana for her brother's sixtieth birthday celebrations.

Jonah sings of love and wonderful roses, and Auntie June catches hold of Mum's hand for a second and gives me a little thumbs-up as we pass—even my cousin Lucy manages to raise a smile from beneath her massive coral hat. I daren't look who's behind her, but whoever it is isn't going to see a thing. Freddie's family have gathered on the other side, distant relatives I'm less familiar with who always turn up at the promise of a free dinner, and the lads from the pub have scrubbed up in their suits that probably do service at weddings, funerals, and job interviews. His mum is up front in a vibrant orangey red dress that's more beach wedding than barn, but it doesn't matter because I'm almost level with Freddie now and he's turning to look at me. Oh, my heart. I step forward alone as his eyes sweep down the length of me and then back up to hold my gaze, and I'm so slammed by emotion that it's a wonder I stay on my feet.

"You're here," he whispers, as if he knows how far I've traveled to be here, and even though it's no doubt off script, he leans in and kisses me, his lips warm against mine.

"And you're here," I murmur, more wondrous still. He holds my hand, and I don't want to let go.

His laugh is soft, his words for my ears only. "As if I'd be anywhere else."

The celebrant clears her throat, ready to begin, and we listen as she welcomes everyone, telling them how thrilled we are they're here to share in our most special of days. She tells them we've chosen to write our own vows, which I nod along to, and then her words actually sink in and I realize that I've no clue what I was going to say. Panic flutters, a paper moth in my throat. I swallow it down as the celebrant turns to Freddie with a smile; at least he is to go first.

Freddie clears his throat, and then he clears it again for good measure. It's pin-drop quiet. For once his nerves are written all over his face.

"To be honest," he says, "I've struggled to know what to say today. Jonah's always been the wordsmith," he turns to glance at Jonah over his shoulder. "I even asked him for help with this, but he said it's the one bit of homework I need to do for myself."

People laugh softly, Jonah too as he shrugs in acknowledgment. He catches my eye, a fraction of a second at most, the ghost of an apology for the things he said on my hen night. I feel a jolt because in my waking life I'm already missing him, wondering if LA will become his permanent home.

Freddie waits for silence before he refocuses on me.

"Lyds, you were fourteen when I first saw you, all blond hair and legs that went on forever, and there I was with a BMX and a dodgy set of highlights put in by my mother," he glances behind him at his mum this time as people laugh again. For a nervous man, he's already got the crowd eating out of the palm of his hand.

"Christ knows why you—" He breaks off and hastily apologizes to the celebrant, who inclines her head, gracious, even though this isn't a religious ceremony. "I mean, God only knows why—" He stops again, and the celebrant does the tiniest of eye rolls as people laugh under their breath. Freddie waits for them to settle before he plows on.

"What I'm trying to say, in my own way and without swearing this time, is that I have no clue why you said yes to me, or how I've managed to hang on to you all these years. You're smarter than me, and you're kinder than me. You're so far out of my league that it's not even funny. But still you said yes, and that makes me the luckiest man alive."

His words are perfect because they are his.

"I know I drive you nuts sometimes, but I promise you this much—we're forever, you and me. I'll always look after you. I'll make sure you wear sun cream, and on cold mornings I'll button your winter coat. You light my world up, Lydia Bird, I don't want to do life without you."

Oh Freddie, I think, if only you knew. That's the deal we make when we love someone, isn't it? Somewhere along the path one person is always going to have to find a way to carry on without the other. Looking at Freddie now, I draw some small solace from the fact that he never had to know such heartbreak as I have in my waking world.

I'm struggling to hold it together. I can see Elle out of the corner of my eye; tears have streaked her makeup.

I won't let myself cry. I can't. I need to speak clearly, to say the things I never got to say.

"Freddie," I say, testing out my voice for steadiness. It isn't perfect. I swallow hard, clear my throat, and Freddie must be able to tell how close I am to falling apart because he reaches for my hand. There's a few moments silence, between us, and in the room all around us. Everyone waits, and I take a few calming breaths because these words matter more than any I've ever spoken.

"I look at you standing here today, Freddie, and my heart . . . well, I wonder how it can hold so many things inside it without bursting its seams." I raise his hand and lay it over my heart. "It's full of wishes and one days and if only's. It's full of our yesterdays, all of them gathered here in one place for safekeeping. It's full of our tomorrows too. The faces of our children, all the places we'd go, our triumphs and our hardships." I lay my hand on his chest too now; his heartbeat beneath my palm, mine beneath his. "My life has been meshed with yours since I was fourteen years old." He stares into my eyes, and we are connected. I feel him profoundly, in every atom of my body, in every version of our world revolving around every version of the sun. "Time changes everything in the end, Freddie, and I've realized now that that's okay, because what we have is more than just here, or just now. You and me, we're all the time, and we're always, and we're everywhere. If I live a million lifetimes, I'll find you in all of them, Freddie Hunter."

I look at him, and he looks at me, and we cry. Not great heaving sobs that make everyone uncomfortable, but small silent streams that become rivers and then seas. I want to remember us this way always.

The celebrant is about to declare us husband and wife, and I can't wait to hear the words spoken aloud, for her to declare us married, and the bells are ringing, and ringing, and ringing, louder and ever more insistent. I'm shaking, physically shaking with the sudden, herculean effort of just staying here. I can't keep a limb still. The bell doesn't sound like a wedding bell anymore, and however hard I try and however much I don't want to, I'm splicing away from them, spiraling through darkness, and my pajamas are damp with sweat from the effort. How can I be wearing my pajamas? I can still hear the wedding bells. But then I realize; it isn't bells. It's my mobile; blaring and fractious on my bedside table, beckoning to me from one world into the next. I can't bear the noise nor the feelings of absolute, savage distress as I grope for it, still half asleep. Maybe I can go back. Maybe, if I can just hang on to the vestiges of sleep, I can tumble through the barn door again before it closes. Even as I cling to these thoughts, I see the neon blue name on my phone screen through my lashes. Elle. I barrel awake, terrified.

"Lyds, I'm on my own." My sister's voice is so pain-twisted I barely recognize it. "The baby . . . Help."

AWAKE

Saturday, July 20

I'M THERE BEFORE the ambulance arrives, still in my pj's. I dialed 9-9-9 from my landline; Elle still with me on my mobile. "Hold on," I told her, panicking because I couldn't find my car keys, shoving my feet into my boots as I stumbled out onto the pavement. "They're coming, I'm coming, blink and I'll be there," I said.

From what she's managed to tell me in short, jerky gasps, I know the baby is coming, David is away with work, and she doesn't know why it's so bad so fast. I don't either; my only experience of childbirth to date has been the pregnant fairground goldfish I won when we were kids. We called her Ariel, for obvious reasons, and watched in fascinated horror when she delivered a snowstorm of eggs several days later, disinterestedly puffing them out behind her like a fake snow machine in need of new batteries. I've got that and a few episodes of *Call the Midwife* under my belt; neither of those things have even slightly qualified me to be the only person around when my sister goes into labor.

All of this flashes through my mind as I screech to a halt on her street five minutes away, feeling through my keys for the one to her front door as I dash up the garden path. I have her key and my mum's; another thing they insisted on after the accident.

"I'm here, Elle, I'm here," I bend to shout through the letter box, finding the right key at last and jabbing it at the lock. I leave the door on the latch for the ambulance crew before I dash upstairs; something from *Call the Midwife* must have sunk in after all.

She's sitting on the edge of her bed, at the end, her arms gripped around the wooden bedpost as if she's on a sinking ship. Her dark hair is plastered to her head with sweat, and her face is a study of panic and relief rolled into one when I kneel in front of her and put my hands on her knees.

"It's too early, Lyds," she whispers, staring at me wide eyed. She's shaking hard enough to make her teeth rattle. "Four weeks."

"That's okay," I tell her, because the ambulance dispatcher assured me it should be when I asked ten minutes ago. "Babies are born safely at eight months all the time."

Elle doesn't answer; she can't because her body is gripped by what must be another contraction, twisting her up with pain, making her moan like a wounded animal. It subsides slowly, and I move to sit beside her, my arm around her shoulders when she slumps against me.

"How long between contractions?" I ask, even

though I don't really know what the answer should be. "Roughly?"

"Not enough," she breathes, when she can. "Nowhere near enough."

"Okay," I say, rubbing her back. There's blood on her legs, but I don't say anything. "Shall we do some breathing exercises?"

I hope she knows what to do because it's a surefire fact I don't. I wish I had taken more interest when she told me about the NCT classes she'd been to. That I hadn't been so bloody self-absorbed. Thankfully, Elle nods and breathes in more deeply than she has since I arrived, exhaling on a long hiss.

"You sound like a balloon going down," I say, and she half laughs, half cries.

"I *feel* like a fucking balloon," she gulps, and we both laugh a bit shaky, a bit hysterical. "What if the baby comes before the ambulance gets here?" she says, more crying than laughing again.

"Then we'll cope," I say, with far more conviction than I feel. If that ambulance doesn't get here before this baby does I'm going to have a breakdown. I can't even watch *Casualty*.

"We won't," she says, fearful. "What if something happens to my baby and no one's here to help?" she says. I notice her breath starting to shallow, and within seconds her face contorts with agony again. By my reckoning, that's two minutes. Definitely not three. Two is a frighteningly small number.

"I'm here. I'll help you. They'll get here, Elle, but if they don't, we can do this together, okay?"

She stares into my eyes, and I look right back, unflinching, cast iron. "Okay?"

She swallows. "It's too late to get to the hospital."

"So we won't go," I say.

"David isn't here," she says, and her face crumples.

"No," I say. "He isn't. I am though, and I won't leave your side until he is, okay? I called him, he's on his way."

She squeezes my hand, and I look down at her pale, tight grip. Elle and I used to hold hands when we were scared as kids; camping in the back garden at five years old, when dad appeared out of the blue on my ninth birthday, at our grandfather's funeral when I'd just turned twenty-one. It's as instinctive as it is comforting. I hope she draws the same strength from it as I do.

"Thank you," she says. Her lip wobbles and she sounds about ten years old, and I realize that right now, I need to step up and be the big sister.

"I think you should probably lie down," I say.

"I don't know if I can."

"Yes, you can," I say, firm. "Come on, let's do it right now before the next contraction comes."

Together we manage to shuffle her up against the pillows just in time, and she draws her knees in and starts to puff. Where's that sodding ambulance? There's fresh blood streaked on the sheets where she's moved. I try not to think about it; I don't know if it's normal or not.

"I'm sorry to do this to you today of all days," she sobs out, breathless with pain.

A fleeting image of my wedding scrolls in front of my eyes; my seafoam dress, Freddie's broad smile, Elle and Mum walking me down the aisle. "Don't be daft," I say. "I was at a bit of a loose end."

Elle and I share an age-old look that doesn't need any words, and then she screws her eyes closed and her hands clench into fists as a new contraction rolls over her. I've never felt so helpless. I reach for her hand when she opens her eyes again.

"I wouldn't," she warns. "I can't guarantee I won't break your fingers."

I laugh because we've heard Mum's labor story so many times. "I wouldn't want you to ruin my chances of being a champion surfer," I say, not letting go.

"Lydia, it's happening now, I think I can feel the baby coming," Elle gasps. "I need to push," she says, urgent, one protective arm around her bump, the other behind her head gripping the headboard. Her knuckles stand out stark white against her skin.

"Can you hold on?" I ask, baring my teeth, bracing for the impact of the answer I know is coming.

"No!" she half screams, her face the color of boiled beetroot with effort. I don't think about it; I move around to the other end of the bed.

"I'm going to have to see if I can see anything, Elle," I say, far braver than I feel.

"Okay." She's crying. "Please don't let my baby die, Lyds. Don't let the cord choke her or anything."

I can barely see through the film of tears, but I can see enough to know that the ambulance crew isn't going to be here in time.

"I think I can see the top of the baby's head," I tell her, moving closer, trying to remember any birth I've ever seen or read about. Ariel isn't cutting it.

"Listen to me, Elle," I say, looking up at her between her knees. "When you're ready, you need to push until I say stop, and then for God's sake stop so I can check the cord isn't around her neck, okay?"

She's terrified but she nods, and in seconds the pain is on her again.

"Good," I say. "Good girl. Now push."

I watch, breathless as the baby's small face slowly, miraculously appears, scrunched up and puce. "Now stop," I say loudly, Elle's knee braced against my shoulder. I gently feel around the baby's neck and thank every god there is that the cord isn't there. "It's okay, she's okay," I say, nodding vigorously. "You can push again when you're ready."

She nods vigorously too, and then she's screaming, and in the distance I can hear sirens.

"Come on, Elle, we've got this," I half shout, my hands on the baby's head as her shoulders start to emerge. I help as much as I can, cupping the tiny body, maneuvering, encouraging Elle for one last push to press the slippery, gunky, wondrous child from her body into my hands.

"Don't drop her, will you?" she pants.

"I won't let go, Elle. I promise." It isn't lost on me that it's the second time I've made solemn promises in recent hours. I can't process it; it's too much. But then all thoughts but here and now are pushed aside; a brand-new life taking her first lungful of air in my hands. "She's here, she's here! We bloody did it! I told you we could!" I'm laughing and crying with sheer relief, we both are, and I drag a sheet from the bed and wrap it around the mewling, wriggling baby. I pass her over and Elle cradles her precious child in her arms.

"The ambulance is coming, I can hear it," I say quietly.

"Thank you," she says, her mouth trembling.

I lean in and hug her, careful not to squash my new niece. The sirens get louder and then stop, here at last.

"You were brilliant," I say.

"You too," she whispers, still sobbing, sagging with relief.

"I've never delivered a baby before," I say, as if this is news to either of us.

"You're forgetting Ariel," she says, as if it counts for previous midwifery experience.

"True. She didn't make half as much of a song and dance about it, either."

"Hello?" a male voice calls, and we can hear boots on the stairs.

"In here," I call.

Two medics dressed in dark green appear in short succession, a balding man and a tall woman with a blond ponytail, both standing at the foot of the bed assessing the situation as they introduce themselves as Andy and Louise.

"Looks like you've had a busy morning, love," Andy says, grinning at Elle.

"She's a girl," Elle smiles.

"Okay if I check her over?" Louise perches next to Elle and carefully examines the baby. I step away to let them do their thing, watching as the cord is clamped and then cut.

"Could I ask you to hold the baby while we check Elle?" Louise asks.

I'm relieved someone else is in charge as she places the swaddled child in my arms. I take her over to the window as the medics tend to Elle, their words washing over me, background noise as I study this new human. I stroke my fingertip down the brow of her tiny nose, featherlight, across the down of her cheeks. My niece. She isn't purple anymore, more of a beautiful peach, downy and still a little blood smeared. Her mouth puckers when I touch her bottom lip, instinctive, full-on Maggie Simpson suction. How clever you are already, I think, knowing how to survive. I hope you always have that in you. When she wriggles and her hand emerges, I place my finger against her palm. Tiny, translucent fingers curl around mine, the most fragile thing I've seen in my life. I stare at her dewy newness, and I realize with a jolt that in the next world over she doesn't even exist. "Oh," I whisper. She's been in my world for only minutes, and already she has widened the space between here and there. There, Elle is not a mother. There, this child didn't make it. I don't know what it all means; but suddenly I realize how very tired I am. The last twenty-four hours have been heavy to say the least. I'm almost relieved when it's time to hand the baby back to Elle, who by now is sitting up in bed looking far more normal than I'd imagine someone could look after jettisoning a whole new person into the world. I overheard Louise soothing Elle's concerns about the speed with which the baby arrived; it takes as long as it takes, apparently. She's delivered more than one baby in the back of the ambulance, even one at the base of an escalator in a shopping center once. Better than toiling through two days of hard labor she said, which I guess is true.

I hand the baby back to Elle and then nip onto the landing to call David to tell him that mum and baby are fine and he should get back pronto. He goes into meltdown; I have to be firm and tell him to stop panicking and pull himself together.

"Do you have to go to hospital?" I ask, sitting carefully on the edge of the bed when Louise and Andy head downstairs.

She shakes her head. "No. Louise is trying to get my midwife on the phone to ask her to come and see me, check me over again." She looks down at the baby. "And this one too."

For a moment, we both gaze at the sleeping child. I'm not surprised she's zonked out; however difficult the last hour or two was for Elle and me, it was even more eventful for her.

"Any names yet?" I ask. They've knocked so many options around in the last few months and weeks that I've lost track.

Elle studies her daughter. "We'd settled on Charlotte, but now she's here I'm not sure she looks like one."

"Hmm," I say, considering. "How about . . . Lydia Ariel Peach?"

Elle's smile is tired but there. "There's only room for one Lydia in my life."

And yet there are two of everyone else in mine, I think. Two of everyone, apart from Freddie and this little girl.

"David shouldn't be too long."

"I can't wait for him to get here," she says.

I eye the bloodstained sheets. "Why don't I make you some toast, and you can sit in the chair and eat it while I change the bed. Make it all a bit less . . . err . . . *Alien*?"

Her mouth twitches. She knows how I am with gore. "Was it awful for you at the business end?"

"Oddly not," I say. "Being the first person in the world to see this little lady was pretty special, to be honest." It's a sweeping understatement. People say all kinds of flowery things when they witness a birth; they call it a miracle, or life changing, or precious. For me it was all of those things and so much more–it was pure, human magic. Elle performed the magic trick of all magic tricks right in front of my eyes today. My sister is a sorceress, and her daughter is a masterpiece.

THEY'RE BOTH ASLEEP when David comes hurtling through the door a little later, taking the stairs two at a time. I'm dozing in the armchair, and I startle awake as he comes into the room breathing heavily.

"They're fine," I say quietly as he approaches the bed, and Elle opens her eyes and sees him. And the look on her face . . . it's everything. It's I love you, look what I did, I'm so glad you're here.

The look on his face . . . it's everything too. It's I love you more, look at this wonderful thing you did, I'm so proud of you, my super human.

He sits beside her, and she slides into his arms, crying again, but this time with sheer joy because her new family is at last together for the first time. I soak in their pleasure, and then slowly back out of the room because I don't want to intrude on their first moments as three. They don't notice, and that's okay. It's as it should be.

I STAYED LONG enough to find out that they settled on Charlotte after all. David carried her cautiously downstairs to give Elle a chance to take a very careful shower. We sat on the sofa examining Charlotte's miniature hands and feet, her gangly limbs waiting to plump out, her shock of dark hair. David thinks she favors Elle; I think he's probably right. The midwife came, brisk and efficient with her scales. Charlotte weighed in at a healthy 5lbs 4oz, which is apparently great going for a month early.

I'm back home again now with a cup of tea. But now I'm here I don't think the house has ever felt this empty, and nor have I ever felt this lonely. The silence is acute; I could switch on the radio, but I don't think I could stand the inane chatter or banal laughter. I sat here in this same chair yesterday morning, sickly nervous with nerves about my wedding. Now I'm exhausted to my bones. I feel strange . . . untethered, which is odd really, having just witnessed something as fundamentally grounding as birth. Perhaps I've hit emotional overload; getting married and delivering a baby all in the space of twelve hours can do that to a person. I can't easily explain it. It's a feeling of disconnection, like distant clicks on the line when you call overseas. Elle has moved to another country now, somewhere I can visit but not stay. Everyone around me is moving forward, away from me; Mum with Stef, Elle and the baby, Jonah in LA.

My poor, strained heart. You know those old-fashioned music boxes lined with mirrors angled to reflect the slowly revolving ballerina from every angle? I have one somewhere with colorful birds painted on the lid; Jonah gave it to me for a birthday when we were still schoolkids. I imagine myself like that ballerina, a myriad spinning versions of me.

I'm so damn tired and it's too much effort to get upstairs to bed, so I drag myself as far as the sofa and collapse, curled on my side, my face in my hands to block out the daylight. I'd cry myself to sleep if I had the energy; I deserve a bloody good sob given the hours I've just lived through. But I don't have the energy, and I don't think I have any tears left in me either. I feel tinder dry, a parched pile of leaves that would catch alight at the merest hint of a flame. As I close my eyes I see the leaves scatter on the breeze, some here, some there, pieces of me drifting away.

IT'S DARK AGAIN when I wake up. I passed out into a dreamless sleep and now I'm wide awake at ten o'clock at night and seized by the urge to do something, to go somewhere, to take myself away from here. I'm not at work this week or next; I booked it off without mentioning that if things had been different, Freddie and I would be in New York on my honeymoon. I told Dawn that I'm planning to redecorate the kitchen, and I told Phil and Susan that I'm going to a spa with Mum and

Elle before the baby comes. I'm not doing either of those things. I've blocked this time out to spend at home, a back-to-back string of visits to my other world. Crazy as it sounds, I'm going on my honeymoon.

But it occurs to me now that I don't need to stay at home; have pills, will travel. In fact, the more I think about it, the more it makes sense to get away. If I stay here there will be demands on my time. Elle, the baby, Mum. If I go away, there will be no one but myself to think about or plan for. My heart is racing with adrenaline; I'm gripped by the idea of being somewhere else. It's a need, not a want. My mind races around the options: beaches, mountaintops, oceans. Where can I go? I mean, I could actually try to get on a plane to New York. I consider it for a few minutes, but then I decide that it'd be too weird even on my scale of weird to be there in both of my lives simultaneously. Upstairs, I practically run through the shower and change, throwing clothes and underwear into my suitcase dragged from the spare room, sunglasses, sandals. I know myself well enough to know that I don't want to end up somewhere cold. *Sunshine.* I need to turn my face up to the sun and feel it coat my skin in hot, sticky warmth. Bag packed in a fashion, I drag it downstairs and hunt out my passport from the kitchen drawer. It's in an envelope with Freddie's, and for a few moments I hold them both against my chest, imagining us queuing at the airport with them clutched tightly in our excited hands. I daren't look at his now; I need to stay in this frame of mind, the one that's going to carry me all the way to a new place. I can't wait it out until morning comes. I can't wait even another hour, so I call a cab and drag my suitcase out onto the footpath and wait in the street. I push some money and a scribbled apology note through Agnes's letter box; I feel obliged to ask her to watch Turpin, even though he practically lives with her anyway, and he won't give a damn if I'm not around. There's no one else to leave a note for to alert them to my madness. I'll message Mum when I'm sure where I'm going, but for now I lock the doors and fling myself into the cab when it pulls up, exhilarated. I can't shake the feeling that someone or something will stop me, grab ahold of my arm and tell me I can't go, but no one does. I'm on my own. Captain of my own ship, albeit one who has no idea where she's navigating toward.

I STAND IN the departures lounge and gaze at the board, bewildered. It's only now that the first fingers of doubt begin to tap lightly on my shoulder. Truth is I feel a bit unhinged, standing here in the middle of the airport on my own with a hastily packed suitcase, a half-empty bottle of pink pills, and my passport. No one knows I'm here. I could turn around and go home, no one would be any the wiser. It's tempting; I consider it. Everywhere I look there are couples and families, tired kids on iPads and hen parties making a beeline for the bar. I definitely don't want to go anywhere where there are hen parties. I don't know what to do so I stand still and let everyone move around me, snippets of conversations, traces of duty-free perfume.

"Okay love?" someone says, and I turn to see a security guard. "You've been standing there awhile now," he says. "Need some help?"

He has a lived-in sort of face, as if he's seeing out the last few years before retirement. I expect he's asking me if I need directions to my check-in desk, but our conversation may as well serve a bigger purpose. He doesn't know it, but he's just become second in command on this ship.

"I do, actually," I say. "Where would you go if you could go anywhere right now?"

Ted, whose name I know from his name badge, looks at me oddly, thrown by the question.

"Home?" he says.

I half laugh, desperate, because it's the absolute wrong answer. "No, I mean abroad. If you could fly somewhere right now, where would you go?"

He eyes my suitcase and then me, assessing. What's he thinking, I wonder? On the run from the police? Jilting someone at the altar? I belatedly hope I haven't asked the least suitable person in the entire building for help; this guy could probably detain me. His hand rests on the radio on his belt, his thick gold wedding ring tucked into a well-worn groove on his finger.

"Well," he says slowly. "I'd probably go for somewhere with good internet connection so I could let someone know where I was when I get there."

It's fatherly; terribly endearing to this fatherless girl.

"I will," I say, and then nod at the departures board again. "So, where?"

Ted sighs, as if he'd really rather me turn around and go home instead. "You might be better seeing what's actually available. Head over to the sales booths rather than the check-in desks."

He points me in the direction of kiosks lining the far wall, illuminated in red and yellows. "Oh, I see," I say. There's quite a lot of them, a dozen or more, so I throw a different question at Ted. "A number between one and twelve?"

He rolls his eyes. "Six."

Six. It's as good as any. "Thank you, Ted," I say, feeling a bit awkward, as if I should hug him or something. "I should . . . er . . . you know. Go."

He steps aside and waves me along. "On your way then," he says. "And don't forget to call home."

I nod. He's right; I should call Mum at least, but I daren't yet for fear of her talking me out of it before I can even get off the ground. Tomorrow is soon enough, Mum's more than busy right now trying to get home from the Lakes to see her new granddaughter.

Right. Six. I approach the wall of kiosks and walk along, ticking them off in my head as I go. Kiosk one: United Airlines. I don't think I can go to the United States without visas and all that gubbins, so that would be a nonstarter anyway. Two: Air France. Bit too close; I can't guarantee Mum wouldn't come and get me. Besides, Paris. Three: Qantas. Too far away. I want to get away, but not as far away as I can possibly go. Four: Emirates. Hmm. I don't think the bling and glitz of Dubai is what my soul needs right now. Aer Lingus is at five; another no-go purely on proximity. Okay. Kiosk six glows orange and red, welcoming me. Beckoning me, almost. Air India. Nerves grumble low in my gut. I'd sort of imagined myself heading out to the Balearics or Portugal, but something about the thought of India feels suddenly appealing. It's far enough away to put me out of Mum's reach, and it's different enough to be exactly what I need—not that I knew it until this very second. I've never imagined myself traveling anywhere alone, let alone somewhere as unknown to me. Some of the desks have been closed up for the night, but as luck would have it, there's a guy perched at the kiosk who looks up and catches my eye.

"You need some help?" he asks, smiling at me. It's welcoming, and I move nearer.

"I think I'd like to go to India," I say, ever so slightly slower than usual, as if I'm testing the words out.

"Excellent," he says. "Where in India were you planning to fly to?"

"Oh," I say, feeling foolish. "Right. Well, where can I fly to soonest?"

If my answer surprises him, he's professional enough not to show it. He taps his keyboard, and I wait, crossing my fingers under the desk that he doesn't tell me there are no imminent flights.

"There's a flight to Delhi in two hours and twenty-seven minutes," he says.

"That one," I say, gripped.

"But it's full I'm afraid," he says, arranging his features into a sympathetic smile.

I'm crushed. I've known about the flight for less than thirty seconds, and already it's a missed opportunity.

The attendant checks his watch. "The next flight after that is at two nineteen, but it's to Goa."

He looks at me as if that might be a deal breaker, but whether it's Delhi or Goa makes no difference to me. "Is there a seat?"

A few more taps, a thoughtful twist of his mouth, and then a decision. "There is."

My credit card is out of my bag and on the desk before I speak again. "I'll take it."

For the smallest of microseconds, his ultra-professional expression falters. "You're sure now?"

"Do I look like someone who isn't sure?" I ask. "I have a suitcase and my passport right here."

"And your visa is in order?"

My heart sinks. "I need a visa to go to India?"

His sympathetic expression is laced with irritation now. "Of course, but you can obtain it easily online."

I have my phone in my hand, hopeful again. "Now? I could do that now?"

"You certainly could, madam, but it takes two days to process."

I could cry. In fact I think I'm horribly close to it as I slide my credit card back into my purse.

"Thanks anyway," I say, shaking my head. "But I need to get away tonight."

He looks genuinely regretful as I wheel my case away, probably at the loss of commission.

The next desk is one of the major holiday operators with their own airline, so I drag my case up to the bored-looking girl behind the desk, and wiser from my India disappointment, I try a new, more targeted tack.

"I'd like the next available seat on the next available flight to a warm country that doesn't require a visa, please."

Her eyes open wide behind her cat's-eye glasses.

"Right," she says, clicking her mouse to bring her computer to life as she shoves the sandwich she'd been eating in her drawer. Looking up at the clock on the wall, she makes a clicking noise behind her teeth, thinking.

"You could just about make the Majorca flight, the desk closes in ten minutes," she says. I know I said the next seat on the next flight, but I've been to Majorca in the past and it summons Freddie memories I don't need right now.

"What's next after that one?" I ask.

She gives me an ever so slightly cynical look over her glasses before she checks, as if she half admired my opening boldness and I've let her down by being picky.

"Ibiza at twenty past one."

"I was hoping for somewhere a bit less touristy," I say.

"Have you been there before?"

I shake my head.

"It might surprise you. There's different sides to the island, it's not party central outside of San Antonio. Or you always could hop over to Formentera if you're looking for somewhere a bit more hippy."

I'm caught in indecision as she taps her long dark blue fingernails on the keyboard again and narrows her eyes.

"Or otherwise it looks like there's one seat left on the three forty-five flight to Split."

"Split?"

"It's in Croatia."

I hand over my credit card.

AWAKE

Sunday, July 21

IT'S STRANGE BEING on a plane when you really think about it, isn't it? Neither on land nor in space, hurtling through the celestial hinterlands in a tin can. The family next to me are trying to coax their disinterested toddler to eat his distinctly unappetizing airline breakfast so I lean my head against the window and try to tune them out. I gaze instead across the carpet of meringue cloud below the plane. Nigella wouldn't be at all satisfied with it, I think, it's wispy and insubstantial rather than stiff, glossy peaks. Burnished rose and yellow streak the dawn skies, and as I gaze out beyond the clouds I can see a scattering of distant stars. Is my other world out there somewhere too? Am I closer to it than usual right now? Would the contrails of this flight be visible there? It's a terribly beguiling idea. Maybe the pilot will take a wrong turn across the heavens and we'll touch down there by mistake. As I close my eyes and drift toward sleep, my brain throws up a memory of a quote Elle used to have on her bedroom wall, a *Peter Pan* poster I think. *Second star to the right, and straight on till morning.*

I HADN'T REALLY considered the reality of being in a foreign land until just now. This trip has been more about getting away rather than arriving. But now as I look down and see landmass ringed by hundreds of tiny islands and boats with frilly tadpole wakes, I feel the first rumbles of doubt. Hundreds of redbrick monopoly houses scatter the verdant mainland as we come in low, the occasional splash of swimming pool blue reminding me that I'm somewhere warmer than home. I don't know anything about this place besides its name, and I have no idea what I'm going to do when I leave the airport. It's an adventure, of sorts, but I'm not someone who under usual circumstances would consider themselves an adventurous kind of person. Under usual circumstances; perhaps that's the difference. I haven't lived my life under usual circumstances since Freddie died.

I make it through passport control and baggage reclaim by following the herd, and then I'm swept up in the bump and swell of suitcases out through the exit doors. I'm instantly enveloped by heat. I step aside and stand still for a few moments, gathering myself beneath the huge, space-age overhead sunshades. Bloody hell. I'm in Croatia. I have no idea what the language sounds like or is similar to, and the money I exchanged at the airport is unrecognizable to my eyes. I doubt I could even accurately pinpoint this place on a map. I think briefly, longingly, of home, of Mum and Elle and the baby, and I resolve to call them as soon as I've found somewhere to be. I raise my hand to my eyes, almost like a sailor scanning the horizon while I take in my options. There are buses around, but I don't know where to buy a ticket. There are coaches, but I guess they're package tour operators. Then I spy a line of cabs, and I'm chewing my lip, considering, when a guy approaches me.

"You need taxi?"

I'm encouraged enough by the fact he speaks English to reply.

"I'm not sure where I want to go," I say.

"You want parties?"

I frown. I don't know if it's a general question or a proposition. He looks decent enough, but you never know, do you?

"Or you need quiet place for reading books?"

Ah, it was a general question.

"That one," I say, quickly. "Quiet. Reading is good too."

He looks at his watch. "My wife has a room to rent."

"She does?"

He nods. "In Makarska."

I've no idea where that is.

"She keeps a restaurant. The room is above. Close to beach."

"Is it far?"

He shrugs. "A little."

Again, I've no idea how to quantify that.

"Umm . . ." I say, trying to decide if it's good fortune

or I'm about to be murdered and thrown off a cliff. Then something tells me to just go for it. "Okay."

He breaks into a genuine smile and it changes his face. "I take you now. Vita will give you chicken for free, on my house."

I'm guessing Vita must be his wife, unless he's talking about himself in the third person, which would be weird. He takes my case in one hand, and wipes his other on his short-sleeved checked shirt before holding it out to me. I really hope he doesn't mean a live chicken.

"Petar," he says.

"Lydia," I reply, and I put my hand in his with a tentative smile. He pumps my arm, briefly and quite unmurderously, I'd say.

"This way," he says. I'm relieved when he leads me to a white people carrier in a line of similar cabs, pausing to slap the shoulder of another driver through his open window. I'm bolstered. People know this man here and appear to like him. I'm starting to believe meeting Petar is a stroke of good luck; God knows it must be my turn for some.

VITA IS MY new favorite person. She looked me over for a few silent seconds when Petar produced me from his taxi, a shepherd with his lost sheep, and she nodded and hugged me. She caught me off guard and I stood there stiff as a board in the middle of their shaded family restaurant, still clutching the pull-along handle of my suitcase. It wasn't an over-enthusiastic, clap on the back kind of hug; it was more of a simple therapeutic folding of her arms around me, and then she stepped back and looked into my eyes and into my head all at once.

"You can stay with me."

She unhooks my heavy flight bag from my shoulder and hangs it over her own as she speaks. "Your secrets are your own here."

It's such a simple yet profound thing to say. Is my life story written all over my face, there to be read by anyone who takes the time to notice? Or is Vita some kind of mystic, able to read my mind without the need for words? I'm not fanciful enough to believe in all of that stuff, but there is something about Vita, about her quiet calmness, that I'm drawn to. She's a little taller than me and probably a decade or so older; slender and understated in jeans and a faded red apron, her dark hair drawn back from her makeup-free face.

"Follow me. I'll show you the room."

She dismisses her husband with a wave and inclines her head to direct me toward the open patio doors.

I do as she's asked and find myself stepping out onto the restaurant's beachfront terrace. For a moment, I'm too dazzled to speak. Dazzled by the quality of the morning sunlight, by the warmth, by the glitter of the ocean. I stand among the simple wooden tables and chairs and turn my face up to the warmth, and a wash of something like freedom slides over my skin. No one knows me here. No one knows my story. I can just be.

"This is you," she says, calling out. "Up here."

I leave my case at the bottom of the stone staircase running up the side of the restaurant and follow her, waiting behind her when she fishes in her apron pocket for a key. The room is spotless and plain; white walls, a low wooden double bed with clean sheets folded on a red mattress. There's a monastic simplicity to it that I appreciate as Vita opens the shuttered double doors to reveal a small balcony overlooking the sea. A single wooden deckchair, low slung with a red cushion. There's no call for art on the walls in here with a view like that.

"There's a bathroom through there," she says, pointing toward a closed door.

"It's just what I was looking for," I say, even though up to now I had no real idea what I was looking for. "Thank you."

She nods as if it's a given as she explains the weekly cost. "Or you can help downstairs, if you'd prefer? Mornings, evenings. It's our busy time."

So I have a room, and now I have a job too if I want one. How easy, I think, to reinvent myself, to be someone else.

"Okay." I smile, and laugh a little. "I might do that. Can I think about it for a day or two?"

"Of course," she says. "Take a couple of days for yourself first. Get used to the place." She hands me the key. "It's yours for as long as you need it."

I fold my fingers around the key as she leaves. As long as you need it, she said. It's distinct from as long as you want it; I get the feeling Vita knows the subtle difference perfectly well.

I sigh as I walk out onto the balcony. This place. It's like something from a postcard, eye-popping colors, a scattering of simple buildings, an easy sense of unhurried calm. I'm in Croatia, in a town I can't even recall the name of. This time yesterday I was at home surrounded by people who know me. Today I'm a stranger in a foreign land. It's a weight off my shoulders.

"WHAT THE HELL do you mean, you're in Croatia?" Mum shouts, the brief delay on her voice evidence of our distance. "You were here yesterday."

"I know," I say. I've been on the phone for about thirty seconds and the conversation spiraled from hello darling to this pretty quickly. "It was, umm, a spontaneous thing, Mum." I falter, trying to explain away the fact that I ran away from home.

"But your sister has just had a baby," Mum says, incredulous even from two thousand miles away.

"I do know that," I say, mild. "I was there."

"But Lydia . . ." she runs out of words. "Why?"

Why. There you go again, Mum, straight to the heart of it.

"I don't know," I say. "I just . . . I needed to get away for a while."

She pauses. I can hear the upset in her silence. "How long for?"

I don't know, so I tell her what she wants to hear. "A week or so. Maybe two. I'm off work."

"And then you'll come home again?"

"What else am I going to do?"

"I honestly don't know, Lydia," she says.

Her tone suggests she's worn out by my unpredictability, which rankles with me because I'm hardly a bloody tearaway.

"What's that supposed to mean?"

I hear her sigh. "Nothing, love," she says. "I just worry about you, that's all."

"I'm just on holiday," I say, brushing her concerns aside as if they are unwarranted and unnecessary. I can see her in my mind's eye, standing in her hallway, frowning, twisting her necklace around her fingers. "I'll message you a picture of the view. I'm going to read books on the beach. Lie in the sun. Eat too much, drink too much. Just chill out for a week or so, that's all."

I don't tell her about the job offer.

I COULDN'T FACE calling Elle after my call with Mum, so I texted her instead, a preemptive strike in case Mum calls her in a tizz. That was yesterday evening and she hasn't replied yet, but then I expect she's got more pressing things on her mind than checking her phone. Counting toes, buttoning sleep suits, kissing the pronounced curve of tiny cheeks. Those kind of things. I press all thoughts of home and the baby to the back of my mind and bring myself back to here, to my now.

I don't tell her about the job offer either.

IT'S A LITTLE after nine in the evening, and I'm sitting on my balcony watching the evening unfold. Vita and Petar made me welcome downstairs for dinner just now, feeding me delicious baked chicken and rice, refilling my glass with local wine, introducing me to the staff. Down below the restaurant terrace is buzzing with activity, every candlelit table alive with families and lovers, suntanned shoulders and flashes of laughter, children perched on the terrace edge with their toes in the cooling sand, the clatter of cutlery on china, babies sleeping in pushchairs. It's a movie perfect scene that's no doubt repeated all across the Med tonight; white lights strung from pine trees, the lingering scent of salt and sunscreen from the beach, people gathered together as stars emerge in the darkening sky. Perhaps it's the sunshine or the holiday vibe but my mood already feels a little lighter here, my heart too.

My phone is in my lap as I flop back in the deckchair, wineglass in my other hand. Petar insisted I bring the rest of the bottle up with me. It's heady with blackcurrants and spice, and it's dulling my edges nicely. Still no reply from Elle. In my haste to get away I didn't stop to consider her feelings, but I honestly don't think for a minute that she'll begrudge me this. Her every waking moment must be filled with baby-related thoughts; she's learning how to be a mum and I have no pearls of wisdom to offer her there. If anything, my absence will probably be a bit of a relief, although she'd never say as much.

I sip a little more wine, and my phone buzzes. Elle at last.

> Croatia? WTF, Lyds, did the sight of my ladybits send you running for the airport? Am already knackered. Come back soon, miss you. x

I smile, and then hold in a little gulp-cry when an angelic photo of a sleeping Charlotte pings in.

> She looks a lot cleaner than the last time I saw her, thank

God! I type. Too beautiful for words, sis, you did good. Blowing kisses in your direction. Xx

I press send, smiling as my words head across the seas toward home. The baby is gorgeous. I'm not going to get a look in with that child. It's as well that I've stepped back for a little while, give everyone else a chance to cluster around and press tiny sleep suits and gifts into Elle and David's hands as they clamor for a hold. David has quite a clan, and Mum won't be able to stop herself from camping out on Elle's doorstep.

Something in me settles, soothed by Elle's acceptance of my leaving.

I ignore my phone the second time it buzzes, then pick it up moments later feeling guilty. My first emotion is relief; it isn't another unbearably gorgeous baby picture. My second emotion is harder to identify so I don't try; it's Jonah calling me from LA.

I scrabble to answer before he hangs up.

"Hey," I say, tucking my hair behind my ear as I sit up straighter in the chair. "Can you hear me?"

"Hey yourself," he says. The smile behind his voice makes me smile too.

"How's LA?" I say. "Have you made your fortune and married Jennifer Lawrence?"

"Yes, that's exactly what I've done," he laughs. "How about you?"

I hesitate. "Same old same old."

I don't know why I didn't tell him I'm in Croatia. Probably because I just couldn't face another "What the hell are you doing there?" conversation.

"What time is it in LA?"

"Lunch," he says. "I'm eating the world's biggest bowl of pasta and I thought of you."

"Stodgy and pale?" I say. My skin looks practically blue here among the sun-kissed crowds.

He laughs. "The waitress's name is Lydia."

"Oh." My limited knowledge of LA conjures up a Cameron Diaz–style roller-skating queen with Jonah's pasta held aloft on a tray as she pirouettes between tables.

"So seriously, is it going well?"

He pauses. "You know what, it really is," he says, half laughing, incredulous. "Scarily so."

"That's good though, right?"

"No, yeah, it is." He sounds unsure. "Things have just moved more quickly than I'd let myself hope they could."

"Did you decide which film company you like best?"

"I did," he says. "The one who asked if I could stay on over here for a while and develop the script. Until Christmas, even. Maybe."

He says it super casual, as if it's normal to be planning to spend an extra half of the year on the other side of the world.

"But what about work and everything?"

"I think it'll be okay," he says. "I've spoken to the head and he's looking into a sabbatical for me."

"That's, that's really great," I say, and I hope he doesn't catch the note of despondency I can't quite keep from my voice.

"So, I thought that, if you can get the time off work, you might fancy coming out here for a week or two?

See the sights? We could walk the Hollywood Stars and you can stalk Ryan Reynolds or someone."

I'm taken aback, really surprised, and relieved that our friendship is back in a place where this feels like a good idea to him.

"I'm in Croatia," I say.

He goes quiet for a few moments. "Croatia?"

"It was kind of a last-minute thing."

"On your own? Or . . ."

I hear the question he doesn't ask me.

"On my own, yeah."

"Wow."

I don't know if I'm offended. "Is it that shocking?"

"No, no, it's not that," he says. "You just caught me by surprise."

"Elle had the baby."

"She did? When?"

"Yesterday morning."

"Oh Lyds, you missed it! Are you going home soon?"

I close my eyes. "I didn't miss it. I was there, I delivered the baby myself."

He laughs, and I realize he doesn't believe me.

"I'm serious, Jonah, I delivered my niece. She's fine, thanks for asking."

"Shit, okay. Right, yes, I'm sorry, I thought you were kidding around," he says, struggling to get the right words out. "So you delivered Elle's baby yesterday, and today you're in Croatia on a spur of the moment holiday?"

He relays all of this back, fact checking, as if I might realize I got some of it wrong.

"Yep."

He waits for me to explain further, but I don't.

"So that's cool," he says. "Tell them congrats from me."

"I will," I say, and again he falls silent.

"It's almost ten o'clock at night here," I say, settling back in my balcony chair. "There's so many stars Jonah, it's a whole new level of brightness and beauty," I say.

"I wish I could see it," he says, quiet against my ear.

"I wish that too," I whisper, suddenly feeling a long way from home.

"Go home soon," Jonah tells me. "Don't spend too much time on your own out there."

"I won't," I say. "You should get back to your pasta mountain."

"True," he says.

"Say hi to Ryan Reynolds from me if you run into him."

"Will do." I hear someone speak to him in the background, and he asks for the bill, distracted.

"Listen, I'll let you get back to your day," I say.

"Yeah, I should probably go," he says, then after a beat he adds, "Call me if you get lonely, okay?"

"Thanks. I'll remember."

"Get some sleep, stargazer." His voice is so clear he could be sitting beside me on this moonlit balcony.

"Night, Jonah Jones," I say, and I click to end the call before I, or he, can say anything else. I didn't tell him about the job offer.

AWAKE

Monday, July 22

NEW YORK, NEW YORK, so good they named it twice. I've just showered after a quiet morning people watching on the beach, and now my stomach is alive with nervous excitement at the thought of seeing Freddie, of being in New York on honeymoon. I have no idea what we'll do or where we're staying, it's all been a closely guarded secret. I could probably hazard an educated guess at a couple of things on Freddie's itinerary; New York has been my number-one dream destination since my slightly obsessive *Sex and the City* addiction, and I've dropped a million hints over the years of things I'd love to do if we ever go.

Breakfast at Tiffany's. Horse-drawn carriage rides in Central Park. Take the Staten Island ferry. I know, I know, I'm a great big cliché and there's a million other brilliant things to do but I can't help myself. New flippin' York! I'm going to be there today with Freddie.

I think fleetingly of home, of Elle and the baby and of Mum. I hope they understand how much I need this time away, that they don't think me too selfish. I shake the niggling worry off my shoulders, assuring myself that they love me, they know me well enough, they'll be okay.

I'm sitting in the middle of my pine-framed double bed, water in one hand, pink pill in the other, almost scared because I'm so desperate for everything to be perfect. I've always imagined New York to have this unique smell: brewed black coffee, the lingering scent of sugar donuts, newsprint and taxi fumes, bagels and beer from bars where everybody knows your name. For clarity, I know *Cheers* wasn't set in New York, but there must be places just like it on every street corner. Or maybe cafés like Central Perk, full of sagging sofas and magazines and women with fabulous hair.

Oh New York, New York, hold on. I'm coming, at last.

ASLEEP

Monday, July 22

"I THINK I'VE died and gone to heaven."

Freddie's disconcerting words are the first thing I hear as I try to orientate myself. We're sitting in a booth, and everywhere is too noisy and too bright. Freddie is opposite me finishing off a burger the size of his face, and in front of me is a half-eaten plate of grilled salmon. We each have frothy milkshakes, and the logo on the menu helps me out; we're in Ellen's Stardust Diner. I check my watch quickly. It feels too early to be eating food like this. I guess you'd call it brunch.

"We won't want to eat again today," I say, hiding the surprise I feel at our restaurant choice. This place wouldn't have made my wish list, but being fair, it's Freddie's honeymoon too, so it's okay.

"Save some room," he grins.

"For . . . ?"

He taps the side of his nose. "You'll see later. It's a surprise."

I smile, glad to know that our day is balanced with things for both of us. And I'm being churlish; this place might not be on my list, but that doesn't mean I can't appreciate it. I flip the gratitude switch on in my head. Freddie booked New York to make my dreams come true, but I can't expect him to get all of the details bang on. Besides, I can see how this is supposed to be fun. Neon lighting, disco balls, and wannabe Broadway actors serving food while belting out show tunes. It's stereotypical America with bells on. It just caught me off guard, that's all.

I watch Freddie (my husband!) for a few seconds through my lashes, trying not to make it obvious that I'm staring. He's in his element in places like this, where the fast-paced, high-energy level chimes with his. My breath catches in my throat at the sight of his platinum wedding ring, still gleaming, yet to wear a groove of familiarity into his flesh. I check out my own hand and find my ring there too: a slender white gold band beneath my engagement ring.

Oh. I bite the inside of my lip because it looks so perfect, exactly the way I'd imagined it would the day we picked out my trilogy diamond ring a few hours after Freddie proposed, because I was too excited to wait.

"So, Mrs. Hunter," he says. "Ready to make a move?"

Mrs. Hunter. First the rings, now the name. In truth, I wasn't sure what to do about my surname when Freddie proposed. I'm Lydia Bird. Mum, Elle, and me—we're the Birds. It's always been us three. I don't feel able to think of myself as Lydia Hunter, even though it's a perfectly good name. Elle had the same concern when she married David, and in the end she settled for double-barreling his name onto the end of hers. I didn't really have that option—Lydia Bird-Hunter makes me sound like something from *The Hunger Games*. It wasn't a question we ever got around to resolving in my waking life, but it seems that here the decision has been made—I'm no longer a Bird.

"Mrs. Hunter," I say slowly, trying it out. I can't help smiling as I say it. I longed to be Freddie's wife, and now I am.

"Sounds good, eh?" he says, holding my hand across the table.

I squeeze his fingers. "It does," I say. "It'll take some getting used to."

"You'll always be Lydia Bird to me," he says. It's exactly what I needed to hear. I'm still the same person, my new name doesn't change anything. I love him for understanding that it might feel strange.

OUTSIDE ON THE STREET, Times Square is an assault on all of my senses at the same time. Everything is bigger, noisier, and brighter than I'd anticipated, and I cling to Freddie's arm and laugh at the sheer overwhelm of it all.

"Wow," I say, filling my eyes with the huge moving billboards and Broadway show trailers, stepping backward to avoid the flow of people as I stand still, look up, and gawp.

Freddie looks at me. "Okay?"

I nod, remembering that this isn't the first time I've seen this in this world. "It's amazing every time you see it, isn't it? So full-on."

"The city that never sleeps," he laughs. "Come on, it's your turn to flag a cab."

"It is?"

I'm guessing that I've made a thing about wanting to hail one of the famous yellow cabs, but now I'm here I feel clueless. It's not as if I've spent much time hailing cabs back home either, to be fair to me. If anyone needs a taxi in my day-to-day life, we call the only local firm in town and Andrew Fletcher's mother dispatches one to us, more often than not driven by Andrew himself. I give myself a shake. How hard can it be?

Freddie tugs me by the hand until we're on the edge of the sidewalk. Traffic and cabs surge past us, and I dither about before bobbing my arm out in the general direction of the road. He bursts out laughing.

"Bloody hell, Lyds, do it like you mean it," he says.

I have another go, but it's as if I'm invisible.

"Might be better to go for one that's actually available," Freddie says. "Just the number illuminated, remember?"

I study the yellow cabs for a few seconds and realize that some of them have "Off Duty" lit up, and some of them have nothing lit at all. Others have their number on; they must be the ones I need to target. Right, I think. I've got this. I spot the next empty and available cab cruising in our direction and I thrust my whole arm out like I mean business. I'm giddy with success when it slows to a stop. It's only when the driver peers out at me that I realize I don't know where we're headed.

"Where to?" I say, turning back to Freddie, my fingers curled around the open window because I'm scared the cabdriver will leave.

Freddie leans in. "Four Seasons?"

The driver nods, and Freddie smiles as he opens the door for me.

I DON'T KNOW how on earth we've afforded this place. In all of my New York fantasies, and there have been many, we never stayed anywhere as fabulous as the Four Seasons. The marble, the flowers, the gilt, the sheer splendor–it's all off the scale. I want to imprint every last detail on my brain forever. I want to remember the exact feeling of walking through the perfumed lobby with Freddie for the rest of my life. This old-school grandeur is so detached from our everyday life that even Freddie must feel as if he's dreaming. I manage to keep a lid on gasping out loud as we take the elevator up to the eighth floor, and Freddie opens the door to our room. Or to our suite, should I say.

"I'm bursting for the loo," he says, ducking into the bathroom.

I'm grateful for his absence, because I need a private minute to pull myself together. Our belongings are here so this must be our room. Some things I recognize, some are new to me. I guess we must have arrived yesterday. I wonder what we did, where we ate, how we marveled at our luck to be staying in a hotel as swanky as this. I spot a pile of loose change on a side table, among it a receipt from last night for cocktails at Bar SixtyFive. I sigh, glad to know I've been to the Top of the Rock in this life at least, even if I didn't get to experience how it felt. One of the hardest parts of falling into this life for hops and catches is trying to find out what I've missed and work out what lies ahead.

This room . . . I look around, blown away. It's so luxurious, so beyond us really. I stand by the picture windows looking out over the New York cityscape I've seen countless times on TV and in photographs. They didn't even remotely prepare me for the real thing. It's alive out there; a pulsing sprawl of metal and glass, Central Park an oasis of green.

"We have a couple of spare hours," Freddie says, coming to stand behind me at the window. The smoke in his voice tells me how he'd like to spend that time, the graze of his mouth hot against my ear. I lean into him. I want the same thing. To know the touch of my husband, to make love to him as his wife. What a precious, precious gift.

"GO ON, TELL ME," I wheedle. "We're here now, and I'll be able to look forward to it more if I know."

I'm lying in the crook of Freddie's shoulder, warm and blissed out, the white sheets tangled around our bodies. My efforts at the gym have clearly been paying off; my arms are more toned here, my thighs too. It's a bit bizarre to look down and see myself altered. It highlights the space between here and there, the subtle and not so subtle differences between the two worlds.

"You really want to know?"

I'm trying to get Freddie to reveal his plans for the next few days so I can work out when to come back, how to wring out as much pleasure as possible from our time together. He's going to tell me; I can see he's desperate to.

"MoMA?" I guess. It's a bit of a long shot. I'd love to go but museums are so not Freddie's thing.

He shakes his head. "Closed for a few months. Renovations, I think."

Disappointment spears me, but now that I think about it, I remember reading about the closure. The important fact is that he bothered to check.

"Breakfast at Tiffany's?" I guess again, holding my breath because reservations at the Blue Box Café are rarer than hen's teeth.

He holds out on me for a few seconds and then laughs, shrugging. "Tomorrow at ten A.M."

"No way!" I say, delighted, sitting up on one elbow to look at him. I've TripAdvisored the café to death and mooned over their blue-and-white crockery, the Tiffany blue leather banquettes.

"And then *Wicked* tomorrow evening," Freddie expands, keen for praise. "That's the one you want to see, right?"

I nod, glad he's listened to me and not gone for something newer. We never seem to make the time for a weekend away in London to catch a show, and grabbing tickets for the big productions when they tour is nigh on impossible. I tried to get *Wicked* tickets a couple of years back but missed out. I'm glad now, because I get to see it on Broadway. Broadway! I laugh, giddy, and flop back down into Freddie's arms. "You're my favorite person in the world," I tell him. Musical theater isn't his bag, so I know this is just to make me happy.

"Your favorite husband," he corrects me.

"That too," I say, pressing my face into his neck and breathing deeply. He smells of expensive hotel toiletries, of joy, and of New York, New York.

THE BATHROOM IS something else again. Floor-to-ceiling marble everywhere I look. I bathe in Bvlgari and envelop myself in a heavy white robe and slippers, feeling as if I've stepped inside a movie. We're due downstairs in a little while for afternoon tea and champagne. How frankly fabulous is that? Our honeymoon is everything I could have wished for. Freddie has pulled out all the stops to make my first days as his wife as memorable as possible.

I expect to find him still in bed when I head back through, but he isn't. I spy him out on the terrace in his robe, and as I step closer to the doors, I see he's on his phone. I can't catch any words, but his animated body language and pacing tell me it's work. It irks me, but it doesn't surprise me that Vince wouldn't respect the fact that we are on our honeymoon. I know Freddie could have ignored the call, but he wouldn't, and I'm sure Vince knew that perfectly well.

I'm detangling my damp hair when he finally comes back inside, and I catch his eye in the mirror, hoping his mood isn't ruined.

"Everything okay?"

He drops down on the armchair and scrubs his hands through his hair. "No."

I place the comb down on the dressing table and scoot round on the stool to face him. "What's wrong?" I don't really want to talk about work but it's clear he needs to decompress after the call, to get whatever it is off his chest so he can transition back into honeymoon mode.

"Babe . . ."

Something in his tone alerts me to incoming trouble. He doesn't generally call me babe. He knows I don't really like it, but I don't comment because he's scrubbing his palms over his cheeks in an agitated, something-isn't-right way. My mind starts to spiral. Is the company in crisis? Has he lost his job?

"What's wrong, Freddie?"

He shakes his head, and then comes over and kneels in front of me. It's unexpected. Submissive.

"I need to go to LA, Lyds. Just for a day or so."

I stare at him, not quite comprehending the problem. "Okay," I say slowly, and then I realize. "So you'll go straight from JFK on Friday? I need to fly home alone?"

He swallows and looks away. "Tonight."

I'm gobsmacked. "Tonight?"

"It's just for tomorrow," he rushes in, pleading. "I'll be back before you even know it."

I feel my blood start to heat. "You're kidding, right? You're on your honeymoon, Freddie. *Our* honeymoon."

He's nodding, fast, clearly conflicted. "Don't you think I know that? I said no, Lyds, but it's crunch time with these clients. They're on the verge of signing with someone else tomorrow, who swooped in out of nowhere offering them the earth. I've been romancing them for bloody weeks now. I even cut my stag night short for them, remember?"

He's asking me to understand, but I don't.

"It's not quite on the same scale though, is it?" I say, staring at him. He can't genuinely think this is in any way okay, that juggling his stag night around is on par with running out on his own honeymoon.

"Say no."

He raises his eyes to the ceiling. "This is Vince, Lyds. You know I can't say no."

"What's he going to do, Freddie? Fire you?"

He huffs. "I've worked night and day for this contract. It's mine. I won't let someone slide it right out from under my fucking nose at the last minute."

And then I see it. Vince hasn't had to force Freddie to go.

"But what about us?" I say, my voice small.

He looks at the floor and then back up at me. "I'll make it up to you, I promise."

I do the maths in my head. We're here for five days, and he's leaving for at least one of them, probably two when you factor in the travel. Almost half of our honeymoon gone at the click of Vince's fingers. It can't happen, I won't let it. I reach out and place my hand on Freddie's jaw, my eyes fixed on his.

"Tell him no, Freddie. Tell him our honeymoon is sacred."

He looks at me, and we have a silent conversation with our eyes. He's asking me to see it his way, I'm asking him to see it mine. There isn't a compromise, no middle ground. Someone has to lose.

"I can't."

He gets to his feet and walks away from me, and hot, sudden fury ignites in my gut.

"You mean you won't," I say, and he spins back around, his arms flung wide.

"Look around you, Lydia. Look at this room. Who do you think paid for us to come to a place like this? Fucking Santa Claus?"

"Oh," I say, feeling stupid as the penny drops. "Oh, I get it now. The *company* paid for this, so now we owe them, right? Was this the plan all along then?"

He's angry now, exasperated. "Of course it bloody wasn't. It's been booked for months, you know that. But things happen sometimes; it's just bad timing, that's all."

"Bad timing?" I half yell. "Bad timing? This isn't bad timing, Freddie." I'm so angry, I'm shaking. I've moved mountains to be here with him, for this precious uninterrupted time. "This is way beyond bad timing. This is us, you and me, our once-in-a-lifetime honeymoon. Doesn't that matter more than sodding work?"

He stares at me.

"Why are you being like this? Surely you can see how hard this is for me," he says, almost as if I'm the one being unreasonable. "Do you think I want to have to do this?"

"I think you could say no if you wanted to."

He looks as if I've slapped him.

"I don't know what's happened to you lately," he says.

"What's that supposed to mean?"

He shrugs. "You're just . . . I don't know . . . different. Always ready for a row."

I laugh, because surely anyone would be argumentative under the circumstances. "Well, excuse me for saying what I think," I mutter. "So what am I supposed to do while you're off in LA? Go for breakfast at Tiffany's alone, watch *Wicked* with an empty seat beside me?"

He wipes his hand down his face. "I'll rebook them. We'll go on Thursday. I can make it work."

We both know he can't, and it isn't even the point.

"If you do this . . . ," I say, not even sure what I'm about to say next.

He stares at me, silent for a few charged beats, and then turns away and pulls the suitcase from the wardrobe. I sink down into the armchair and watch him throw things into the case. It's desolate, just awful to see our honeymoon in tatters.

"Please don't go." I stand up and try one last time. "This is too important."

He looks at me, and I know from his face that he's not going to change his mind.

"You could make this easier on me," he says. "You could use the spa, wallow around in the bath, enjoy the city for a couple of days until I get back. But you won't do that, will you?"

We stare at each other. He means it, and it dawns on me that the woman I used to be would probably be able to find it in herself to do the things he's just suggested. To allow him to leave without guilt, to make a silk purse from a sow's ear, to grudgingly accept the change of plan. Only I'm not that woman anymore. I've been through the worst thing life could possibly throw at me, I've had to find strength I didn't know I had, and it's changed me. I'm not the same person anymore. Lydia here hasn't lived through disaster. It's not just the toned arms, or the good thighs. It's the way my brain is wired, the way my heart loves. Freddie's right. I am different, and the realization that I don't really fit here anymore breaks my heart.

He's dressed now, his case packed.

"I'll see you when I get back," he says, raw. "Try not to hate me."

I look at him, hurt beyond measure. I don't say anything, because I'm not capable of offering the soothing words he wants to hear.

He nods, hesitates as if he wants to say more, but he doesn't. He just picks up his suitcase and leaves.

AWAKE

Tuesday, July 23

EVERYTHING IS WRONG. I came to Croatia to be with Freddie, blissful and uninterrupted. To picnic in Central Park, take in a show on Broadway, to try on diamonds we could never afford in Tiffany's. We were going to throw away the guidebooks and wander the backstreets in search of our own adventure, admire brownstones, eat delicious things in cafés that don't rate well on TripAdvisor. We were going to do all of those marvelous things, but I've now realized that making new memories with Freddie means I'm trampling on my old precious memories of him.

I've turned our bruising argument over in my head a thousand times, examined it from every angle, trying to find something that isn't there because my stubborn heart is desperate not to admit the truth. That the girl I used to be would likely have found it in herself to let Freddie leave, she'd have understood that he needed to go. *Try not to hate me,* he said. I feel sick remembering the look on his face. But I can't shake the fact that the girl I am now knows it would have been wrong to accept him leaving. Damn it, Freddie should have said no to Vince; he should have put us first. But he didn't, and I can't square that with myself.

The thing about losing the love of your life is that you get to make up what would have happened afterward. You're entitled to dream that all of your tomorrows would have been perfect, because you loved him so much, you're allowed to flex and bend every situation in your head so he'd say and do all of the right things. Your love story never really ends, because your brain paints him into every photograph and he's there beside you on all of your special days. He doesn't argue with you or fall short of your expectations, he doesn't make questionable decisions, and he absolutely, categorically never runs out on you halfway through your honeymoon.

I'm in a terrible mess. I've cried the frightened, body-racking sobs of a lost child. I crave the comfort of my mum's arms and Elle's everything's-going-to-be-okay hug, but they're oceans away. I came all this way to be with Freddie, but I've never felt more alone in my life.

AWAKE

Saturday, August 3

"TAKE MORE WATER with you." Vita turns to the glass fridge behind her and pulls out a couple of bottles and pushes them across the counter to me. "Here."

It's relatively early on Saturday morning, just after seven, and Vita insisted that I take the day off. I've been here for almost two weeks now, and I haven't taken another pill since that terrible trip back when I first arrived.

I've worked most days, by choice rather than demand. At first I did it just to get out of my head, but soon I realized there's something freeing about tying the restaurant's red apron around my body and picking up the notepad and pen. It beats any kind of paid therapy. I've toasted the blueness out of my skin on the beach for a couple of hours most mornings, and come lunchtime I've thrown on shorts and slicked on a little lip gloss to morph into Vita's wingwoman. More often than not my evenings have ended chatting to Jonah on Skype, my feet propped up on the balcony and my eyes on the stars. It's a simple, soul nourishing routine. Clean and cathartic, as if by some miracle I've ended up exactly where I needed to be, in a safe place to hide from both of my lives.

In quieter moments Vita and I have taken refuge inside from the heat, swapping stories and photographs. I've seen her on the day she married Petar eight years previously, a man of few words but good heart. I know she's one of six siblings, aunt to more than ten, and that she and Petar long for a child of their own. In turn she's heard news of Elle and the new baby, seen photos of my folks, and is vaguely aware that I do organizational things in my local community center. I'm sure she's also aware that there are elephant-sized chunks of my life I haven't been able to share yet, and I greatly appreciate that she hasn't asked. Truth be told, I've got a bit of a hero worship–style crush on her. What I wouldn't give for even half of her serenity; she radiates quiet strength and good humor in a way that makes her addictive company to me. She seems to run the restaurant with little more than the occasional flick of her fingers and a smile; I expect she could run the country in the same way if she was of a mind. Lucky Petar, and, for a little while, lucky me.

"You remember the way?"

I nod. "Think so."

I'm going to see some of the local sights, taking Vita's moped to save the walk. I don't think I'd have ridden one myself if I'd come here with Freddie, he'd have picked the biggest thing going and asked for a second helmet for me. It's kind of liberating traveling under my own steam like one of the locals. People here have already become accustomed to me, greeting me by name thanks to my status as one of Vita's friends.

"It's a straight road," she says. "Don't hurry yourself back."

I roll my eyes. It's Saturday so bound to be extra busy around here and I don't especially feel the need to take the time out.

"And don't grumble," she smiles. "It spoils your lovely face. You have to see the tourist sights while you're here."

"You sound like my mum."

"In that case, your mother is a very wise woman." She reaches under the desk for the moped key. "It has enough fuel if you want to explore."

"I'll be back soon. Before lunch."

"Don't be."

We lock eyes, and then laugh as I swing my backpack over my shoulders. She follows me out to the moped and puts a paper bag in the basket on the front. I spy the end of a baguette poking out.

"Your lunch," she says, unsubtle.

I swing my leg over the moped and fasten the helmet beneath my chin.

"See you in a while," I say.

Vita nods, her arms folded across her chest. "I'll be here."

* * *

I'M NOT RELIGIOUS, but at Vita's suggestion I find myself parking up at the Shrine of Vepric on the outskirts of the town. It's early enough to still be quiet here, intensifying the volume of the crickets and the pervading sense of peace. The shrine is nestled at the base of a wooded hill. Croatia seems to have been created from a paintbox of vibrant turquoise and verdant green, never more so than here as I climb the wide stone steps toward the shrine. A couple of other people mill around, as quiet in their observation as I am in mine.

Wooden benches fill the space in front of the shrine. Right now they stand empty, so I lower myself onto the front pew for a few minutes and breathe.

A stone altar sits inside the cave-like natural shrine, and a delicately painted statue of the Virgin Mary presides from an alcove set high into one of the walls. It really is spectacularly peaceful. I drink in the silence and let my eyes wander over the scene, and after a little while a woman comes and takes the next pew along. She bows her head, twisting dark beads around her fingers as she prays. I've had moments since the accident when I fervently wished I believed in God or some higher purpose; it must bring comfort to feel that the pieces are moved around down here for some greater reason. I don't hold any such beliefs, but that doesn't mean I can't draw solace from a place like this. People believe this shrine heals. Can it mend broken hearts too?

I sit now and think back over the last couple of years. I acknowledge how far I've come since Freddie's death, and how far I still have to travel. Decades, if I'm fortunate.

I think briefly of New York, calamitous, everything it shouldn't have been. I don't know when I'll feel strong enough to go back, and bigger questions are hovering on the edges of my mind waiting to be answered.

As I close my eyes and turn my face up to the sun, I consciously remind myself that I'm still here, anchored. My sneaker-clad feet are planted on this dry, dusty earth, my flesh and bones rest on this plain wooden bench. My heart may be a loose cannon in my chest, unsure if anyone owns it, but I'm still here. I take slow, measured breaths, focusing on the scent of pine needles and the chatter of birds, until a steady, all-encompassing sense of sanctuary wraps itself around me like an invisible shield. It's the safety of my grandparents' dinner table, and the strength of my mother's hug. It's Elle holding my hand, it's Freddie making my perfect bacon and beetroot sandwich, it's Jonah at the piano in The Prince on New Year's Eve. It's all of those things and all of those people, as surely as if they're filling the pews around me. It's Vita's serenity, and Petar's kindness, and it's Dawn and Ryan picking up the slack for me at work. It's Kris expecting nothing from me, and Julia's secondhand flowers. But moreover and most of all, it's me. Right here, right now on this bench, it's every version of *me*. My sunburnt shoulders, my too-long hair twisted into a knot on top of my head, my makeup-free face, the frayed cotton braids around my wrist from the beach seller, the chipped green polish on my fingernails, it's me, it's me, it's me.

I feel a tide swell inside me, this sense of myself as a whole, loved person, as owner of my own heart, a whisper and then a roar.

Me. Me. Me.

If I was somewhere other than a shrine, I'd shout out at the top of my lungs. I'm Lydia Bird, and I'm still here.

I RUN INTO Petar washing off the pavement outside the restaurant as I park the moped up in Vita's space.

"Did you find it?" he asks, leaning on the mop handle.

I climb off the bike and unclip the helmet. "I did. It's quite an amazing place, isn't it?"

"I love it," he says. "Did you pray?"

I wrinkle my nose, apologetic. "It's not really my thing."

He nods, philosophical. "Everyone is different."

"Yes," I say. "Although I did feel something . . . I don't know how to put it . . ."

"Not alone?" he suggests.

I think about it. "Sort of, but not exactly," I say. "More like," I touch my fingertips against my breast. "More like acceptance. I found the old me, still in here, and the new me sitting right alongside her. We made friends."

"The old you and the new you," he says, slowly.

I don't expect him to understand because I'm not sure I really understand myself.

"I think . . . I think I've been trying too hard to be

everything to everyone," I say, working through my jumbled thoughts for my own benefit as much as for Petar. "It's hard to accept that life always marches forward, isn't it? Always forward, never back. I was forced to change when my life suddenly changed around me, but even if it hadn't, I'd have changed in one way or another sooner or later, wouldn't I? Because people do, don't they, no one stays the same forever. Everything is just so fragile, isn't it? We make our decisions dependent on the day, the weather, our mood, the phases of the moon, what we had for breakfast . . . I can't keep questioning choices I may or may not have made, blaming myself for being too soft there and too hard here. I see now that I've been walking in circles, making crazy patterns." I stop and draw breath. "I need to walk in a straight line, Petar."

Petar stares at me, taken aback by my ramble. I'm not sure how much he understood, or even how much I understood.

"It's not always easy to accept the things you cannot change." He takes the moped key and helmet from me. "Go and rest for a while."

Vita has been into my room while I was out, leaving behind a mason jar of wild flowers and a note to tell me she's replenished my linen and bottled water supplies. I lay down on the fresh sheets, thinking about Petar's words just now. It's a clichéd line from a million posters and fridge magnets, but the concept of acceptance is settling itself on my bones.

Sitting at the shrine today, I felt almost like two people. The old me, the girl I was before Freddie died, and the new me, the woman I've become since the accident. It probably sounds ridiculous, but as I sat there in the silence this morning, it was as if the two versions of me inched closer and closer on that pew until finally, finally, they became one whole person.

AWAKE

Wednesday, August 7

I'VE BEEN HERE for seventeen days now. It feels auspicious because it's more than the usual package holiday. More than my leave allowance at work too. I emailed Phil a couple of days ago to try to explain, or rather to beg for a leave of unpaid absence because I'm not ready to go home yet. I know I'm taking liberties; he's already been so generous and accommodating, and I have no right to expect him to understand. He's replied that he'll try to juggle things for a while longer, a weight off my peeling shoulders. Mum was a little trickier. We haven't argued as such but she couldn't keep a lid on her simmering discontent. Elle's daily texts and photos have slipped to every other day or so too. It pains me that my absence is difficult for them; I honestly wouldn't stay away if being here didn't feel vital for my sanity. I need to stay here for a little while longer yet, be Lydia the beach waitress, just passing through.

AWAKE

Wednesday, August 14

I'M SITTING ON my balcony stargazing before going to sleep alone, a starfish in a too big bed. I've been thinking about making some changes when I go home. Getting my hair chopped, maybe replacing the kitchen if I can afford it. Our Savoy bed is on my mind too. Much as I love it, I'm not sure I'll ever be able to sleep in it without imagining Freddie there right before I close my eyes, and that's a forlorn way to fall asleep indefinitely. I'm not sure, it's just something I've been thinking about.

I stare at the night skies, trying to untangle the knotted, multicolored strands of my life. I had quite a tense conversation with Mum earlier. She thinks I'm being irresponsible staying on here, that I'll lose my job, or else that I'm going to decide to stay here forever. I entertained that idea for a while; I could do it. I could sell my beloved house, move out here, live a barefoot beach life. Vita would help me, I'm sure of it.

But what of Elle, and my friends, and Mum? I can't bear the thought of being so far away from them forever, even if it suits me right now, today. They are my anchor, my fingerprint. And there's the baby. Charlotte. My heart aches a bit whenever I think of her, because she's going to be a month old in a couple days' time and I haven't held her since the day she was born. Work is another anchor; I know I'm not running the country, but the community center is my place and I don't want to lose it.

And then, of course, there's Freddie. I haven't slipped through the back door in the universe since that terrible day in New York for fear of making everything worse. I feel as if I'm navigating the map of my heart with a faulty compass, trying to work out where I live now.

And finally there's Jonah Jones. When Freddie was here Jonah had a defined role in my life as his best friend, which somewhere along the way meant he couldn't be my best friend, too. We settled into that dynamic, our own friendship shelved because we had to vie for Freddie's attention. And now that he isn't here standing between us anymore it's as if we're remembering what drew us to each other in the first place, what we mean to each other. He is my oldest friend. His name on my phone lifts my heart.

AWAKE

Sunday, September 22

"I THINK YOU should go home."

Vita and I are drinking coffee on the restaurant terrace. My skin is only a few shades off hers now, the seasoned color of someone who spends all their days in the sun, rather than shoehorning two weeks into their fluorescent-lit, office-based life. The summer rush is over, and life here has slowed to a more leisurely pace.

"I know," I say. I've been thinking the same thing. Mum and I have resorted to communicating by text in recent weeks because talking has become so fractious, and it's easier to chat to Elle that way too. The last couple of times I've called she's had to dash because Charlotte was screaming or had just thrown up down David's clean work shirt.

"You can always come back. We're not going anywhere," Vita says, sipping her coffee.

"You're lucky to feel so sure," I say, envious of her seemingly simple life.

She winds the string of her apron around her fingers. "You make your own luck, Lydia."

"Do you think so, really?" I ask, not sure I agree. "Because sometimes I feel as if life just sweeps me along and it's all I can do not to hit the rocks."

She snorts through her nose. "Rocks won't kill you."

"They might," I mutter.

"So hide out here for the rest of your life to avoid the rocks?" She shrugs, her dark eyes full of challenge.

I look out at the sea. "Is that what I'm doing?"

Vita shrugs again. "Isn't it?"

I know she's bang on the money. I've been here for sixty-five days now. Sixty-five days without seeing my family, and almost as many without seeing Freddie.

"What would you do if you weren't afraid, Lydia?"

Her question goes straight to the heart of me, as usual. I mull it over.

"I'd have my hair cut off," I say. Getting it cut feels like such a big deal because Freddie loved it long, chopping it feels like I'm not taking his feelings into account. Which is crazy, I know.

"Want me to do it right now?" she offers. "I used to cut my sisters' all the time."

I'm not sure if she's kidding, but I shake my head. "I'm not ready yet."

Vita pushes her chair back and stands up, her hand on my shoulder. "Don't leave it much longer."

AWAKE

Tuesday, September 24

"SHE'S FUSSY AT the moment, won't go to anyone else," Elle says. "Not even David."

I came straight here this morning after a late flight last night. I've been here for ten minutes and I can't shake the feeling that Elle wishes I'd leave. I should probably have called ahead; the house is a bit of a mess and she looks as if she's been wearing the same stained T-shirt for a few days. It's very un-Elle; I know how much she'll dislike appearing so un-put together.

"Can I help?" I feel really useless. Charlotte is tomato red from crying and seems to have the lung capacity of a small horse. "I could, I don't know, wash up or something?"

Elle's eyes fill with tears. "I can't help the mess, Lydia. You try looking after another human on two hours sleep a night, broken sleep at that, and then see if you feel like cleaning up."

"Shall I make a cup of tea?" I'm walking on eggshells, trying to work out whether to stay and help or go.

"I don't have any milk until David gets back from work," she says, and then laughs, wide eyed and hollow. "Unless you count these." She gestures down at her boobs, the baby squirming on one shoulder. "Because this dairy is never allowed to run out, night and day, on bloody demand."

"I'll nip and grab some," I say, glad of a job. "Is there anything else you need?"

She snorts. "A good night's sleep? More than five minutes to myself? My sister not to piss off right when I needed her most?"

"Elle, I'm sorry . . . I didn't realize things were so . . ." I'm stricken. "Tell me what to do, how to help—"

She cuts me off with an impatient wave of her hand. "Do you think I knew what to do when Freddie died? How to help you through the worst thing that had ever happened to you? I'll tell you the answer—no. No, I had no bloody clue. But you know what I *didn't* do? I didn't catch a flight to fucking Croatia!"

I'm wounded. I want to argue, to say that you can hardly compare losing someone to gaining someone, but I don't because my sister is in a state.

"It's bath time," she says, clipped, switching the baby from one shoulder to the other. "I better get it done before she's hungry again or she'll have a meltdown."

I hear it; she's telling me to leave. I swallow hard. "Can I help you bathe her?"

She sighs, as if the fight has left her. "Not today, okay Lyds? I'll be faster on my own."

Because I have no other option, I pick up my keys. "Shall I call you later?"

She tips her head to indicate the baby. "Text's better in case she's asleep."

I expect she means it's better because she won't have to speak to me, either.

THERE'S A CAR in Mum's drive I don't recognize when I pull up there ten minutes later. But I don't really register it in my eagerness to surprise her.

I let myself in, kicking off my Converse by the door as I head for the kitchen. And I walk in on my mum stripped down to her bra and jeans having a good old-fashioned snog with Stef, the now shirtless computer mender. My raised jazz hands freeze in the air at the sight of them, and they jump apart as if they've been electrified.

"Bloody hell, Lydia!" my mother half shouts, red faced, covering herself nonsensically with a tea towel.

Stef literally crawls under the kitchen table and re-emerges from the other side with his jumper on inside out and my mum's blouse in his hand. She whips it off him and drags it on without saying a word.

"Nice to meet you again, Lydia love," Stef mutters, and then shoots past me down the hall and scoots. I don't blame him; Mum looks ready to blow a gasket.

"Nine weeks," she shouts, still flustered. "Nine weeks you've been gone, and then you swan in here without so much as a phone call to tell me you're home again?"

I stare at her. I knew both Elle and Mum were put

out but I didn't think they'd react to my homecoming this badly.

"I wanted to surprise you," I say.

"Well, you certainly did that."

"Sorry," I mumble.

She sighs, running her hands over her hair to tidy it. "When did you get back?"

"Last night," I say. I don't tell her that the house was colder than I've ever known it when I finally got back at around six yesterday evening, or that there was an officially worded letter from Phil telling me that they had had to take someone on to cover my job and to call him, or that my time away has changed something in me. "I'm sorry I've been gone so long."

I can see that she's struggling between being angry and being relieved I'm home.

"You shouldn't have stayed away so long."

I nod, miserable.

"Have you seen your sister?"

"Just now."

"How was she today?"

The question implies that Elle's health currently changes on a day-to-day basis. Organized, calm, reliable Elle.

"She seemed stressed. The baby was crying, I didn't stay long."

Mum huffs. I don't know if it's at me for not staying long, or Elle for being stressed, or the baby for crying.

"She isn't just stressed. She's struggling, Lydia. You'd know that if you'd been here."

Ah. Me then, obviously. "I didn't realize."

"No," Mum says. "Clearly."

It's as if my prolonged absence has soaked up any residues of sympathy they had for me and flushed them down the sink.

"I'm sorry for interrupting you . . . you know."

She glances down at her blouse, knowing she's buttoned it up wrong.

"Poor Stef," she says, shaking her head.

"Sorry."

"Will you stop bloody apologizing? It's not helping."

I clam up, unsure what to do or say.

"Have you eaten?" she asks, eventually.

I shake my head. Shopping is next on my list today; the cupboards are bare. She opens the fridge and pulls out a half empty glass dish of lasagne and pushes it into my hands.

"Here. Take that with you."

I stare down at it, stupidly close to tears because both of my most special people have dismissed me from their homes today. "Thanks," I say.

She nods and then looks away out of the window.

"I'll be off then," I say. "Shall I call you tomorrow?"

She nods again, tight lipped.

"It's really nice to see you, Mum," I say, quietly. "I missed you."

I turn away and leave, and she lets me.

I climb into my car, tearful and rejected, and as I drive the familiar streets toward home, I know it's finally time to go back.

ASLEEP

Tuesday, September 24

HE ISN'T HERE. I've found the courage to return at last, but the house is empty. Further inspection tells me that the fridge is empty of Freddie's favorite brand of beer, and the washing basket has only my clothes in. Where is he? We've only been married a couple of months. I start to panic; was our argument in New York the catalyst for change? Did I derail our happiness to the extent that our fledgling marriage has hit the rocks? I pour myself some juice, my hand shaking as I pick up my phone in search of answers.

Two messages flash up on my screen. From Elle: do I fancy going to theirs for fish and chips later? From Mum: the offer of a spare ticket to a play she's seeing in Bath at the weekend. They're rallying around me here in this world. I rub my finger over my wedding ring, still in place on my third finger. Where are you, Freddie Hunter?

I click his name and wait for it to ring out, hoping I don't get his answer machine. It's seven in the evening, so I'm hopeful that he won't be working, wherever he is.

It takes longer than usual to connect, and when it does it isn't the regular ringtone. It perplexes me, and then my heart jumps because he answers.

"Freddie?" I say, uncertain. It's noisy wherever he is.

"Lyds?" he half shouts. "Hang on a sec. I'll go outside."

I can hear the bustle of conversation and background music, laughter and raised voices. I think he's in a bar.

"It's bloody hot here today," he says, clearer now. "My shirt's sticking to my back."

"Where are you?" I say, confused.

"Right now?" he says. "Outside a beach bar. Vince is in there flashing the company credit card around in the hope of sealing the deal."

"All work and no play, right?" I say, vague, trying to force lightness I don't feel into my voice.

He laughs. "When in Rome. Or Rio, as the case may be."

Rio? Freddie's in Brazil? Distant bells ring in my head, he might have mentioned something, but I'm certain I didn't know he was going to spend any significant time out there.

"I miss you," I say, because it's true, especially now I've heard his voice again.

"You too," he says. "It won't be for much longer now. Two weeks, three at most."

"Another three weeks?" I say, downbeat. The things I said in New York obviously didn't land at all if he's allowed this to happen. Or if I have. By the looks of our fridge and the messages from Mum and Elle he's already been gone for a couple of weeks.

"Don't start again." He sighs, irritated. "You know I can't help it."

It's clear we've reached a pinch point here.

"Did you say you're on the beach?"

"No," he says, over-patient, mildly pass-agg. "I said I was with Vince, trying to seal a deal for the PodGods. This whole place revolves around the bloody beach, Lydia, it's not my fault, okay?"

"I didn't say it was," I say, miserable. I haven't spoken to Freddie in weeks, and now I am and it's like this again. If we were together we'd be able to talk our misunderstanding out, but it's not so easy down the telephone line. It strikes me now how reliant our relationship has always been on physical closeness; on touch, and on being able to read each other's visual cues. We don't have the luxury of any of that right now, and what we're left with feels disappointing and riddled with the potential for angst. I can hear someone shouting Freddie's name, Vince probably, telling him to come and grab a Caipirinha. He mispronounces it. It doesn't surprise me, he's a bullish sort of man, not someone who'd take the time to learn something like that. I'd lay money on the fact that he's flown himself and Freddie to Brazil without even finding out how to say please and thank you in Portuguese.

"I need to get back inside," he says.

"Sounds like it," I say, feeling dejected, wishing I could find the right words to heal this.

"I'll call soon," he says, and then he's gone, back to his cocktail, back to the beach bar, back to his life without me.

AWAKE

Tuesday, September 24

I SIT ALONE in my lamp-lit living room, a mug of hot chocolate clasped in my hand in the hope it'll help me sleep. What a hideous, crappy homecoming. Mum and Elle probably wish I'd stayed in Croatia, and Freddie is out in Rio knocking back cocktails on the beach.

I can see now how much I've relied on my other world to offer me an escape from this one; an escape from the hard, unforgiving coalface of grief. This afternoon though . . . it didn't do that. It left me feeling jaded and despondent again, lower than I've been since New York, and thinking things through this evening has led me closer to an undeniable truth.

I've traded healing here for living there. I've used visiting the other place as a way to try to outrun grief, even when every grief manual I've ever read tells me that just isn't possible. Maybe my bloody doctor was onto something–I haven't moved sentiently through the process. I've zigzagged between worlds, taking the long way around, slowing myself down without realizing.

I didn't take any more pills in Croatia after that night in New York, and as a consequence I slept at night. The circles faded from beneath my eyes, and my heart beat easier in my chest because it wasn't putting in double shifts. My days were simpler, because living one life is less stressful than living two.

I can't ignore the fact that I'm changing anymore, that the me that visits Freddie in the other world is less and less like the Lydia he knows. And in truth, I like this new version of me better. She's still really messed up, but she's plucky. Adventurous and strong. She's been trying to move slowly forward, walking against the tide, and all this time I've been trying to pull her back.

AWAKE

Saturday, September 28

"ARE YOU ABSOLUTELY SURE?"

I meet my hairdresser's eyes in the mirror. "Yes."

She's standing behind me with her scissors in her hand, and for a woman paid to cut hair, she looks particularly reluctant.

"I haven't cut more than an inch off your hair in the last ten years," she says, biting her lip.

It's true. I've flirted with layers, every now and then I've had a fringe put in, but that's as exciting as it's been.

I pick up the weight of my plait one last time. "Do it, Laura."

She takes a deep breath, and doesn't ask again.

AFTERWARD I SIT in the car, my plait coiled in a clear zip-lock bag in my lap, much more than a physical weight off my shoulders. Dawn donated her hair a few summers ago, so I looked last night and found a charity that makes wigs for teenage girls. My hair was my pride and joy when I was fifteen; you need something to swish and hide behind at such a tender age. It warms me to think my hair might in some small way brighten the life of another girl who's struggling. I have no need for it anymore.

In the hallway I drop my bag and examine myself in the mirror from every angle, smoothing my fingers down the back of my revealed neck, fiddling with the short strands around my face. I can now put a tick in that classic "get all your hair cut off" box on the grief reaction checklist. Laura nearly had a heart attack when I asked for a pixie cut. She grabbed a pile of magazines to show me photographs of short cuts, imagining that I'd got it wrong. I hadn't; I knew what I wanted, and looking at myself now, I'm glad I was brave enough to go through with it.

Brave. I turn the word over in my head, and then I say it out loud. My reflection looks steadily back at me, telling me I've done the right thing. I add brave to the collection of words that describe my life right now.

IT'S FIVE IN the afternoon here, which I reckon makes it nine in the morning in LA. I texted Jonah a photo of my new haircut a few minutes ago, and just when I think he's having a Saturday morning lie-in my phone lights up with a message.

"Calling you right now."

I grin and drop down into the corner of the sofa

with my legs curled under me as my phone buzzes and then he appears, laughing, still in bed.

"Let me get a proper look at you then," he says, and out of nowhere I feel shy and wrinkle my nose up, embarrassed as I twist my head from one side to the other and await his verdict.

"What do you think?" I ask.

He's the first person besides my hairdresser to offer an opinion.

"You look . . . you look Australian," he says, and then he laughs again, shrugging because he knows it's a ridiculous thing to say.

"Australian?"

"I don't know," he says. "It's the tan and the hair combo I think. You look like you should be a lifeguard on Bondi Beach or something."

"That is such a weirdly specific description," I say, rolling my eyes. "Did I disturb you in the middle of some *Baywatch* dream?"

He runs his hand over his stubble and pulls a face that suggests I might have but he's too polite to say so.

"When did you get home?" he asks.

Jonah and I speak quite a lot now, usually last thing at night for me. He was the main thread connecting me to home back in Croatia, the only person who hadn't judged me harshly for going away—probably because by his own admission he'd done pretty much the same himself.

"A couple of days ago," I say. "Not the warmest of welcomes, it has to be said. I stayed away too long."

"They'll come round," he says. "They love you."

"Yeah, I know," I say, because he's right of course. I

change the subject because thinking about Elle and Mum lowers my spirits. "What's new with you?"

He reaches for a glass of water from his bedside table then flops back, his LA tan stark against the white sheets. He looks better than I've seen him for a long time; healthier, vital, like he's found his shine somewhere in the bottom of a wheatgrass smoothie. I settle in and listen as he tells me about his days, developments with the script, the people he's spending his time with. Enthusiasm shines from his dark eyes. I can't imagine he'll ever come home, he moves in different circles now.

"What's it like to be back?" he asks me.

I sigh. "Same old," I say, then I catch myself. "Actually, it's not. It feels weird. As if I don't quite belong here anymore."

He nods slowly. "You've been away a fair while, you'll settle back down."

"I know."

"Back to work soon?"

I nod, my heart heavy. "Tomorrow. They've taken someone new on though. Phil told me to come in, but I don't know if there's still a place for me there."

Concern flickers in his eyes. "Sure you're feeling okay?"

"I will be," I say. "Just missing the sunshine, probably."

"It's a big world out there, Lyds," he says. "There's always sunshine somewhere."

"Not here," I say, unsure if we're even talking about the weather. "Any plans to come home?"

He shakes his head. "I'm here for a little while yet. My sabbatical ends at Christmas, so by then, I guess?"

I swallow hard, and I don't tell him how much I wish he'd come back sooner. "Okay."

"If Phil gives you the boot, come out here and stay with me for a bit," he smiles, messing around. I don't tell him how appealing it sounds.

"Yeah, because that'd help smooth things out with my mum," I say.

"Maybe not then," he laughs. "Anyway, Phil's not going to give you the boot. He's practically family."

I raise a smile. "Yeah, it'll be all right."

His eyes flicker to the top of his screen. "I better go," he says. "Stuff to get done."

"Windsurfing? Movie premiere?"

"Both," he says. "Then lunch with Kate Winslet."

"Nice," I say.

"You know it," he says. "Catch you later, stargazer."

He clicks to end the call and his image is frozen on the screen, hand raised in farewell. Stargazer. I'd sometimes show him the late-night Croatian skies from my balcony, but the nickname doesn't really apply anymore. I can't imagine he'd want to see our gray hometown skies and streetlights.

I run my hand over my new hair, still getting used to it. It's almost boy short, a feathered cap.

"I don't think you'd like it, Freddie," I say. "In fact, I know you'd bloody hate it."

I don't hate it though. It's going to take some getting used to, but I think, in time, I'm going to love it.

AWAKE

Monday, September 30

"OH MY FUCKING GOD!"

Ryan's desk is closest to me when I walk into the office, and he jumps to his feet, startled. "You're back and you look amazing!"

He skirts around the edge of his desk and runs his hands over my cropped hair, staring at me. "What did you do? I mean, I totally love it, but it's a bit radical for you, you know?"

By now everyone else has drifted toward me too, all of them looking at me as if I've had a limb chopped off rather than my hair.

"It's gamine," Julia offers.

"Shows off your eyes," Dawn says. "Wow, look at the color of you." She puts her pale forearm next to mine.

My eyes drop to her rounded belly and she laughs. "Yeah. Not just cake."

"I'm really glad," I say, pleased for her.

Phil appears at my side and squeezes my shoulder. "Good to see you, Lydia," he says. "Grab a cuppa, then a word in my office?"

Everyone looks slightly uncomfortable as they scatter back to work, and it's only then I notice the new girl at my desk. I know about her, of course, but still the sight of Louise, as I believe her name is, makes me sickly nervous. She looks efficient, her fingers flying over the keys as she glances up at me and smiles. I'm sure she's perfectly nice and obviously can type fast enough to make her fingers bleed, but I'd still really like it if she vanished in a puff of smoke about now. I watch her for a second in case she does, but she remains stubbornly present, so I take Phil's suggestion and head for the kitchen.

SO, THE GOOD news is I still have a job. The not-so-good news is that it isn't the one I left. Phil tried to frame it as kindly as possible and clearly didn't enjoy being the bearer of bad news, but Super Lou (he didn't call her that) is here to stay and by all accounts doing a stonkingly good job. His hand was forced when Dawn's morning sickness kicked in, he said. Of course I've got no grounds to be angry because it's my own fault for staying away so long. I've been ever so nicely shunted downstairs to the library. Delia has finally decided it's time to hang up her inkpad and stamp and someone needs to step into the breach.

He sold it to me as a challenge, a chance to get my teeth into overhauling the place, a project. And I'm grateful, I really am. I'll still be at the community center and able to see everyone upstairs, just in passing, rather than working together every day. I won't lie, I feel like the black sheep of the family being banished downstairs for my misdemeanors, but I know the reality is that I'm lucky to still have a job at all.

And actually, when I think about, taking on the library revamp might be good for me. There's a couple of part-time staff to manage and the system needs digitalizing. I could start some reading events. Meetings, author visits. A book club, even. Phil really wants me to see it as something I can take charge of and make my own. He even gave me twenty quid out of petty cash and told me to go and buy myself a planner and pens from the fancy stationery shop in town. I appreciate the gesture. I'll try to do as he suggests; make some plans for the future.

"SUPPORT HER HEAD," Elle says, lowering a naked and rather angry-looking Charlotte into my waiting arms. We're kneeling on the floor in Elle's bathroom; she's allowed me up to help with bath time, an olive branch of sorts. The baby bath is inside their regular bathtub, and as I lower the wriggling baby into the water, miraculously, she calms.

"She loves it," Elle says, resting her face on her arms beside me as she gazes down at her daughter. "I bathed her four times the other day just to stop her from crying."

"She'll be a mermaid," I say.

"A prune, more like," Elle says.

I smile, scooping up handfuls of warm water to

ladle over Charlotte's tummy. She really is a water baby, it's like magic.

"Maybe it feels womb-like," I say.

Elle reaches out and tickles Charlotte's foot. "Maybe. Thank you. For being there for me when she was born. For us."

I hear the struggle she has to get the words out, and my throat thickens as I remember the day Charlotte was born. My wedding day.

"I wouldn't have missed it for the world," I say.

And it's then that I know. If I'd had to make a conscious choice between the wedding and delivering Charlotte, hard as it is to acknowledge, I'd have stayed here in this world. The baby's tiny fingers grip around one of mine, acknowledgment that there's more holding me here than there is for me there. That it's time to face up to the inevitable.

I've been through this catastrophic, all-consuming event. The worst thing happened. I lost the love of my life, and then miraculously, I found my way back to him again, but at what cost?

In the beginning it was dazzling, all of my dreams come true, and it's taken until now to understand that however beautiful it was, it's unsustainable–for both the woman I am here, and the woman I am there. The woman I am there should enjoy her long, beautiful life with Freddie. God knows I need to believe that there is a world out there where Freddie and I make it, where we're happy and have time to build a family of our own, where we're lucky enough to grow old together.

Traveling back and forth, visiting a place where my grief doesn't exist, where extraordinary pain hasn't irrevocably changed me; it was magnificent. Honestly, it was. Who in the world wouldn't grab the chance to see their lost loved one again? And not just once, but often?

The human brain is wired to cope with grief. It knows even as we fall into unfathomably dark places, there will be light again, and if we just keep moving forward in one brave straight line, however slowly, we'll find our way back again. But I didn't do that. I stumbled in every which direction, blindfolded, two steps forward, three steps back. The pills have been my comfort, my crutch, and my escape, but they've also been the blindfold sending me in the wrong direction. For every version of me that exists, I need to remove it. I need to say goodbye.

ASLEEP

Tuesday, October 1

I KNEW FREDDIE wouldn't be here, of course. I could have waited a couple of weeks in the hope that he'd be back from Rio, but there are no guarantees when that would be and now my decision is made, I need to see it through.

The bedside lamp is on, a low nightlight glow, and the clock tells me it's just after five in the morning. My iPad is where I hoped it would be, on Freddie's pillow. I'm a nighttime reader, sometimes a middle-of-the-night reader when I can't sleep, which is often the case when I'm alone. I reach for it now and check the battery level. Eighty-seven percent. That's okay. So I'm here, in our beautiful Savoy bed, and I have my iPad ready. FaceTime isn't the way I'd ever have imagined or wished to say goodbye, but it's all I have. Coming back here again after tonight isn't an option I can allow myself.

I put the iPad down and lay back against the pillows. I can afford a few minutes to myself before I make the call. I'm warm and comfortable, and for a few minutes I soak in the stillness, try to slow down my breathing, to be calm in these last moments because they matter so much.

And then, when I'm sure I'm ready, I prop myself up on the pillows and reach for my iPad.

HE'S NOT GOING to pick up. I feel my calmness start to ebb as the ringtone beams out somewhere in the darkness on the other side of the world. He's not going to pick up. The beginnings of panic tighten my throat; I can feel my heartbeat racing too fast as I gaze at my pale reflection on the screen. I brace myself for the message to flash up telling me Freddie Hunter is unavailable. Of course he is; it's the middle of the night in Rio.

Come on, Freddie, I whisper. Please hear me one last time. Of all the times I've ever needed you, this is the time I need you most of all.

And then, miraculously, as if he heard my plea, he does. The screen flickers as it connects, and then he's there and I could cry with sheer relief.

"Lyds? Hang on." He reaches across to switch his bedside lamp on. It washes him in an intimate glow, the kind of welcome you might see through a pub window on a winter's night. "Is everything okay?"

He's bleary eyed, concerned.

I nod, already choking back tears. "I just wanted to see your face again."

I spent most of yesterday trying to think of the right

things to say to him, but now he's looking at me, all I want to do is fill my eyes with him. Eighty-seven percent could never be enough.

He flops back against his pillow. "It's one in the morning here, babes," he says.

"I know, I know. I'm sorry," I whisper. "I just miss you so much, Freddie. I hate it when we argue."

"Me too," he says. "Especially when we can't have makeup sex."

I shake my head and laugh softly. "Promise me you'll never change, Freddie Hunter."

"Hey," he says, low and familiar now. "It's felt like forever for me too, you know."

"Has it?" I say, a sob catching hot in my throat, because I never truly realized how long forever is until the day I saw Freddie's name etched in gold on his headstone.

"Of course, it has," he says, like it's obvious. "I won't stay away this long again, Lyds, promise. It's driving me nuts."

It's been a million times harder for me, I think, but I don't say it.

"I haven't been sleeping so well," I tell him instead. "The bed's too big without you."

"Don't knock it. This thing's like a plank of wood." His arm is flung behind his head and he raps his knuckles on the cheap pine headboard. "Make the best of it while you can, Lyds. Starfish all you like."

Make the best of it while you can; I store his advice to live by away for later.

"I'll try to," I say. "Every day. I promise."

"Just don't go getting too used to life without me, okay?" he says, after a beat.

My mouth tries to form words, anything at all, but I can't, because getting used to life without Freddie Hunter has become the story of my life.

"I love you very much," I say.

He smiles. "Love you more than Keira."

"Straight in at the top, huh?"

"Tired," he stifles a yawn.

"Shall I let you go?" In all of my days, I don't think I'll find any other words more difficult to say.

He nods, and I hold his gaze, knowing he's ready to leave me.

"Goodbye, my love," I say, tracing my finger over his cheekbone, the familiar curve of his bottom lip.

"See you in the morning," he murmurs.

It's something we always used to say last thing before sleep: a promise, an endearment, an I'll be here waiting for you when you open your eyes. Mum always used to say it to Elle and me when we were little, a reassurance because she was our rock.

"See you in the morning, Freddie." My voice burns in my throat as I say it back one last time. "I need to go now," I tell him. "Sleep easy, my love."

He half smiles, too far toward sleep to see that I'm crying. "Over and out," he whispers, and then he sighs just one more breath.

Oh, Freddie Hunter. I try to smile through my tears, and I look at him for a few more last-me-a-lifetime moments before I make myself press the end button. He's frozen on the screen for a second, already sleeping, and then he's gone—and this time it's forever.

AWAKE

Tuesday, October 1

I WAS SO terrified about the idea of saying goodbye that I didn't really think too much about how I'd feel once it was over. If I had to guess, I'd probably have predicted I'd be a tearful mess, exhausted and broken, too lonely for words. And I'd have been right, to an extent at least. But what I wouldn't have imagined is that I'd feel my own strength, that I'd be able to look at myself in the illuminated bathroom mirror right now and feel quiet pride. That I'd know in my bones that it was the right thing to do. Right for me here, me there, and right for the people who love me. *What a journey you've been on,* I whisper to my reflection, unscrewing the lid on the bottle of pink pills.

I catch my own eye in the mirror and smile, because it's the kind of comment that Ryan would take the piss out of me for. Maybe I'll tell him one day, if I can find a way to word it that doesn't make me sound insane.

Right, I say, resolute, the open pill bottle clutched in my hand. I have to do this. I need to show the girl in the mirror that I have her back. It's one in the morning. I need to do this right now, and then go back to bed and rest.

Vita asked me a while ago what I'd do if I wasn't afraid. It's a question I've thought about quite a lot since getting back here, and one I ask myself again now as I stare at the pills. There are eleven left in the bottle. That's eleven more visits. I could keep them. I could. I could eke them out, allow myself just one visit a year. I could absolutely do that. Spend one splendid day each year with Freddie. My birthday or his. One every other year, even. Or I could space them out even more, every few years or every five, slip in and see what becomes of us. I'd get to see our children. Just imagine. I could make their breakfast, help them with their homework. A tear slides down my cheek, because it's too tender a thing to imagine rocking my child to sleep in my arms even once.

But if I do that, if I keep these pills safely tucked away, what will it mean for my life here? I swallow hard, because I know the answer. It would mean life here is always second best, forever a waiting room, and that isn't fair on me or anyone else in my life. This life has to be my only option, but more than that, my best option. I need to do the thing I'd do if I wasn't afraid. It's time to leave the other me to her own devices, let her know the joy of making breakfast for her children and birthdays with Freddie unencumbered by the occasional visit from a sharper-edged, world-weary version of herself.

My hand is shaking when I hold the bottle out over the sink, and that's okay, because this is hard. I turn the tap on full and hold my breath, my heart racing, and then I do it, fast, all in one rush so I can't change my mind and stop midway through. The pills upend into the gushing water and swirl around for a few seconds, turning the water pink as they jostle to leave. I watch them, feeling everything: proud of me, heart-sore, relieved, shattered. And then they're all gone, vanished at last, and I turn the tap off and look myself in the eye in the mirror.

"Just you and me now," I say.

I belt my dressing gown more securely around my body, and feel a quiet sense of peace.

Saturday, October 12

"HAPPY BIRTHDAY, JUNE!"

We all raise our glasses and toast my Auntie June.

"Sixty years young!" Uncle Bob says, cliché-proud, and loud enough to earn himself a tight, sit-down-before-I-throttle-you smile from his wife.

We're gathered in the packed local steakhouse, shiny balloons tied to the back of the birthday girl's chair. Mum is beside me, Elle opposite with the baby on her shoulder, Charlotte's first official family gathering. I'm greatly relieved that things are steadily thawing between us all since my return. Elle and I aren't where we used to be yet but she has at least fallen back into texting me daily videos of Charlotte, and Mum burst into tears and hugged me when she saw my new hair. "You look too fragile, Lydia," she said. "I don't know what to do about you."

The truth is I don't need people to do anything

about me. My time away from my lives was transformative, necessary despite the strain it put my relationship with my family under. I'm not as fragile as my haircut makes me look.

My cousin Lucy gives me the side-eye from down the table. "How was backpacking, Lydia?"

Backpacking. Gah, she always knows what not to say.

"Croatia's beautiful," I say. "You should go."

She picks up her wineglass. "I'm a bit old for that kind of thing."

"More of a package holiday girl." Elle catches my eye over Charlotte's head.

Lucy shoots her a look. "Maldives actually, for Christmas."

"Then you should both come to us for Christmas lunch this year, June," Mum says, smiling at Auntie June.

David takes his daughter from Elle so she can eat, a well-oiled tag team, and I don't miss the amused look that passes between them at Mum's lack of tact. She'd never have made the offer if Lucy wasn't guaranteed to be out of the country.

Uncle Bob considers it. "As long as I can carve," he says. "Tradition and all that."

A moment of solidarity passes between the four of us at the memory of David hacking away at the turkey last year.

"I think that can be accommodated," Mum says.

Auntie June leans forward and looks at me. "How's your friend doing in America, Lydia?"

I lay my cutlery down, done with eating. "Yeah, he's really well." In a town the size of ours, everyone hears about it if you so much as graze your knee, so Jonah's LA scriptwriting venture has become a rich source of local gossip. The hairdresser asked after him, everyone at work too. "He's staying out there for a while longer anyway, so that's encouraging," I say.

"Well, I wouldn't come back here if I was him," Lucy says. "Miami or here. Here or Miami." She makes weighing scale motions with her hands as she speaks and rolls her eyes.

"It's LA," I say, trying not to let her rile me.

"Same difference," she says. "Sun, sand, Americans."

I think of Vita, serene, cool, drinking early morning coffee on the terrace. She wouldn't let someone like Lucy get under her skin. Since Freddie died, both Jonah and I have broadened our horizons, an instinctive reaction to the fact that he isn't here anymore. We've sought out places and experiences you'll never find in a holiday brochure. Lucy hasn't been through that kind of transition; I let her sweeping inaccuracy slide.

"If you say so."

The conversation ebbs and flows around me. Elle and David still speak about Charlotte in terms of weeks; she's twelve weeks now and hitting all her milestones like a boss.

"Takes after her mother," Uncle Bob says. "You always were the organized one, Elle."

I don't think he intended to imply that I wasn't, but that's what I take from it. It's probably fair. I wonder what my children would inherit from me. Courage, Vita whispers. I only hope she's right.

* * *

SOMETHING BRUSHES PAST my ankles when I open my front door a little later; Turpin has come home. He jumps up on the kitchen work surface, watching me dig out some food for him.

"Need a bed for the night, old-timer?"

He tolerates an ear rub in return for dinner, and although I open the back door to give him the option, he decides not to chance the rain. I take my cuppa up to bed to read, leaving him asleep on Freddie's armchair.

Thursday, October 31

"THERE YOU GO," I say, sitting back on my haunches to admire my handiwork. "It looks suitably hideous."

I've decorated Freddie's grave with garish orange and purple flowers and a small ready-carved pumpkin for good measure. I realize it's not in the best taste to make a thing of Halloween in a graveyard, but Freddie loved it; Frankenstein's monster was his default fright-night alter ego. I know he'd get a laugh out of this if he could see me now. In fact he'd urge me to add fake cobwebs and cut-out ghosts, really go all out. I still visit him often, weather permitting. It's where I feel closest to him, or where he feels closest to me, especially these days.

"Library's going well," I say, clearing up the flower cuttings and wiping the stone. "Mary and Flo are hilarious, they can't even switch the computer on between them so how they're going to manage the new system is anyone's guess."

My work days are different now, but not in a bad way. I've traded my upstairs colleagues for two ladies from the local sheltered accommodation unit; Mary can't see very well and Flo is stone deaf in one ear, but all the same they've folded me into their circle. I haven't actually been to their bingo evening yet, but I can see it coming. They're the kind of women I hope Elle and I turn into when we're in our nineties, full of stories and trouble, with better social lives than most twenty-one-year-olds.

"You should see Charlotte," I say. "She seems to get bigger every day. She's holding her head up herself, and she has Elle's eyes." I laugh. "She's quite the madam. She filled her nappy when I was there this morning, I could hear David literally gagging when he changed her."

I pull my coat sleeves down over my cold fingers. "Jonah's still in LA," I say. "I think they're haggling over the script."

We speak most weekends, it's fast becoming one of the best parts of my week. He's fluent in the terminology of the world he moves in now, his conversation peppered with writing room talk and contractual meetings.

"I think they've been having some creative differences," I say, as if I have a clue what that means. "Reading between the lines the studio are pushing for some changes to give it more mass appeal and Jonah has been fighting their urge to cookie-cutter his story. I don't pretend to follow everything he tells me, but that's the gist of it."

He called me last night distinctly down in the mouth about it all. But life in LA has put the spring back in his step and the color back in his cheeks, so I hope he can find a way to ride out this bump in the road.

"I even offered to read it for him," I say. "Not that I know anything about it."

But I did know Freddie, and if this story is about their friendship, perhaps I'll see something Jonah doesn't, or at least help him find a way to compromise.

Movement in the distance catches my eye. A funeral cortege pulls in through the gates, two black limousines rolling down the central path. I bow my head, world-weary as they pass; my heart is heavy for whoever sits in those cars today. I know the long road they have ahead of them all too well and I can only stand sentry and send out quiet thoughts of solidarity and fortitude.

It's bitter here this lunchtime, the nip of winter well and truly on the wind. I button my winter coat, then kiss my fingertips and touch Freddie's gravestone before I head back into work.

It was never about getting over Freddie Hunter. It doesn't work that way, despite what my doctor's chart might say. There isn't a handy grief blueprint. You don't get over losing someone you love in six months or two years or twenty, but you do have to find a way to carry on living without feeling as if everything that comes afterward is second best. Some people walk up mountains, others throw themselves out of planes. Everyone has to find their own way back, and if they're lucky they'll have people who love them to hold their hand.

Monday, November 4

"ANY BOOKS FOR cranky babies?"

I look up from the box of books I'd been unpacking and find Elle standing in front of me. She looks so much better than she did a few weeks ago, pink cheeked from the cold and less drawn thanks to the fact Charlotte has started to sleep for longer stretches. I peep inside the pram at the bundled-up baby, positively angelic as she naps.

"I won't hear a word said against her," I say. I've spent as much time as I can with them lately, anxious to make up for the time I missed. Elle and I are mostly over the blip in our relationship, we need each other too much to let it linger. We had a couple of glasses of wine last weekend and sniveled together over a movie, and I found the words to tell her how sorry I was for not being there when she needed me.

"Mum thought I had postnatal depression," she

says. "But I knew it wasn't that. I was just so bloody furious with you for leaving me and too knackered to be able to talk myself out of it."

It's only now that I understand how much my absence hurt her, Mum too.

"I wondered if you'd be able to watch her for half an hour or so?" Elle says. "It's David's birthday next week, I'd kill kittens for the chance to walk around the shops without this pushchair."

"Right now?" I say, smiling, because she's just turned my day from humdrum to the best kind. This is the first time she's asked me to watch Charlotte.

"Unless you're too busy?"

I shake my head. "No. Perfect timing, I'm due for my lunchbreak."

Elle rattles off a whole bunch of instructions about nappy cream and bottles in case Charlotte won't stop crying, and I try to listen but all I can think is how glad I am that Elle trusts me again and wonder if it's possible to pick a sleeping baby up without waking them because I'm bursting out of my skin for a cuddle of this child.

And then it's just us, Charlotte and me. I wheel her slowly up and down the aisles of the library, absently talking her through the nonfiction sections, heading slowly toward the children's corner. When I pull back the blanket and peer into the pram, Charlotte gazes right back at me, her wide-awake eyes fringed with dark lashes.

"Hello you," I smile, unearthing her from her pram. She's still doll-tiny, delicate even in her snowsuit, and she fixes her solemn, Elle-like eyes on me as I settle us into one of the new armchairs.

"You know me," I remind her. "I was the first human you saw."

I like to think she remembers, that she's content in my arms because she recognizes me as safe harbor.

"What do we do now?" I whisper, even though there's no one in this part of the library for us to interrupt. "Shall I read to you?"

It feels like the appropriate thing to do given our surroundings, so I pick out a book I know well from my own childhood.

"It's a story about a caterpillar," I say, balancing the open book on my knees. "He's a pretty greedy guy, from what I remember."

I move her more securely into the fold of my elbow, and she watches me intently as I tell her how the caterpillar hatched on Sunday, ate an apple on Monday, two pears on Tuesday, and three plums on Wednesday. I swear she's taking it in. I tell her how he eats so much cheese and chocolate cake and salami that he feels ill, but then it's Sunday and he starts all over again until he's neither hungry nor little anymore.

I close the book and put it back on the stand, even though the story isn't over yet. Everyone knows how it ends.

"And then, Charlotte, the caterpillar spins himself a cocoon and he goes to sleep," I say. "And while he's sleeping he dreams of all the wonderful things he's going to see, the magical life he's going to live, and all the far-flung places he's going to go."

I stroke her palm, and her hand closes around mine,

a flower closing its petals, just as she did the morning she was born. Already her fingers are longer, less translucent, her grip more firm.

"And after a while he's had enough of sleeping," I tell her. "So he wakes up and stretches his new wings to test them out, and then he flies away in search of new adventures."

And that's when this small, precious child smiles at me. She's already been doing it for a few weeks for Elle and Mum, but she's made me work for it–the price of leaving her in the lurch, I guess. I smile back, and then I laugh, and she just keeps giving me that ridiculous beam that's split her face wide open like a small tree frog's.

"You're really something, you know," I tell her, my throat tight. "Thank you for being here."

And I am thankful. Maybe her impact would have lessened had I not been there to help her come into the world, if she hadn't gasped her first breath in my hands. But she did, and in doing so, she laid her tiny palms against the edge of my sleeping world and pushed it just far enough away to make my journey there perilous.

As she grows I'm going to be on hand to help her learn colors and take her to the movies and warn her off the wrong boys, but I don't think I'll ever be able to teach this little girl more than she's taught me just by being here.

"My little butterfly," I say.

Saturday, November 9

"I BLOODY HATE FIREWORKS."

Jonah laughs at me on my screen. "No, you don't. You were always the one who wanted to go and see them."

My phone is propped against a vase of flowers on the kitchen table so I can chat to him hands-free while I work. It's Saturday night here, Saturday lunchtime for him, and I'm being particularly dull and catching up on library paperwork with a glass of wine. I don't feel too sorry for myself though. In fact I'm glad to have so much to think about at work, it's helping to fill the empty spaces in my life. It's been almost six weeks now since I washed the pills away, and I'm honestly doing okay, in the daytime at least.

"Yeah, well, I've changed my mind," I grumble. Our local park display is tonight, and it sounds like war has broken out.

Jonah turns from his kitchen counter and comes to sit down at the table.

"Looks good," I say, nodding toward the bacon sandwich I've just watched him cook.

"I had to go to three shops to find thick-sliced white," he says. "It's practically illegal here."

"You're just too British for your own good, Jonah Jones." I roll my eyes, laughing.

He shows me his Heinz ketchup and grins. I put my pen down and reach for my wineglass.

"Any new news? Tell me something good."

He pushes his hair back from his face, and my eyes flicker to the scar across his eyebrow, bleached silver by LA sunshine. In one of our conversations recently he told me that he unscrewed his bathroom mirror from the wall not long after the accident because he couldn't stand seeing the constant reminder every morning; it's a relief to know that he's doing better now. I listen as he shares snippets of his LA week, eating his lunch as he goes.

"Oh, and guess what?" he says suddenly. "I ditched the car and hired a motorbike instead. Fancied the thrill of the open road."

I smile, biting back my desire to tell him to be careful, because he always is. I wonder if he ever got around to buying that classic bike off Gripper Grimes he talked about with Freddie in our other life.

"Vintage?" I say, casual.

He frowns and shakes his head. "Brand-new, why?"

"No reason," I shrug off his question. "Just trying to picture it."

We do this most days; use technology to make it feel

as if we're in the same room rather than on opposite sides of the world. My brain makes a hop, skip, and jump and wonders if there might come a time when similar technology exists to casually place a call across universes rather than continents. I'd quite like to be able to offer myself some advice; I think I've been through enough tough stuff to gather some pearls of wisdom.

"You look knackered," Jonah says.

I sigh as I swallow some wine. "Yeah, I am a bit."

"Still not sleeping?"

I run my hand over my forehead. "Not great, no."

Sleep is becoming an issue for me, in all honesty. I washed those pills down the sink, and with them my ability to sleep at night. I don't know why, but I do know I won't be going back to see the doctor about it anytime soon.

"Want me to sing to you?" Jonah laughs. "I do a good line in lullabies. Or death metal. Whichever you find more soothing."

I pick my phone up and relocate to the sofa.

"Go on then," I say, settling down. I pull the throw over me and drag a pillow under my head, and then I look at Jonah. "I'm ready."

"You actually want me to sing to you?"

"Don't tell me you were kidding," I say, even though I know he was. "It's been a long time since I heard you sing."

He stares at me, seeing me more clearly than most people do, even though he's on the other side of the world. I see him clearly too; his eyes tell me that he still doesn't sing very much these days, and he's trying to decide if he can do it right now for me.

"Close your eyes," he says.

I prop my phone where he can see me and burrow into the pillow, the blanket pulled up, more comfortable than I've been in a while.

"Any requests?"

"Surprise me," I whisper.

He falls quiet, and for a while all I can hear is his breathing, which is kind of soothing in itself. And then he begins, low and soulful, and my grateful bones sink into the cushions. I've heard Jonah work his way through the Beatles' back catalog countless times in the pub after hours. In The Prince he usually goes for crowd-pleasers, but tonight he strips it back and sings "The Long and Winding Road" just for me.

Wednesday, December 18

"I WOULDN'T WEAR this beard for anyone else," Phil says, pulling the frothy white wool down over his mouth. "I've swallowed at least half of it."

"Don't hock up a hairball," Ryan says, every inch Santa's helper in his elf outfit.

My upstairs buddies have all been roped in to do their bit for my library Christmas party this morning. It's nothing big or grand in the scale of things, just an open day with activities and games, a chance to get parents in to see the improvements I've made to our preschool corner. I used the lure of seeing Santa to pull in the preschool crowd, and it's been more effective than I anticipated. The place is heaving with harassed-looking parents, too warm in their outside jackets and holding onto tissues, changing bags, and half-eaten snacks.

Dawn is in charge of the coloring table, her Christmas jumper stretched over her beachball bump, and Julia is handing out punch to grateful mums and dads. I can't guarantee she hasn't laced it with vodka. She hasn't gone near a Christmas outfit, of course, but her bright red lipstick is a good match with Phil's Santa suit. And then there's Flo and Mary, my library ladies. They've come in dressed as a pair of Christmas baubles, which would be fine except for the fact that they can barely fit between the aisles in the library. Ryan laughed until tears ran down his cheeks earlier when Flo got wedged in the history section and needed him to give her a good shove from behind.

"Someone wanted to see Santa."

I turn and find Elle behind me, Mum beside her with Charlotte in her arms. There's something magical about that child; I only have to see her and a light switches on inside me. It's a mutual appreciation society, thankfully—she laughs like a drain at my really bad jokes and it's an undisputable fact that I'm her favorite. Well, undisputable to me, at least.

"You came," I say, kissing their cold cheeks.

"As if we'd miss it," Mum says, taking it all in. "Look at all these people, Lydia!"

"I hope Santa has enough gifts," Elle says.

I know for a fact that Santa has enough gifts. I've shaken local businesses dry for donations and used the money to bulk buy copies of *The Very Hungry Caterpillar*.

"I hope Santa doesn't choke on his beard," I say.

"I think that's the least of his worries," Mum laughs.

Phil is on a throne in the corner basically being mobbed by two-year-olds, all desperate to lodge their

Christmas demands. Ryan is turning out to be terrible at queue management, unable to organize people who barely reach his green Lycra-clad knee. In fact, they're crawling up him, using him like a climbing frame to launch themselves at Phil. He looks across at me, all big eyes and help me hands, and I just laugh and throw him a double thumbs-up.

"I think we need to call the police," Julia says. "The small people are out of control. There's jelly on the new rug."

That isn't what I see though. I see my library full of people, and my friends and family all gathered to support me. I see knackered parents leaning on the bookshelves getting to know each other with a glass of punch in their hands, and I see kids fizzing with the joy and anticipation of the season. What I see is life. Noisy, messy, complicated life, and I love it.

Tuesday, December 31

"SEE YOU TOMORROW," I say, blowing a kiss through my phone screen to Elle and Charlotte as the call cuts at her end, freezing them on my screen. She's grown ridiculously fast—Charlotte that is—filling out all of her creases with juicy, gorgeous baby rolls. We're spending the first day of the New Year together tomorrow, lunch at Mum's. Stef's coming too. I've met him a few times now, thankfully with his shirt on, and I really like him. He's not much of a talker but what he does say is usually quite pithy; his dark sense of humor appeals to me.

Tonight though it's just me and a glass of fizz. Jonah is still in LA; we talked a couple of days ago and even managed to make light of the fact that he isn't able to come and bang on my door at midnight this year. God, that feels like so much more than a year ago. I feel snakelike, as if I've shed a whole layer of myself and emerged the same but different, part of me left behind.

It's been three months since I last walked through the back door to another universe. I've done a lot of thinking since then; I've even been for a couple of sessions with a therapist. I told her everything; about the pills, the lot, and to her credit she didn't reach under her desk and feel for the panic button.

I've made my peace with the fact I'll never know for certain if the pink pills truly allowed me to move between worlds, if they inadvertently illuminated the flightpath to another place beyond our own.

I've also made my peace with the possibility that it was a sophisticated self-preservation technique, vivid lucid dreams as my subconscious unjumbled my thoughts, layering my actual life over an alternative version. It could have been that; my new therapist certainly thinks so. But you know what? I wouldn't stake my life on it.

I STEP OUT of my back door before I turn in, and I scan the clear night sky. If Jonah was here he'd be able to point out the planets and faraway constellations, but it's enough for me to just look up and let my eyes travel slowly across the darkness. It's really quite something. Every now and then, if I narrow my eyes and try hard enough, I think I catch a glimpse of something, the faint outline of a door standing ajar. I imagine myself there, so close to it I can hear distant voices; the rumble of familiar laughter, the excited shriek of a child. I smile as I pull the door gently shut, then I turn the key and let it float away across the stars.

2020

Thursday, January 2

I'M IN A turkey- and gin-related slump. Yesterday's lunch at Mum's turned into a bit of an all-day party; half the neighbors came in and there may or may not have been an ill-advised conga along the icy pavements, all very silly and led by Stef of all people, who it seems turns into a party animal after a couple of drinks.

And now I'm home again and I've got a tender head, a house brick–sized parcel of turkey in the fridge, and the esteemed Turpin as a companion.

"*Shawshank Redemption* or James Bond?" I ask him.

He stares at me from his favored perch on Freddie's chair.

"Wink once for Bond, twice for *Shawshank*?" I suggest, amusing myself even as he ignores me.

"You're a tough audience," I tell him. "Are you sure you don't want to go back and see what Agnes is doing?"

I think he recognizes my tone as sarcasm and turns his backside toward me.

"Fine," I mutter. "I'll decide myself."

I'm trying to work up the energy to go for a walk. I've got post-party lethargy, and because it's a brand-new year, I feel obliged to at least attempt to shake it off and make something of the day. My conviction carries me as far as the front step, new striped bobble hat and woolly gloves on courtesy of my mum. She gave Elle a similar but different set, we switched them when she wasn't looking. Left or right? Shops or park? I've no real intention or destination, so I just strike out toward the corner, and as I do someone else rounds it toward me.

He's tall, his shoulders bunched into his coat and scarf, but even from this distance I recognize him. Jonah Jones looks my way and I see the precise moment he knows it's me under all these stripes; he slows for a moment and then speeds up until we meet in the middle.

"What are you doing here?" I reach out and clutch him by the arms, incredulous, blindsided by the sight of him in person after seeing him so often on the small screen. "You're in LA!"

He laughs, pulling his navy woollen hat off. He needs a haircut, as usual, but my goodness, his unguarded smile is a sight for my sore eyes. I don't think I'd gauged from the iPad screen quite how much he'd caught the sun or how much LA has given him his spark back. He's not the same man who boarded the plane all those months ago. He isn't the Jonah I remember as Freddie's sidekick, either. He looks older, more grown up, as if he's stepped into bigger shoes and found them a better fit.

"Evidently I'm not," he grins. "All that wall-to-wall sunshine, Lyds, it drives you nuts."

"You've come to the right place then." I can't stop looking at him. "I'm just so glad to see you, Jonah," I shake my head, still in shock.

"You too," he says. "Come here."

He pulls me into his arms, and honestly, it's like a dam bursting. It's not a polite hug. It's a you matter to me, I can't believe you're here, let me look at you, you've just lit my world up hug. We rock, and we laugh, and eventually I step backward, thrilled to my bones.

He reaches out and pulls my bobble hat off.

"Wow," he says. "It's like feathers. I love it."

He's seen my haircut countless times on screen but this is the first time in person.

I run my hand over it, self-conscious. "I miss my long hair in this weather," I say.

He pulls my hat back on over my ears. "Better?"

I nod. "Better."

"Were you going somewhere?" he asks.

I blink, trying to remember. "Not really. Just blowing away the cobwebs, making sure my legs still work, that kind of thing."

"That kind of New Year?" he says.

"Lunch at Mum's got a bit out of hand yesterday," I laugh. "Headache today."

He rubs his cold hands together. "I was coming to see you," he says. "I can come back later though, if you like? Or tomorrow?"

"No," I jump in. "God, no. Come on, let's go inside,

it's too cold out here anyway. I don't know what I was thinking."

I slide my arm through his as we turn toward mine. "*Shawshank Redemption* or Bond?" I say. "You can choose."

He screws his nose up. "Which Bond?"

"I don't know," I say. "James?"

Jonah shakes his head, laughing as I slide the key into the lock. "Happy New Year, Lyds."

I turn back and smile.

"You too, Jonah."

IN THE BACKGROUND, Roger Moore messes around with a guy with metal teeth, and in the foreground, Jonah and I sit either end of the sofa and trade news as we work our way through a pile of turkey sandwiches.

I tell him silly work stories about Flo and Mary and show him pictures of Charlotte on my phone, and he tells me he spent last night at The Prince catching up with Deckers and co., who haven't changed at all. Which is odd really, because Jonah and I are barely recognizable as the people we were a couple of years ago. I listen and nod in the right places, building up to asking him the things I really want the answers to.

"*Lion King*?" he says, flicking through the TV guide. "Or some shite about midwives?"

"Err, hello?" I say. "Who in this room delivered a baby with her bare hands last summer?"

Jonah lays the guide down. "I'd forgotten you did that," he says. "And with your bare hands too. You're an everyday miracle worker, Lyds." He laughs as he tilts the neck of his beer toward me in salute.

"I'll take that," I say, gracious.

"Good," he says. "It's true."

"So . . ." I sit up straighter, cross-legged on the sofa facing him. "What's really brought you home, Jonah?"

He picks at the corner of the label on his beer bottle. "I just needed to clear my head."

I take an educated guess. "Script woes again?"

"Yeah," he sighs. I know he's sometimes found it difficult to walk the line between staying true to his story and accepting the studio's vision for the script, but it seemed to have gone quiet lately.

"I thought you'd ironed all that out?"

He twists his head until his neck cricks, a giveaway of his anxiety to me because I know him so well.

"We did," he says. "We had. Or at least I thought we had."

I reach for my wineglass without interrupting.

"But then we broke for Christmas, and they must have all watched too much of the Hallmark Channel or something, because they've decided the ending needs to change. Again."

Ah. "And you don't agree?"

He casts his eyes to the ceiling, as if the answer to his problems might be hidden somewhere up there. "No."

"So you've come home to . . . ?" I leave it open ended for him to finish, but he just stares at me in silence.

"Hide?" I suggest.

He huffs softly. "Something like that."

"But you will go back again, right?" I say, because I couldn't bear to see him lose this now he's come so far.

He drains his beer. "Yeah, I'll go back. Of course, I will, but I've no idea what I'm going to say to them because the end matters, Lyds. It makes all the difference."

"I know," I say, even though I don't really know much about stories. "Is there any chance they might have a point?"

"More hopeful. That's what they said. It needs to be more hopeful."

I swirl my wine. "People need hope, Jonah," I say, softly. "Surely we know that better than anyone?"

He looks away. "We also know that not every story has a happy ending," he says.

"Maybe not," I say. "Not in real life anyway, but I don't go to the movies to be depressed. I go to be inspired, and to feel like everything's going to be okay even when it isn't, to think the good guy always wins in the end. I mean, who'd watch James Bond if the bloke with the metal teeth won?"

"Jaws," Jonah mutters.

"Exactly," I point at Jonah. "That shark got what was coming to him."

"No, Jaws as in . . . it doesn't matter."

"Would it help if I read it?"

He looks at me, quiet. "I don't know."

He hasn't told me what happens in his script. Obviously, I know it's inspired and informed by his friendship with Freddie but he's been reluctant to share too much, and I haven't pushed him because I'm nervous about it too. I know it's going to stir up a million memories, and I don't want it to damage the friendship Jonah and I have worked so hard to rebuild over the last couple of years. But I look at him now, in trouble, and I know that I'm the only person in the world who might be able to help. The studio execs might know their business, but they didn't know Freddie Hunter.

"Let me read it," I say, resolute. "I'd really like to."

Hope flickers in his eyes. "You would?"

He looks so down in the mouth, I just want to see his smile again. "I'll do you a deal," I say. "I'll read it if you watch the midwives shite with me."

He looks at his empty beer bottle. "I think I might need another beer for that."

"You know where they are."

He comes back from the kitchen with a fresh beer and the wine bottle in his hand, topping me up before he sits down again. It's such a simple, second-nature gesture, yet it hits me right in the gut because I've grown so accustomed to doing everything myself. I refill my own glass, I eat alone, I watch TV on my own.

"I'm really glad you're home," I say.

Jonah looks my way, surprised. "I wasn't sure it'd feel much like home anymore," he says. "But it does."

I know exactly what he means.

Friday, January 3

IT'S THREE IN the morning. I've tried all of my usual tricks to get to sleep, but it won't come to me, even though I'm done in. Reading strains my eyes, sleep sounds make me want the loo, and it's a well-established fact that counting sheep is a crock of shit.

Jonah's stayed over, he's downstairs on the sofa like he always used to be. I wonder if he's awake too, or if sleep finds him easily at night. The floorboards are cool against my feet when I get out of bed, quiet so as not to disturb him. I sometimes make a cup of tea if I can't sleep, but the kettle might wake him so I don't bother tonight. I stand at the sink with a glass of water instead, yawning, and then I put my head round the door to look in on Jonah before I go back up to try for sleep again. He's fast out, one arm flung out toward the floor, his dark hair black in the shaded room. He's always possessed an innate calmness, even back when we were kids and his home life was anything but. Sleep only amplifies it; he's guru-level relaxed right now, his T-shirt discarded on the floor. Something draws me closer, until I'm sitting on the floor next to him, resting my head on the bunched-up quilt. God, I'm tired. I close my eyes, comforted by the sound of his breathing.

"Can't sleep?"

Jonah strokes my hair, soothing. I must have dropped off. I'm cold and my arm's gone numb where I've been leaning on it.

"Struggling," I admit. It won't come as news to him, he knows I've been battling insomnia for a while.

He moves back and lifts the quilt. "Come up, there's room."

I don't hesitate, not really. I crawl into the space he's made for me, my back pressed against his chest. He wraps his arms around me and pulls the quilt up to my shoulders, his knees behind mine.

"Go to sleep now," he says, his mouth close to my ear. "I've got you."

Jonah Jones cradles me in his arms and shares his beautiful calmness with me. The steady beat of his heart against my shoulder blade, his body heat radiating into my blood and my bones. I sleep.

Monday, January 6

"YOU LOOK A BIT PEAKY." Flo rummages in her cardigan pocket and pulls out a tube of mints. "Bit of sugar, that's what you need."

I shake my head. "Thanks, Flo. I'm all right, just tired."

Jonah flew back to LA on Saturday. He called round on the way to the airport and left me with a kiss on the forehead, a hug that has to last until I see him again, and a copy of his manuscript.

Be brutal, he said. *I trust your judgment more than anyone else's.*

I spent yesterday reading it, and all of last night rereading it, and it's in my desk drawer right now. I keep going back through it, trying to read the empty spaces in between. It's such a tender story, teenage angst at its poignant best, and at its raging, hormonal worst, the horror and heartbreak of losing your best friend, the confusion and heartache of silently loving his girl. It's all there, the story of us; Jonah's vulnerable teen heart, Freddie's bravado, and me, the thread that pulls the two of them together and apart. As is often the case in real life, no one wins in the end. They grow up and drift apart because seeing each other hurts too much. It's raw and melancholy beautiful, but it's not the kind of ending this story deserves.

"Are you sure we can't go back to the bonkers, Lydia?" Flo grumbles. "I can't make head nor tail of this computer."

I look up from sorting a pile of recently returned books. "Bonkers?"

"You know," Flo says, miming the old library date stamp action. "The bonkers."

"You're bonkers," I find a smile because Flo deserves it. "You and Mary, you're both bonkers."

"Best way if you ask me," she says. "Makes life more interesting anyway."

I look at Flo. "Is Flo short for Florence?"

"Florence Gardenia," she says, then laughs. "Bit of a mouthful. I used to tell Norm I only married him because his name was Smith."

I don't know a great deal about Flo's past. She mentions Norm, her GI husband, every now and then, and I know they celebrated their golden wedding just before he passed away. She has sons, but I get the impression she doesn't see as much of her family as she'd like to.

"Where did you meet him?"

Her face softens. "He turned up one Sunday evening

at the dance hall, all swagger in his fancy uniform. Gave me his cigarettes, I gave him my heart."

"Easy as that," I say.

"Not always." She rests her face on her hands, thinking. "He was away too much in the early years." She pauses. "Wrote me some saucy letters, mind, I still have them in a shoebox in my wardrobe. I might have to burn them before I die to stop the boys from reading them."

That's one of the things I appreciate most about being around Flo; she always looks for the laugh.

"Did you send him any back?"

She raises her eyebrows. "Do I look like a girl who'd write mucky letters, Lydia?"

"I'll take that as a yes," I say, and she just laughs and taps the side of her nose.

We look up as the doors open and a class from the local primary troops in, filling the library with noise and wet Wellingtons.

TURPIN COVERS HIMSELF in glory just now when I empty the contents of my old school bag out onto the rug. I've been up to the loft and I am pretty sure what I'm searching for is in here somewhere. A dried up Lypsyl, a magazine with a band on the front I can't remember the name of, a pre-smartphone envelope of photos. I delve deeper to lift out the stuff at the bottom, and one of those things happens to be a spider the size of Jupiter. Already loft-jumpy, I let out a bit of an OTT scream as I shake it off my arm, alerting the cat, who shoots off Freddie's chair and lands on it with terrifying precision. I can't say for sure if he squashed or ate it, but I don't think it's going to be troubling me anytime soon.

I take a few deep breaths and sit down on the rug, my teen life spread around me. Exercise books covered in doodles and graffiti; I flick through them, nostalgic for easier days. My careful handwriting, bubble dots above the i's, red ruler lines, teacher's marks in green. For a girl who didn't like chemistry, I scored pretty well in the homework I copied off Jonah Jones. I set the books aside and pick up the thing I went to the loft in search of; a small wooden music box decorated with colorfully painted birds.

It's been years since Jonah gave me this for my birthday. At the time he told me he saw it in a charity shop window and thought I might like it because of the birds and all; nonchalant, no big deal. I accepted it in the spirit it was given and used it to stash the bracelet Freddie gave me that same morning. It isn't in there anymore, lost somewhere along the passage of years. I pause to smile when I find the yellow plastic flower ring Freddie gave me, and a couple of knotted necklaces, and a pair of earrings I think might have been Elle's rather than mine. Nothing else of worth or note, and underneath them all, a small, smooth pebble. I take it out and lay it in the palm of my hand. It's pale gray and marbled with white, no bigger than a Brazil nut. It's nothing special to look at, but as I close my fingers around it I remember the day Jonah slipped it into my hand as we filed into the school hall for our first exam. *For luck,* he whispered, folding my shaking fingers around it.

I glance at my mobile on the coffee table. I haven't

heard from Jonah since he left for the airport on Saturday. I don't think I will. He left me with his manuscript, the trace of his kiss on my forehead, and the ball in my court. I think back to my earlier conversation with Flo, to those letters she still has in a shoebox in her wardrobe.

Something soul-deep and undeniable has shifted inside me lately when it comes to Jonah Jones. I've realized that you can love people in different ways at different times of your life. He's my oldest friend, but I turned to him as a man the other night. I turned to him in the small hours of the morning as someone I love, and he gave me sanctuary and protection without question.

I turn the small gray pebble over and over, thinking about the ending to the story he's written, and then I get up and find some paper and a pen. Words have always been Jonah's thing, really, not mine, but maybe tonight I can find the right words for both of us.

Dear Jonah,

So I read the manuscript and I love it—of course I do. I cried on page one, and to be honest all the way through because Freddie is there on every page. You've brought him, and us, to life with your magic words.

I'm not surprised people have fallen in love with your story. I have too—I'm so very, terribly proud of you, but Jonah, here's the thing. I think they're right—you should change the ending.

Every story has a beginning, a middle and, if you're lucky, a happy ending—your characters deserve that much after everything they've been through. Your audience does too. Let people leave the theater with empty popcorn buckets but hearts full of hope, because surely there's more than one happy ending for everyone?

I wish I could say all of this to you in person, but I think we both know Phil would fire me if I ask for any more time off at the moment! Besides . . . some things are difficult to say out loud, so maybe it's as well.

You and me . . . it's complicated, isn't it? But then again it isn't really, when you think about it. We both loved Freddie—if he was still here I'd be his wife and you'd be his best friend, and I don't for a minute think that would have ever changed. We'd have all grown old, although I don't think he'd have ever truly grown up.

But he isn't here. There's just you and me. We're forever changed because we loved him, and things changed forever because we lost him. But aren't we lucky to have shared so much? We have a forever bond. I can't imagine sharing my life with someone who didn't know him.

Change the ending, Jonah.

Love, Lydia x

Wednesday, January 29, 2020

I ALMOST DIDN'T mail the letter, because I'm not sure our friendship can survive it. I queued in the post office, anxious, and in front of me a small child reached up and slid his hand into his mum's. It reminded me of that gray pebble being slipped into my hand for luck, and it gave me just enough courage to hand the letter over.

That was more than three weeks ago, and he hasn't replied. I've imagined any number of reasons why. Perhaps the letter got lost in the post and he's out there in LA thinking I haven't bothered to read the script, or worse, that I read it and hate it. Or maybe he's read it and is mortified because I've read the signs all wrong and he doesn't know how to let me down gently. Or it could be that he's moved to Vegas and married a showgirl, my letter still unopened on his doormat. If it's that one, I hope someone does me the kindness of scrawling "return to sender" on the envelope.

"I wish your mother had never introduced me to these," Ryan says, unwrapping his mint biscuit. He's surreptitiously eating his lunch behind the front desk in the library, breaking my no food or drink rule. I don't mind; he comes down every now and then to spend his lunch break with us, drawn as much by Flo and Mary as me, I suspect. They're both in this afternoon, sitting either side of Ryan behind the desk.

"How's it going with Kate?" I ask. He's been seeing Kate, the Uma Thurman look-alike who ran the speed dating sessions, for a while now. They bumped into each other in the supermarket a couple of months after the event; as he tells it their eyes met over the cucumbers, but I think he's embroidering the truth for the sake of comedy.

"Good." His ears turn pink. "She's . . ." He puts his biscuit down while he thinks. "You know that place in town next to the dry cleaners?"

I frown as I try to bring the high street to mind. "The butchers?"

"Best pork pies for miles," Mary says.

Ryan rolls his eyes. "The other side."

"The fancy dress shop?" I say.

Ryan nods. "She's into all that stuff."

Flo rubs her hands together. "Does she want you to dress up as Batman?"

He blanches, and we all laugh, even though it's terribly indiscreet of him to say anything.

"I'm going to go and put this lot back in the children's section." I pick up an armful of books. "Don't go bonking anything while I'm gone."

I'VE GROWN TO love my library. The kids' section is my haven, set off in a side room to contain the noise, with graceful bay windows overlooking the street. I've reshelved the books and tidied the tables, and I take a breather for a few minutes on one of the deep window seats to watch the rain-damp street scene. People coming, people going. I don't realize anyone else is in the room with me until I turn back and find Jonah Jones leaning on the door frame in his winter coat, watching me.

I'm held bone still by the surprise of seeing him here; we stare at each other for a few silent beats across the room. His dark eyes tell me he's crossed the ocean to see me and now that he's here he doesn't know how to play this, and I can't help him because I don't know either.

He breaks first.

"I changed the ending."

"You did?"

He walks toward me, almost within touching distance. "You were right. There's more than one happy ending for everyone."

I swallow hard. "Did the studio prefer it?"

"They love it," he says softly, his lashes rain spiked as he looks down.

"And you?" I sit on my hands because they're desperate to reach for him. "Do you love it?"

He lifts his eyes to mine again.

"I was worried it might feel too fairy tale," he says. "Too clichéd. But it doesn't. He tells her he's loved her for as long as he can remember. That he wants her to be his Friday nights and his Christmas mornings, and that every love song he's ever written has been about her. He tells her he wants to be the one who holds her to sleep every night. That he wants his happy ending to be with her."

I slide off the window seat, and step toward him.

"And then, because she told him there's more than one happy ending for everyone, he kisses her."

"Wow," I whisper. "It sounds like a smash hit. I love it."

I reach for him and he folds me inside his coat, close enough to feel his heart banging against mine. The studio will probably set the final kiss outside in torrential rain and lay a romantic soundtrack over it, but they'll never come anywhere close to capturing the reverence in Jonah's eyes as he lowers his head, or the tremble of his mouth when it touches mine, or the beautiful ache of our slow first kiss. It isn't the bittersweet teenage kiss that never happened. It's adult and electric, soft yet urgent. I hold his face between my hands and press myself against him, and he sighs my name and lifts his head just enough to be able to look down at me. We stare at each other, breathless, wondrous, and I realize it isn't rain on his eyelashes. He's crying.

ACKNOWLEDGMENTS

Huge thanks to Katy Loftus, editor, genius, and friend, and to the brilliant team at Viking for your continuing support. Thank you more widely to everyone at Penguin, notably the mighty foreign rights team for sharing Lydia around the world.

I'm immensely grateful to Hilary Teeman and the fantastic team at Ballantine in the U.S. How lucky I am to work with you, your input and support mean a great deal to me.

Many thanks to my overseas publishers, I'm honored to work with you all.

Thank you to Jemima Forrester and everyone at David Higham for your help.

Much love and thanks to Kathrin Magyar for your generous charity bid to have your name appear in the book—I hope you approve of your character!

I must say a special and affectionate thank-you to all of the people who have shared their stories with me, both online and in person. Grief is such a difficult subject to talk about; you have informed, inspired, and touched me beyond measure.

I am, of course, unendingly grateful to everyone who reads Lydia's story. Thank you for choosing to spend your time with the Birds, for chatting to me on social media, and for helping to spread the word. I'm unfailingly blown away by your fabulous pictures and blog posts.

Last but not least, my family, past and present. This book in particular has been richly informed by you all, you lovely, crazy bunch! A word or a glance here, a laugh or a memory there—you're all fabulous and I love you lots.

The Two Lives Of Lydia Bird

JOSIE SILVER

Random House Book Club

Because Stories Are Better Shared™

RANDOM HOUSE BOOK CLUB

QUESTIONS AND TOPICS FOR DISCUSSION

1. After the unexpected death of Lydia's fiancé, she discovers that—with the aid of sleeping pills—she can visit a world in which he didn't die. Soon, she is spending her days waiting to go to sleep to see him. Do you think this was a healthy way for her to cope with what happened?

2. Lydia wrestles with placing the blame for Freddie's death on Jonah's shoulders for quite some time; do you think this is an understandable reaction? Why or why not?

3. Lydia is not the only person struggling with Freddie's death—Jonah is also mourning his best friend. In what ways are Lydia's and Jonah's journeys through grief similar? In what ways are they different?

4. Throughout the novel, Lydia's friends and family try to help her heal and put her life back together. Have you ever helped a friend or a family member through a difficult time? What obstacles do friends and family face when they try to help their loved ones through this kind of loss?

5. Elle is perhaps the person Lydia leans on the most as she copes with the changes in her life; in what ways is Elle there for Lydia, not just as her sister but as her best friend?

6. After some time, Lydia tentatively begins dating again. How did you feel when she began to get close to Kris? In what ways is their relationship important for Lydia? For Kris?

7. Lydia had an unexpected reaction after the birth of her niece. Did you sympathize with her or find her selfish? Did you view her time abroad as running away from her problems or as giving herself space to process her feelings? How did you react to Lydia during this part of the novel?

8. As Lydia spends more time "asleep" with Freddie, their relationship hits several discordant notes. What did you attribute the tension to? What, if anything, did these moments reveal about Freddie and Lydia's relationship?

9. While the primary difference between Lydia's "asleep" world and the real world is that in the for-

mer, Freddie is still alive, there are a number of other differences as well. What are some of these, and why do you think the author emphasizes them? What do you think they are meant to show?

10. As Lydia emerges from her grief, we see her begin to take care of the people who have been taking care of her since Freddie's death. Were you able to relate to Lydia's journey back to herself and her family? Have you been on any personal journeys of your own that helped you relate to her?

11. After reading the novel, do you believe that a person can have more than one "happy ending" in life? Why or why not?

A PLAYLIST FOR
The Two Lives of Lydia Bird

1. "Ocean Breathes Salty" • Modest Mouse
2. "Tears in Heaven" • Eric Clapton
3. "Keep Me in Your Heart" • Warren Zevon
4. "I'll Be Missing You" • Puff Daddy, featuring Faith Evans and 112
5. "It's All Coming Back to Me Now" • Céline Dion
6. "Un-break My Heart" • Toni Braxton
7. "How Do I Live" • LeAnn Rimes
8. "Like the Deserts Miss the Rain" • Everything but the Girl
9. "My Heart Will Go On" • Céline Dion
10. "Fire and Rain" • James Taylor
11. "See You Again" • Wiz Khalifa, featuring Charlie Puth
12. "Don't Get Around Much Anymore" • Ella Fitzgerald

13. "My Immortal" • Evanescence
14. "To Where You Are" • Josh Groban
15. "One Sweet Day" • Mariah Carey and Boyz II Men
16. "Together Again" • Janet Jackson
17. "Who Knew" • P!nk
18. "If I Have to Go" • Tom Waits

RECIPES FOR
The Two Lives of Lydia Bird

★ COFFEE AND WALNUT CAKE ★

PREP TIME: 25 minutes
COOK TIME: 20 minutes
TOTAL TIME: 45 minutes

FOR THE SPONGE

1¼ cups self-rising flour
2 tablespoons coffee powder (or instant coffee granules ground in a spice grinder or using a mortar and pestle)
⅛ teaspoon salt
3 medium eggs
5¾ ounces butter
¾ cup soft light brown sugar
1½ teaspoons milk
2⅔ ounces chopped walnuts

FOR THE BUTTERCREAM

3 tablespoons instant coffee granules
1½ tablespoons boiling water

9 ounces softened butter
4¼ cups confectioners' sugar
¼ teaspoon vanilla extract

TO DECORATE

1 ounce chopped walnuts
A handful of walnut halves

MAKE THE SPONGE

1. Preheat your oven to 320°F (or 285°F in a convection oven).
2. Line three 8-inch cake pans.
3. Sift the self-rising flour and coffee powder into a large bowl and add the salt. Add the eggs, butter, light brown sugar, and milk and mix until fully combined (either by hand or using an electric mixer on a low speed). Fold in the chopped walnuts.
4. Divide the mixture equally between the three pans.
5. Bake for about 20 minutes, until a skewer inserted into the middle comes out clean. Leave the cakes to cool in their pans for about 10 minutes, then remove and place on a wire rack to cool fully before decorating.

MAKE THE BUTTERCREAM

1. Mix the instant coffee granules with the boiling water and set aside to cool.
2. Cut the butter into cubes and beat on low-medium speed until soft. Add the confectioners' sugar (gradually, to stop it from flying everywhere) and beat until fully combined.
3. Add the vanilla extract and then add the coffee a teaspoon at a time, beating in each addition before adding more.

4. Check the consistency of your buttercream. It should be soft and perfect for piping at this point. If it's still a little stiff, beat in a little milk.

DECORATE

1. Place the bottom layer of your cake onto your chosen dish.
2. Cover with a third of the buttercream. Sprinkle half of the chopped walnuts over the buttercream.
3. Place another cake layer on top and repeat the previous step.
4. Place the final layer on top. Decorate with the remaining buttercream, then finish with the walnut halves.

SOURCE: charlotteslivelykitchen.com/coffee-walnut-cake

★ CRUSTLESS MINI QUICHE ★

PREP TIME: 10 minutes
COOK TIME: 25 minutes
TOTAL TIME: 35 minutes
YIELDS: 16 to 18 muffins

BASE

12 large eggs
½ cup heavy cream
¼ cup milk
2 tablespoons chopped fresh parsley
2 tablespoons chopped fresh basil (or herb of choice)
¼ teaspoon salt
¼ teaspoon pepper

OPTIONAL ADD-INS

1½ cups grated cheddar, Gruyère, mozzarella, or other cheese, divided in half
1 pound bacon, sausage, or other meat, fully cooked

VEGGIES*

1 cup broccoli, cut into teeny tiny florets
1 cup roughly chopped fresh spinach
1 red bell pepper, chopped small
¼ to ½ cup finely diced onion
1 jalapeño pepper, seeds and veins removed, diced fine

* Feel free to sub in whatever veggies you like or have on hand. I usually use 3 to 4 cups of chopped veggies in total and wouldn't suggest using much more; if you do, you won't have enough egg mixture to go around.

TO PREPARE

1. If using meat (bacon, sausage, etc.), cook it fully first. Set aside to cool, then cut into small pieces.
2. Optional: you can sauté your onion with a bit of olive oil to soften it and take away some of its bite. Set aside and allow to cool.
3. Preheat oven to 375°F and thoroughly grease a muffin tin.
4. In a large bowl, whisk together the eggs, cream, milk, parsley, basil, salt, and pepper. Set aside.
5. Get all your veggies diced up and ready to go.
6. Add all the veggies to the bowl with the egg mixture, and stir to combine. Stir in half of the cheese and all of the meat, if using.
7. Using an ice-cream scoop or ¼-cup measure, scoop the mixture into the prepared muffin tin. Fill to about a quarter inch from the top, then sprinkle a small amount of the remaining cheese over each. Place in the oven and bake for 20 to 25 minutes, or until the egg is fully set and the cheese has just started to turn golden on top.
8. Remove from the oven and let cool for 5 to 10 minutes before running a butter knife around each muffin and gently removing it from the tin. Enjoy while warm, or let cool completely before storing in an airtight container in the fridge. Leftovers can be reheated for several seconds in the microwave or for a few minutes in a preheated oven or toaster oven.

SOURCE: willcookforfriends.com/2014/04/crustless-mini-quiche-single-serving-breakfast-muffins.html

If you enjoyed

The Two Lives of Lydia Bird

read on for a preview of
Josie Silver's next novel.

One Night on the Island

CLEO, SEPTEMBER 28 LONDON

Finding my flamingo

"YOU GENUINELY WANT to send me to a remote island to marry myself?"

A warm flush creeps up my neck as I sit across the desk from Ali, my terrifyingly enigmatic boss at *Women Today*. She's asked me to do some fairly out there things over the years, but this one tops the lot.

"It's not legally binding," she says, as if that makes it better.

"Look." I pinch the bridge of my nose, choosing my words carefully. "It's one thing for an A-lister to declare she's 'self-coupling' for an interview in *Vogue,* Ali. It's altogether different for an almost thirty-year-old dating columnist to claim she's doing it too."

I stumble as I say my age; the number sticks like glue in my mouth. Thirty felt like just another year until I was twenty-nine and three-quarters, but now that my landmark birthday is a few weeks away, I've started to experience all kinds of unexpected and unwelcome anxieties. I was, I *am,* determined not to be someone who makes a big drama out of it, but with every passing day it's as if someone adds an extra weight onto my shoulders—one of those mini cast-iron ones you see in old-fashioned kitchen scales. I'm disappearing under tiny, invisible kitchen weights, and Ali has noticed my diminishment because Ali notices everything. She didn't get to be the editor of one of the UK's leading online women's lifestyle magazine by resting on her laurels; her meteoric rise is well documented in the industry with both green-eyed envy and huge respect. I consider myself lucky to work for her; I'd even go so far as to count her as a friend. A laser-eyed, ball-of-energy friend who terrifies me and makes me do things I don't want to, such as decamping to a remote Irish island I've never heard of to marry myself.

"Honestly, Clee, I came across that old Emma Watson interview again over the weekend and all I could think about was you." She gets up from her chair to pace, too excited by her own idea to sit. "A string of dating failures and disasters, about to turn thirty"—she ticks the list off on her fingers as she speaks—"trying to define her place in the world as a single woman, pressured by the media and the expectations of others."

"I feel sick with sorrow for her, I really do," I say. "It must be a shocker having to snog R-Patz for a living." He made a lasting impression on teenage me—all that immortal glittering. Is it any wonder I've struggled to find love after being set such unrealistic expectations? There's a whole other column for another day.

"She's never had to snog R-Patz. Don't minimize

Emma's contribution to make yourself feel better, you know I'm onto something here."

I pick at a loose thread on the arm of the office chair. "It's not strictly fair to say I've had a string of dating disasters. It *is* my job."

"I know, I know. We pay you to swipe right and wear your big, beautiful heart on your sleeve. We love you for your optimism and your faith in finding your flamingo."

Finding My Flamingo is the name of my online column, so called because flamingos mate for life. We experimented with other animals that mate for life too, but Finding My Gibbon suggested red bums and picking each other's ears, and Finding My Beaver lowered the tone in a most unstylish way. Finding My Flamingo felt appropriate, but as time has gone on I've become somewhat less invested, in no small part because I've been gifted so much flamingo-related shite that I could open a flamingo-related shite shop.

"Look, Clee, you need to do something to mark turning thirty. It's a seismic moment in a woman's life." Ali pauses in that specific way she does when something bad is coming next. "It's this or the tattoo."

I sigh; I really should have seen that coming. The tattoo has become a bit of an in-joke at team meetings. Any time I'm struggling for column content, someone gives me the side-eye and then suggests I get a flamingo inked indelibly on my skin, preferably in a place it can't easily be concealed.

"Okay. Look, I always kind of liked what Emma said about self-coupling," I say cautiously. "I get it. She was saying she's enough already, alone but not lonely."

Ali nods. She doesn't interrupt me; I know she's hoping I'm going to talk myself into it. She's excellent at deploying silence to get what she wants.

"She's a vibrant, independent woman who understands that there's more than one way to achieve a fulfilled life," I say. "She isn't a failure because she doesn't have a partner and a bunch of kids, and *she* doesn't let the fact that both of her sisters and her brother are married with their own broods pressure her, or feel forced to defend her singledom at every family gathering, even if she is drowning in an ocean of wedding and baby shower invitations—I mean, I'm genuinely happy for them all, but do they really need to wave it in my face in gold italics, for God's sake?"

I stop, realizing my voice had grown loud and somewhere in there I'd switched from talking about Emma Watson to talking about myself. Besides, it was unfair of me to include my brother, Tom, in my list of grievances—he's the only member of my family who never mentions my waning egg supply or lack of a significant other. Of my three siblings, he's furthest in age from me, seven years to be precise, yet we're closest in every other way. It'd be easy to cast him as a father figure in my life, given that I was a baby when our father died, but Tom was the one slipping teenage me an illicit cigarette under the table and covering for me when I stayed out late at night. We both take after my dad, apparently, dark hair and eyes full of trouble, if Mum is to be believed.

Ali sits back down, absolutely unfazed by my speech, her fingers steepled in a way that suggests she's either thinking or praying. "Exactly my point," she finally says. "This is the perfect opportunity to get away from the pressure of the huge surprise party your family is planning for your birthday, a valid reason to politely duck out of any impending weddings and baby showers, and the chance to catch your breath for the first time in three years."

"My family is planning a surprise party?"

Ali nods. "Your mum emailed me last week to check if you'd be able to take some time off and to ask for a list of all of your 'London friends.' I use air quotes because she used actual quotes. She also mentioned looking up your old schoolmates on Facebook. Old boyfriends. Your funeral without you dying, basically."

My fingers itch to text Tom for the lowdown. I love my family dearly, but surely they know me well enough to know that the ghosts of my past jumping out at me in a darkened room would be my personal hell? I'd rather get that flamingo tattoo. On my face.

"So basically, it's a huge birthday party, or I accept your proposal that I self-couple alone on a remote island no one's ever heard of off the Irish coast," I say, summarizing the meeting.

"Salvation Island," Ali says. Her satisfied expression tells me how pleased she is by the serendipitous name of the aforementioned remote island. She probably changed it herself by petition, or whatever it is you have to do to change the name of an island. It's the kind of stunt she'd pull if she thought it would boost readership.

"All expenses paid," she adds, as if that's going to be the clincher.

"Can't I self-couple in my flat?"

"No."

"The Maldives?"

"Not all expenses paid, no."

"Will it be cold?"

Ali's face contorts with the effort of trying to turn a grimace into a smile. "Come on now. Who ever wrote their best work under a beach umbrella? Think inspirational log fires and steaming cups of ambition."

"You totally stole that line from Dolly Parton," I grouch, not at all happy with the situation.

Ali's eyes gleam. "No nine-to-five on Salvation Island," she says, slowly reeling me in.

I weigh up my options. Just thinking about turning thirty spikes my anxiety levels again; marking it with a huge party surrounded by people I no longer know, who will no doubt be sporting wedding bands like medals, has my heart reaching for its suitcase.

"I do love Ireland," I say quietly, feeling Ali's web closing around me. As it was always going to.

She nods. "The lodge is so beautiful, totally off grid." She pauses. "A writer's dream."

She's saying words she knows will speak straight to my heart. I may be a dating columnist right now, but thanks to wine-fueled confessions, she knows about the secret novelist hiding out inside me, the fragile teen dreams all but buried under London life. I begrudgingly admire the way she says just enough to trigger a flare of tender hope. "How do you even know about this place?" I say, wavering.

Ali sighs. "Carole sent me the details. One of her hippie friends used it as a Reiki retreat, or for rechanneling her negative energy, something like that. You know what she's like, always thinks I'm on the edge of a breakdown." Ali's sister-in-law, Carole, expresses her concern through birthday and Christmas gifts: cupping vouchers, life-decluttering manuals, a Tibetan gong Ali sometimes whacks when she wants everyone's attention. "Think of it as a honeymoon," she says, getting the discussion back on track. "Or a . . . unimoon." She doesn't even try to hide how thrilled she is with herself at that.

"Is there Wi-Fi?" I ask, clutching at straws. I can't go if I can't file my column.

"Technically no, but would I send you somewhere without it?" She shudders. "They have it in the village—it's just a ten-minute stroll away apparently."

Great. Cold, damp, and no checking Insta while I'm on the loo. "You've already booked it, haven't you?" I say, resigned.

She hums the bridal march as she reaches into her drawer and slides a red pom-pom hat across the desk. "You fly on Friday."